TURF WARS – Ing

by Richard T Weston

TURF WARS – Ingleton Manor
ISBN: 978-0-9956172-1-6

Limited 1st Edition Review Copy – Print Run: 200

First published November 2016 – Language: UK English

Cover Artwork by Nick Hare at Nick Hare Design
nickharedesign.com

Enquiries foreign language rights and permission requests may be sent to the Author: richardweston247@gmail.com

DISCLAIMER

TURF WARS – Ingleton Manor is a work of plausible fiction.

With the sole exceptions of Karl Vasey and the late Dr Nigel Hill,

all of the characters and storylines are fictional. None are based

on actual persons either alive or dead. Any similarity to real

persons is coincidental.

Products, politicians, and all businesses mentioned are used in a purely
fictitious manner. No judgements or conclusions should be derived from this
fictional portrayal.

This work does not represent the opinions or beliefs of the author.

This book is dedicated to the memories of:

May 'Murray' Weston 1930-2013

Dr Nigel Hill 1961-2010

Acknowledgements

A book is rarely created without the support of others and this project was certainly no exception. I would like to thank all of the following in equal measure.

My wife Liz, and our children, for accepting that for ten months I would come home from a full-time job and retreat to my keyboard. Then, for not questioning that this keyboard was to accompany us on two family holidays. Also for showing such patience when dragged along for research visits to Ingleton, Langton, Barnard Castle, and Appleby.

A special mention to Zoë Coxall, who gave me an insight into the complexities of autism and social anxiety, that helped give depth to Paul's character.

To Sophie & Richard, for sharing their vast gardening knowledge and for the many conversations, over countless cups of excellent coffee, that assisted my research, inspiring some of my writing.

To my wife Liz, who spent hours removing my dyslexic errors and for removing so many, unnecessary, commas!

Also, my son, Tom Weston, who identified even more errors prior to the book going off to press. He'll make a good editor!

Finally, to my friend Pauline Day who encouraged me to consider gardening as a career and who's wisdom and personal self-sacrifice supported my family during some tough years.

VI

Contents

Preface

Human society has evolved into a fascinating and complex system supporting billions of people. In the West, we benefit from a food production and distribution network able to overcome major catastrophes. This system is robust, capable of adapting to counter the disruption of war and natural disasters.

However, sitting just below this man-made system, there is our food chain; its fragility, so far, not seriously challenged.

Our beautiful blue planet and its many ecosystems may appear to be self-balancing: Life would almost certainly recover after a break in the food chain; but will that life continue to include mankind?

People are not all brave, selfless heroes and should our society collapse, what would be the outcome? Would you be an early casualty or one of the few who might survive?

George Craven enjoys gardening at Ingleton Manor but he certainly isn't a hero. He means well but he is inclined to both act before he thinks and prefers to run away from his problems. However, when his name is given to a virus that may have disastrous global consequences, he has to man-up quickly. Lord Quail over-estimates his abilities and sends him behind the curtains of a secretive and back-biting government. This head gardener has a lot to learn and some difficult personal relationships to manage at Ingleton Manor, while an ecological disaster unfolds before him.

1. Chapter1 — A Tennis Court

The day we first noticed the white grass wasn't just like any other…

The warm morning sunlight was being randomly scattered by the formal pond's fountain, creating fleeting, miniature prismatic rainbows. These danced across the walls of my little gatehouse like a thousand demented butterflies at just before seven.

But something else had woken me and it wasn't my alarm. As I stirred, I struggled to recognise the regular, urgent buzzing. Fearing at first, that it was the doorbell, I grabbed my pants, and staggered towards the door, only then realising that the sound was the old intercom buzzer from the Manor. I cleared my throat and pressed the small cream button on the brown Bakelite panel.

"Ah, good morning, George. I trust I didn't wake you? Some news, so staff meeting in the drawing room at nine sharp. Don't bother to dress up."

Staff meeting? – That was a bit of a joke; there was me - the underpaid 'head gardener' and Karen Jenkins, the cleaner, who now only came in on Fridays. It was Friday. I was starting to wake up. I began analysing Lord Quail's brief message. I hoped his cost-saving regime wasn't being further extended? Maybe he was reducing my hours or was about to let Karen go, leaving me to do the cleaning *and* all the gardening? We hadn't had a proper staff meeting since Lady Quail had left two years previously.

I enjoyed gardening for the Quails despite the problems the family were experiencing. Ingleton Manor is lost in stunning scenery, nestled in beautiful rolling hills, deep in Durham County. From my bedroom window in the gatehouse, I can see my short walk to work - straight down the drive which circles a raised fountain before continuing to the large Tudor house that is Ingleton Manor.

As I walked towards the Manor, I was reminded of that day, five years earlier, when I first walked, nervously, up the drive. I had been more than a little apprehensive having applied for the job with little experience and hoping I could 'blag' my way in and learn on the job. I hadn't expected it to be such a large and beautifully maintained property. I was in awe of both the size of the gardens and the house. Either side of the yellow-walled, 'H-shaped' house, dark green topiary box sculptures dominated. Expertly trimmed, these served to hide the garages and outbuildings as well as add majesty and grandeur. This job was going to involve more than mowing lawns, trimming rough hedges and deadheading roses, and that was about the limit of my experience.

I'd never addressed a Lord before and was worried about etiquette, even imagining that I might have to bow. I also doubted my decision to wear my gardening greens; I soon felt sure that I would not be successful in my application and would certainly not be put to work the very same day. After climbing the nine stone steps to the large ornate oak door before me, I hesitated. Turning back to survey the view across the garden from this vantage point, 'I should have worn a suit.' I said to myself, as I gazed upon acres of rich green grass and the mature trees that lined the drive beyond the fountain. 'And I've turned up in a green boiler suit!' The gate, my escape route, was hidden by the gatehouse. 'I've bitten off a lot more that I can chew.' I muttered under my breath. I turned once more to the door, 'Oh, what the heck... they can only, sneer, with their noses in the air and send me away once!' I lifted the heavy brass knocker that hung from an angry looking lion's mouth and let it fall against the solid door. Then, instinctively, I took one step back.

My initial fears and preconceptions were dispelled when Lady

Quail answered the door herself and said: "Hello, you must be George, I'm Jayne." She shook my hand warmly and called out, "Arthur? – George is here about the gardening job!" Then she whispered, "He likes to be called Arthur when he is at home, with family and the other staff. Please only call him 'Lord' if we have visitors. I *do* prefer to be called 'Lady Jayne', but I promise not to bite if you forget!"

Those last five years had flown by, yet that first encounter with the Lord and Lady of the house was still fresh in my memory. I'm trusted with my own key to the side door now and, through this, I headed along the corridor, past the kitchen, study and Melissa's homework room to the drawing room. I realised that I had only been in the drawing room twice since that first, very informal interview.

The drawing room looked bigger than I remembered, probably because it was missing some of the furniture: The large portrait of Lord and Lady Quail had gone leaving a lighter patch of wall where it once hung directly above the now cold inglenook fireplace. The porcelain statues had gone too, as had the pair of bulbous jardinière that had dominated either side of the window.

"I'm not *staff* Daddy!"

It was not unusual to hear Melissa before you saw her. Their footsteps slowed and stopped as her Father whispered some calm explanation before they composed themselves and came in together.

Melissa was 15 and that week her hair was bright pink. She blamed her Father for her Mother's sudden departure and was certainly not impressed by the cost savings he had initiated because he had been expecting a painfully expensive divorce settlement to arrive every day since she had left.

3

Melissa now spent much of her time trying to find ways to shock or upset her Father. And, because she was now attending the local comprehensive, rather than the private boarding school, she was under his skin much more of the time. His irritation had started to show; the always reliable, very correct and calm Lord Arthur Quail, had twice exploded in rage at Melissa during the previous month.

I did have a lot of sympathy for Melissa: Her Mother left suddenly, without any explanation or even 'goodbyes' and had not sent so much as a postcard or text since. Now both she and her Father seemed like two, small, pieces of different jigsaw puzzles, rattling around in a huge house that had once been so full of life, love and activity. While I continued to enjoy gardening at the Manor, I no longer felt relaxed in the house. It had changed, becoming a place to receive bad news and where thin smiles failed to hide a deep sadness. Lady Jayne's departure had left a permanent shadow - a coldness. I felt fresh apprehension as Melissa and her father approached.

Karen the cleaner walked past the windows. It was nearing the end of the school summer holidays, and she had brought her son Paul with her. He was heading off towards the back garden, past 'Melissa's fountain', towards the lake. There he would likely spend most of the day searching out wildlife, taking photographs on his little digital camera and constructing his hidden den on the hillside beyond the lake. He seemed to enjoy his own company more than that of others, though he and Melissa got on well.

"What's this all about Daddy?" Melissa sighed as she sat on the arm of a chair and crossed her arms.

"Ah, Good morning George. I hope you are well? – Melissa-Jayne a little patience please, we must wait for Karen; we should all to hear this together."

"Don't call me that! – I'm Mel – just Mel!" Then turning to me, "Oh, Hi George! Yum, you're looking good this morning ..."

In her Father's company, I had become accustomed to her false flirting and ignored her attempt at a sexy wink that accompanied her flopping back into the chair, her legs unnecessarily akimbo. She rarely missed an opportunity to try to upset or embarrass her father and we'd both seen this little act before.

The previous week Melissa had asked me to tell her father that she was a lesbian. I doubted it and told her so. Saying that, should it be true, then she should tell him herself. I had made it quite clear that I wasn't going to be party to any of her childish games.

"Good morning Melissa." I dismissively replied, acknowledging her father's raised eyebrows with a slight sympathetic smile.

"Ah, Karen, you got my message. Thank you for coming in early" Arthur Quail welcomed Karen and ushered her to a chair next to where I was standing.

"I trust I'm being paid for this extra hour, Arthur?" she asked coldly.

Karen struggled financially especially since her hours were cut from full-time to just one day per week. She had never really liked 'Mrs Quail' refusing to refer to her as 'Lady Quail'. The consequences of her sudden departure had done nothing to improve her, already low, opinion of her. Karen had become bitter and often abrupt. I rarely saw her smiling unless in the company of young Paul. She was now a stressed, single mum, who I thought, was likely to stay that way. I figured she probably had depression, for little remained of the cheery young woman I had first met five years previously.

"I'll come to that in due course Miss Jenkins. – Please do take a seat, George."

Lord Quail is of short stature and rarely dressed in anything other than grey or tweed. I vividly remember, five years earlier, his being pulled into the large dining room by Lady Jayne. She had brought him and forced him to wear, bright orange trousers, purple shirt and a yellow cardigan for his 60th birthday party. We couldn't help it - everyone laughed! It just wasn't 'him'. Molly, the cook, had produced a truly magnificent banquet with much fayre from James Granger, the estates' gamekeeper, who was also proudly in attendance. But before the dessert arrived, Arthur had slipped away and changed back into his favourite tweed. When he returned some cheered and others applauded, much to Lady Jayne's annoyance. 'Well I looked like a damn blancmange!' he declared.

Lord Quail propped his silver-topped stick by the fireplace and gathered two official looking letters from the ornate mantelpiece. He then put on his half-lens reading spectacles before removing the papers from the first envelope. Arthur Quail proceeded to unfold them carefully and deliberately slowly. Finally clearing his throat before he spoke, "Melissa has reminded me that this meeting should not have been called a *staff meeting* rather a meeting of my trusted advisors and friends. Friends whom I have each asked to make sacrifices as I reacted to try to ensure that my blood line retains the house and as much of this estate as possible."

Lord Quail lowered his head and sucked on his top lip. I knew this meant he had something difficult or emotional to say. I had seen him do this before he told us that Molly the cook and James the gamekeeper had been dismissed, and again when he had asked Peter Rutherford, my mentor and head gardener to take early retirement, although he *was* seventy-four! I had automatically been promoted to 'Head Gardener' but without either a pay increase nor any other gardeners to be *head* over.

"As well as freezing staff pay these last two years, I have let four good people go. I significantly reduced your hours Karen and increased everybody's workload. For that, I apologise and remain truly grateful for your loyalty and continuing hard work."

I quickly tried to account for the four staff he had *let go*… Cook, Head Gardener, Game Keeper… then I remembered Sandy Rutherford; Sandy was Peter's granddaughter and had left shortly after he did, to have her first child. She was 'Maid', although her duties had mainly involved assisting Molly and Karen, as well as doing the household laundry. She never returned after first suffering a miscarriage, then having to deal with the death of her Grandfather. I last spoke to her at Peter's funeral; she was bitter that he had been retired and suggested his death, within a year, was caused directly by Lord Quail. Apparently, she had been offered her job back but had refused, telling Lord Quail exactly what she thought of his foolishness in marrying someone so much younger than him. She'd said that what had followed had been inevitable. Sandy had never been replaced; Karen, Melissa and Lord Quail himself now shared her duties.

"I believe you know that I have applied for planning permission for the 30 acres of land beyond the lake. Selling the land with planning permission for 90 dwellings could alone, raise enough to cover half the value of the Manor and gardens."

I had been actively involved in discussions concerning the impact of this proposed housing development on the hill beyond the lake. The effect they could have on the water course and the impact on the view from the house were my primary concerns.
Personally, I hated the whole scheme. I loved how the lake beautifully reflected the sheep and copse-dotted hill beyond. The

thought of a housing estate being reflected instead appalled me. However, if it saved the house from being sold to settle a divorce claim, then it was the lesser of two evils. I had suggested screening the new development with a line of Totem Cypress trees and creating a new bog garden should the additional water displaced from the hill overwhelm the lake.

Arthur continued, "Well, on Wednesday, I finally received a decision from Durham County Council, granting permission, subject only to certain height restrictions and access approval from highways."

After a brief murmur of surprise, Karen burst out, almost shouting, "Great. Just build the sodding houses, pay the bitch off and let's all move on."

"Shut up!" Screamed Melissa, turning and pointing angrily at Karen. "My Mother's not a bitch, and you don't know why she left any more than I do. How would you like to go down to *no* days a week, you lazy cow?"

"I beg your pardon? You stuck-up little wannabe whore! – Lazy, am I? - Well, see how you cope with *no* cleaner!" Karen snatched her bag and headed straight towards the door.

"Please, Karen, wait." insisted Lord Quail "Melissa, *please,* you must allow me to continue *without* interruption."

I quickly pushed Melissa back into her chair, as she was rising for a fight. "Please Mel, calm down and just hear your Father out."

Lord Quail guided Karen back into the room "Karen, Melissa, please! We have all been guilty of jumping to conclusions and this fighting between ourselves is not helping."

Neither Karen nor Melissa said anything – they sat opposite

one another arms crossed, bolt upright, glaring at each other until Lord Quail continued.

"So, as I was saying; we have been granted provisional planning permission for the hillside, and that has significantly increased its value. However, I received another letter yesterday morning that rather throws the cat amongst the pigeons." He paused, "It is from Lady Jayne's solicitor..."

"Oh, here we go…" muttered Karen.

Melissa leapt to her feet and tried to grab the letter. "From Mummy – How is she? Where is she? Can I visit her? Is she coming back? Please, Daddy, tell me what she says? Does it say why she left? – Please, Daddy, let me see!" Tears started pouring down her face, the tough-girl facade collapsing as rapidly as a pyramid of playing cards. She had heard absolutely nothing from her mother for two years, and I felt for her. I also thought it wrong of Lord Quail not to have told her about this second letter, privately, beforehand.

"Melissa, my darling, this letter is not *from* your Mother; this is merely her instructions via her solicitor and, I'm afraid, it doesn't answer your questions but let me just read all that it does say." Melissa remained standing by her Father so she could read alongside him.

'Lord Arthur James Quail, I write to you as the appointed legal representative of Mrs Jayne Anne Cavendish formerly Lady Jayne Anne Quail. My client has reverted to her maiden name legally via deed poll on 20th August 2013. Certification of this is included herein. She wishes to revoke the title of Lady and not to be addressed as such in future correspondences.

My client seeks a divorce from you and a petition for this is also enclosed. To summarise the petition, my client wishes you do agree to grant a divorce on the basis of two years' separation.

And, providing you make no claim to my client's assets, estate, pensions, or claim for child maintenance, is agreeable to an 'as is' financial settlement whereby she will make no claim to assets held by you personally nor those of the Quail Estate.

My client reserves her right to reconsider the financial settlement should you choose to contest the divorce.

Please forward this to your legal representative as soon as possible so that this can be concluded promptly as per my client's wishes. Mrs Jayne Cavendish does not wish to be contacted directly.'

"That's it. The rest is just a copy of the name change certificate and the divorce petition."

Melissa took the papers and searched through them, was pale but said nothing at all.

Karen held a shaking hand in front of her mouth asking only for confirmation that it really meant Jayne didn't want any money at all.

"It does appear so." Stated Lord Quail solemnly as he turned to his daughter to offer an arm of comfort.

She pulled away throwing the papers on the floor. "That's it? – I don't even get a mention – What the fuck did you do to her Daddy?!" She ran off, slamming the heavy oak door, and could be heard thumping up the stairs all the way to the second-floor.

Nobody said anything for a while.

Karen quietly gathered up the papers and handed them back to Lord Quail, who was standing motionless in front of the fireplace staring at the cold hearth. "I'm so sorry Arthur. Do you want me to go after Melissa?"

Arthur Quail took a deep breath, "Thank you, my dear, but no, she'll not be comforted."

"And how about you? A brandy perhaps?" Karen asked, indicating towards the drinks cabinet.

"You know, I've spent the last two years worrying about losing the house and only now I realise that actually, I've lost much more: My wife whom I love dearly, the love and respect of my only child, and the small community that once made this house a home. Thank you, but I don't think a brandy is going to help me, nor poor Melissa, who deserves so much more than this."

Karen gave him a quick hug "You're all she's got. She'll come around. And I'm sure she still loves you. I just can't believe that Jayne doesn't want anything including poor Melissa. She's not even asked how she is. She was never that heartless."

I realised that I had said nothing for a long while and that I should also offer some words of comfort, but I had nothing. Why is it that any woman will, apparently with no effort, manage to do and say the right things in emotional situations while men just become useless spectators? I just couldn't understand how a mother could abandon a child and not show any interest in her welfare. I thought changing the subject back to the planning permission might help, "Well, I guess the hill is safe from development now?" Karen shot me a look that said 'shut up!' So I quickly added 'Well the grass isn't going to cut itself. You know where I am if you need anything."

"Yes, thank you, George," replied Lord Quail as he turned away from the fireplace, "I will find you later - there is something I've seen on the croquet lawn I'd like your opinion on."

Nodding politely to them both I made a hasty retreat.

"Good morning, George. Another lovely day!" The postman had just arrived at the bottom of the steps and, straddling his push bike, was fishing out Manor post from his rather worn bag. "Not more letters" is what I wanted to say but, "Thank you. Yes,

another fine morning, but rain at the weekend," is what I actually said as I took the little pile. Usually, I would just put them on the reception table inside the door but today I glanced at each, hoping to see a hand-written letter for Melissa now that her mother had resurfaced, but no; just business mail. The postman was just about to pedal away when he stopped again. "Oh, George, did *you* sign the petition to save the tennis courts?"

"Yes, young Melissa insisted I sign it, and more than once!" I grinned and winked.

"Yeah, both she and the 'Wonder Boy' had me put my name to it too. But I have some bad news: The dozers were there early this morning, and the changing rooms have been torn down already!"

"Oh no!" I replied with a pained expression. Though I wasn't personally bothered by the loss of the two tennis courts in the village, Melissa had been a leading campaigner and had actively been trying to save them. "She's already had bad news today — that's not going to improve her mood."

"There's progress for you; a bit of space? — Cram in some more houses. Always profit before fitness or the possible future of our Wonder Boy!" He gave a resigned shrug and cycled off down the drive.

The 'Wonder Boy' he referred to was Stuart Gilly. Stuart was the village celebrity because he had won national youth tennis championships. His family had raised money to pay for a professional coach, who seemed to believe he had real talent and that Stuart was likely to become a Wimbledon star of the future. Melissa fancied Stuart but so did every young lady from the surrounding villages. He had apparently turned down all advances, being completely dedicated to his sport. When passing through Ingleton, he could often be seen practising in one of the two 'community courts'. If demolished, according to the Westmoreland Gazette, Stuart would have to travel some 20 miles to the nearest public courts and even then, he would not be guaranteed the court time that he could rely on in Ingleton.

I was edging the drive that led from the gatehouse to the Manor when I saw Arthur Quail walking towards me. Between the gatehouse and the small formal pond, with its fountain, the drive runs through an avenue of ancient horse chestnut trees. On a hot day, the shade of each tree provides a refreshing pool of relief from the scorching sun. I adjusted my edging pace so as to meet with him under one of these spheres of shade.

"Ah, George, there you are."

"Sorry about this morning Arthur, I just didn't know the right thing to say."

"Ah not to worry, I did have time to think and was still struggling myself. I didn't say much of what I intended to, especially once Melissa threw all her toys out of her pram!"

"How is Melissa now?" I asked, wondering if she had resurfaced after her outburst.

"Ah, Melissa… Yes, well she has had some other news this afternoon that has distracted her for now. George, if I were to say to you 'I would like to have a tennis court built,' where would you suggest it could go?"

I laughed, "Do you mean *Melissa* would like a tennis court

built?" It wasn't really a question and received only a brief nod as an answer. "I honestly can't think of anywhere in the garden that wouldn't disrupt one of the four views."

The garden had originally had two avenues; the narrow one that led from the front of the house and appeared to lead the drive directly to 'my' symmetrical gatehouse, rounding the circular

formal pond with its fountain midway, and the considerably wider, walnut and oak South Avenue, at the back. That included the large rectangular pond, rose beds, annual beds and the view of the lake and hill beyond.

Peter and I had created two new avenues; 'East' and 'West' that formed a cross with Melissa's fountain in the middle. East was planted with Azalea, Camilla and Rhododendron with a box-edged path and East, created from dwarf cherry and apple trees with a lavender edged path. Neither had yet fully matured, but both were taking shape nicely. The paths both ended in a circle of grass with a semi-circular box hedge beyond that screened the view of the boundary fence and farmland beyond. These were intended to display statues or sculptures that were yet to be purchased and had been put on hold after Lady Quail left.

"The only places in the garden that are big enough and won't disrupt a view would be very close to the house. Either the chamomile lawn, which is probably too narrow or the croquet lawn which I don't think sees any use?" I added, knowing full well he loved this space, often having his breakfast out there and reading his papers there in the afternoon.

"No, I often sit out there in the late afternoon sun with my Pimm's and take in the wonderful aromas of the sensory garden. No, while I do want to do something to make up for all that's happened to Melissa it is not going there!"

14

I remembered that most of the surrounding land had once been part of the Quail Estate, "What about on one of the tenant farms rather than in the garden?"

"I did think of that, but I think I want to be able to keep an eye on her. I fear this is probably just a man-trap to lure that young tennis chappie." We both paused to think for a moment then he spoke again. "Is there any chance that some of the hill beyond the lake could be levelled?"

"Possibly but it's a very long walk, quite steep, and there isn't any access for builders at the moment."

"True. With hindsight, I should have purchased the land those two courts were on in the village. I will have to see if there is any other public land available that just happens to be well overlooked. It is high time I regained some favour in the village anyhow. She will just have to be patient, and maybe this whim will pass before I find anything. Remember last month she wanted a horse? That I can now afford and likely accommodate!" Arthur laughed.

"Maybe remind her about that horse?" I asked.

"Yes, maybe I should?" he answered thoughtfully, "Now back to the croquet lawn; can I bring something to your attention?"

"Yes, of course," I replied. We started to walk back towards the house as Karen's little red Fiat headed towards us.

She slowed as she passed. Young Paul was imitating a Royal wave from the rear window, and Karen seemed happy. She was actually smiling!

Lord Quail called to her as she drove by, "See you *Tuesday* Miss Jenkins!"

"Tuesday?" I exclaimed, assuming she had already been given extra hours in light of the 'as is' financial settlement.

"Yes," Arthur explained with pride, "she can only do Tuesdays and Fridays for now, but she's going to give notice to her other clients and return to full time as soon as she is able."

"Oh, I am so pleased, and she's visibly happier already!" I wondered about asking if he could also take on another gardener because I was struggling to maintain everything on my own. However, I thought this was not the right time, and I did have the use of the gatehouse for just peppercorn rent since Peter had vacated it.

"Yes, well I have also offered her a couple of rooms on the 1st floor that she can move into once her current tenancy is up."

"Oh! That's so kind of you Arthur – no wonder she's cheered up."

We rounded the house and continued towards a wisteria-laden stone archway that led to the side door, then through the walled kitchen garden, and towards the croquet lawn.

"I had previously considered letting her the rooms, but my solicitor advised against taking in tenants while a divorce settlement was pending. I think it is safe to take that chance now. George, would you be so kind as to assist her with the move when the time comes?"

"Yes certainly," I replied without hesitation. "Paul and Melissa get on very well together now they are both at the same school. I take it Melissa is staying at the school in Bishops Auckland?"

"Yes. You know that young Paul is a quiet chap but he's certainly helped Melissa to settle in. She's now achieving better than predicted and, dare I admit it; she's doing better there than she ever did at Abbotsholme."

Ducking through the wisteria, Lord Quail again reminded me that the wisteria needed cutting back again before adding "Shall I advertise for a gardener's assistant or would you like to find someone yourself?"

That was just what I was hoping he was going to ask. The position I had originally applied for was 'Under one' which is an old term, dating back to when estates employed several gardeners. It just means you are one below the head gardener and in charge of all the other gardeners. However, I quickly discovered there weren't any other gardeners, so I had referred to my post as simply 'assistant gardener' and it seemed that Arthur now accepted this too. Since Peter had retired, I was trying to do everything myself. Arthur did agree that two large lawns facing the lake could be turned over to meadow, and these were now harvested and maintained by the neighbouring farmer, but there was still too much to work for one to complete alone.

Realising that I didn't have the time to find an assistant myself, I replied, "Can I leave that with you, Arthur? I'd like to be there for the interviews, though."

"I'll organise it as a priority," Arthur gave me a little shove in the arm, "and don't think I haven't noticed you working way into the evenings and some weekends George. I really am most grateful. However, squeezing extra hours from you was an unforeseen consequence of me letting you have the gatehouse and certainly not the reason I offered it! From now on, you will be paid by the hour rather than fixed salary and at the proper rate! Will be the same for the new guy. Oh... And when did you last take a holiday George?" Arthur stopped for a second to peer at me as if over glasses though he wasn't wearing any. This habit of Arthur's I found very endearing.

I smiled, "Last holiday I took was with my wife, and we've been divorced six years! But I don't fancy holidaying on my own. I don't even like to eat out alone. I just feel too self-conscious so it's been no sacrifice, honestly."

"18-30's holidays are not for you eh, George?" Arthur was smiling at his own suggestion.

"Absolutely not!" I replied sternly.

Lord Quail laughed. "I thought not! But I insist that you take some time off once we have the new guy aboard."

"You do know that we can't advertise for 'a *male* gardener' don't you?" I seriously wondered if he might place an ad for a 'Very fit, white man, aged 20-30 with no disabilities.'

"Ah, I see George... you want a pretty one! Karen not good enough for you, eh? – Young Paul reckons you two are a perfect match!"

"Hmmm. Yes, I am aware of Paul's wishes - as are half of Ingleton - but 'no.' Lovely though she is, there's just no chemistry there and the feeling's mutual. Also, no... unfortunately, you can't include the words 'only attractive young ladies need apply'!"

"No?!" he winked. "Ah well. Where's there's a will ..."

Arthur had led us to the far corner of the immaculately flat and well-tended croquet lawn. This was part of the garden I had to pay particular attention to and, weather permitting, it was roller- mown and edged twice a week from Mid-February until the first frosts of winter.

"You seem to have cheered up a bit since this morning" I stated.

"Yes, well it was all a bit of a shock, but I hope we will soon be able to draw a line under the whole episode. I believe things will improve for us now. And once Melissa and I get over our feelings of loss, I sincerely hope and believe that we can repair our relationship. Now to change the subject entirely; what do you think that is and is it a problem?"

We stood looking down at the edge of the lawn which was bordered by my recent installation of a sensory bed; brimming with stocks, fragrant lilies, curry mint and various scented herbs including thymus and hyssop. The grass in the far corner had gone a dusty white colour. Although only a small area had turned white, that patch didn't look at all well.

I bent down and carefully tugged a bit out, roots and all. "It's a fungus. Not too uncommon to find fungus where it's been wet and is shady, but it usually appears much later in autumn. I've not seen it here before nor anywhere quite as dense as this."

"Can you do anything about it? I do not like the look of it. Imagine if it spread to the whole lawn... Could your edging tool have spread it from the other lawns?"

"Well, I'll take a sample and send it off to RHS Wisley for analysis as a precaution. Then spray the whole lawn with a general fungicide. One thing Peter instilled in me was to disinfect all bladed tools between jobs and areas, so spreading by tools here is unlikely. The roller mower used here isn't used anywhere else either, and I've haven't noticed this elsewhere in the garden anyway."

"Spread by those damn rabbits, is it?" Arthur began pointing his stick like a gun.

"I'm sure we don't have any rabbits in at the moment but,

yes, squirrels, voles, mice, etc., they can all spread fungi and other plant diseases."

"OK, deal with it as soon as you can. I'm not losing my croquet lawn to either a tennis court or to a fungus!" Lord Quail patted me on the shoulder and headed towards the conservatory.

The following Tuesday was cloudy and threatened rain. Karen had arrived with Paul, and they had stopped by the gate and were chatting to the postman. Karen was clutching the post, saving him the long ride up and down the drive. She was also explaining why she was there on a Tuesday.

"Morning, all," I said, "Anything for me?" I asked wondering if Wisley had responded already.

"Just your Garden magazine," replied Karen, as she passed it over.

"Mum can I get out here?" called Paul from the back seat. He had spotted Melissa apparently fishing in the fountain half way up the drive. He had left the car and was running up the drive before Karen had answered. "Yes, dear!" she muttered sarcastically. Postie said his 'goodbyes' and Karen asked if I'd like a lift to the house. I declined, explaining that I had many tools to take up and that I'd need to use the tractor & trailer.

I finished my tea, wondered why Melissa was up so early, and read my work list for the day. That involved checking my emails because if Arthur had any special requests, he would often send them the previous evening. I had nothing from the Manor, but there was a brief reply from RHS Wisley.

They had examined the grass sample and concluded it was infected by *myxomycetes* or 'Slime Mould' as it is more commonly known.

They included a brief cut 'n' paste explanation stating that it was common on turf in very shady spots and damp areas. They even felt it necessary to tell me that grass requires sunlight and without it, fungus might thrive. However, these conditions were all contrary to ours, as I had described in my covering letter, so I was slightly niggled with the standard reply. They did ask for an updated photo of the patch so they could compare this with the photograph I had already sent. The problem with that was that I had already applied a fungicide, and the white mould had gone. Though the grass in that patch did still look very unhealthy, so I added 'camera' to my list of tools needed for the day's work.

I got everything I needed in the trailer and proceed up from the shed towards the Manor. Melissa was still sitting on the edge of the fountain, but Paul was looking decidedly bored and was wandering away by the time I arrived.

"Morning Mel, you OK?" – I had not seen her since she ran out of the meeting on Friday.

She looked up dreamily. "Yeah, we were just looking for the fish in here," she pointed into the water, "but Paul can't see them."

"Really?" I asked, knowing full well that there were no fish in the fountain unless she had put them there.

"Yes," she replied, "they are very tiny. Oh, and I just saw a rabbit coming in just over there," she pointed towards the fence between the gatehouse and the equipment sheds, partially hidden behind a screen of fir hedging.

"Oh great," I did wonder if the rabbit she claimed to have seen was as real as the fish, but Lord Quail hated rabbits. Once in, they usually made their way to the kitchen garden and destroyed the vegetables before descending on the croquet lawn where they contoured it with small holes, trenches and hillocks. So I'd have to start checking the double layered rabbit fencing for holes, and for any signs the little beasts had been in, right away. "Thanks, Mel," I said, climbing down from the tractor and heading back towards the equipment sheds.

I couldn't see any of the usual tell-tale signs that rabbits had been in, nor find any hole in the fence, and after 10 minutes searching I began to further doubt Melissa's sighting. I looked back towards the fountain to see if she was laughing at me. Instead, I saw her running towards me. Melissa rarely ran anywhere and so had my full attention. She kept looking towards the gate as she ran and following her glances, I saw a strikingly handsome young man with jet black hair starting to walk up the drive. I recognized him from the local newspaper: This was Stuart Gilly the 'Wonder Boy' with whom Melissa was undoubtedly smitten.

"George!" panted Melissa as she got to me, "Please, please can you pretend to be my Father and just go along with whatever Stuart says? Oh, please, George?!"

"Mel. What on earth have you said? I'm not quite thirty. I'm not old enough to be your Father!" Then, as Stuart spotted us and turned off the drive towards us, it dawned on me; "Oh, tell me you have not promised him that your father has agreed to build a tennis court?!"

"Yes, I kind of did," then with pleading eyes she added, "Just tell him you are going to need planning permission first or something. Please!?" She was now hanging off my arm, her big blue eyes desperately searching mine.

"Before I agree to anything just tell me, honestly Mel, was there a rabbit or was it like the fish?"

"Oh, thanks, George!" she hugged my arm tighter as Stuart approached and said loudly, "No Daddy, I've not seen *any* rabbits in the garden for ages... Oh, hi, Stuart, wow, you're looking fitter than ever!"

'Oh God', I thought, I'm about to impersonate my boss who is more than twice my age!

"Hello, Mel. Sir," Stuart began. "Mel, is it OK for me to go up to the house and thank your Father in person?"

Mel laughed and said, very convincingly I thought, "*This* is my Father! Daddy, this is Stuart Gilly, a future Wimbledon champion! Stuart, this is my Father, Arthur Quail."
"Oh, I'm so sorry, Arthur – Sir – Lord? Er, I'm so sorry. I thought you were the gardener!"

"It's a common mistake," I shot a look at Melissa "I do a lot of the gardening myself." I decided that I could have a bit of fun with Melissa, who had positioned herself slightly behind Stuart's shoulder, thinking she could direct me without him seeing. "Please just call me Sir, no one ever calls me Lord."

Melissa was scowling fiercely now as I struggled to tell as many truths as possible.

Stuart seemed ill at ease and slightly confused, "Well, Sir, I just wanted to thank you in person for agreeing to build a tennis court for me. It's so wonderful of you. I couldn't believe it when Mel, sorry, Melissa said you had agreed so quickly! – I am truly very grateful, as are my parents."

"Oh, it's nothing Stuart, really; it is nothing at all. Mel and I are really close, and since she has come out as a lesbian, I'll do anything to cheer her up and assist her good causes."

Melissa, taken completely off guard, was wide-eyed, glaring and shaking her head. She mouthed 'No!' and 'why?' at me.

Her expression had to switch back very quickly because Stuart turned to her, and patting her on the shoulder said: "Oh, that was so very brave, especially for someone as young as you. I was 17 when I came out to my parents, and I'm still not openly gay because both my Father and Coach think it would be better if I built a fan base and had some successes before making it public knowledge. I don't want to be defined by my sexuality."

"Oh... Well yes... That's good advice I'd say," I replied, assuming that Melissa had no idea, as did I, that Stuart was gay. I could have mimed 'exaggerated laughter' at her behind his back but thought better of it as she was now clearly in some distress, seemed confused and certainly wasn't appreciating the humour that I was finding in the situation.

"Excuse me, Sir, it's quite a long walk from the village. May I use a toilet, please?" I directed Stuart to the gatehouse. "Yes. Please use the one in the gatehouse, the gardener won't mind. First door on the left – it's not locked." I pointed back down the drive to my gatehouse.

As soon as Stuart disappeared inside the gatehouse, I felt a punch land on the top of my arm. "He's not gay!? Oh, he *is*, isn't he? Oh, and I so totally hate you!" But now she was smiling, just slightly, and that worried me.

"So Melissa, now are you going tell him there's not actually going to be a tennis court for him here?" I asked.

Melissa laughed, "Well, you see, now that's *your* problem; 'You *are* going to build him a tennis court', then he tells you he's gay and suddenly you're *not!*" Then she strode back up the drive towards the house turning to swipe the surface of the water in the fountain causing a dramatic wave of spray right across the drive and all over my tractor as she called out "That's game, set and match... *Daddy!*"

24

Chapter 2 – Northern Grass Fungus

Weather forecasts are of particular importance to gardeners; we carefully watch television forecasts, the full week-in-advance projections, as well as keep a constant eye on the sky for any rogue showers. Each day I organise my tasks based on the conditions the weather is likely to bring.

On this Thursday morning, there was a further indication that the day was to be another fine one. Melissa's shadow was interrupting the little butterfly patterns dancing on my wall. My bedroom window is the only window facing the house, and it looks out, right down the middle of the drive, past the fountain to the house. I looked out to see her heading down the drive on her bicycle in a lacy white blouse and thin cotton skirt. Confirming the TV forecasts: *North Yorkshire and Durham County could look forward to another warm and dry day.* I also concluded that any oncoming male drivers could be distracted if the breeze continued to catch and lift her skirt.

I wondered who in Ingleton she was after now? Or maybe she was going the nine miles to Barney – That's what the locals call the lovely market town of Barnard Castle and, as Melissa had exclaimed many times: "The only town for miles with a shoe shop!"

I waved as she passed. She smiled and returned the wave but didn't stop for a chat as she did some mornings. 'Good,' I thought – 'I've got lots to do.'

Checking my emails reminded me that I had still not got around to revisiting the croquet lawn to photograph the grass. I decided to do that straight away and check on what deadheading and weeding might be required in the sensory bed while I was up there. The surrounding hedge and the wisteria on the arch also needed attention, and I'd see if the lavender had finished and needed cutting and… I really couldn't wait until I got an assistant to share the workload.

Viewing the croquet lawn on the camera's LCD, I wondered if it was going to be able to capture what I was seeing? I would have to compare this new image with an earlier photograph.

Behind me, I heard the conservatory doors open. Lord Quail's stick appeared first as he carefully stepped out with his two papers. Possibly because he had been the Westmorland MP, until that constituency was broken up, he liked to compare the right and left views of his two papers. Politics hadn't been my 'thing', but I did listen when he read out how each managed to report the same story differently, the political bias of each, often only becoming evident when compared to the other.

"Ah, Good morning George. I've placed an ad for an assistant gardener," he said, tapping the newspapers, "front page both papers."

I grinned. Arthur may be a little eccentric, but he wasn't going to put an ad in a national newspaper for an assistant gardener. "What, not the Sun and the Daily Mail too?" It had been a long while since I felt I could joke with Arthur.

Lord Quail frowned, "Absolutely not! Even you deserve a young lady with some degree of class! – No, actually the ad was in this week's Westmorland Gazette, but they, in their infinite wisdom, omitted to print our phone number! Though, Melissa thinks, I forgot to include it? … Hmm, anyway they, have kindly agreed to reprint it - with our number - next week." Then craning his neck towards the far side of the lawn he asked, "How *is* the grass looking? I can't see any white."

"Well the fungicide has worked on the fungus OK, but the grass still doesn't look very well. Do you think it all seems a little yellow? Like it's been under a cover for a couple of days?"

"Is it overdue for a feed?" he enquired.

I'd applied a grass fertiliser in May, and it wasn't due for another feed until September. "No, it's been feed and got plenty of rain Friday night. What's also odd, is that I didn't cut it Monday because I'd applied Fungicide, and I'd usually be cutting it again today, but it still doesn't need it."

Arthur poked at the grass with his stick. "It looks considerably better than it did with the fungus. Are you sure it is unwell?"

"Well I'm not completely sure but it's definitely a bit off colour. I'm wondering if it has a virus that made it more susceptible to the fungus, and so I have only treated the symptoms? I'm going to take a couple more photographs including a close-up and send them to Wisley with another sample. Also, I'll see if I can find some comparison images taken this time last year."

The phone started to ring in the house.

"Well do what you need to, but if I lose my lawns you are not getting an assistant, you understand?" He winked and turning to the house, he called out, "Melissa! – Please… The phone!"

"Sorry, she's gone out," I stated.

"Ah, I'd better get it then. See you later George."

On the way back to the shed, I began to doubt my observation about the grass being more yellow than usual. It all appeared yellow now I was taking the time to look at it more carefully. It could be the yellow of the late summer morning sun, or maybe it was just the recent heat? Summer had arrived late after an unusually wet June and July. But I had my sample and, when back in my gatehouse, compared the new images of the croquet lawn with those I'd taken the previous August. I could see instantly there was, more than a subtle, difference in colour.

If the grass did have a virus, it occurred to me that the species on the croquet lawn were 'Chewings Fescue' and 'Browntop Bent' - both very fine varieties of grass. Very different to the Rye mixes used by the drives and open lawns, and different again to the 'Velvet Bentgrass' and 'St. Augustine' mix I'd sewn on the shadier areas such as the East and West avenues. If a virus could infect different lawn grasses, could it also infect other members of the grass family like wheat and corn?

I included these suspicions in my email to Wisley. I then packed the new sample, sealing it well just in case it *was* infectious, and included another copy of the email.

Just south of the Manor is the little hamlet of Langton. I'd missed the postman, who unofficially, would take as well as deliver mail, so I chose to walk to Langton because they have a little post box alongside a real old red telephone box. It would also give me a chance to look at the condition of other lawns and grass verges as I passed.

The drive swings sharply around the gatehouse to both hide the gate from the house and also the house from anyone in the lane. The lane is unnamed and signposted as a 'No Through Road', it runs past the Manor gates allowing farm machinery to access the fields and hill behind the house. Almost directly opposite the Manor gates, there is a public footpath that leads to the main road just where the turn off to Langton is. This route is quite a bit shorter than following the lane down to the road, but the path isn't well used, is steep, and is liable to get very overgrown.

After a few minutes, I was fighting off brambles and shoulder-high nettles and not making much progress. I considered turning back, but I heard a car on the road ahead so battled on. I decided that I would definitely not be going back the same way. I had been stung by nettles more than once and was sporting a scratch right across my chin. Cursing the brambles, I wished a virus on them out loud. Suddenly, without any warning, there was a violent clatter and noise of leaves being scattered and torn as a grey shape flew right at me. I jumped in alarm and ducked out of the way. "Damn pigeons! – and you can all get a virus too!"

Finally, I staggered out onto the road. I rounded the corner towards a yard where refrigerated vans and mobile canteen trucks were parked. Then the little post box and telephone box finally came into view. I remember feeling that I'd actually achieved something by making it there with only minor injuries and proudly pushed my padded bag into the slot. Noted that collection wasn't for another hour, I headed back – via the road.

Just before I got to the left turn into the lane, I spotted Melissa walking towards me from the direction of Ingleton; she looked a little dishevelled, her head was bowed and she held a hand over her face. It looked from that distance that she might have been crying. Then I realised she was without her bike and concluded that she must have had an accident. I ran past the lane entrance towards her.

As I approached, she heard my steps and looked up as if terrified I was an attacker.

"Hey, Mel, it's only me. I've just been to the post box. What's happened? Are you hurt?"

She continued to walk head down. I stopped her by firmly placing my hands on her shoulders. She reluctantly let me carefully pull her hand away from her face. She *had* been crying, and her hand was covering a bruising right eye. She started sobbing again as soon as I grimaced.

I put an arm around her and guided her towards the lane. "Come on. Let's get you back to the house and clean you up. It doesn't look too bad." I hoped that her injuries looked worse than they were due to her smudged makeup but didn't want to spend too much time examining her by the roadside.

She said nothing all the way back. Occasionally sobbing and sniffing. I was hoping she hadn't been assaulted or worse but decided to wait until she was ready to tell me.

As we passed my gatehouse, she pulled away. "There," she pointed at my door. "I don't want *him* to see me like this," and she nodded towards the Manor.

My kitchen is dominated by a large, rustic oak table. I picked Melissa up under her arms and plonked her down on it opposite the window and sink. She just sat there slumped in silence looking at the floor.

I found and wetted two clean flannels and without turning to her quietly asked, "Should I be calling the police Mel?" turning back to face her for an answer.

She shook her head slowly and muttered, "No point."

The majority of the pale pink was coming off onto the first flannel as I carefully dabbed her foundation away. She was clearly sensitive around her eye but otherwise appeared unhurt. I handed her the 2nd flannel and asked her to hold it against her eye to reduce the swelling.

"I am going to have a black eye?" she asked quietly while looking straight at me for an honest answer.

"Yes, I think so, but not a great shiner."

She sighed. "Will it have gone by my birthday?"

I knew her Birthday was in September but couldn't recall the day. "When's that?"

"10th September – it's a Friday so I'll be at school. Oh crap, school starts again next Wednesday! Can you pass me a mirror?"

"You'll probably be back to beautiful by your sweet sixteenth and the red will probably have cleared by Wednesday. I think there maybe still some bruising, though. – As for a mirror… Er, no, there's one in the bathroom, but it's kind of attached to the wall."

She looked at me with one puzzled eye. "You don't have a hand mirror!?"

"Er, no, it's a *man thing*" I retorted.

"Stuart always carries a mirror," she stated.

"Hmm... yes. You don't surprise me."

"Oh," she sighed, "The signs were all there, weren't they? Pocket mirror, those yellow shorts! Oh, and that high-pitched giggle!" Melissa smiled just a little and, imitating him, said, *"My most favourite group ever is ABBA!"*

We both laughed, and a pretty smile briefly flashed across her face again.

She sniffed and had completely stopped crying as she slowly pulled the flannel away from her eye. It was bloodshot and a little bruised just below. She passed me the flannel. "Can you put some more cold on this?"

I took it and turned to the sink. I felt it was time to try to get her to tell me what had happened. I wondered if Stuart had maybe hit her for deceiving him about the tennis court. With my back turned to her, I casually asked, "Did you meet up with Stuart?"

"Yes," Melissa replied despondently, "we met up at the Black Horse but after only about fifteen minutes, his trainer showed up. He'd been looking for him because he'd found a court at Appleby and took him over there. Stuart asked me to come along, but I don't think his trainer approved, and I'd forgotten to bring my bike lock anyway."

Turning back and handing her the cooled flannel, I continued to probe; "So you and Stuart are OK? I did have to tell him everything, including that I was *not* your father!"

Then she noticed the scratch on my chin. "You have blood on your chin! What happened to you?" Melissa attempted to wipe my chin with the flannel, but I stepped back out of her reach.

"It's just a scratch. I lost a fight with a bramble," I assured her. Then remembered that I had failed to look out for yellowing or fungus-infected grass while I was out.

Melissa managed a small smile that evaporated as soon as she replaced the flannel on her eye. "Ow! – That's icy! Yes, Stuart was cool about it; he actually found it all rather funny, what with me making promises to lure a gay man, the lesbian thing, and you, unconvincingly, pretending to be a Lord. We're still going to be friends and for now, he's going to let people assume that I *am* his girlfriend."

I frowned, "I'm not so sure that's a good idea? – When the truth comes out it could make you look a bit of a fool. Anyway, where's your bike now?"

An angry look appeared, "Mad Mick has it," she stated.

"Oh great!" 'Mad Mick' was Michael Duguid. Mick was my age, or maybe even slightly older, but dressed and acted like a teenager. Rarely alone, he had a small following of real teenagers to whom he was a mentor in petty crime and general anti-social behaviour. Mick probably orchestrated most of the petty crime around Ingleton, but the inmates at Deerbolt, a young offenders prison at nearby Startforth, usually got the blame.

A natural bully whenever his 'gang' were to hand, but far less aggressive when on his own. So probably not as tough as he acted. He seemed unable to complete a sentence without the use of terrible puns and childish sexual innuendo. Gaining him the alternative nickname of 'Killer-the-pun.'

Before Lady Quail had left, Peter and I used to walk down to the Black Horse of an evening and often met up with fellow gardener Richard, who worked at Ingleton Bury. They were pleasant evenings. Together we would share gardening tips, listen to Richard's endless supply of bad jokes, and then we'd put all the world's wrongs to right.

Mad Mick and his little gang were often there too but left us alone. Occasionally they would cause a fight or loud argument with some poor lone drinker or elderly couple. However, one evening, Richard arrived early, and Mick took the opportunity to break his nose and threatened him never to return - something he never did. That left just me with Peter, in his seventies. Mick got braver and would taunt us too. The landlady did her best to prevent Mick losing her yet more custom, but his menacing presence, rude interruptions, and terrible puns reduced our enjoyment and we went less often until, without ever deciding to, we just stopped going altogether.

I could imagine Mick hitting a young girl. "So Mick hit you?"

"No," Melissa replied fiercely, "he held me so Sandy could hit me – Twice!"

"Not Sandy Rutherford! – Peter's granddaughter? I know she's got some dubious issues with your father but why would she hit *you*?"

Melissa took a deep breath, slid off the table and casually discarded the flannel in the sink. "Can we sit somewhere more comfortable?"

"Sure upstairs." I pointed to the foot of the stairs and then, noting her slightly suspicious look, added, "My bedroom is through *there*." I pointed to the door behind her.

"Oh! – Downstairs? – I've never seen beyond the kitchen since Peter left. His bedroom was upstairs," she explained.

I nodded. "Yes, that's right, it was; I swapped them around because I didn't want such a big room just to sleep in."

I've never been up here! She looked back as she climbed the creaking stairs and smirked. "You can do more than sleep in a bedroom you know? – And no looking up my skirt!"

"Hadn't crossed my mind!" I replied as I quickly averted my eyes.

We entered my 'man pad'. The whole of the upstairs is a single, well proportioned, loft room. The room is basic with panoramic windows and blackout blinds at each apex and four large, square, skylights in the roof. On one side: Two, large, leather cinema chairs face the obligatory 52" plasma TV with huge hi-fi speakers either side. To the left of the door a small bar complete with optics and to the right an original, coin-operated Pac-Man machine. My telescope dominated the far end and pointed up

34

towards one of the two skylights at the far end.

"What on earth is that?" Melissa pointed at the Pac-Man machine.

"You are too young to have encountered Pac-Man? – You need educating. But not now. Now you can take a seat and tell me exactly what happened today."

She stabbed the [Start] button as she passed but the machine was unplugged, and nothing happened. She gave a brief and a rather dismissive look around the room, before falling back into the nearest chair and was almost swallowed by it. She looked so tiny in it, and I tried hard not to laugh. She found and quickly mastering the chair's remote control, she raised the back and retracted the foot rest so she sat forward without having her feet in the air. "You waste your money on some weird shit George. This place needs a woman's touch. Where in Hell did you get that black wallpaper?"

"Never mind that, I should be gardening. Now tell me what happened to you?"

"Do you have any make-up?" Melissa was now up again and looking at her reflection in the big screen.

I sighed. "Why would I have any makeup? - Sit down and spill the beans!" I was starting to get irritated and felt the weeds were going to go to seed before she answered.

She sat back down, and I swivelled her chair to face the other as I sat down.

Melissa looked serious again and let out a big sigh before starting. "I'd gone to meet Stuart, but he went off with his coach - like I said. But I'd not finished the J2O that Stuart got me, so I sat out front with it so I could keep an eye on my bike. Well,

Mick and Sandy turned up arm-in-arm with his band of Muppets following behind. Sandy said something about 'the little rich bitch', but I ignored her. Mad Mick shouted out that I charged 50p for a screw but that I'd do it for a J2O on Thursday's. I ignored that too."

I nodded. "Wise, he thinks he's so funny… Sorry, go on."

Shifting in the chair her legs sticking to the leather she continued. "Mick spotted my bike and told his Muppets that it was a gift from *Daddy* to him and told them to take it for scrap. I said that's they'd better not else they'll be down the nick for theft! That's when Sandy kicked off; she got right in my face asking if I was really going to report a theft to Mick's dad? Then she said I had to be a 'Daddy's girl' because my mother had fucked off with all the money to screw another ancient Lord."

"Ah!" I remembered her reaction to Karen's comments the previous Friday. "So you had *words*?" I asked.

"Too right! I told her how she wasn't taking any money so had been completely wrong about her. And do you know what she said?" she paused, "she said 'So *Daddy* had killed her Grandfather for nothing!' – Then she just went mad and tried to hit me! I dodged her, but Mick had got behind me. He held my head down to the table, his other filthy hand everywhere, and that bitch hit me twice before I managed to get away, and I had to run because the Muppets had still got my bike." Melissa started to cry again.

"Oh Mel, I'm so sorry. Those complete bastards have got it coming. We can't let this go unreported. You said Sandy mentioned something about 'reporting it to Mick's dad' what did she mean by that?"

Melissa looked up and wiped her eyes. "Didn't you know? –

Mad Mick's father is Simon Duguid, he's only a desk sergeant. Oh, and a Parish Councillor. That's why there's absolutely no point reporting this or anything else that Mick and his Muppets do."

"No, I didn't know. So, you're saying that Mick's dad uses his position to protect him!?"

"Yes," she sighed, "you know Mad Mick broke Richard's nose?" Melissa had hopped out of the chair and now, and on tip-toes was trying to look through my telescope.

I nodded. "Yes, that was outside the Black Horse too."

Then she started running her fingers down the blackout blind making it clack before turning back towards the chair.

"Well, Richard did report it; he had witnesses, hospital report, and everything. He asked to have another officer deal with it too. But, when the witness statements were collected, every single one was useless; either claiming they were drunk - at 6 pm! - and so couldn't remember, or that they didn't actually see *anything*."

I couldn't believe what I was hearing "Jesus! That's totally corrupt! I didn't think that kind of thing still happened."

Mel sighed. "It gets worse; I hear his Dad then threatened to prosecute Richard for wasting police time and warned *him* to stay away from Mick and the pub!"

I'd never liked Mick, but now I was beginning to feel real anger towards him "I'd like to catch that Mad Mick alone – I can just imagine the pleasure I'd get holding his head under the water and leaving his body in Langton Beck."

"George! – You're not serious?" Melissa looked

anxious. "No. Much as I might think it, I…"

"Or say it!" She interrupted.

"Alright! - As much as I might like to think it - and say it," I agreed, "the only things I could kill are weeds and maybe the odd rabbit."

Melissa was now looking at her reflection in the TV again. "Can I use your bathroom? – I'm OK now, I just want to clean myself up. Thanks for listening, George."

"Sure. Look, I'd better go and do some gardening. Are you sure you're going to be OK?"

Melissa nodded, gave me a weak smile and headed off down the stairs. I followed her down and called through the bathroom door: "Obviously, you're just too young to have a real drink, but should you want a small one today, just help yourself."

"Thanks. You are so kind, George. Please don't mention any of this to Daddy."

I thought that she should, but left her to give him an edited version in her own time.

I left Melissa and headed back to work, but the unfairness of all that had happened continued to bother me for the rest of the day and felt sure that Melissa would be feeling worse.

I had thought 'Ingle' was a happy little village but Mad Mick and his gang, now surprisingly including Sandy, were just spoiling it. I also wondered what had happened to Sandy's fiancée; the father of the child that she had lost. If Sandy was really with Mad Mick now, they must have broken up. That was another sad thing because the couple had seemed so happy when, only about 18 Months earlier, in the Black Horse, they'd announced she was both expecting and that they were engaged. I wondered too about Melissa's bike, was there any way I could safely get that back to her?

I was getting a headache, and the intense sun wasn't helping.

I didn't sleep well that night; I kept waking up, and spent most of it going over all that Melissa had said. I was particularly concerned about what had happened to Richard, and I felt guilty that I hadn't attempted to contact him since his nose had been broken.

No 'butterflies' were dancing on the wall the following morning. It must be cloudy, I thought. I looked out of the window hoping the rain that had been forecast had passed by, and it had.

The forecast had said nothing about frost! But, I could see that the whole of the hill beyond the house was frosty white. My heart sank; as well as being a very early sign that winter was approaching - and it was only the 4th of September - I hadn't moved the many pots of frost-tender geraniums into the shelter of the walled garden, and they may now have suffered as a result.

A car beeped twice. Karen had arrived for her Friday cleaning duties, and the twin beeps indicated she wanted to ask me something. I'd overslept so I hurriedly dressed and went out to see her.

"Morning George! – Can you confirm that this bike belongs to Mel?" Paul was sitting in the front with the bike both in the rear and sticking out the back of the little car. Puzzled I took a look.

"Morning Karen. Er, yes! – How come you have it?" I enquired.

"Great, can you help me get it out of the car? It was a real job to get it in. Simon Duguid found it abandoned and thought he recognised it as Melissa's so he kindly dropped it round to me last night."

"Oh did he now?" I asked suspiciously.

As we struggled to pull it from the car, she said: "It was very kind of him. He's a nice bloke and nothing like his son!"

"Does Mad Mick still live with him? - With his dad?"

Paul had got out of the car and interrupted: "Can I ride the bike up to the steps? Please, Mum?"

Karen looked like she was about to say 'No.' but I knew Melissa had let him ride it before, so quickly said: "That will save me walking it up later, thank you, Paul!"

"OK," Karen said with a familiar resigned tone, "but put that tin on the seat carefully."

Paul clumsily climbed out of the car holding an upside-down biscuit tin in both hands. He then, very carefully put it back on the passenger seat before taking the bike. Though it was clearly too big for him, he managed to get it going by standing up on the pedals.

"Be careful!" Karen called out after him before finally answering my question. "Yes, Mick still lives with his Dad." Karen sighed and shrugged, "You know he is 34 this year, and I can't see him leaving anytime soon! Although… village gossip says he's hooked up with Sandy Rutherford! I wonder what happened to that lovely fiancée of hers? What was his name? Oh! And I bet you didn't know there's a story circulating about Mel? Well, apparently, she attacked Sandy yesterday for no reason! It was outside the pub, so she was probably drunk! Have you heard anything? I know first-hand that she has a very short fuse!"

I thought carefully before answering. "Well, Melissa's version is rather different; I can tell you that she had not been drinking. I don't know if she's told Arthur anything about it yet? Probably depends on whether he has noticed her black eye or not. So please don't say anything up at the house in his earshot."

Karen's eyes widened. "A black eye?! – Is that why she left her bike behind?"

"Have you and Mel made up after last Friday?" I enquired.

"Oh yes, …" Karen took in a deep breath. "Yes, on Tuesday I apologised and ate a great deal of humble pie. Seems I had completely misjudged her Mother, and I said so. I've known Mel since she was a baby; until recently we got on really well. We have both been stressed out and we've talked, kissed and made up. Though I still just don't understand why that woman doesn't want any contact with her own daughter?"

"No, nor do I, but it's good you are friends again. She's up at the house so you can ask her yourself, but *not* in Arthur's earshot," I reminded.

"Hmmm. I see," Karen said coldly as she got back into her car, "well, I have made cakes! You can join us for *tea and cakes at eleven* like we always used to on a Friday, even if you won't share the gossip!"

"Oh nice! – I look forward to it. Thank you."

"Well, it was Arthur's idea; a regular get together and *not* a staff meeting he said."

I had forgotten the 'tea and cakes at eleven' tradition. It must have ended after Lady Quail left. Every Friday Karen or Molly the cook would make, or bring in, cakes from the bakery, and at eleven we would all have tea, some cake, and a chat. It was a special, end-of-the-week, treat, and I was very pleased that the

41

tradition was to be reinstated.

Just as Karen was about to pull away, I caught sight of the hill above the house. "Oh Karen, was there a frost in Ingle last night? The hill is covered in it!" I nodded towards the hill.

"That's not frost! – It's some grass fungus that's going around. Didn't you see the local news this morning? – Our Ingleton got a mention! Apparently, someone from the village was first to report it."

"No, I missed it. I didn't sleep very well and then overslept. Did they say who reported it?" I wondered if it might have been me, "and did they say if there was there a cure for it?"

Karen shrugged as she put on her seat belt, "I don't think so. I wasn't really listening. It was only a short report about some boring grass fungus. I did see quite a lot of white grass on my way in this morning, though."

She waved and drove off, beeping at Paul, who had stopped to look in the fountain.

I headed towards the hill wanting to confirm that the white was fungus and not frost. Unable to choose which I'd prefer it to be. But I never got that far; the grass under the trees was covered in the fungus, as were the lawns behind the house. I stood, frozen to the spot, at the back of the house; staring down the broad South Avenue, to the hill and beyond, in shocked wonder.

Arthur had seen me and came out to join me. "It all looks like a bizarre Christmas card does it not?" he asked solemnly. "Heavy frost with roses in full bloom and leaves still on the trees."

"It's scary: If it all dies what will take its place? Weeds or just mud? I thought it was just an early frost. Now I wish that's all it was. This looks like a different garden – with a different view.

"Yes… It would make a great film backdrop for an alien planet! George, can you do something about the croquet lawn? The grass has gone all slimy, and it has attracted masses of tiny black flies – most unpleasant."

"Oh no! I'll see if I can mow it to zero and pick it up. I just hope the wheels, and my feet, have traction on the slime and that it doesn't clog up the mower." I let out a deep sigh.

The gravity of the situation and inevitable increased workload was starting to dawn on me. "If all this dies and turns to slime, I just don't know what I can do?" I waved my arm from left to right taking in the frosty looking view as I did. As far as the garden extended and almost right up to the house, the grass was a dusty white. Beyond the garden, right to the horizon, where there had been green there was now white. "Imagine twelve acres of slime here and another six at the front. Even if I could pick it all up, where can I take it all?"

My eyes were starting to water. I suddenly realised that I was close to tears. I had been gardening at the Manor for just over five years, the last two on my own. I had worked extremely hard and was proud of my achievements. Peter and I had both received much praise from Arthur. But now, we stood looking at a completely ruined landscape. I felt like quitting, there and then.

I felt an arm around my shoulder, not something that came naturally from Lord Quail. He must have noticed my sudden depression or watering eyes. "Hey, none of this is your fault, George. Sort the croquet lawn as best as you can. We'll just have to let nature, time or the science bods sort out the rest. Might be wise to buy up grass seed, though. Take a trip to Millers End and pick up as much as you can fit in the car. Then we can be ready to reseed when this passes. We won't be able to buy turf. This has spread from Newcastle and, according to the news this morning; has gone west as far as Barney, south as far as

Darlington and is nearing the Borders to the north."

"Thanks, Arthur. I appreciate that this is not the view you want to see. I'll do what I can for the croquet lawn, and I'll go for the seed now before it sells out." It was then that I decided, rather than this being a destructive problem, this was going to be a new challenge; one for me to solve. Running away wasn't an option this time – I felt sure this virus would follow and catch up with me anyway.

"Chin up, George, I fully trust you to do whatever is possible. I'll see you for tea and cakes at eleven, and we'll talk some more then." He released my shoulder and gave me a hearty pat on the back.

Behind me, I could hear a window opening. We turned to see Melissa, wearing large sunglasses, waving some pieces of paper. "There you are!" she called out. "The phone has been going non-stop and you two… Oh, my god! The grass!" Melissa, lifted her glasses to confirm what she was actually seeing, briefly revealing wide, astonished eyes. Agape she took in the alien landscape that had replaced her usual view.

We walked towards her. "Morning Mel. Thanks, Arthur, I'll let you get on and get your phone messages."

"No!" insisted Melissa as she quickly replaced her glasses. "The messages are all for *you* George." Looking at her notes she said: "There's been …" In the background, we could hear the phone ringing again. "I've just switched it to go straight to message," she assured. "There's been Deefra - twice, RHS, Plant Pathology at Imperial College, Fera PC and Sky news!"

Arthur chuckled "Melissa I think you have your first job!"

Melissa looked puzzled.

As she leant out of the window, Arthur tapped her on each shoulder with the end of his stick as if knighting her and bellowed: "I hereby appoint you – Melissa Jayne Quail - Secretary to the Head Gardener of Ingleton Manor!"

"Get lost!" Melissa replied, tossing her notes out of the window and slamming it shut.

Arthur chased the papers and looked at them. "Was that a 'no' do you think?" Putting on his reading glasses, he began to read, "Hmmm, I think 'Deefra' will be DEFRA no idea who 'Peta PC' are?"

I didn't feel like talking to any of them. I just hoped the RHS hadn't given them all my mobile number and was glad that the gatehouse didn't have a land line. "Should I call them back?"

Folding the papers up and putting in his breast pocket he looked over the top of his glasses at me and said simply, "No, they can all wait until you have had some thinking time and we've had our chat at eleven. My twelve years as an MP has given me some valuable experience dealing with both the media and government departments. I also still command the respect of some useful contacts, so may be able to smooth your path somewhat."

"Thanks, Arthur. I'd much prefer to get grass seed and deal with that slime than speak to that lot! Is it OK to use the car?"

"Yes, of course, I've no need of it until tomorrow. I will see you at eleven."

Between the house and the gardening sheds, where the tools, barrows, tractor-mower and trailer are stored, is a double garage. This is connected to the drive by a narrow spur road. A walkway of arches - a recent addition - offers some shelter for those walking from the car to the side door of the house. Originally, the chauffeur would have taken the Lord and Lady directly to the main door then return the car to the garages himself. There are still photographs in the house of a beautiful deep red Bentley and Rolls Royce Silver Shadow with a smartly uniformed chauffeur standing proudly between them.

The electric door opened slowly to reveal a 6-year-old, silver, Toyota RAV-4 and an empty space in the garage next to it.

Things had changed a lot at the Manor even before Lady Quail had left. I recalled how Peter had surprised me, one evening at the Black Horse: He told how, in 1958, aged just nineteen, he had originally been employed as the Quail's chauffeur. He recalled that Arthur was only eight years old when he started but that the post was retired, by Arthur, in 1972 after Arthur's father died.

I stopped at the gatehouse on my way out. What with oversleeping and then Karen turning up with Mel's bike, I'd forgotten to either check my emails or pocket my mobile phone.

I was relieved to find no missed calls on the mobile. But there was an email, sent the previous day from RHS Wisley; replying to my message, it first asked me, in bold, not to send any further samples of possibly infected grass to anyone. "Oops!" I thought.

It also stated that they had kept my original sample and divided it between DEFRA's research labs, Peta Plant Care, and Plant Pathology at Imperial College. They had also included a copy of all of my correspondences to each. "So that explains those phone calls," I muttered to myself. The final paragraph said that, should I have discovered a new plant virus, it could be named after me. I wasn't sure how I felt about that; a little pride but then, did I want to put my name to something most people are going to associate with a destructive fungus?

As soon as I drove into the lane, I became aware of yellow grass on the verges and at Langton, many lawns were either white with the fungus or had gone very yellow.

Once at Millers End, I grabbed a trolley and headed straight for where their 25Kg bags of lawn grasses were displayed. I saw another trolley already there, loaded with five sacks. As I rounded the corner, I immediately recognised Richard from Ingleton Bury.

"Hello George!" he said, "I thought I might see you here today!" Then grinning, he added, "I've left you one split-open bag of rye!"

"Oh, Richard, long time no see! Thanks such a lot for leaving the rye grass!" I had already scanned the shelves, and there were still, at least, ten bags of fine grasses remaining. "The Bury has got white lawns too?"

"Yeah we got it almost everywhere," he sighed, "if it's not white it's gone yellow." Pointing at the bags, he asked, "Not sure planting this is going to help, is it?"

"No, I'm sure there will be no point sowing it now, but when this passes or is cured there will be a significant seed shortage." I saw, with his bags of grass, several boxes of fungicide. Pointing at those, I stated: "That stuff doesn't help I'm afraid; it clears the fungus, but the grass still dies."

"Oh, I did hear that but thought I'd try it for myself. Are you sure?"

I told Richard about the croquet lawn remaining sick and the slime and flies that Arthur had said was there now.

"Oh shit. Do you know who called this in?" Richard asked, "On the news, it said someone from Ingleton but that it spread here from Newcastle."

"Er, that might have been yours truly; I did send a sample off to Wisley last week," I explained as casually as I could.

Richard raised his eyebrows, "Really! – So you were the first to notice it?"

"Well actually no… Lord Quail himself saw just a small patch on one corner of the croquet lawn last Friday. He brought it to my attention."

Remembering what Melissa said about his run-in with the Duguid's, I thought I'd try to verify the story; "I'm sorry to hear you had a run-in with the Mad Mick and his dad."

"Oh that was almost two years ago, and Simon Duguid's not a bit like his son."

"Didn't he caution you for wasting police time and tell you not go near the Black Horse again?"

"No!" Richard laughed, "that's just so typical of Ingle Gossip! He probably did have a hand in persuading my witnesses to sign useless statements, but I certainly didn't get a caution nor a Black Horse ban. I chose not to go back - why risk running into Mick again? And, I think it was Simon who paid for my nose to be straightened."

I had been secretly looking at his nose and couldn't see any signs of a break. "What?! Simon Duguid paid for your nose to be fixed?" I gave him my most disbelieving look.

"Well, I can't be sure; I'd had an NHS quick fix, but it was twisted and not very pretty. When I reported the attack, I was asked how much compensation I was seeking to have it straightened privately. Well, I didn't know, I hadn't considered it.

I just wanted Mad Mick locked up. Anyway, a week after the charges against Mick were dropped, an envelope full of cash dropped through my door."

"You're kidding?"

"No, it really happened. By then I had got a quote from Ramsay Newcastle to fix it. They wanted nineteen hundred quid! Well, of course, I couldn't justify that on gardener's wages. But in that envelope, there was ...?" Richard raised his eyebrows waiting for me to answer.

"No? Not nineteen hundred?!"

"No," replied Richard smugly, "not quite, it had two grand in it! – So I had it done - what do you think?" he turned his head from side to side.

"I can't see the join!" I joked. "No, honestly, it looks no different to when I last saw you… Oh, look, Richard, I'm so sorry… Sorry that I didn't keep in touch with you.

Richard looked down and paused before replying. "I wasn't so upset by that; My Doctor had just told me I need to cut out the beer anyway. But, I would have liked to have been told that Peter had died. I'm a bit isolated up at the Bury and don't get much local news. I read it in the Westy Gazette the day after his funeral. I would have liked to have gone - shown my respects. He was such a lovely old chap. I do miss him."

"Yes, he was one-of-a-kind, and I miss him too. Sorry, I just didn't think. Karen only told us on the day of the funeral, and we only just made it ourselves. It was a bit of a shock. I know he was in his mid-seventies, but he seemed so fit and well when I last saw him."

We stood there in silence remembering Peter. Then Richard

said, "Well, I'd better get this lot, less the fungicide, back to the Bury. See you around George."

Once back at the Manor, I stored the seed sacks in the spare garage and completed the watering. I checked my watch: 10.50 - I just had time to take a quick look at the croquet lawn before 'tea and cakes at eleven.'

A foul stagnant smell greeted me as I came through the wisteria arch. Not the usual bouquet of sweet scents from the sensory bed. The lawn was now a mix of mostly grey and very pale yellow. As I approached, a cloud of tiny black flies rose up, triggering a ripple effect as the flies took to the air from where I stood. As more and more ascended, I realised that I could barely see the ground through them. I stood back as they formed a dense black fog that filled the air from shoulder height down to the ground. Slowly, starting from where I stood the process reversed as the flies settled back down on the slime that was all that remained of the once perfect lawn.

There was a knock on the conservatory window. It was Karen indicating that I should come in, but not via the door leading directly onto the croquet lawn. Young Paul was by the door also and was and pointing frantically back to what had been the croquet lawn, but I didn't understand what he was trying to say.

Arriving in the conservatory, via the side door, I was pleased to see the table, complete with a white lace-edged cloth, laid out with tea and coffee pots, decent sized cups, and a silver platter of Karen's homemade cupcakes. Karen and Arthur were already sitting in two of the large, high-backed, wicker chairs. Paul was squatting by the window under the dragon tree and was banging the window loudly. Karen indicated I should take the vacant seat and then chastised Paul: "Paul! I've told you to stop hitting that window. Do it again and you'll have no cake!"

Paul turned to look first at the cakes then back to the window,

"Doesn't work anyway," he muttered gloomily.

Curious, I asked, "What were you trying to do Paul?" He didn't answer and just continued to stare out of the window.

Arthur chuckled, "Paul saw all the flies rise up when you walked up to them. He was trying to get you to make them fly up again. It was quite a show!"

Karen screwed up her face, "It's disgusting that's what it is. I don't want to be sweeping or wiping those up, so everyone, please keep those windows and doors shut."

"Come and have some cake, Paul." Arthur beckoned him from the window. "They are both fascinating and a little disgusting. Not the cakes you understand, Karen! But I concur, we certainly do not need those flies in the house! Now who's for tea?"

Karen served the drinks, and we helped ourselves to the dainty little cakes. Paul took his back to the window and sat crossed legged on the floor so he could keep an eye on the flies. Arthur and Karen discussed which areas of the house could now be cleaned and reopened. They decided since both he and Melissa had taken a liking to cooking, and that Karen had promised to help once she moved in, that there was no need to re-hire a cook. I was barely listening, being deep in my thoughts about the many consequences of the grass dying.

My thoughts were broken when Karen looking past me said, "Wow, you do look smart!"

I turned to see Melissa entering the room. She still wore the large sunglasses but had now changed into a very stylish outfit consisting of a glossy white blouse, short black jacket, and matching pleated skirt. Unusually for her she was also wearing tights and her trainers had been swapped for black, flat shoes. But to our further surprise, her formerly pink hair was now back

51

to blonde and considerably tidier.

"You look absolutely beautiful my dear," Arthur stated.

Karen and I both nodded and smiled encouragingly in agreement, Paul just glanced at her, seemed most unimpressed, and returned his gaze to the window, propping his head up with a hand on his chin.

"So you're applying for a job?" joked Karen.

"Got one thanks," replied Melissa smugly.

"Er... You do?" Arthur enquired as if peering over glasses.

"I am PA to the Head Gardener!" She said proudly, briefly placing her hand on my shoulder, before sitting down between Karen and Arthur. We all watched as she carefully placed a small notepad and pen down on the table before sitting unusually upright in the chair and crossing her legs. "Oh, Daddy, I will require a new laptop. Did you make these cakes Karen? They do look most delicious!" Melissa then very daintily took one and nibbled at it, most delicately.

Karen looked completely puzzled as well as slightly amused. She looked to both Arthur and me, for an explanation, but all she saw were two men trying to hide their amusement.

Noting that Arthur was clearly pleased with her new appearance, even if it had arisen from Melissa having misinterpreted his flippant comment early that day, I said: "I'd be delighted to have you as my personal assistant Melissa. Are there any more messages?" I asked nodding towards her blank notepad.

"Er, hair!" she responded pointing at her head with both hands,

"I can't take messages and get to look like this at the same time you know!" Then realising she'd fallen out of character, she quickly added, "But you may be assured that I will play the phone messages and summarise them for you just as soon as possible."

Arthur smiled, "Well you do look lovely my dear; the job is yours. I'll put five hundred pounds on your card for the laptop but ..." he looked sternly straight at her, "you are still going back to school on Wednesday come what may!"

"Oh." Melissa sighed slightly.

"When did you get the outfit?" Karen asked.

"Last week. I got it for the sixth form – we don't have to wear uniforms anymore just be 'smart.'"

"I see." Said Karen still looking puzzled, "And George, why should *you* need a secretary all of a sudden?"

"PA!" Interrupted Melissa, answering for me. "It's because he's going to be famous and people from all over are calling him, even Sky News! – He needs someone to take notes and... Um, other Personal Assistant stuff like... Em, holding his stuff and standing next to him when he's on the telly."

Karen and I laughed, and even Melissa joined in. "Well you know what I mean!" she added, "I only started today!"

"OK... So George, what's this all about? You dark horse, you!" Karen asked.

Arthur and I updated Karen as the cakes slowly disappeared, mostly to Paul, who would sneak two at a time and take them back to his fly monitoring. We discussed the possibility that the virus could be named after me and some of the many consequences that could result should all the grass die.

Melissa was at first only concerned about it spreading to Wimbledon, and if tennis could be played on Astroturf or not? Then she added horses being unable to graze, and milk, to the growing list of potential casualties.

Even Paul entered the debate when I mentioned my theory that cereal crops could also be affected. "No Weetabix!" he stated, "I love my Weetabix."

"Nor bread" Added Karen,

"Good! I don't like bread," replied Paul.

"Or cakes!" said Arthur and Karen in perfect unison. Paul snatched the last cake and took it back to the window.

Arthur contributed: Grazing sheep and deer as well as grass being ground cover for many nesting birds. "I can live without football and rugby, but I'll miss the cricket. But you know what worries me the most? ... Whisky; made from rye!"

Karen was concerned that people, once realising crops might not grow the following spring, would hoard food or could start looting, causing premature shortages that may lead to rioting.

Melissa, who had been taking notes, looked to me, "What do you think George? Is this going to destroy crops? Could it spread around the world? Can it be stopped?"

My head had been just buzzing with thoughts each leading to a series of scenarios that seemed worse than the last. I shook my head slowly, "I really don't know… But there could be massive problems, even if it's only the grasses that dies."

"The state of my croquet lawn you mean?" joked Arthur.

"No." I wasn't really in a joking mood. "Flooding for one. Think of this… You look around the countryside, and you see mostly green? Well, that green is the top half of grass. All of the grass is holding water. Where's all that water going to go? Then, once the roots have died, what remains to bind the soil together? – Road and rail embankments will be washed down onto the tracks and roads. Every time we get heavy rain, there would be total transport chaos!" I had everyone's full attention. The mood in the room became solemn. "There could be food shortages caused by distribution problems even if cereal crops aren't affected. Ambulances and…"

"Thank you, George," Arthur interrupted, wanting me to stop.

I realised that both Karen and Melissa were looking scared. "You are clearly looking at this from a different perspective, and your views and ideas may be a valuable asset. Now I need to make a phone call, and you have some calls of your own to answer.
However, keep *those* thoughts under your hat for now. Especially when you speak to Sky, just tell them what you know and how you discovered it. I strongly advise you don't include any 'disaster scenarios' or predictions, nothing that might instil panic. Maybe you could just play dumb and 'wonder about the football'?"

I nodded in agreement realising that my words could be influential and might encourage reckless behaviour. I also wondered who it was that Arthur needed to phone so urgently?

Karen asked Paul to bring his plate back and to go and play in the garden. "Keep well away from those flies!" she insisted. Then she started tidying up the table before returning to her cleaning duties.

Melissa led me to her homework room, which she stated could be 'our' office. She played back the messages, then she briefed me, very professionally, as if I'd not just heard them. She even put them in order importance.

I spoke to Miss Parker, an epidemiologist at Imperial College; she had successfully isolated a new virus from my sample. She sounded quite excited about it and insisted we agreed on a name for it. She rattled on about 'gene vectors' and 'transient protein expressions' before I interrupted her and explained that I was sorry, but I just didn't have a clue what she was talking about! She sounded a little disappointed, but after some less detailed scientific explanation, we agreed the virus should be named: 'Potyviridae Craven-Parker'. I didn't fully grasp what 'Potyviridae; actually meant, but apparently, it had to be there.

Peta Plant Clinic also blinded me with science for a while and seemed very disappointed that the virus had been isolated and already named. However, they were kind enough to offer lots of practical advice that may slow or stop its spread. They suggested that it was unlikely to spread much further south because not so much rainfall had fallen there as had in the north of England.

DEFRA would call me back. They failed to recognise either my name or the name of the person who had called me earlier and we simply agreed to end the call.

I refused an offer to go live on Sky TV News but allowed them to record a brief phone interview that was unlikely to cause any panic and concentrated instead on the football and effects on tourism in the Lake District. When asked if I thought it was possible that a meteorite had brought the virus with it? I replied cagily "I can't comment on that." And, promptly, put the phone down.

"Stop winding them up, George!" grinned Melissa.

I tasked Melissa to take any further calls, responding as I had done if she felt she could, also to watch news reports and do social media searches on related stories.

It was now 1.30 in the afternoon, and I had barely even started gardening. "I've got all that slime to get rid of. Don't suppose my PA wants to help with that?" Melissa carried on reading her notes and just raised a middle finger without even looking up.

The flies rose up again in a great plume as I approached the croquet lawn. I thought of calling Paul over to look, but he was probably down by the lake. What remained of the grass was a smelly, stringy slime, barely visible through the millions of tiny flies. Using one foot, I quickly established that this stuff was very slippery and that mowing it wasn't an option. Scraping my boot sideways cleared a narrow patch down to shiny wet mud. The slime only partially flowed back, so scraping it off was the answer.

I returned armed with a wheelbarrow, greenhouse mister, snow shovel, four large gardening buckets and the heavy metal gravel rake. The water mister created a fine mist which successfully kept the flies down. The back of the gravel rake has a long flat bar, and this worked well scraping the slime off the level surface. I shovelled up the thick, stinking slime with the snow shovel. The bucket quickly filled with a mixture of the green slime and dead flies, and it stank. The pungent, stagnant smell made me retch, and I regularly turned my head to one side to try to breathe some fresher air.

I filled the four buckets and quickly realised they were so heavy that I could only put two in the barrow at a time. So, just two buckets at a time, I took them right around to the far side of the lake and emptied them on the far shore. After those initial four had been emptied, I filled another four and did the same.

Finally, the flies and slime were gone. Just a large, very flat, patch of damp mud remained.

By the time I'd cleaned and put all the tools away it was early evening. Karen and Paul had long since gone home, and I was about to retire to the gatehouse. First, I thought I'd better check in on Melissa and see if there had been any further calls or news and also check with Arthur that it was alright for me to continue my work over the weekend.

I looked for Arthur first in the conservatory then the sitting room before finally finding him napping in the library - a brandy glass, empty but still in his hand. I gently slid it out from between his fingers and put it on the little table beside him.

Melissa was still in 'our office'. I could see her notes had expanded onto another page, and there was now also an empty coke can, a side plate with a few crumbs and half a cold cup of tea on the desk. The little television was on BBC News-24, and she was asleep in the chair, with her head resting on her folded arms, on the desk.

I glanced through her notes.

DEFRA called: "They wouldn't speak to me! – So I hung up."

Radio Borders: "Will call back this evening" – looking for comment on fungus spreading into Scotland."

Sky News (on the TV) – "Northern Grass Fungus threatens Lake District" – "George Craven (!!!) from Ingleton, first reported the white fungus last Friday blah blah..." Spread from Newcastle... Some maps showing spread and where the meteorite hit the sea. Air traffic controller interviewed – "Thinks meteorite fell too slowly, and it was unusual for them to appear on radar." Sheep farmer interviewed – "Thinks grass will recover, but some of his sheep died after inhaling flies."

BBC National News. "Newcastle City match cancelled at St. James's Park due to Northern Grass Fungus." Biologist interviewed "This is just an ordinary grass fungus and is only bad because of amount of rain followed by warm spell" (Dick brain!!)

Peta Plant Care called to remind you not to send any grass samples by post and complaining that Imperial College had prematurely published their 'assessment'.

Miss Parker – Imperial College: She hopes you don't mind that they have made a statement to BBC re 'their' virus discovery.

High Peak Radio: "Can you do a phone interview tomorrow morning?" - Minster FM: "Are going call you for interview at 7.30" (cheeky gits –I gave them made up mobile number ha ha!) - BBC Tees (not Radio Tees?!): "Can you call their researcher?"

I'm so bored! – Why is your mobile phone in the gatehouse and not your pocket? !!!'

I left her a note thanking her for her good work and promising to keep my mobile with me from now on. I added that I'd be around in the morning if she needed me. Then I disconnected the phone on her desk, leaving the plug end of the cable in front of her so that she'd know it was unplugged.

I realised that I hadn't eaten anything other than a couple of Karen's cupcakes and that I was both exhausted and hungry. Ingleton's small population of only about 650, doesn't support a takeaway, and I didn't fancy freezer food. I briefly considered going to the Black Horse but, firstly I'd be self-conscious eating alone, and secondly, Mad Mick would probably show up. I decided that beans on toast then a shot or two of white rum followed by sleep would suffice. I could still smell the slime on my fingers, so a shower first.

As I opened my door, I became aware that a big black Nissan was crawling, very slowly, past the gate in the direction of the hill. I couldn't see anything through the windows in the failing light because they were heavily tinted. 'Lost,' I thought to myself. If they went much further, they'd have a job turning around.
Soon after the Manor entrance the track climbs steeply, narrows, and the tarmac changes to a rough track. Sure enough, I heard a clunk as it was put into reverse and it crawled back, reversing into the gateway to turn around. Curious, I waited until it got to the junction with the main road. It was very unusual for any vehicles, other than farm machinery to enter the lane. It seemed to have stopped again at the junction and I didn't hear it pull away.

'Yes, definitely lost,' I said to myself as I shut the door.

Chapter 3 – Just not Croquet

Arthur was up early. His Saturday newspapers were both neatly folded back and left on the table by the conservatory door. I assumed the fly problem had passed because the doors were left wide open.

He would leave out newspapers if there were any articles that he thought would be of interest to me. I decided to look later; I needed to catch up with work I'd not got around to during the week.

I started on the lavender, which was no longer buzzing with bees and hover flies. The upright flower heads were turning dusty-grey and had lost some of their pungent scent, both indicators that the flowers had finally finished and that autumn was approaching. I bagged up some of the flower heads for Karen, who would use them to make pretty lavender bags for her mother.

Moving on to the long sensory beds that border two sides of the former croquet lawn, I started to dead-head and cut back some of the many fragrant plants that were each fighting to dominate the space and available light. The rich peppery aroma of the hyssop filling the air as my shears sliced through the wayward stems that dared to hang over lawn.

I was so engaged in my work that Arthur's, "Ah, morning George," made me jump. "Oh dear! Sorry George, I didn't mean to sneak up on you!"

"Not to worry, didn't hear you coming," I stood up, slowly realising I'd been kneeling for a while, and my legs had become stiff.

"Did you look at the papers? You get a mention and, according to the Guardian, you have become a biologist!" Arthur pointed to the papers.

"Really?! No, I've not read them yet. I thought I'd see if Melissa, in her capacity as my PA, would make me a coffee later, and I'd read them then."

Arthur chuckled. "How is she doing?"

"She's quite vicious, judging by the notes she left me last night - she'll make a good PA!"

"Well," Arthur pointed back to the newspapers, "you have managed to get yourself quoted in both papers! And between them, they have found the cause; It is... 'A result of global warming.' *And...* 'The virus came from a meteorite or UFO, that apparently landed in the North Sea near Newcastle.' Oh, and do take a look at the story in the sports section in this one!"

I walked over to the table with Arthur, and we read the articles. The most serious reporting was actually in the sports section, under the dramatic heading: '**DEATH OF ENGLISH SPORT!**' It started, as expected, by listing all the races, matches and events that had already been cancelled. Then predicting those that would follow if the fungus continued to spread south. Lots of little pictures of iconic sports venues were crossed out in red, with lots more having a big question mark printed on them. The report continued to examine the spread; speculating on how the virus that caused the fungus was distributed. It stated that it was spreading considerably faster than Dutch Elm Disease had, when that arrived in the UK in the late 60's. As in the other articles 'Potyviridae Craven-Parker' had been abbreviated to 'PCP'.

I was quoted as having said that global warming was a contributing factor and that the PCP was probably wind-borne. However, unlike the other reports, it considered more than just the loss of private lawns and sports venues; the writer 'wondered' if there was a potential threat to agriculture or even our food chain?'

I looked up and sighed, "So, just one writer is starting to get a handle on this, and that's buried at the very end of the sports section!"

Arthur smiled, "Well, that's not going to cause panic buying at least." I looked up to see Arthur biting his top lip again.

"Ah, now George, after hearing what you said yesterday, I took the liberty of talking to the Secretary for the Environment, Food & Rural Affairs – Maria Trellis - We're old friends. Well, anyway, I recommended that she should maybe seek your views in a sort of advisory capacity."

"Oh!" I hadn't expected that. "What, she'll phone me?" I was quite sure that Arthur had overestimated the importance of my opinions. I certainly did not consider myself an 'expert advisor'.

"Well, that's what I thought, but she's hoping to meet with you. You see, with your name being attached to the virus, it gives you greater credibility, and this allows you to share your, shall we say, 'more global' thoughts on the potential problems. In turn, that makes her look better qualified to contribute to the meeting herself." Arthur peered over his glasses and added, "What do you say?"

"I don't know? This Maria, she does know that I'm just a gardener?"

"Yes, she knows that you are *not* a biologist and isn't expecting a highly qualified, professional advisor. She just wants you to share your assessments. It is what ministers often do. Only this time it is rather more urgent than usual."

This was bothering me. I wondered why a quick chat on the phone wouldn't suffice, and thought Arthur knew more than he was letting on. "Arthur, what's this meeting and is she coming here or am I going to her?"

Arthur just smiled slightly and looked a little uncomfortable.

"Is there something you know that you're not telling me?" I probed.

"Well, George, I didn't tell you this, and you don't repeat it to anybody, you understand?" He looked serious now.

I just nodded unable to guess what he was about to divulge.

"Well, it has been established that, should the virus still be active in the environment by spring, it *will* infect and probably destroy all our cereal crops. So far, everything in the grass family they have exposed PCP to has become infected. Your new friend, Miss Parker, has been leading the research and is also going to be advising the ministers." He paused, waiting for a reaction, but was chewing his top lip again.

"Go on ..." I knew that there was something he was still withholding. Any virus that could wipe out all our cereal crops was a severe and substantial problem that would urgently require the government to act decisively.

"Yes, sorry George; you are going to be advising a minister, possibly ministers, prior to, or perhaps in, a civil contingencies committee meeting in Cabinet Office briefing room A. Or a 'Cobra Meeting' as the press usually refers to them."

I was stunned and also annoyed that this all now appeared to be a fait accompli. I'd had neither discussed nor approved anything. "Shit! At Number 10? You have booked *me* to advise in a Cobra

meeting at Number 10 without asking first? Arthur, please tell me you're joking?"

Arthur, who had been standing by the table, sat down and closed the papers. "I am sorry, George, I do have a habit of breaking news badly and not necessarily in the right order. It was never my intention to invite you to a Cobra meeting. I too believed that you would simply have a chat with Maria beforehand.
However, as our discussion progressed, she disclosed the seriousness of the situation and everything just spiralled from there. However, Cobra meetings are not held at Number 10, they are convened in a Westminster Cabinet Office."

"Arthur, I am beginning to wish I'd not agreed to putting my name to this virus. I don't like where this is going. I certainly don't feel I have anything to contribute to what will be the Country's top experts. Surely, I can just decline?"

"Ah, George, I remember you telling me how you liked to solve problems and that you intended to face challenges head-on and not run away again. Well, try to imagine this as just one big practical problem and that you have received a rare opportunity to contribute towards a solution."

I thought for a moment, remembering that I had said, just that, at my 2nd interview, when Arthur confronted me with my real christian name and got me to admit that I had effectively run 200 miles away from a situation I could no longer face.

Arthur continued, "Also, and I shouldn't tell you this either, but Departmental Ministers are rarely experts in their particular office. Indeed, I have often wondered why some deserve to get into the Cabinet at all. Some eventually do become experts, or at least knowledgeable but by then, they will be liable to be sacked due to some scandal, a Cabinet reshuffle, or a General Election will throw the whole lot out."

I considered all he had said. Could I get a grip on my fear and just interact with these people as if they were merely pawns in some problem-solving exercise? Or would these people be judging me and likely discover that I was an unqualified fool who was way out of his depth? Though it filled me with dread, I decided I would have to accept the challenge. "OK Arthur, I guess this situation will escalate into something that will affect us all anyway. This way I will learn what the government intends to do and maybe also learn what other consequences there could be."

"That's the fellow!" Arthur stood up on patted me on the back. "It will be an experience that's for sure. You may soon be privy to the very heart of the British government!" Arthur stood for a moment tapping the side of his head trying to remember something. "Ah, there are two other things I need to tell you."

I thought that he couldn't possibly have dropped me into anything else. "There's more?"

He clicked his fingers as it came to him. "Oh, nothing to worry about. Ah yes, firstly I'm off to Newcastle today; I'm collecting unsold items from the auction and those I recalled from sale last week. I'll be eating out, so won't be back until late afternoon. I hope you didn't need to use the car?"

"No, I've got all I need. Thanks." I was a little relieved that he was going out, he'd not be able to drop any more on my plate if he was elsewhere.

"And George, I see you've stored the grass seed in the garage.

Well, Karen's going to want that space for her car soon, so can you carry it all up into the garage loft?"

"Er, Sorry... The garage has a loft?"

Arthur looked surprised. "You've never been up there! Well, the hatch is hidden I suppose. It can only be accessed when the garage is empty. If you look, from the inside at the centre pillar, you will see a short orange nylon rope hanging down. That pulls down the stairs. But you have to use the small step ladder hanging on the pillar below it to open the four catches to the hatch first. Once unlatched, pull the rope hard, and the steps will come down. Stand with your back to the pillar as you pull else they will clout you on the way down!" Arthur mimed the actions as he spoke. "It is a bit of a fiddle getting them all the way back up and do remember to turn the four catches back just in case it falls down. Oh, and turn the light off *before* pushing the steps back up!"

"Oh OK, I didn't even realise there was a loft room. Has it got any windows? And, where's the light switch?"

"Well it did have two skylights on the back, but they were covered when the solar panels went up. Once the steps are down you will see a small switch on the right side. Probably be very dusty up there but it has a solid floor, and there should be plenty of space for the sacks. You know, I haven't been up there myself, for a decade or more!"

"OK, I'll do that this afternoon." I thought a bit of exploring would take my mind off the impending Cobra meeting.

"That's very kind of you. Now I must get to Newcastle." Arthur called back as he disappeared into the hallway "Have a good day, George."

A few minutes later, while working on the sensory bed, I heard the garage door open and the car pulling away.

I completed the sensory bed by about 11.30 and wondered about getting a coffee and taking another look at the papers. I looked over towards the little table to see Melissa looking out of the window at me. She seemed deep in thought, but I wondered if, as my PA, she could be persuaded to make me a coffee or maybe I'd just get to see her wave her middle finger once more?

As I walked towards her, I mimed pouring and drinking coffee. She smiled, nodded and headed towards the kitchen. 'That was too easy!' I thought.

Melissa returned five minutes later with a tray; complete with a coffee pot, two cups and a plate of biscuits. "Good morning George. How are you this morning?" She was still dressed smartly as before, but the little black jacket had gone.

I abandoned my trimming and joined her at the small table. She'd put the tray down on the newspapers, and I noticed her notepad was also on the tray. It didn't appear to have anything new on it, though.

"I'm very well, thank you, Melissa, and how's my PA today?" I thought calling her 'Melissa' would test her new character, and I instantly regretted it because she was making a real effort and hoped she wouldn't react badly.

"Your PA is also very well, but she does like to be referred to as 'Mel' if that's OK with you… Sir?"

"Oh, Touché! Mel!" We laughed together. Her smile, in the late morning sun, that day, reminded me that Melissa was blossoming into an exceptionally beautiful young lady who was, before my eyes, maturing into a bright and quick-witted young woman.

I also realised that I felt very comfortable in her company. All too often, Melissa had been more of an irritation; she'd play annoying practical jokes, like letting the tractor tyres down, tying the legs of my overalls together or sneaking up behind me to either make me jump or to take and hide my secateurs. She had even filled one of my Wellington boots with water and a fish

from the main pond! I'd probably have found these things funnier if I wasn't always so pushed for time. It wasn't all bad, though. She often came to me for advice, either because she thought her father was too old or just because they had fallen out again. We'd had some fun moments as well; only a few weeks earlier we had spent a happy couple of hours bowling apples down the drive, into a dustpan, on a wet Sunday afternoon.

"What are you thinking?" She broke my thoughts.

"Oh, just how things are changing around here and all for the good, well, except for the grass anyway." I nodded back towards the large brown patch that had been the croquet lawn.

"Did you unplug my phone yesterday?" She enquired.

"Yes, I saw from your notes that someone planned to call and thought I'd let you sleep on."

"You are very thoughtful George." Melissa scanned the garden. "It's so perfectly flat. I never realised that before."

"That's from many years of mowing it with a heavy roller mower. Though it's seen a lot more of the lawn mower than it ever has a croquet ball." I remembered that Arthur, Lady Jayne, Peter, Melissa and myself had tried to start a game about 3 years earlier, but Melissa had gone off in a tantrum when her ball control proved to be wildly inaccurate. Arthur and Jayne both went after her and never returned to the game.

70

"Let's play now!" Melissa stood up. "I'm sure it will be much better without the grass anyway!"

I shook my head "No, the ball will roll too fast and go too far. It needs the grass to slow it down."

"It will be the same handicap for both of us. We'll just have to tap it more gently. Come on – take a break," she turned on her big blue-eyed pleading look, "please!?"

I was beginning to think that the 'old Melissa' had returned, and some silliness would follow, but I conceded: "OK, but no more than an hour. I do have lots of work to catch up on."

She ran straight inside the conservatory to get the loops, balls, flags, peg and mallets. Returning with all the equipment balanced precariously in her arms, she dropped 3 of the four balls on exiting the conservatory. "You want to be red and yellow, or black and blue?" She excitedly asked referring to the ball colours.

I joked, "I think you ought to be black and blue! How *is* the eye now?" Realising that the sunglasses had gone and I'd not noticed anything.

"Bit sore but I tried to hide it with extra foundation. Can you see it?" She came right up to me and turned her face slightly for me to take a closer look.

That close I could just see that it was still a little darker under her right eye, but I chose to say I couldn't see anything.

Happy with my answer she danced around setting up the six loops while reminding me of her interpretation of the rules as she went. "We both start here in the corner, and when we've got through all six, we come back the other way with our other ball. "As you chose the colours - I'm going first."

She swung the mallet and hit the black ball with a clunk. It shot off at high speed, past the loop, right across the entire long side of the 'lawn', continued straight through the sensory bed and disappeared under the lavender beyond.

I fell to my knees laughing, "Oh, good shot Mel!"

"That was obviously just a test shot to see how far it could go without the grass," she joked as she crossed the garden to recover the ball, "that wasn't my go." She looked back at me. "Get up!" she laughed, "no kneeling on the brown!"

I was still wiping away tears of laughter when she finally returned with the ball. I got another punch on the top of my arm for my efforts.

"There will have to be a penalty if we go off the lawn from now on," she declared. Then, replacing the ball, she drew the mallet back only a little way and let it swing to hit the ball, this time, much more gently: The ball barely moved at all.

I bit my lip and suppressed a snigger.

Melissa gave me a stare that dared me to laugh, "Don't say anything unless you want me to swing at *your* balls! That was my last test shot." She took another shot and, this time, got it just right; straight through the loop and maintaining a straight line towards the next one. "Yes!" She exclaimed happily.

"Well done. Now let me make a fool of myself." I placed my red ball down and picked up my mallet.

"You are already making a fool of yourself! I get a continuation stroke for getting it through the loop." She marched up to her ball and swung again. This time, it hit the loop and didn't make it through."

I lined up my shot and just before taking it, asked: "Didn't we each have two balls going together, last time we played?"

"Yes, but I don't play it that way, the balls get in the way of each other too much."

I accepted what she said, though did think that was all part of the game. I said nothing and lined up my first shot again trying to match the same amount of energy she was now putting into her shots.

Just as I started to swing, she piped up, "I know! The penalty for going off the lawn is you have to remove one item of clothing!" Clunk. I had hit the ball too hard. "No Mel!" I said firmly as I watched my yellow ball go through the first loop but then curve right into the far left corner way beyond the second loop.

Melissa whooped, "Ooooo! You so nearly lost your shirt there! – You get a continuation shot, but you've got to go through that loop from the other side!" She pointed at the second loop which my ball had passed.

"Yes, yes, I know," I said as I walked to the very corner. "and we are *not* playing forfeits."

She followed me into the corner where the ball had settled. "That's really going to be hard George, going to take a few shots to get it through. Oh, and we are playing by my rules."

"Get out of the way Mel." She was standing too close and getting flirty again. She'd never done this unless her father had been watching before and was starting to make me uncomfortable. But, at the same time, I was starting to enjoy the challenge of the game and was wondering if I could strike her ball from the ideal position she'd left it in?

Melissa took a few steps back, and I took my shot. It started off in the right direction, but it curved a little to the left and struck the side of the loop. This deflected it back towards Melissa's black ball, and it settled directly between the two.

"Ha!" I exclaimed, "Get out of that one without pushing mine through with it."

"Maybe I'd like yours pushed through!" She pouted and blew me a kiss.

"Cut the innuendo's and just take your shot, Mel! Come on, this looks like it could be a good game."

"OK, I'll give you my best shot" Standing side on to the two balls it appeared she was going to give her black ball just a little tap so that the yellow one was no longer in the way. She took her time carefully aiming and considering the shot. Then she suddenly just whacked it straight off the lawn.

I was just starting to laugh when she proclaimed, "Oh look, it's rolled off the court. I lose my skirt!" In a single movement, she violently pulled down her pleated skirt to reveal a small and lacy pair of white knickers. Then as she stepped out of her skirt, she said, "Oh, George! I see where you're looking! – Now it's your go…"

Angrily I shouted, "No! - I just glanced. And I told you no forfeits! Game over!" Trying not to take another look I marched around pulling up the loops and the peg. I snatched the mallet she was posing with and stormed into the conservatory.

The far, oak panelled wall contains a hidden, full height, closet that had formerly been the gun cupboard. Luckily Melissa had left it open because it's hard to find when closed. I marched in and began placing the mallets and loops into slots and holes in a shelf that had been specially engineered for them. The cupboard was a bit gloomy, and I hadn't had a hand free to turn the light on, but I could just make out the holes and slots. I was just replacing the last loop when it got even darker.

I turned around. Melissa hadn't given up! There she was, still without her skirt and now with her blouse completely unbuttoned, revealing a lacy bra matching her knickers.

"Mel! - Go away!" I yelled straight at her. I was sure she'd turn and run, probably in tears. But she just advanced on me pushing me up against the croquet rack. Her arm came around me, she tried to kiss me, but I raised my head back taking my face out of range. She started kissing my neck, pushed herself hard against me and then I felt a hand fumbling between my legs.

I tried again to shout 'No!" but only a strange, choked, muted sound came out. She felt so warm and close, I could smell her perfume, feel her young breasts pushing urgently against my chest and even her kisses, raining on my neck, were becoming exciting.

A strange, sleep-like feeling started to come over me, it was almost as if I was becoming hypnotised – my defiance was dissolving, and I was losing my free will. Her closeness and desires were creating waves of emotional overload that swept away my resistance. I'd been holding my arms high above my head, both to show her I wasn't interested and also because I was afraid that I'd touch her. Only they were relaxing and descending behind her. I needed her. My arms fell low behind her, stroking her back and falling below her waist. Feeling her

75

soft, cool buttocks through her flimsy knickers, I felt an urge to pull her even tighter against me, I could struggle no more. She was a stunningly beautiful virgin with an hour-glass figure and we had the house all to ourselves. I lowered my head; I needed to return her passionate kisses and to feel her lips pressed against mine.

It was then that Melissa herself broke the spell that she had cast; she passionately whispered, "Oh George I can feel you're getting very interested!"

The sleepy feeling suddenly just evaporated, as her words brought me back to the dangerous reality of the situation. I snatched back control, suddenly pushing her away with all my might. She fell backwards, heavily into the doorway. "I said No!" – I quickly strode over her, preventing her from getting up and then ran all the way back to my gatehouse, knowing that Melissa was unlikely to run that far. Besides, I locked the door as soon as I got in.

Panting, I filled the kettle and put it on. I then realised, as I took a mug out of the dishwasher, that my hands were shaking uncontrollably. I held them out in front of me willing them to stop, but I was unable to influence them. Had I lost all control over my entire body?

I went to the window, at first, just to ensure that she wasn't following me down the drive. Then returned to look again, only this time, I started to imagine her, still skirt-less, running towards me, her breasts bouncing in that thin, lacy white bra. A dark part of me wished she was coming and if she was… I think I might have unlocked that door…

But she wasn't coming. During the next few minutes, I kept going back to the window to check. Finally, on about the fifth look, I caught sight of her, not on the drive but above the fountain. She was in the house, walking past the window at the top of the stairs. She stopped to look out, and I dropped to the floor and hid under the window my heart racing once more.

I'd run away again and was now hiding. This time, from a fifteen- year-old girl! – However, this time, I didn't feel any guilt about it. I felt slightly proud that I'd done the 'right thing'. I was also deeply disappointed that Melissa's unpredictable behaviour had surfaced again and that our relationship, one that I had just begun to feel more comfortable about, had been soured, possibly irrevocably.

Maybe I had somehow encouraged her? I cared about her, and I *had* started to find her attractive. Could she tell? I also felt pity for her because her Mother had left her devastated.

Had I unintentionally, manipulated her because she couldn't relate to her father who was so much older? Was I a father figure gone badly wrong? I was sure that I was going to have another sleepless night, what with this and the upcoming trip to Westminster.

I waited until I heard Arthur coming back before I went to rescue the tools and wheelbarrow that I'd abandoned. For some reason, he beeped as he entered the lane, giving me an advance warning that he was returning and so had reached the fountain before he passed me.

I waved, but he didn't look at all happy and stopped just after the fountain. I wondered if Melissa had called him and, in anger, had invented a story. I approached the driver's side slowly, wondering if I was soon going to have to find a new job and lodgings.

Through the open window, Arthur complained about a young woman who, looking only at her 'i-Thingy', had walked out into the road in front of him causing him to swerve and brake hard. He was also angry that the auction house had charged him £10 for each item he'd removed from sale even though they hadn't even been catalogued yet. He finished by complaining about a big black car that he'd twice had to beep at because it had parked, blocking the lane entrance.

After collecting and cleaning my tools, I returning once more, to the sanctuary of my little gatehouse and I had a few drinks. I really wanted to sleep but couldn't. Just after midnight my mobile buzzed. I'd received a text from Melissa.

Sorry! :-(2.00am

I didn't reply. During the next hour, the phone buzzed twice more. I didn't even look at the phone - I turned it right off before finally going to sleep.

Three things surprised me on Sunday morning: Firstly, I'd actually slept quite well, only waking once and running through what Arthur had dropped me in and what Melissa had wanted. Secondly, there was un-forecast light rain tapping on my window. And, thirdly, all the grass right up to the gatehouse was now dusty white.

Since I no longer had a car of my own, Karen had kindly offered to take me into Barnard Castle every other Sunday. We both did our shopping, and it also gave her a break from Paul, whom I would attempt to entertain, while she did hers. We'd usually meet back up again, for a coffee and a chat, at 3 pm. She always sent a text at 9.30am to see if I was coming despite the fact that I'd not missed one of these bi-weekly rendezvous since they started. It had become a routine, not entirely necessary, but it was Barnard Castle that had originally attracted me to 'The North', and I enjoyed these regular outings that took me away from the Manor.

I was annoyed with myself for not having returned to work the previous afternoon. I couldn't continue to work at the Manor and have to hide from Melissa whenever Arthur was out.

I remembered that I'd promised to put the seed sacks into the garage loft and had not done so. Arthur would have seen that when he parked the car and may well ask me why. Remembering that he was already in a bad mood, I thought I'd better do it straight away. I glanced at my phone for a time check and remembered, only then, that it was switched off.

Upon switching it on it buzzed twice more and displayed four unread texts and a missed call. The call was from a withheld number, and the texts were all from Melissa. I decided to read them later. The time was just before 8 am – I'd thought it was much later. I guessed that I would have a chance to get those sacks into the garage loft and still go to Barney.

Once inside the garage and upon seeing the RAV-4 parked there, I remembered that Arthur had said the stairs could not be lowered if cars were there. The spare keys were hidden inside an old Marmite jar on the shelves that ran right along the right-hand side. These shelves had been slotted for various tools and car cleaning accessories, in the same fashion as those in the old gun cupboard. I found myself reliving Melissa's 'croquet game' all over again, sure that I'd be revisiting those memories repeatedly in the future.

I drove the car out a little way and on returning to the garage heard a faint, sad, voice behind me.

"You are going out today?" I turned to see Melissa standing in the rain, head bowed. She looked up briefly I could see she had been crying. She had little or no makeup on, and her bruised eye was visible again. "You're never going to talk to me again, are you?" She half sobbed, her head bowed once more. She looked wretched with her hair all wet. She wore her scruffy jeans and a coat she'd grown out of. Clearly, she didn't intend to seduce me. In that, I took some comfort.

I felt a very strong, instinctive urge to run over to her, hug her tightly and say 'It's alright Mel!' But I restrained myself. I knew that I was going to have to be very careful that I didn't give out any more 'wrong signals', everything I did had to be controlled and not left open to misinterpretation.

I turned away as if disinterested and unhooked the step ladder from the central pillar before I answered. Melissa didn't follow me in. She just stood there in the rain. "We will talk Melissa, but I don't think we can be friends now. It's not all your fault, but we can't." As I said those few simple words, a feeling of loss, almost like grief, swept across and engulfed me. This was so unexpected and although brief, it caused me to question both the harshness of my reply and my own feelings for Melissa.

"Please just answer my last text," she said as she turned away and walked slowly back to the house. I watched her until she disappeared into the arched pathway. I thought of calling after her. I didn't. She never raised her head. She never looked back.

After a moment, during which I felt very subdued, I climbed the little step ladder and turned the four catches. The hatch dropped slightly, and I could see it was hinged. I moved the ladder out of the way and pulled on the rope. Nothing happened. I used two hands and pulled harder, still nothing. Then furiously I let all my pent-up frustrations and anger out on that rope, tugging at it with all my might - I was almost swinging on it. The hatch screeched and juddered as it started to drop. The screeching noise continued as the metal stairs, reluctantly, came down and finally crashed into the concrete floor.

'I'm going to need to oil those before putting them back up,' I muttered to myself. I saw an electrical cable had come down with the stairs and followed it to the light switch Arthur had described. A single fluorescent tube slowly flickered to life above me, as I carefully climbed the steep steps.

The loft space was much bigger than I thought it would be; I could stand upright under the apex, the floor seemed very stable, and the room was dry. Cobwebs hung everywhere, and there were piles of plastic plant pots and empty compost bags. Peter had never been one to throw anything away.

At the far end, I could see what looked like a standard lamp and a white box with an orange light on it. I'd investigate that once I'd got the sacks up and was sure I'd have time.

I quickly realised that I could only carry one sack of grass seed at a time up the steep steps. I took each of them two-thirds of the way up and then tossed them in. Once all twelve of the 25Kg sacks were up, I climbed right up and stacked them properly.

The little orange light was bothering me. I checked my phone for the time and was reminded about Melissa's texts as I did so. It was just after 9 am. I sat at the top with my legs dangling into the garage and read the texts.

After her first 'Sorry!" she had sent: "I feel so stupid - please forgive me?" then at 1 am: "Can we please just forget this ever happened? x"

Finally, at 6 am: "George I am so sorry, I think there is actually something wrong with me – I feel like I am more than one person and sometimes I'm out of control. Please, can you help me once more by talking about this then never again if that is what you really want?"

'Out of control? - I can agree on that', I thought to myself. "I am not falling for a 'split personality' excuse, though.' I said, out loud to the phone.

I got up and walked across to where the light was. I saw first a battered armchair with a timeworn standard lamp next to it. But it was the source of the orange light that interested me. As I got closer, ducking the cobwebs, as I did so, I realised it was a small fridge and that it was switched on! I wondered why it was there and what was in it? I opened it cautiously.

Beer! 3 bottles in a row from front to back. In the door was also a miniature bottle of brandy, an empty brandy glass and a bottle of coke. I pulled out the first bottle of beer. Newcastle Brown! - "You, sneaky old sod, Peter!" That had always been his beer of choice. The next bottle was a Guinness, which was a favourite of mine. Propped up on the last bottle was a small envelope. I removed that to expose an Adnam's Broadside "Oh my God, that's Richard's beer!" I said out loud.

The light was too dim to read by, so I studied the ancient standard light with its large, and yellowed tasselled shade. I assumed it had come from the house, probably in the 1940's. The dusty flex was a twisted wire covered in some kind of brown cloth. I half expected a bang and then all the lights to fuse when I switched it on. Instead, an energy saving bulb slowly started to illuminate the chair and a little coffee table that I'd not noticed before. There were a couple of paperbacks on the table. I remembered that Peter liked to read. The top book was titled 'Four bowls of soup.' Peter liked to read some weird stuff, I thought.

I sat back in Peter's chair and carefully opened the slightly damp envelope, being careful not to tear the letter inside and hoping the moisture hadn't made the ink run. I recognised instantly Peter's neat handwriting, a skill I'd never mastered. It brought back memories of the little notes he'd leave for me if he had taken a rare day off, or was ill.

Hi George,

I'm assuming two things: Firstly, that it is you who found my hidey-hole. If not, whoever you are - go find George Craven and give him this note and his beer!

I wanted you, Richard, and Arthur, to have a final drink in my memory and 'thank you' all for your valued friendship.

That's my second assumption - that I am no longer with you. I know I have only a few months left on the clock, but I haven't worried my family with this news. I've had a good life, and my only regrets are that I will miss Sandy & Graham's wedding and not get to greet my great grandchild.

I had hoped to pop my clogs while working in my favourite garden, but it seems I must retire and depart elsewhere - that's life (or death!). If it's not too late, I like you to ask Arthur and my family, if my ashes could be scattered by the lake?

Cheers! And good luck to you all.

~ *Peter* ~

P.S. Look after 'my' garden - And no more bluebells! Oh - And the coke is for Mel

I let out a big sigh. Such a short note that said so much, I read it again, twice.

I was not sure how I felt about Peter not having told his family he was unwell. That had led to Sandy blaming Arthur for his death and her not accepting her job back. But how could Peter have possibly known that would happen?

Graham! – That was Sandy's fiancé's name. No wonder I'd forgotten it.

On first reading, I'd been upset that Peter never knew that Graham & Sandy never married and that his first Grandchild hadn't lived. But then… maybe it was better that he didn't? He died thinking happy thoughts about Sandy's future. He certainly would never have approved of her new relationship with Mad Mick!

I was also relieved that Peter didn't die in the garden because it was likely I'd be the one to discover his body!

As for the drinks and request for his ashes to be scattered by the lake: I'd arrange a little memorial drink by the lake and see if Arthur had contact details of his family. Maybe take the opportunity to tell Sandy that he knew he hadn't long to live? – I wasn't sure on that last point. I'd take the note with me and show it to Karen - she'd know.

Bang on cue, my mobile buzzed; Karen was confirming that I wanted to be picked up at 10 am. I'd better grab a quick shower I thought, as I folded Peter's note and clicked off the old lamp.

Chapter 4 – Waterfalls

The call that I had been dreading came just as I was stepping out of the shower, 'That will be Karen – she's been held up again,' I told myself as I reached across my steamy bathroom, for my phone which was nestled safely on top of a pile of soft, warmed towels. The screen was misted up, and I'd pressed 'Answer' before realising that it was a withheld number.

"I need to confirm that I am speaking to Mr Simon Craven." The cold voice stated rather than asked. I wasn't able to determine if it was a man or a woman who was speaking. The caller seemed to lack any vocal range or connotation. It was flat, expressionless voice, almost computer-like.

My heart rate increased; firstly, because this was almost certainly the call that would take me to Westminster the next day, and secondly because the caller had already discovered that my real christian name is 'Simon', despite the fact that I'd not used that name, nor been called it, for over five years.

"Yes. I am Simon Craven, but I go by the name George now." I found myself almost imitating the caller with a flat reply. With the phone tucked under my chin, I continued to dry myself and get dressed. I think that this was my way of trying to normalise a bizarre situation, but I also feared that they could be outside and were about to collect me.

The conversation that followed continued in monotones; firstly, confirming my identity, with a series security questions rather like those a bank might ask. I confirmed that I would sign the Official Secrets Act and not disclose anything about the meeting unless it was agreed that I should. I was not to make any public statements nor accept any media interviews that had not been arranged by the government's press office. I would receive additional information and screening on route, and a car would collect me at 6 am. I was to bring photo identification and all notes, research and documents, in my possession, that related to either the grass fungus or virus.

Finally, with maybe just a slight hint of human emotion, the caller told me that they would continue to refer to me as 'George Craven' so as not to cause any confusion with the press or public. I decided the caller was probably a woman and hoped it wasn't this 'Maria' that I'd be advising.

Strangely I wasn't nervous anymore; I decided, there and then, that whatever was going to happen, I'd not be scared. I told myself that the following day would be over just as quickly as any other and that I'd just contribute as little as possible so I'd not make too much of a fool of myself.

Then the doorbell went. My heart raced again, and I realised that it was not so easy to simply *decide* not to be scared.

I opened the door slowly and peeked out of the narrow opening. No one appeared to be there, but the gates were open. Suddenly Karen's face appeared right in front of mine. She'd been hiding right behind the door. I jumped back. "Karen! Don't do that!" I barked.

Karen pushed the door open further and gave me a puzzled look. "What's going on George?" she asked suspiciously "Your phone is hardly ever engaged, and you've certainly never answered the door like that before!"

"Sorry, you made me jump. I'll just get my coat. Oh good, it's stopped raining! I'll take Paul for that walk up Galgate and around the castle to the other side of the river." I quickly retreated inside to find my coat, hoping I'd successfully dodged her question. I grabbed my coat from the kitchen table and, upon turning back to the door, saw that Karen had followed me.

She was standing in the doorway and, damn, she'd made me jump again!

"No, no, no!" Karen shook her head while frowning. "You, sit down and tell me what's going on," she pointed to one of the two rustic wooden chairs that were either end of the table.

"There's nothing to tell, and we can't just leave Paul in the car. Come on let's go." I headed towards where she was standing in the doorway with her arms crossed.

She didn't move, blocking my path. "Paul's not in the car. I've left him watching the diggers clearing the old tennis court site." Again, she pointed firmly to the chair.

Reluctantly I sat down, as did she. I let out an exaggerated sigh and said: "There's nothing to tell, it's *your* time that you're wasting."

I'd come to know Karen quite well over the years, and realised that once she'd got the bit between her teeth she wasn't going to stop probing until she's got some answers.

Karen and I had first met at the Manor, on the day of my second interview, and we just hit it off from the word go. She was just under a year older than me. I'd recently taunted her about hitting 'The big 3-O' and being in her thirties while I was still in my twenties. Karen is actually a very attractive woman, but she never dressed to show off her figure, nor enhanced her appearance with makeup. I didn't understand why I felt little physical attraction towards her, yet was able to confide in her and joke with her, like a lifelong friend, within just days of our first meeting.

In fact, Karen was the only one in Ingleton, other than Arthur, who knew I was a divorcee. I soon found I could openly discuss my feelings, doubts, and fears with her, and also discovered that she had a knack of worming out any details that I might try to conceal.

Paul liked playing matchmaker and it was likely that some of the locals thought we were a couple simply because we'd often be seen out together. But I never felt that special 'spark' that lovers share. We just enjoyed a comfortable friendship, and that's the way I liked it.

Now, I'd got the Cobra meeting that I couldn't talk about and a 'croquet game' I'd be both too embarrassed to discuss even with her. I did want to, but I feared she might too odiously misinterpret my genuinely innocent intentions of human kindness for those of a 'grooming pervert', and our friendship could also become damaged.

Quickly I needed to find a third option. Then I remembered Peter's note. "You got me!" I gave her my best, 'resigned look'. "I found this note from Peter. It's kind of messed me up a bit, and I need to talk to you about its implications and what I should do." I pulled the note from my coat pocket and placed it on the table. "It can wait 'till we have our coffee, though."

My prop may have persuaded Karen, but her suspicious look didn't fade, and she pushed the note back to me. "Has your ex-wife found you?"

"No!" I said firmly.

"Were you hiding from Arthur?" She continued to probe, apparently not convinced there wasn't a bigger story to be unearthed.

"Why on earth would I be hiding from Arthur? – Come on let's get Paul and go to Barney."

"Mel?" She probed, searching for a subconscious reaction.

"What about Mel?" I asked as casually as I could.

"Ah!" A little knowing smile appeared on her face as her eyebrows raised.

How was she doing this? Was she suddenly a body language expert? What had I done or had said that was feeding her my thoughts?! "There is no 'ah!' Karen, except the one in Barn'*ah*'d Castle. Now… can we go?"

Karen was still smiling and slowly shaking her head. She had a glint in her eyes that told me I'd been rumbled. "Well, I know that Mel's had a bit of crush on you for a while and, just recently, I've seen your little glances in her direction too. I'm an expert at spotting covert glimpses you know!"

Her expression and tone then changed to become much more serious, "She may have well developed into a sexy young thing, but she's messed up at the moment and very vulnerable. I'd be more than disappointed if anyone were to pursue or exploit her and take advantage of her innocence. You do understand, don't you George? – *Very* disappointed!"

I laughed. "I see. So, I'm having a relationship with Melissa, Arthur has found out and now I'm hiding where I live, coz he'd never think to look here? Well, Karen, I can't fault your observational skills, but you're not quite such a good judge of character!"

"Hmmm, well I'm sorry George, I was just clutching at straws. It wasn't a serious accusation, it's just that she should wear a t-shirt that says 'Caution! A lot younger than I look!' She reached across and patted me on the arm.

"Well, it was not my character that I was referring to. However, while I'll admit that my eyes have wandered just a little recently, I can assure you that my hands will *not* be following."

"I should think not! Good. So …"

Her expression told she was piecing together another part of the story, "So nothing!" I interrupted, wanting Karen to stop investigating and worming out more of the story.

"So… S*he* went for *you*!" Karen grinned broadly, "The little minx! Oh, do tell – what did she do?"

"No," I replied sternly, "I'm neither confirming your assumptions nor giving you any details. Now can we go to Barnard Castle, please?" I stood up as if to go.

Karen remained sitting, crossed her arms again and gave it one more go "Oh well, I could always ask Mel?"

I gave her a most nonchalant look and said, "Yes you could." knowing full well that she would certainly not.

"Hmmm, maybe I will?" She looked at me for a reaction, but I gave her a dismissive look and shrugged.

She let out a resigning sigh, "OK, I give up. Let's go and get Paul. Oh look, the sun's come out!"

The drive isn't wide enough to turn around in quickly, so Karen continued up towards the house and drove right around the fountain's pond to turn back. "Are there any fish in that fountain George?" Karen asked.

"No!" I laughed remembering why Melissa had created that story. "But remind me, when we have our coffee this afternoon, to tell you why I tried to convince Stuart Gilly that *I* was Arthur!"

As we waited for the automatic gates to let us out again, Karen gave me a bemused look. "Oh, that does sound like a fun story! Have you much shopping to do yourself? I've got loads to do!"

"Not much really, the freezer is running a bit low, and I'm right out of coffee and butter."

"Well, I do have something I'd like to talk to you about so don't be later than three, will you? Oh no, not again!" Karen slowed and beeped her horn at a black Nissan that had stopped at the entrance to the lane. "I had to get that to move out of the way twice on Friday." The car crawled forward to the junction and pulled to the right. As Karen pulled alongside to turn left, she wound her window down and shouted at the heavily tinted windows "Doggers! – Go do your stuff somewhere else." Getting no response, she continued towards Ingleton, raising her window as she went.

I turned to look at the Nissan as we passed and noticed it had a small aerial on the roof and another on the front wing. "That car's been up and down the lane a lot recently. Arthur has complained about it too, and I've seen it before as well," Then added: "Not a good idea to shout at it though - we don't want to start a road rage incident!"

"Did you get its registration number? We should maybe report it?" Karen took a second look at her rear-view mirror. "Oh …"

I stretched my seatbelt to turn around. Some way behind the Nissan was following. "Karen, drive straight to Ingleton Police Station in case it is following us."

"We don't have a Police Station! There is only the Police office, and that's shut at the weekends. Nearest one that's staffed is probably Bishops Auckland."

I knew that was too far to go only to probably find the Nissan wasn't interested in us at all. "Simon Duguid's house?"

"No. I'm not going there," Karen replied firmly.

"But you said Simon was OK, and he is a policeman?" I looked around again. The Nissan was not in sight because of the crest of the hill, but it reappeared once it reached the top.

"I said No!" Karen replied abruptly.

"OK. Keep your hair on! – We've got to pick up Paul where there are builders working right? So it will pass us there for sure. Whoever it is won't want to mess with builders!"

"I hope so. Look - there he is," Karen pointed to where Paul was standing on white fungus-ridden grass. He was looking through a high wire fence with his arms crossed above his head. "exactly where I left him!"

Karen slowed down and beeped. I kept an eye on the road behind us. No Nissan. "It's OK - it must have turned off, I think."

Paul got in the back without saying anything or even acknowledging his mother's 'Hello Darling", but that was not unusual for Paul. He didn't say much unless it was about the topic that he was currently focused on, and then it would be hard to stop him.
Instead of pulling away as soon as Paul had belted up, Karen sat there looking at the rear-view mirror for over a minute. Satisfied that the black Nissan was not following, she finally continued.

The traffic started to build up before the turn off to Barnard Castle. Karen turned on the radio for traffic news. "That's a lot of traffic for a Sunday. If it's the A67 again, I'll bet someone's jumped the lights at the bridge and has met something head on."

We'd been held up before entering Barnard Castle. There is a sharp turn onto a very narrow, single file, stone bridge as you enter the town from the south. It's controlled by traffic lights, but sometimes a car would go too slowly over the bridge while a vehicle, coming the other way, would jump the lights early. Reversing back around the narrow, 90-degree turn, with high stone walls either side, is a slow process and often the lights would change again before the bridge was clear.

Sure enough, the queue was right back to the A66 turn-off. Karen looked over at me "Appleby?"

"There's no shoe shop in Appleby you know!" I said, imitating Melissa's frequent complaint. "But I think Paul prefers the walks around Appleby, don't you Paul?"

"Yeah, Appleby!" came an excited voice from the back seat.

"Maybe the grass will still be green in Appleby, eh Paul? I didn't get a reply. This time, because something else had caught his attention.

"Millions and millions more flies," he stated.

I followed his gaze. The view to the left is usually quite a steep drop into a picturesque valley, with a pretty river meandering through it about 80 meters below.

The verges were white, as they had been since leaving the Manor, but the whole valley was black as if filled with a dense storm cloud or smoke. The flies had formed an impenetrable fog

94

that completely hid its depth and all sight of the river somewhere below. A few people had stopped to photograph this strange phenomenon.

A side road ahead briefly looked like a cloud of smoke was pouring up out of it onto the road. This was followed by a blackened car that had crawled up out of the valley, blinded by the billions of tiny flies. The flies pushed ahead of it seemed to flow back around it to return to the dark depths of the valley.

Paul was now also trying to take pictures of it through the window. While Karen and I sat in silence unable to believe what we were seeing.

"Can we stop please Mum? I want to get out and take better pictures." Paul pleaded from the back.

"Shit!" Karen had lost concentration while looking at the flies to our left. There was an explosion of the dense black smoke right across our lane, just a few meters in front of us. An unknown vehicle, blinded by the flies, had burst onto the carriageway and careered straight out onto it. Karen braked and swerved hard to the right taking the car into the cloud of flies pushed ahead of this unseen vehicle. It went dark as the flies engulfed us and we braced ourselves for the impact.

But there was no impact; slowly light returned from the top of the windows first as the flies cleared. Then I saw the stationary bonnet of a van right under our near-side wing mirror. An equally terrified van driver could be seen behind the wheel of his van. He waved a meek apology as his wipers whizzed back and forth across the blackened slime on his windscreen and he reversed slightly so we could go on.

"That was too close!" I said, as we pulled forward just a little more and stopped. Karen said nothing. She was clearly shaken. "Would you like me to drive?" I asked. Karen just nodded. "Are you OK, Paul?"

"Yeah! That was awesome! Can we go down there?" He pointed back to the little side road that the van had emerged from.

"You won't see anything if you go down there, and it would be like driving with my eyes closed, so no!" I replied. Paul didn't contest my answer.

As I got out of the car, to swap seats, and Karen slid across to the passenger side, I looked back up the road to see what kind of a queue we had caused. About twelve cars were waiting patiently for us to move. Among them, six cars back, sat the black Nissan with the two aerials.

It was only then that it occurred to me that the black Nissan could have something to do with the Cobra meeting, but then what was the point? I chose not to tell Karen that it was back.

We drove on in silence for another few miles before I asked Karen if she wanted to go on or abort the trip?

"Please go on, I really must get my food shop," she replied, "and those flies are all behind us now. Look there's even a few patches of green grass ahead."

There were some distant patches of green and, as we continued to travel west, we could see that the virus hadn't been so destructive; the grass was mostly in the yellow, first stage of the infection with few patches having any white fungus.

We passed the sign for Appleby Manor Hotel, which indicated we were just about to enter Appleby itself. As we headed downhill, towards the town and river, I spotted a parking space right by the Co-Op. "That's handy," I said, quickly taking the space. "Now, meet up again at three at Eden River or Ruby's?"

Karen turned to Paul "You choose today Paul!"

"I choose Ruby's – for massive scones! And can George take me to Rosie's too?"

Karen smiled, "Oh OK, but don't pester George to buy you two ice creams again! Or no jam scone for you!" As was usual, Karen tried to slip me a fiver, and I pushed it away again saying "No, my treat." as I did so.

That day, however, Karen insisted "No. Take it. I can easily afford this now," as she pushed it firmly into my jacket pocket. "There is something I desperately need to talk to you about today. Can we meet for coffee earlier today, say at two?"

"Yeah sure we can," I replied, hoping she didn't intend to continue to probe for more about Melissa, but I could tell something was bothering Karen. I just didn't know what.

Appleby is another very pretty little town: The river Eden meanders through it, offering many picture postcard views as it does so. The grass on the riverbanks was yellow, but no sign of any frosty-looking grass. Paul and I walked in silence until we reached the bridge.

"Rosie's first!" Paul pointed excitedly across the bridge, "then walk all the paths in the wood," looking ahead of us along the bank of the river and lowering his tone to show disappointment, "then shopping only if you have to."

The sunshine continued and Paul got all of his wishes - not

finishing his ice cream until we started to climb the steep path into the woods. He ran ahead, choosing the even steeper path off up to the right, while I continued on the slightly lower one that followed the curve of the river below. I knew, at some point, before we got to the bridge by the farm, he'd jump out at me from behind a tree or maybe the hay stacked up near the metal footbridge.

I was deep in my thoughts about the meeting the following day; did I need to contribute, or was I just a name to put on the resulting press release? What was this 'screening' that was to happen on route in the car? Was the black Nissan going to be my transport? If so, should I demand to be told why it had been stalking me?

Paul had decided to climb the hay bales but didn't get a chance to jump out at me. Ahead, I could hear a gruff voice shouting "Oi! Get off my hay! That's bloody dangerous that is. S'not a playground, an 'as you any idea how much hay is worth now? Come on - get down!"

I quickened my pace in case I needed to calm the situation, catching up with him in a little clearing by the metal footbridge less than a minute later. Paul had worked his magic on the farmer already; tractors being one of the things he'd decided to study, he'd become very knowledgeable about them. Apparently, he'd told the farmer all he knew about the John Deere tractor he'd arrived on. They were both climbing into the cab of the bright green and yellow tractor with the farmer showing him all the controls! 'Nice work Paul!' I said to myself as I approached.

The farmer saw me coming. "This lad yours, is he?"

"Well, yeah… I'm *supposed* to be looking after him. Sorry if he's been a nuisance… Come on Paul."

"No, he's been no trouble really. He sure knows a lot about tractors and heavy plant too. Apparently, I chose the wrong model! But, he's er, a bit um …" he mouthed something to me, but I didn't catch it. "You stay right there lad, I'll just have a word with your dad a minute." He climbed down and led me behind the tractor a little. "Your lad, he's a bit autistic, aren't he?"

That question caught me off guard. "Well, I'm not his dad and, well, no… I don't think so? His mum's a good friend, and she's never mentioned it anyway."

The farmer scratched his head. "Well, you see one of mine 'as it. He went right through primary with it, and no one noticed till secondary. Thought he was just quiet and couldn't make friends easy. But *he* has a thing for facts and figures, just like Paul here, and there're other things too – hard to describe, but the way he walks an' he don't often look you in the eye an' he suddenly goes on about what he knows, all excited and opinionated."

"Oh, I don't know anything much about autism. He's about to start year 8, secondary now. But it's a rural school, so maybe no one there is qualified to recognise it?"

Paul was now trying to climb down from the tractor, and the farmer went to help him jump down. "Well, do have a quiet chat with his mum if you gets a chance."

As we waved goodbye to the farmer, Paul asked, "What were you talking about? You're not going to tell mum about climbing the hay, are you?"

I smiled at him broadly and noted that he wasn't actually looking right at me. Maybe he never did? "No. That can be our secret Paul, just don't do it again, OK?" We may need that extra time over coffee today, I thought.

We completed our walk, and I watched Paul more carefully than usual as we walked through the town to the shop. As I put my products in the basket, he appeared to glance up at the shelf where each item had been. Maybe he was counting the remaining product? Often Paul would tell me I'd not brought an item that I had before and, that day, he usefully reminded me to buy butter. Remembering that cows may be low on grass I put two in my basket. 'That's hardly hoarding!' I said to myself.

On approaching the checkout, I wondered if Paul was one of those mathematical geniuses I'd read about? I casually asked if he knew how much my shopping would come to? But he just looked confused, and shrugged. At the checkout, Paul mimicked each of the beeps as the items were passed over the scanner by the bored-looking checkout girl. He'd always done this, and I'd not paid it much attention before. Was this behaviour symptomatic of autism? Not having any children of my own. I had no one to compare him with.

We walked back through the town, and a digger on a large trailer thundered past, clinking and clanking its chains which were straining to secure the heavy load as it lurched from side to side on the rough road. That started Paul off: "That's a JS370. It weighs 37 tonnes. It has a closed box revolving frame and has a six-cylinder turbocharged engine ..."

He continued to rattle off facts about it and its sister models all the way back to Bridge Road where I was happy to see Karen waving to us, finally stopping Paul's regurgitation of JCB specifications.

"Hello, Paul! – Hello, George! – You had a good time?"

Paul answered babbling excitedly, "I was on the hay and a man on a John Deere 6150 crop tractor let me go in the cab, and he showed me all the controls and then we saw a JCB JS370!"

Karen hugged him, maybe a bit more enthusiastically than usual and more lingering too. "Well you have had a good day haven't you! How about you George, get everything you need?" Karen asked as we headed into the café.

"Yeah, got all I needed, and now know much more than I'll ever need to about JCBs!"

As we looked for a place to sit, Karen patted Paul on the head and said, "Well, I've got a special treat for you today Paul. How about, after your jam scone, you go get yourself *another* ice cream from Rosie's, *and* go down to the river bank to watch the ducks while you eat it?"

"Yes! Yes! Yes! Yes! Yes!" Paul danced wildly in the doorway of the café, and Karen had to hold his shoulders to calm him down.

"OK, Paul; calm down! You must stay by the ducks, and we'll come and find you when we've finished, OK?"

"But mum, can you come with me to choose what ice cream I want?"

Choosing things was always a slow process for Paul, earlier we had created a small queue in Rosie's while he'd 'um'd and er'd' for some minutes before I'd eventually chosen for him.

Karen smiled at him warmly, "I think you *definitely* want to try their new 'mango sorbet'. Can you ask for a large one of those?"

I realised that Karen must have visited Rosie's herself, to have seen the poster advertising the new sorbet. She would have briefed the staff that Paul was coming too, and told them what he wanted. Only quite recently had Paul found the confidence to go into any shop on his own, and he would often return empty-handed, sometimes in tears.

"Large mango sorbet please," Paul repeated as he got up to go.

"Hold on Paul!" Karen held his arm. "What about some money to pay for it and what about your jam scone?" Karen handed Paul the exact money.

"Mango sorbet with the ducks trumps scone!" Announced Paul as he took the money and headed out.

"Do you think he'll be alright?" Karen asked as she watched him go.

"Sure he will." I confirmed. I was glad Paul had gone as it gave me an opportunity to discuss what the farmer had said about him without him overhearing. I was never sure when he was listening, or if he was concentrating fully on his phone.

We ordered a coffee each, and a couple of sandwiches, then sat together waiting rather awkwardly. The silence wasn't usual for us because conversation usually flowed.

"That was a close call this morning - with that van. I hope there haven't been any serious accidents caused by those flies." I attempted to get a conversation going.

"Yes," Karen replied quietly, "George, I've got something difficult to tell you and also something to ask you to consider. but after we've been served, if that's OK?"

"Yes, sure. I've something rather sensitive to ask you too, and I was also waiting 'till I knew we'd not been disturbed."

The coffees and toasted sandwiches arrived, and we tucked in, but Karen still appeared distant and troubled, not catching my eye as she usually would. We sat there sending each other little reassuring smiles like strangers do.

"Shall I go first?" I asked, hoping she'd say 'no.'

But she nodded. It was then that I saw, crossing the bridge right behind her, the black Nissan creeping along. The front passenger window was open slightly, but I still couldn't see the driver. I again chose to ignore it and not worry Karen about it, especially because Paul wasn't with us.

"Em... Yes, OK. Well, it's about Paul; has he had a diagnosis for anything that I don't know about?"

Karen looked up at me in surprise, "Oh, George! You knew! Why didn't you tell me before? What kind of mother am I if I'm the last to realise? I'm so very disappointed that you didn't say anything, I really am! – I thought you were my friend?!" She crossed her arms angrily.

"No. Karen I don't *know* anything – honestly! Only today did I suspect something. It was that farmer who suggested it to me. Honestly, I wasn't keeping anything from you."

Karen said nothing but her eyes were welling up.

I continued quietly, "The farmer, today, he said that Paul might have autism. Is that right?"

Still, Karen said nothing but her arms unfolded and she attempted to take a sip of coffee, failing because her hands were shaking too much.

I continued, "He said that one of his children has it, and that it wasn't spotted until he started secondary school."

Karen looked up, and with tears now freely flowing, she asked, "Why? Why does my Paul have to have autism?" She then burst into floods of tears.

I'd never known Karen to be openly upset before. I'd seen depressed, angry, sarcastic, prudish - even drunk, but she was always strong. It would be more likely that I'd be crying on her shoulder than she would on mine. I moved around to sit next to her, pulling her onto my shoulder and handing her my napkin.

Between sniffs and sobs, she explained that, before the holidays, the school had called her in and that they had already involved County, who'd arranged for a specialist to talk to and test Paul. A diagnosis of 'high-functioning autism' had arrived by post only the previous day.

Then something occurred to me, and I hoped it would be encouraging for Karen. I whispered: "He is *still* Paul. That diagnosis isn't going to suddenly change him, is it? He is still the Paul we know and love. But what that diagnosis does mean, is that he will be better understood and will probably now get an education that's more tailored to his needs."

She sniffed and wiped her eyes then kissed me on the cheek. "Thank you, George, I hadn't looked at it quite like that. But I'm so worried about his future now... They say he might have to go to a special school, but he likes it where he is, and the school they were talking about is in Sheffield. He'd have to board, that's way too far to travel every day."

"What problems are the school having with him? I can't believe he's badly behaved."

Karen was crying quietly again. "I'm not sending him away. I just can't, he's only 12 and he needs his mum!" Composing herself again, she continued through intermittent sniffs, "The school said he is good at learning and remembering things that interest him, but he just switches off if he's not. Apparently, he will either fold his arms on the desk and put his head on them, or he sits bolt upright with his hands over his ears. Well, I've never seen him do anything like that!"

"Oh? Well, maybe, if we both talk to him about the need to learn everything, and explain that if he does, then he could probably stay there?" I suggested.

"We… You said, we…" Karen smiled a little. "That kind of brings me to my second thing. But yes, I've been told he may be able to stay in mainstream school if he can, at least, concentrate
on four subjects. At the moment, he's only really learning two: Maths and History. He's got a 'thing' for dates and numbers - he just loves them."

"What about computer studies? He'd be good at that."

"You mean 'I.T.' For some reason he's not down for doing it next term, but I've already emailed the head. She's been very understanding and helpful; she said that they don't want to lose Paul and will do everything she can to keep him there if that's what I want."

Still trying to be encouraging I continued. "Well that's three out of four in the bag. How about English? He needs to record his facts; I guess?"

"One of his weakest subjects, though." Karen managed a sip of coffee and had cheered up a little. "We get on don't we George?"

I nodded. "Yes, to be honest, since Peter died, you're my only real friend up here."

"And I can tell that you do care for us – for Paul and Me," she squeezed my arm.

I was confused, "Of course, but where are you going with this Karen?"

"Can you please answer just one more question first please George?"

"OK?" I replied cautiously.

"When Mel made her pass at you, were you tempted?" She looked me straight in the eyes. I noticed they were still a little wet and slightly bloodshot, yet still retained a piercing quality.

"Oh Karen, I thought we'd agreed to finish that conversation this morning? But, yes, OK, I *was* tempted. I'll be completely honest with you - I was, briefly, *very* tempted. And it wasn't entirely all her fault either, I'd not seen the signs, let her get too close, and she misread my concerns for her. What I'm saying is; I tried to make her a friend and that I kind of left the door open for her. I also mishandled the whole thing, so now she's upset, and I'm in the awkward position of having to try to avoid her."

"I thought so. I could tell something was wrong this morning. Call it 'women's intuition' but I could see you were troubled. I am just checking that I can rely on you to always give me straight answers."

We finished our toasted sandwiches in silence. Both of us deep in our thoughts. Then she said, "You do know Mel's probably only chasing you to prove something to her father? What with her mother being twenty years younger than him and you...?"

"Hang on a minute! I'm not 20 years her senior!" I
protested. "Not sure that's why she did it either?"

Karen finished her coffee. "Well, I need you to give me
an honest answer to this proposition too."

I nodded, wondering what she had in mind, and why she'd
been unusually hesitant to ask?

"George, when Paul and I move into the Manor, would you
consider moving in with us? Make a sort of family? I mean
I've got no one... you've got no one. We all get on really well,
and now we know Paul has this autism thing, you can help me
deal with it... and Paul too?" She squeezed my arm again.

I really wasn't expecting that! My instinct was to simply say 'no',
but she'd been in tears just minutes before, and Karen was right
-

I didn't have anyone else, and as things were, I was very
unlikely to meet anyone, so what she was asking did make
some sense.
Finally, I spoke and immediately used the wrong phrase:
"You are suggesting a sort of marriage of convenience?"

"Marriage?! Oh, I wasn't jumping that far ahead. I mean I'm
not saying 'no', Paul does need a dad and all that, but not
straight away!"

"Oh Karen, no, that's not really what I meant." I was struggling
and felt pressured. I feared I could so easily lose another friend.
I neither wanted to upset Karen nor did I want to completely
dismiss the idea when it was the only offer I'd got. "Karen, I
just don't know. I do like things the way they are. Maybe, once
you've moved into the Manor, we - just you and I - could maybe

spend a few evenings out or something, see how things go?"

Karen looked unimpressed but not hurt. "Sorry, I shouldn't have asked. We haven't even dated, you're quite right, and I was wrong to just ask like that. I'm Sorry. Please just forget I ever suggested it."

"Karen," I whispered, "do you love me?" I was fairly sure I knew the answer already.

After a pause, she replied quietly, "No, I don't think I'm wired to 'do' love? I've just turned thirty and have never been 'in love'. I love my Paul, but, obviously, that's different. I've read books and seen films showing people falling in love and how they feel all wonderful, excited, passionate, etc., but it's just never happened to me. How about you? You loved your wife, didn't you?"

I took in a deep breath. Karen knew already that I'd foolishly married at 19, the first girl that had let me sleep with her. By 23 we'd divorced. I had never gone into the details because it wasn't a topic I was happy discussing. "Well I thought I did, but things got messed up even before we were married, when we first slept together, and that started unravelling everything really."

Karen had sniffed a story and perked up a bit. "What on earth happened when you first slept together?"

I sighed. Remembering how what should have been a magical moment had been soured. "Well I wasn't her first sexual partner, but she had made out that I was. She claimed I was her first 'proper' boyfriend."

"Go on." Karen probed.

"Well, she'd resisted my charms for about four weeks before she finally agreed that we'd 'do the deed' that night."

"This was *your* first time too, was it?"

"Yes… Yes, it was. Well, she thought I'd be able to tell that she wasn't a virgin so she told me that she'd been raped by someone she barely knew."

"Oh, my God! – She'd been raped?" Karen said rather too loudly, gaining us a few looks from other customers.

"Not so loud!" I said quietly but sternly. "Well I believed her, I broke down in tears, the girl I loved, my first love, had been abused in the worse possible way. Sure, I lost my virginity, much later that night, but I was in a devastated state. I don't remember the sex at all. I just remember being so sad, upset and angry."

Karen was squeezing my arm again. "Oh, George that's so awful. She must have been raped, though, surely?"

"No… I found out soon after we'd married, from *her* family, that she'd had a boyfriend before me and that she often made up terrible stories about her childhood. Then I met him, quite by chance; he'd seen us together and boasted about how they'd slept together on their first date. He had even taken a sneaky self- timer shot of the two of them naked on a bed. The rape story was complete fiction, and I was never able to trust anything she said again."

"What a total bitch!" Karen had shouted again, but this time realised and continued in a whisper as the other customers appeared to strain to hear. "I have no sympathy at all for women who make up rape stories; they make it harder for those who have genuinely been attacked to be believed. Some might not even dare report it because of women like her. Oh, what a cow! – Did you ever challenge her about it?"

"No, no I never did. It made me too angry just thinking about it. I tried to forgive her, but we rarely had sex, that story… that bloody, stupid, story… it just haunted me. Then she wanted kids, and sex was kind of required. So, I told her I didn't want children, she got angry, and we just started drifting apart after that."

"What if you two did have a child, would you have still divorced?"

"God, no! We'd still be together now with our love in tatters, bankrupt and probably with no house, but we'd have stuck together for a child. I certainly wouldn't leave a child and don't think even she could do that. No, she was unfaithful, a fantasist, an attention seeker, and almost permanently jobless, but I'm sure she'd not abandon her own child. So, I'd have been seriously buggered if I had fathered a child with her."

"Did you want a child? I think you'd make a good dad; you're ever so calm and patient - I've seen you with Paul, you're a natural." A reassuring smile returned to Karen's face.

"You are really dragging it all out of me today aren't you Karen? But, I didn't want a child when I was that young; I was only 20 when she started pestering. Maybe if we'd really got on well… Anyway, we couldn't afford one; we had just got a massive mortgage based on us both working, when she just left her job, expecting me to just 'earn more'. Apparently, that's what 'the breadwinner' is expected to do if the woman decides she just doesn't want to work."

Karen frowned, "And yet you still feel guilty that you left her with that debt?"

"Well, it *was* 'our' debt. She accepted the divorce settlement because it left her the house and the car. She didn't realise she'd also taken on the mortgage that was in arrears. I came out with nothing and ran away before the bailiffs turned up. I do feel guilty about doing that. Maybe she sold the car to pay off the mortgage arrears and then got a job? But, more likely, she just found just herself a new 'breadwinner'?"

Karen sat back and crossed her arms. "Well, I'd have done the exactly same. It was fair payback for that rape story that screwed you over!"

I sighed again, "Hmmm? But, going back to your original question Karen, can I have some time to think about what you asked?"

Karen kissed me on the cheek again. "Yes, of course, you can. Take as long as you need. I thought you'd already decided against it, to be honest, and we'll still be fine if you say 'no'. I don't want you to feel bad or pressured into anything. We'll stay friends, though, won't we, whatever happens?"

I smiled back, her idea suddenly not seeming so strange. I couldn't imagine telling anyone else all the details of the car crash that had been my marriage. I was also sure that I could completely trust her, and that she wouldn't be so demanding, nor make up terrible stories. Karen was a bit hard, but she was honest and straight talking. I just didn't love her. Did that really matter? Maybe we'd grow to love each other like couples in arranged marriages sometimes do? I realised I'd been gazing at her for a while and that I'd not answered her question. She was now giving me a puzzled look with her head tilted slightly to one side. Without thinking, I just leant across and kissed her on the lips. She returned the kiss and smiled slightly questioningly. It felt good. "Sure, you and me, we will stay friends, whatever."

"George, you do know you are a master of mixed messages,

don't you? Come on, we'd better go find Paul" We got up together and an elderly couple sitting by the door, apparently having seen us kiss, gave us a warm smile and I suddenly felt a little proud to be with, and to be needed by, Karen.

As we crossed back over the bridge, we stopped to look down to see where Paul was. I felt her hand tap my pocket, I put mine out, and we held hands as we watched Paul gazing at the ducks and swans. We continued to hold hands as we went to collect Paul. I glanced back, remembering the black Nissan, but it was nowhere to be seen.

Paul didn't seem to notice that we were hand-in-hand, and I felt that we were, maybe, just playing at being a couple? It didn't feel wrong; it felt comfortable, but not special.

Karen said she was OK to drive back, and so Paul and I looked out for the flies. We couldn't see down into the valley, now across the other carriageways to our right, but there was a police car assisting a convoy of vehicles up and out of one of the side turnings and 'road closed' signs had been put across the others.

To our left, the hills looked very frosty with the tops appearing unusually dark and misty. The flies were up there but not in such

great numbers. Karen regularly switched her wipers and screen wash jets on to clear the windscreen.

The Nissan wasn't in the lane when Karen dropped me off. After a quick peck on the cheek, I returned to the sanctuary of my little gatehouse with yet more to think about. Then I saw a note from Melissa on the floor, and my heart started to race again. I walked past it into the kitchen, filled the kettle and switched it on. Then I switched it off again. Something from my little bar would be better. I walked past the note again and went upstairs for a drink. Thoughts of running away had returned. I threw back a large Glenfiddich allowing the strong whisky to burn my cheeks and throat and numb my feelings slightly.

Life had all been so much simpler just a couple of weeks earlier; I may have been a bit lonely sometimes, but decisions were all easy, and everything in the garden ambled along in a safe and predictable manner. Now the grass was all dead, there was the mysterious Nissan, I'd got to go to Westminster in the morning, somehow I'd developed some very wrong feelings for Melissa, as had she too. Added to that, Karen was on my case with a most unexpected proposition, and Paul had just been diagnosed with autism. Then I remembered we'd still not discussed Peter's note and its implications.

I felt that I'd become a bit like a small boat on rapids: I was being pushed and pulled towards any number of different waterfalls, my paddles, though thrashing wildly, were no longer controlling my passage. I was making rash and almost panicked decisions. I realised Karen was right when she'd said 'I was master of mixed messages.' The truth was, I just didn't know what messages I wanted to convey. I was overwhelmed with all that was happening. I needed a lot of time, alone, to be able to analyse and consider everything properly.

I poured a second drink. I wasn't going to get that much time. My thoughts turned back to Karen and Paul. I doubted that I'd sleep much, so I'd spend some time researching both grass and autism on the internet. See what I might be letting myself in for if I decided to paddle, or just drift towards, that particular waterfall.

Chapter 5 – Snakes and Ladders

I'd set my alarm for 5 am. I'd done a little more research on the properties of grass and autism during the night, then, probably after my third whisky, I'd formed a plan: I was going to outwit and humiliate the driver of the black Nissan, assuming that was to be my transport to London. This was not one of my better ideas…

The sky was glowing on the northern horizon, but it was still dark outside. I washed, shaved and dressed without turning on the lights. I'd got my photo ID and everything relating to the grass virus together in a small folder. I added some cash and my fully charged mobile phone that I'd just switched off; thinking that they could track the phone if it remained on.

I opened the door very quietly and as the cool morning air hit me, stood on something. It was Melissa's note, so I quickly picked it up and pocketed it. Then I closed the door as quietly as possible behind me.

The car, probably the black Nissan, would be in the lane waiting for me. They'd be asleep, not expecting me for another 45 minutes. I opened the gates with my remote control. In the gloom, they swung open almost silently, but I knew they would close with a clang. I needed to find the car before they closed again. I was going to sneak up on it, then bang on the drivers' window and shout "TAXI!" – That would be payback for it following us and for blocking the drive.

The gates would stay open for thirty seconds, to allow a vehicle through before starting to close automatically. I'd have only about 50 seconds before the clanging gates would alert whoever was in the car. I crept through the opening gates and looked up the lane to the right. I searched the shadows but saw nothing. All I could hear was my own heart starting to race. My senses were all intensely tuned as I scanned for the vehicle. Suddenly I was bathed in bright light from behind me. Startled, I turned back to the drive, shading my eyes from the blinding light of the two headlights on full beam. "Shit!" Somehow a car had got in and was already on the drive facing the gate.

The lights dimmed, and the driver's door opened. A man's deep voice barked: 'Get in!" Then the rear left door swung open as the driver's door slammed shut. Meekly and feeling a complete fool, I walked to the car, recognising it as the black Nissan, only as I got closer. I glanced up towards the house, hoping that maybe someone was up to witness my voluntary abduction but the windows showed no sign of life; they merely reflected the reds of the brightening sky as I entered the black Nissan.

There was a stern-looking woman, probably in her mid-fifties, sitting in the rear. She didn't even turn to look at me, making me feel irrelevant. She appeared to be reading from a tablet. She had short, tightly curled, black, almost certainly dyed hair, a long sharp nose, and was wearing a dull grey suit. I imagined that she was very short, although I couldn't really tell. I glanced at her shoes, dismissing the thought that a poisoned blade could snap out of one at any moment. I had watched too many James Bond films, I assured myself. The driver, from what little I could see of him, was a large black man in a glossy leather jacket that looked slightly too tight for his muscular frame. He didn't turn around to greet me.

"Going somewhere Mr Craven?" The woman asked coldly, still without looking up from her tablet.

I instantly recognised the monotone voice as that which I'd heard on the phone the previous morning. This wasn't going to be a fun-filled trip I thought.

"I was just coming to find you." I lied pathetically.

"I see," she responded without conviction, "do you have your mobile phone with you?" she asked.

I nodded sheepishly as I sat down, and noticed that the seat felt slightly warm. I wondered if the woman had just moved over to the other seat but also noted that she was already buckled up and that I'd not heard a sound from the car before the doors had opened.

"Turn it back on and keep it on until you get to the Cabinet Offices. There you will give it to security on entering. Do *not* try anything else," she instructed in a manner that resembled a policeman reading out a caution. The car started and passed through the gates just before they began to close. I heard the driver say something into a headset, but he sounded distant and muffled. Then I realised that a glass partition separated the front from the rear, and that the woman also had a headset.

Briefly, I considered questioning her authority; did she actually have the right to be giving me orders? But I'd been stupid once already, so just meekly switched my phone back on as instructed. I'd got my passport in the folder and waved it between her face and her tablet as I.D.

"I don't need to see that," she waved it away. While still continuing to read her notes, she started to question me, "Mr Craven, on Wednesday of last week, RHS Wisley sent you an email requesting that you do not send any further samples of infected grass by post. The following morning you sent at least one other sample by post. Why are you trying to spread the virus, and how many other contaminated samples have you sent, and where exactly have they been sent?"

"I wasn't trying to spread the virus!" I protested. "I sent just that one, and *before* I read that email. And I sealed it up really well to prevent infection."

"You are trying to climb ladders aren't you Mr Craven?"

I wished she would turn to look at me, I was wasting my genuine expressions of disbelief and bewilderment, "I don't understand – ladders?"

"Mr Craven, it is evident you are seeking fame by first putting your name to the virus, secondly by attempting to spread it to the South, and thirdly by persuading a senior cabinet minister that you can advise her, while being completely unqualified to do so." She still didn't look up from her screen for my reaction.

This was no friendly chat. This sour-faced woman wasn't easing my fears about the forthcoming meeting, nor teaching me the etiquettes of addressing high-profile ministers. This woman's accusations and assumptions were completely false, and I felt myself getting angry.

"Listen, Lady," I reached across and snatched the tablet from her to get her full attention. "I don't even know your name, but you can take me back right now, remove my name from the virus, and tell Maria whatever-her-name-is, that I'm unable to advise her because I didn't go to university."

The car braked sharply throwing me forward, as the partition came down. The driver reached back, grabbing my collar, and with his right hand formed a raised fist that hung menacingly above me. He was huge and not in a good mood! I passed the tablet back to the woman, keeping a close eye on his fist as I did so. The woman took it back gently and calmly as though nothing had happened.

She also appeared to have completely ignored my rant, as well as the fact that I'd briefly taken her tablet. Instead, undistracted, she spoke quietly into her headpiece "You are in? OK, are you able to confirm when that email was opened?" Then she nodded a

the driver, who released me and turned back to drive, as the glass partition returned.

From what she was saying, I assumed she was talking to someone in my gatehouse. I was still angry but also now terrified of the driver and more cautiously stated, "So someone is in my house messing with my laptop? I guess the same person who was sitting here?"

She tutted and turned to look at me for the first time with a most unimpressed look. "So Simon or is it *'George'*? should we be calling you Sherlock now?"

"If you are going to do jokes, lady, try smiling - maybe someone will laugh if you let them know you've come to the punch line. Now get that person out of my house and take me back!" I was so glad that I'd picked up Melissa's note, and prayed it couldn't be seen sticking out of my pocket.

She turned away, ignoring me again, and spoke once more into her headset. "OK see what else is there."

Suddenly the car swerved, bumped over something and then another before the car slowed considerably. My inquisitor pressed a button, and the glass partition lowered again.

"What's the problem, Nigel?"

"Rabbits, Ma'am, loads of them, all over the road," replied the driver.

We both leant forward to try to see. Ahead the road was bathed in the bluish glow of the headlights. Dotted all along the road were rabbits, many only appearing as a pair of glowing eyes.

Some had already been hit by overnight traffic, while others were frozen in fear, awaiting their fate.

My inquisitor turned to me and asked, with just a hint of emotion showing on her face, finally breaking her mask of sternness, "They are all looking for food? They only eat grass?"

I resisted the temptation to say, 'Surely I'm not qualified to advise you?' instead, to try to diffuse the situation and maybe prove my worth, I chose to reply sensibly: "During the warmer months Rabbits' principal food *is* grass, they supplement their diet with dandelions, clover, thistles and other weeds." She appeared to show an interest in my answer, so I continued, "In the colder months when they are less active, they'll eat much less grass and rely on more woody things like bark, twigs, seeds and the remaining green parts of wildflowers and weeds." Then, pointing at the road ahead, "This mass migration to look for more grass should slow down as the temperature drops so, hopefully, will be temporary as it's September already."

A car ahead had stopped completely, blocking the narrow road, and Nigel, the driver, got out to investigate.

"So as this spreads south and the temperature drops this will become less of a problem?" She inquired with a softer, more human voice than I thought she possessed.

As I watched Nigel talk to the driver of the car ahead, I answered, "Yes, but deer switch from woody things to grass as the temperature drops, so we might see more of those and other animals on the roads during the winter." Then, taking advantage of the fact that this 'ice woman' was starting to thaw, added,

119

"Excuse me, but can I ask, 'what's your name?' We were never properly introduced."

She actually smiled! – Not a big beaming smile, but a small warm one. She offered a hand "I don't usually *do* introductions," We shook hands, "I am Susannah Coburn; Cabinet Office Security."

"And you live in this car, and spent four days stalking me, why?"

"I don't live in this car! I came up last night, you've only had Nigel for company until now."

Nigel had moved the car ahead into a passing point and returned to the Nissan.

"What was the problem, Nigel? Oh, and say hello to George."

Nigel didn't turn around to answer. Instead, he continued to pull away. "Morning George. She's hit a rabbit. Won't drive until the road is cleared."

Susannah and I looked at the car as we passed. The poor lady was sitting in the passenger seat, clearly still upset, and likely not going anywhere for quite a while.

Susannah continued: "Nigel followed you because the car you have access to, the RAV-4 registered to Arthur Quail, had been seen on CCTV in Newcastle where the outbreak spread from. We are concerned that you either created the virus or are responsible for it spreading so quickly to Darlington and Barnard Castle where the car was also monitored. It would be most embarrassing for the government, should an advisor on the virus later be discovered to be responsible for it!"

"I see. But it was Arthur - Lord Quail - who regularly went to Newcastle to the auction house, and to Darlington where his

solicitor is. I don't use the car very often for personal use."
There was another bump and swerve as another rabbit met its
maker. "Nigel, the sky is brightening a bit, if you could switch
your lights down to just parking, the rabbits won't just freeze
and may be more likely to hop out of the way." Nigel waited for
permission from Susannah, who quickly agreed. Then she
replied to someone on her headset again, but with only single
word acknowledgements.

I was about to return to the matter of someone rummaging
through my belongings, when she brought up the same
subject. Sighing exaggeratedly into her headpiece, she relayed
the question: "George, your house guest is asking if that's
really an original Pac-man machine you've got? And how
would you feel if he beat your high score?"

Few people appreciate an original, 1980, coin-operated Pac-
man machine, or could play it well enough to appear on the
high score list. So, strangely, I felt far less aggression towards
my unseen burglar. "Tell him he's welcome to try, but he'd be
there for over two hours to get close. Can he also confirm he's
not taking anything away, and will shut the door on his way
out?"

"Did you hear that?" – "Yes, OK" – "That will do."
Susannah then turned back to me. "He has taken nothing and
has confirmed that you opened that email after you posted
that sample."

"So I'm off the hook?" I asked.

"Yes. Though I trust you will not repeat whatever you were
trying to do this morning! We also received some
information last night that the virus probably arrived via the
Tyne docks."

"From abroad?" I asked.

"I don't know, but I would assume so. No doubt you'll probably be privy to more information this afternoon. Now, my work here is done. Could you drop me off at York Station, Nigel? – I do much prefer travelling by train, and I've got to divert via Cambridge."

Nigel answered "Yes Ma'am. Be about 25 minutes."

I was confused "I thought you were going to brief me on what to expect at the Cobra meeting, correct etiquette, etc.?"

"No. Just be yourself and don't, whatever you do, try to act like them. You'll be fine. Just one more bit of advice; if they ask you to confirm something, the answers should be 'yes' or 'no', *only* if you are 100% sure of your facts. If you are even very slightly unsure say 'to the best of my knowledge ... Yes or no.' Got it?"

I nodded.

We were on the A1 now and the warm orange of the dawn light exposed, with long shadows, a scene like a battlefield across the road and hard shoulder. Mostly dead and injured rabbits, but we also saw some small muntjac deer. Magpies and crows were already picking and tearing at the remains, dodging the building traffic themselves. I imagined that Kites and Kestrels would join them as the temperature climbed during the day. I saw a fox dragging the lifeless body of a rabbit up the brown mud of the embankment. Then we saw two sheep, one severely injured, baying and crying. Neither Susannah nor I could bear to look anymore.

As we approached York, I hoped that the A1 would be closed, and I'd have to take the train too, but the morning light must have also reduced the number of animals searching for food, and I guessed we were also travelling through the furthest South the virus had reached. We were now passing through the powdery-white landscape of the fungus stage of the virus.

We had arrived at York station and, just before Susannah left the car, she leant over and whispered to me: "Don't take it personally, but Nigel doesn't really do 'chatting' – not with anyone! Good luck at the meeting, and don't worry!"

"Thanks, Susannah. You know, you do a really good battle-axe, fierce-bitch act!"

Then, as cold as ice, she turned back slowly and said, very firmly: "That was *no* act." Then gave me a long hard stare that sent a shiver down my spine. She turned away again and headed off into the station. I heard a brief snigger from Nigel, then the glass partition slid back up.

We passed horsebox after horsebox, as well as many cattle trucks with rows of curious sheep or cows peeking out. People and farmers were obviously manually migrating animals south. I wondered if rules had already been put in place to ensure they were all free from the virus before they travelled, and also if they all had somewhere to go?

As the hills and valleys slowly changed from all white to patches of white on yellow, I thought that maybe I *was* going to get that thinking time alone after all. I estimated that it would take at least four hours to get to Westminster.

I started with Mel; this was something I urgently needed to fully understand and sort out. I pulled her note out of my pocket and read it with some trepidation. However, it was just a list of phone calls and her summary of media reports. She obviously wanted to keep her 'job', and didn't include anything that could embarrass either of us in writing.

There were only two requests for interviews. I had hoped that after having declined so many others, the media would forget me.

Melissa had summarised the news very well; the press was still principally concerned with cancelled sports and the threat to training athletes expected to compete at the Olympics. They also considered if the possible loss of grass at Woburn Safari Park and around Buckingham Palace would have an impact on tourist revenue. There was a report about the rocketing price of hay, claiming that many horse owners were complaining that they would be unable to afford to pay for hay over the coming winter. There was nothing else in the note, nothing personal. I hoped that Melissa had come to the same conclusion I had: That she was simply too young for me and I, too old for her. We both had to disregard any ill-conceived feelings for one another and certainly ignore any animal instincts that we shared. Maybe, if she'd not been snatched up by the time she was twenty - unlikely I thought for such a beauty - we could get together then without raising so many eyebrows? But that assumed we still both felt the same. I'd be 33, and even I could have found someone else by then, maybe Karen?

So that was it then. I'd thank Melissa for her continued work, and just make it clear that we could never have a relationship other than that between work colleagues. If she came to me for advice or anything social, I'd refer her to Karen, who would be around at the Manor much more.

But if Karen and I got together, how would that affect dynamics at the Manor between Melissa and Karen? Would that threaten either Karen's job, or her new accommodation?

Then I started to think more about Karen and Paul. I was not sure how I felt about this 'instant family'. I knew that I always felt very comfortable and at ease with Karen. I was a bit lonely, and I'd have someone to dine out with, maybe even go on holiday with? But then, I also liked my little gatehouse, and that had only the one bedroom. Maybe I could keep it as a retreat, or call it a 'games room' for Paul… with a bar? I somehow doubted I could sell that idea to Karen.

I looked up from my thoughts and saw that the grass was 'proper' green again. We were approaching Peterborough where there was now no sign of the rural devastation we'd left behind.

My thoughts returned to the forthcoming meeting. I still wasn't sure if I were to be included in the meeting, or would be just advising Maria beforehand. But the fact that I could have briefed her over the phone in advance led me to suspect that I *would* be attending the meeting. I wondered too if the Prime Minister would be chairing, or present?

What would the worst-case scenario be, should the virus wipe out all our cereal crops? What if the loss of grass did cause flooding and mud slides? Riots, looting, people could even be murdered for food as supplies dried up. Who would continue to go to work if there was no food to buy? Would power and transport workers continue to go to work if they could spend their time better searching for, or maybe growing, their own food?

Society as we know it could quickly collapse into anarchy if hunger broke the infrastructure we'd all become so dependent upon collapsed. Food producers might demand huge sums for their products, and I wondered if the government would, or could, freeze prices to prevent this.

As the miles whizzed past, I started to get nervous again. We were passing through a tunnel; the flashing, orange lights, whooshing past caused a strange strobe effect. We'd reached the Hatfield Tunnel, and I knew that London was looming.

What solutions could I possibly offer these ministers? Over the next few miles, some ideas started to form. Foundations of a plan that would not be at all useful to those at the Cobra meeting. Quite grand ideas that could maybe work at Ingleton Manor? If I could ever sell them to Arthur, and of that I wasn't at all sure. I started to think about Friday's 'tea and cakes' meeting, where I'd offer these ideas up for discussion, and not about the Cobra meeting I was about to attend.

I looked at the time, and was surprised to see that it was only 11.35am, when it felt like mid-afternoon. We were passing the closed gates at the end of Downing Street. The Cabinet Office was very close. I felt myself sweating in fear and anticipation.

As we passed a grand but dirty white stone building, the car drew up opposite a huge and imposing black door atop three stone steps. Almost as soon as we came to a complete stop, this door opened, and a security guard appeared briefly in the doorway. He was replaced by a smartly dressed woman, probably about sixty, who sported short, curled-under, dyed blonde hair. She carefully negotiated the steps and spoke to Nigel, who had opened his window. Then, smiling, she opened my door and beckoned me out.

"Good morning Simon, you are early. We weren't expecting you until noon. The committee is convening at one o'clock, and we are the first to arrive!"

I got out, and my legs chose that moment to remind me that I'd been sitting in a car for over five hours. I staggered for the first few steps. "Ouch! Sorry. I've been sitting for too long."

She took my arm and helped me up the steps, making me feel like an old man. "I'm Maria Trellis, in case you didn't recognise me."

The security guard reappeared and asked me for my identification and phone before I could proceed. I'd expected this and had my passport ready. He then patted me down while Maria excused his actions "Just standard precautions for when the PM is attending. We need you to sign a copy of the Official Secrets Act; you are to agree to never repeat anything you learn from the committee today unless we tell you to do so." I signed without reading the long document, then printed my name as 'George Craven' underneath.

"OK. Let's go through to the greeting room." She ushered me through a large white door into a room which rather resembled an old gentleman's club, dotted with rather worn armchairs with red velvet upholstery and bronze studs. If it weren't for the two desks with flat screen monitors, I'd have thought the room had been stuck in time since the 60's. "Take a seat Simon, or is it George? I can't recall what Arthur said."

I sat down in one of the oversized chairs and caught a whiff of ancient cigar smoke. "It's been agreed that I should remain 'George', though my real name *is* Simon. So, the Prime Minister is going to be in the meeting with you?"

Maria nodded "Oh yes, this is a 'big one' or, at least, it looks like it's going to be. How far south has the virus spread?"

"It's heading south down the A1 corridor quite fast. It's got as far as York already. I don't know how far North it's got? But it is approaching the M6 to the West."

Maria continued to nod and started to scribble some notes as she did so. "If the M6 doesn't stop it, it will be in the Lake District then?"

"The M6 won't stop it. Rabbits searching for food are already migrating to uninfected areas, and they will be carrying the virus with them. I think that all the grass from Keswick to Penrith will be yellow by as early as tomorrow."

Maria pulled a pained expression and sucked in air through her teeth "I heard about those poor rabbits on the radio this morning. Did you see any on the way down?"

"Yes hundreds of them, and some deer too." I solemnly replied.

Looking up, as the door opened, I saw a group of three men entering the room, talking quietly as they did so. I recognised one of them as a politician, but I couldn't name him, nor his post. There was a chief constable in full uniform I also knew only from news reports, and a thin weasel-like man who looked like a used car salesman.

Whispering to Maria, I asked, "Should I know who these people are?"

Maria glanced over at them and called them over "Good morning gentlemen." They looked up, and slightly curiously looked me over as they came across.

Maria and I stood up to greet them.

"George, this is Yorkshire's Chief Constable; Adrian Parker, Graham Stubs you know is Chancellor of the Exchequer and" indicating to the weasel-like man, "Norman Griffin, our newly appointed Home Secretary. Gentlemen, this is one of my special advisors, George Craven, who, along with my other advisor, identified the graminoid virus."

We shook hands and shared the usual meaningless gratitudes. Then the Chief Constable asked Maria, "So what exactly is a graminoid?"

I jumped in with the answer "It's the scientific name for grasses, I think Maria has been on Wikipedia!"

Maria looked slightly uneasy, and the Home Secretary, Norman Griffin, said dryly, "I do hope his advice is better than his humour." Then, as one, the three of them turned and quietly walked away. They sat around a table at the far side of the room and continued to talk between themselves.

Maria shook her head at me and pointed to the chair I had risen from, "Listen, George, there are already mutterings about the need for non-qualified, civilian advisors to attend Civil Contingency meetings. Please don't make me look like a fool for including you."

"I'm sorry! I was just trying break the ice - lighten the mood. 'Wrong place', I realise that now." I could have kicked myself. I had acted on nervous impulse without thinking first.

Another group of four entered the room. Two men and a woman joined the others, while another younger woman in a light blue suit came over to Maria. "The PM wants to see you now, in room A." She whispered.

"OK, thank you." Turning back to me and retaining her stern look, she said, "I'll be back as soon as I can, please... no more 'jokes', George."

As Maria disappeared through the door, the young lady in blue asked if I'd like a coffee? I accepted, and she left too, leaving me alone in a room slowly filling up with more people, all engaged in animated conversations in little groups. I couldn't wait for either my coffee to arrive or for Maria to return. I was feeling very self- conscious, and was aware that I was getting questioning glances from the many groups of people gathering in the room.

I fiddled with my notes in my folder. Sorting out all three

pages several times, and pretending to be reading them as I did so.

After what seemed an age, the lady in blue reappeared. She passed a cup to someone standing in the far corner, then gave the remaining one to me. I thanked her, and I was alone in the crowded room once again.

Glancing around, I caught sight of the recipient of the other beverage; standing rather uncomfortably with her cup, in the far corner, was a very tall and slim young lady. She had straight blonde hair, tied back, and a large pair of black, thick-rimmed glasses. She had a bulging yellow folder under her arm and also was rather furtively looking around. I judged from her composure that she was as out of place as I was. She caught me looking at her, and she nervously smiled. Praying that I wasn't

about to make yet another foolish mistake, I got up and carried my coffee across the room to her. As I did so, I realised she was also making her way through the cliquey groups towards me.

We met in a space near the middle of the room.

"Hello, we appear to have gravitated to one another," she said, "Would you be Mr Craven?"

"George, yes. Please call me George. And I guess you are Miss Parker?" Each balancing our drinks in our right hands, we attempted an awkward handshake, making us both smile at our clumsiness.

She abandoned the handshake. Instead, she leant in towards me and whispered, "Help me, George! My name is Andrea, and I've been transported back in time to a land before manners!"

"*Very* pleased to meet you, Andrea, shall we just elope now?" I nodded towards the door.

We laughed and got a few more irritated looks in the process, but I didn't care anymore. I was no longer alone, and Andrea appeared to share my 'inappropriate' sense of humour.

"I've never advised anyone other than microbiologists before," she explained, "I was just sent in here to meet with Maria Trellis, and was ignored when I came in – what a rude bunch! Have you met anyone yet?"

"Hmm… I had a very brief chat with Maria and was introduced to the Home Secretary, Yorkshire Chief Constable, and Home Secretary…" Nodding to the group sitting to our left "but I gaffed, and it didn't go well. I made the smallest of jokes and they just walked away!"

"Oh, my God! Well, I hope Maria gets back here before the meeting starts, else I've wasted my time. Do you know where she went?"

"Er, I am fairly sure that we are both *attending* the meeting. I'd hoped to be just advising beforehand, but apparently not. Maria was called away by the lady-in-blue to meet with the Prime Minister."

My new friend put her hand over her mouth, and wide-eyed said, "Oh no. The Prime Minister is *here?* I really can't do this. I just can't." She turned towards the door and started towards it.

"Andrea!" I followed and whispered urgently "you can't just leave me here. Just think, in a couple of hours, this will all be over." I caught her arm. It was rigid and tense, but she did stop walking. "I'm sure Maria will be back very soon, and she seems much nicer than this lot."

Maria had appeared in the doorway. "I am back and," she increased her volume "I *am* the nicest person here for sure!"

She continued in a quieter and kinder voice: "Sorry to have left you on your own, and that I wasn't here to greet you, Andrea. Are you OK? You already know George, don't you?"

Andrea replied: "Actually, we've just met. Look, I'm sorry Maria, but I don't think I can do this. I thought I was just advising you, privately, before the meeting." Andrea clearly hadn't been comforted and was still looking past Maria and towards the door.

Maria took her cup from her shaking hand, and placed it down on a table, "Andrea, you're not here to make friends, nor to impress people. You know your science - they don't. They need *you*. The Prime Minister is aware that this experience is entirely alien to you both. He is pleased that you are here to try to help. This lot won't dare to be so rude to you in his company – trust me, they are just a bunch of arse-lickers! – well, the men are anyway. Now, Andrea, did you confirm the rice protein resistance?"

"Yes," Andrea replied quietly.

"And is that coincidence, or something more sinister?" Maria probed.

I had no idea what they were talking about but assumed it would have to be converted to layman's terms for the ministers to understand in the meeting.

Andrea was gaining in confidence: "The chances of a DNA, rather than an RNA, virus evolving naturally, with both the fungal key and rice protein rejection, are infinitely small. I have been unable to identify even an RNA plant virus containing both those attributes or even similar functioning ones."

"OK. that question will be passed to you in the meeting, for you to answer directly. It is a grave concern to the PM. George, the

Transport Minister will be asked, at some point, what the risks are to the transport network. If he doesn't cover the issues Arthur had told me you'd thought of, or any others, then that's your cue to speak up. Just don't add any humour or sarcasm – stick to the facts. If you speculate, make sure they understand that is what you are doing."

Andrea and I nodded in agreement. I smiled at Andrea, "Are you happier now?"

"No, not really. I am saying to myself over and over 'I'm going to be fine', and I'm taking deep breaths, but I think I'll be OK now. Thanks to you both." Andrea managed a smile.

"And you, George? You do look more relaxed than when you arrived." Maria stated.

"Well yes, Andrea and I *were* planning to elope together," I winked at Andrea, "but we'll put that on hold for now."

"Well, I'll let you both into a secret: I've only attended one Cobra meeting before this, and that was about the Ebola crisis, and I contributed absolutely nothing at all!" Maria checked her watch. "The uninvited will be leaving shortly, then we'll be called in."

"Boris not here?" I always wanted to meet Boris Johnson. Though he is a bit of a buffoon, I can relate to people who have a tendency to open their mouths before fully engaging their brain.

"No!" Maria answered, "The outgoing Mayor doesn't hold a ministerial appointment, well not yet anyway!"

Some people started to leave the room. I quickly realised that they were all the younger ones. I guess they were ministers' staff or other advisors. All those who remained were all, except the Secretary for Education, probably twice as old as Andrea and myself.

I was counting those who remained and decided there were 17 of us, including Andrea and myself, when the 'blue coffee lady' appeared at the door. She coughed loudly, and the room fell silent. Then in a clear voice, she announced; "As directed by the 2004 Civil Contingencies Act, a Committee is to be formed in Meeting Room A. The Prime Minister chairs, and instructs those present to attend. Please follow me."

We then filed out in silence, rather like school children being shepherded to an assembly.

The security officer stood to one side of a thick plain wooden door, and the 'blue coffee lady' on the other. Beyond the door, there was a huge table with six pairs of microphones on stalks, and what looked like mobile phone induction chargers along each side. There were also glasses, and water in small jugs, all symmetrically laid out.

The Prime Minister was standing to my right, between two empty seats, at one end of this enormous table. I quickly counted the chairs - three at each end and six either side. He nodded to each person as they entered. There were printed name markers on the table in front of each chair. Instinctively I turned left, away from the Prime Minister, once I had received my nod and a reassuring smile. Sure enough, my place marker was at the opposite end, to the right of Maria and Andrea's. I briefly wondered if I could keep the smart little marker with its government crest and the words 'George Craven – Special Advisor'. 'That would look so cool on my bar,' I thought.

This room was a total contrast to that which we had just left: Behind the Prime Minister, the wall was a bank of 8 42" HD Screens, five of which were on. I recognised the two news channels of BBC and Sky News and there were two screens where the camera was pointed at an unoccupied desk. One was that of the Whitehouse situation room that I recognised from so many films. The other looked more British palatial, and I wondered if the grand seat and desk could belong to the Queen or maybe Angela Merkel?

The fifth screen was displaying a map of the UK, with rings of different colours expanding from Newcastle. The outer yellow circle extended as far north as the Scottish Borders just short of the outskirts of Edinburgh, West to Penrith, and South to York. This confirmed my own estimates of how far the first stage of the virus had reached.

Noting that nobody had sat down, I did as the others were doing and stood, with Maria, then Andrea to my left and the Weasel- like Home Secretary to my right. We did not acknowledge each other.

Once everyone had found their place, the Prime Minister spoke. "Good afternoon ladies and gentlemen. This Civil Contingencies Meeting is now convened, and I remind everyone that this meeting is recorded. To save long introductions I will ask you to sit down as you are identified. Firstly, apologies from the leader of the House of Lords and the Secretary for Culture, Media, and Sports who are unable to attend because of duties overseas. From my right, present here today are: Chancellor of Duchy – Sir Maurice James, Party Chairman - Lord Francis," As their names were called each bowed slightly and sat down. "Transport Secretary – Peter Stubbs, Foreign Secretary – Alistair Green, Work & Pensions – William Grey, Defence – Christopher Darling, Health – Justine Clarkson, Special Advisor - Andrea Parker MSC, Secretary for Food, Environment and Rural Affairs - Maria Trellis, Special Advisor to Maria Trellis – George Craven,"

I nodded and sat, reminded of primary school registration. "Home Secretary – Norman Griffin, Welsh Secretary – Cefni Norris, Yorkshire Chief Constable – Adrian Parker, Education Secretary – Anne Phillips, Scottish Secretary - James Barratt, and Chancellor of the Exchequer – Graham Stubbs."

The Prime Minister sat down himself. "Sir Maurice James will outline the situation we face. Beforehand, I would like to state that we face an unusual threat, and one for which we have no pre-planned contingencies."

Sir Maurice twisted a microphone towards himself before he spoke, in a clear, calm, and authoritative manner. "At 10.15am on Monday 21st September, a shipping container was unloaded at Tyne Side docks, Newcastle. Port operators reported that the container was punctured and that soil was falling from its underside as it was lifted dockside. It was then lowered onto plastic sheeting and taken to the customs inspection area for investigation. The manifest stated that the cargo was coconut fibre compost from Sri Lanka. It was packed in 50Kg bags, many of which appeared to have split at the side seams. The container ship, 'Agnes Rickmers' had indeed departed from Sri Lanka three weeks previously. However, the ship had just installed a new cargo camera. This recorded that the container was already on board when it arrived in Sri Lanka. Unfortunately, no video footage remains prior to this. However, I can confirm that the Agnes Rickmers had sailed to Sri Lanka from Shanghai, China, departing on the 7th August."

There was a murmur around the table with many heads turning to the Foreign Secretary, who merely nodded to confirm he already knew this.

Sir Maurice continued. "It has now been confirmed that the compost was heavily infected with the virus that is responsible for the loss of grass in the North." He turned to point at the map on the screen. This map then also appeared on flat screens on each side of the wall. "The yellow area indicates how far the virus has spread in just 13 days. The grey area indicates where the fungus has started to attack the dying grass, and the inner red zone where absolutely no grasses remain at all."

As if scripted, Sir Maurice paused, and the Prime Minister interceded, "Can we predict the rate of spread if this isn't contained?"

"Yes, we can Prime Minister." As if by magic, a graphical animation appeared, complete with a flip calendar on one of the previously blank screens as well as on those on each wall. Someone was sitting in a side room controlling the screens, I thought. This reminded me of a swish theatre production.

As the animation ran, a gasp went up as the virus swept down the A1 corridor and across London. The whole island, right down to Lands' End turning red on January 20th.

Tapping the table for silence, he resumed: "Obviously, this is only a prediction based on current spread rates. Many variables may influence the actual rate of infection, such as temperature or vehicular spread." Sir Maurice looked towards the Prime Minister, who nodded.

Norman Griffin took the opportunity to throw in a question during the pause. "Why wasn't the container quarantined immediately?"

Sir Maurice and the Prime Minister shared glances again, and the Prime Minister answered. "The Home Secretary has interrupted with a question before questions were thrown open," To my immediate right, Norman Griffin sank back in his chair, and I suppressed a grin. "however, there is little doubt that the press will be asking the very same question; therefore, I will ask Peter Stubbs to answer this."

The Secretary for Transport, caught a little off-guard, cleared his throat before speaking. "Firstly, a leaking container isn't that unusual, and the cargo did appear to match that of the manifest. As a precaution, it was checked for noxious gases and radiation and was cleared. It is probable that by then, the virus had already entered the environment, and that it was too late to try to isolate it. Although grass in Newcastle did start to yellow, and subsequently attract the white fungus, no one reported until it reached Ingleton. That's the Ingleton in Durham, to prevent any further confusion."

There were a few grins shared around the table - I had missed the joke. 'I thought this lot didn't do jokes?' I thought to myself. Then Maria whispered in my ear "Helen Goodman mixed them up, ages ago!" I was still no wiser; I recognised the name but who was Helen Goodman?

"George Craven sent a sample from Ingleton Manor to the RHS on the 25th September. But it was initially not identified as having a virus, just a 'slime mould' - a fungus that is common in the UK. It wasn't until Tuesday 29th, the RHS having now received many other reports from the region, that they divided the sample and couriered it for detailed analysis to Peta, DEFRA and Imperial College. The latter being where Andrea Parker here identified a new virus 'Potyviridae Craven-Parker' or 'PCP' as it has become known. It is this virus that makes the grass susceptible to the fungus. Spores of which were also found in the container's load."

Sir Maurice continued, "Thank you, Peter. We will continue with the details of the virus and its potential biological threat, and ask Andrea Parker to confirm some of these points, in language that we will all understand please Andrea." I saw Andrea was nodding and spreading notes out in front of her. "Firstly, can you confirm what other plants in the grass family have been shown to be susceptible to infection?"

Andrea started to speak quietly but clearly. "We – Imperial College - have conducted a range of tests, as have the RHS, DEFRA and Peta Plant Care. I was given authority to compile, analyse, and present only the confirmed findings. To answer your question; almost every plant in the graminoid (grass) family will become infected if they come into contact with the virus, or the fungus that is hooked with the virus. Grasses tested included almost all natural varieties and modern cultivars of cereal crops: maize, corn, wheat, barley, rye, millet and sugarcane. So far every variant we germinated became infected, and died, well before maturing enough to flower."

An audible intake of breath could be heard from those around the table, as the gravity of the situation dawned on them.

After a pause, Andrea continued: "Looking at the DNA of the virus, we can assume that all wild grasses, some 70,000 varieties worldwide, will also be vulnerable. Exceptions are rushes, reeds and bamboo, all of which are not true grasses."

Sir Maurice asked further questions: "Could you explain how the virus works? – How does it kill the grass, and what is the 'fungus hook' you referred to?"

"The virus defeats the process of photosynthesis by protein modification. This changes the colour of the chloroplasts to yellow and prevents absorption of sunlight, causing the grass blade and sheath quickly die. The virus would only be spread by direct contact with other infected grass if it were not for the unusual 'hook', that the virus also possesses; this latches onto the fungus (myxomycetes) or 'slime-mould'. This fungus is native to the UK and quite common. It is spread by foraging animals, and perhaps birds too. Now the virus is attached, it is spread along with the fungus." Andrea looked up from her notes.

Sir Maurice asked another question: "Is there an exception in the true grass family – one that will not contract the virus?"

"Yes, we have, thus far, only identified one group of grasses that are not affected by the virus - those of the rice family."

There was a murmur from around the table and several ministers turned to look towards the Foreign Secretary, and again he nodded, solemnly, indicating that he already knew this.

"I'm going to ask you one more question, please, Andrea. In your qualified opinion, can you state that this virus, having likely arrived from China - does not threaten rice or bamboo - and has this 'unusual hook' to enable it to spread, has occurred naturally, or if it has been artificially developed, perhaps as a biological weapon?"

Everyone in the room turned to look at Andrea, who clearly was uneasy with the term 'weapon'. She finally took in a deep breath and spoke. "As with almost everything, it *is* mathematically possible for this to have evolved naturally. But it is the opinion of my respected colleagues who specialise in DNA analysis that, while the primary virus may have evolved naturally, there are strong indications that it has been genetically modified: Firstly, the fungus hook sequence appears to have been grafted on, and we know of no other example of DNA virus having a symbiotic relationship with a fungus. Secondly, we can't explain why the DNA includes the string that makes it impossible to infect rice. I am afraid I have to support their conclusions based on the results from studies to date. However, I must state, for the record, that we have had less than a week to analyse this and research must continue."

The Prime Minister spoke, "Thank you, Andrea, you were very concise. Undoubtedly there *will* be further questions for you later. I also understand from the RHS that it was a communication from George Craven," he nodded towards me, "that stimulated the research that confirmed the virus could jump from lawn grasses to cereal crops. For this advance warning, we should also all very grateful. Now back to you Sir Maurice."

"Thank you, Prime Minister. The Chancellor of the Exchequer Graham Stubbs has some serious concerns."

I felt really proud that the Prime Minister had thanked me personally in front of this bunch of doubters - maybe they'd show a little more respect now? I looked over at Andrea, who also looked a lot more relaxed, and was probably pleased with her performance.

Meanwhile, the Chancellor of the Exchequer groaned on about the potential damage to their projections on growth, reduction to GDP, value of pensions, loss of share values and if trading in shares should be suspended. He made assumptions that food shortages would create inflation, and if so, they could be forced to react by increasing benefits. He'd then face claims of a U-turn from the opposition, and any increase in benefits would further damage their projections. There were graphs and numbers – lots of numbers - before he ended his very lengthy statement by stating that there was a significant likelihood that this PCP crisis would push the UK into another recession, and that they urgently needed to seek support from Europe and America to try to prevent this.

Maria leant over and whispered, 'Well he has certainly covered his arse!"

"Oh, please don't wake me up!" I whispered back.

Sir Maurice then asked Peter Stubbs, the Transport Secretary, to make a statement. I pricked up my ears – 'I might get my chance to contribute', I thought.

Peter Stubbs was probably the eldest around the table. He spoke with old school authority but also very slowly. "There will be extra demands put on the transport network to ensure essential services have sufficient food, and to get additional food imports distributed. This will increase dramatically from the middle of next year, when we would usually be harvesting our own crops. Assuming, of course, that the virus is still in the environment and we haven't developed resistant crops by then."

Andrea's raised her hand "May I make a comment on that?" Receiving a nod from Sir Maurice, she continued. "I'm sorry, but developing then producing quantities of any resistant crops is not a 12 Month process. Even if given enormous resources to research and modify a new hybrid, it would be the fourth year, at the very earliest, that we would be able to harvest it. It could take a decade."

Sir Maurice spoke again: "Alistair also queried if the virus will still be in the environment by spring? What will sustain it if the grass has all been destroyed? Does this virus leave spores or will it burn itself out?"

Andrea replied after a pause to think "We can't really be sure. Viri don't leave spores like fungi. So, the virus should die after just a few days without a host, especially if the fungus is attached because that lives on the same proteins. The problem is; where there *was* grass, there *will* still be viable grass seed. As these seeds germinate, the virus will start again. It is possible it will travel up and down the country in decreasing waves until all the viable seed has germinated. This process could, theoretically, sustain the virus for two or three years."

"Could I ask a question?" Something had just occurred to me and I found myself talking without really meaning to.

Maurice gave me a puzzled look. "Well, advisors usually provide the answers to *our* questions, but, please do proceed."

"I'm sorry, but I wasn't aware the virus could self-perpetuate up and down the country like that. Could this be stopped or shortened if we deliberately spread the virus so that the whole country is infected at the same time?"

My question provoked lots of muttering, and much shaking of heads, before Lord Francis, the Party Chairman, spoke for the first time. "That sounds to me like an interesting theory. – May I ask Andrea Parker comment on its worthiness?"

Maria passed a scribbled note to me. It read; 'Arthur said you think 'out of the box!'

Andrea, too, looked over at me with raised eyebrows before answering, "That is a *very* risky strategy and one that would be difficult to simulate until we have a better understanding of the spread rates and other variables. We'd need to know the temperature that all of the various grasses require to germinate, and their distribution, as well as predict animal migration. However, I think it could reduce the chances the virus would self-perpetuate in the environment for so long, and is, therefore, something we actually should consider. Assuming it doesn't spread to and from Ireland, and the rest of Europe; in which case, we'd have to ask them to spread PCP too - a virus they may think they aren't going to get!"

The Prime Minister spoke again: "Research this by all means but I don't like the idea at all. I was hoping we could somehow create a firewall with weed killer or something to halt the spread, not deliberately infect the whole of the South! Relating to the question of it spreading to and from the continent, the French president called me this morning. If the virus remains unchecked and reaches Peterborough, he is going to turn back all cross-channel ferries and close the tunnel. It is likely this reaction will be duplicated throughout mainland Europe. Passengers, arriving from the UK, already have to paddle through disinfectant in Australia, New Zealand and Canada."

Sir Maurice continued, "The Foreign Secretary's statement will be next, but first, was there anything else that concerned you, Peter. I was thinking of the impact of those flies, and animal reports from the North?"

Peter began to speak slowly again, "I have reviewed video footage of the black flies that have caused accidents around Newcastle. There have been temporary road closures to the A1 north of Newcastle, the A68 through Northumberland National Park, the A69 at Hayden Bridge, the A68 Darlington, the A66 to Penrith and the A67 Barnard Castle, as well as countless minor roads in the region. The flies appear only during daylight and not during rainfall. They tend to congregate in low-lying areas, and can reduce visibility to less than one meter. We need to advise people not to drive into these 'swarms' because they are blinded as soon as entering them, and have to stop. There was a fatality reported at Hayden Bridge this morning where an HGV hit a car that had stopped under a cloud of flies. Lorry cabs are generally above the level of the flies, and can continue provided there is no obstruction below about 1.4meters. I would like to ask Andrea Parker if there is anything we can do to kill these flies?"

I could hear Andrea sigh a little before answering, "My expertise is that of a plant epidemiologist – that's plant diseases. However, I have discussed this with eminent entomologist Dr Nigel Hill. He states that there are naturally occurring nematodes that can be sprayed in water to kill these flies. These microscopic nematodes will kill the larvae stage of the flies (which he identifies as Sciarid flies or Fungus Gnats), But he questions the reasoning behind the killing of the flies when they are eating the very fungus that carries the virus, which, in turn, kills the grass. He believes that by killing the flies we may prolong the time the virus remains active in an infected area, and that it might be better to either not interfere or treat the soil after the infection has passed."

The transport secretary coughed and turned over his notes: "I see. Other temporary problems are animals, in particular rabbits, migrating from infected areas. These are also responsible for causing accidents on roads in the region. People need to be reminded not to swerve or suddenly brake to avoid them, and also to slow down in areas where deer are present. With your permission, Prime Minister, I would like to oversee the production of TV and radio Public Information films to warn the public about these dangers as soon as possible? Enforced speed restrictions may also help reduce accidents?"

He looked up for reaction from the Prime Minister, but the Prime Minister appeared to be reading from his own notes, so he continued. "I don't anticipate the rail network will be seriously affected, and the flies and migrating animals appear to stay in one area for only one or two days. I have been reliably informed that the flies pose no risk to commercial aircraft, and that major airports are spraying surrounding grass with weed killer and fungicide now. That is all. In summary, the transport network will be affected only temporarily, and I believe it will be able to cope with the additional demands upon it next year."

That was my cue to jump in, but Sir Maurice got in first: "Thank you, Peter. The Prime Minister and Maria Trellis have already discussed the need for public information media, and I ask you to liaise with Maria this afternoon to get something organised as soon as possible."

"May I make a couple of points, please?" I spoke up urgently.

Sir Maurice looked at me over his glasses, "Does this relate to transport, Mr Craven? We do need to hear from the Defence Secretary."

"Yes, most definitely." I could see Maria nodding firmly to my left too.

"Then please proceed, but keep it brief." Sir Maurice agreed.

I cleared my throat: "Grass is 85% water. Each square meter of grass retains approximately 9 litres of rainwater. Effectively it is a vast reservoir containing more water, across the British Isles, than all the lakes of the Lake District put together." I paused for effect - I'd certainly got their full attention. "So our drainage and waterways will have to deal with considerably more water until other plants establish themselves in place of the grasses. Additionally, grass serves to bind the soil together. Without it, road and rail embankments steeper than 10 degrees will turn to mudslides with the first heavy rain. Those of just 3 degrees or more will contaminate the water flowing off it with mud or silt that could block drains."

After a few seconds of silence, Peter Stubbs, the Transport Secretary, responded, "So Mr Craven, I find myself a little embarrassed having not fully explored these *possible* implications. What are you suggesting as solutions?"

'Shit!' I thought to myself. I hadn't thought that far ahead. Time to try to think on my feet, "Um, well we could try seeding the most critical embankments with other soil bonding, rapidly self- seeding plants. Maybe marigolds or clovers?"

"Marigolds! – Really?" Responded the Prime Minister, looking up from his notes. "I think you and Peter need to get your heads together after the meeting. Peter, I need fully costed solutions in my inbox by tomorrow afternoon. Now we *must* hear from the Foreign Secretary," he nodded towards Alistair Green.

My big moment had soured. Though marigolds *might* have worked? I should have suggested Mint or Cow Parsley? I sat back in my seat. I wasn't any good at this. I was the wrong person in the wrong place. I would resist the temptation to speak again, and couldn't wait to get back to Ingleton Manor, even if it no longer had any grass. I was beginning to form the opinion that this group of people were probably powerless to significantly avert this nationwide crisis anyway.

Sir Maurice called on the Foreign Secretary, Alistair Green, to speak.

He looked around the room before he spoke, and looked uncomfortable. "Our European partners have offered scientific and technical assistance to deal with this problem. Additional supplies of cereal grain may be available, providing the virus does not spread to mainland Europe. I fully understand their concerns, and we should do everything possible to prevent this from spreading to *our* islands as well as to the rest of Europe. The United States has significant reserves of cereal, and has offered unconditional support." Alistair Green paused to read his notes, "From today, all passengers and vehicles will have to be disinfected upon arrival in the US as well as Canada, Argentina and Mexico. The President has asked if we would also oversee a disinfecting process for people, containers, vehicles, etc. as they leave the UK. Clearly a massive undertaking, and I will liaise with Maria because of her expertise with Foot and Mouth containment."

He looked around the room before continuing, "Late last night, I put it to the Chinese Ambassador that the contents of a container from Shanghai appeared to be responsible for this virus. He had been expecting the question, which he declined to answer. Instead, he retaliated by claiming that the UK had conspired with the US to mass-sell Chinese stocks which caused the SSE crash in June. He claimed we did this in retaliation to US computer hacking attacks that he insisted, China was not responsible for."

Without introduction, the Secretary for Defence Christopher Darling threw in a comment, "Well that was a short 'Golden Age' wasn't it? Are we still going to let these people build nuclear power stations for us?"

The Prime Minister scowled at the Defence Secretary and was about to reply, when the door opened, and everyone turned to look, not expecting this interruption. It was the blue coffee lady. She headed straight to the Prime Minister and whispered something to him. He asked a short question of her, to which she nodded.

He looked back at the bank of screens behind him. People were fussing around the big desk in the US situation room, then the feed was cut, to be replaced with an image of the Seal of the United States. The Prime Minister stood up. Grimly he stated, "You must excuse me; I have a red call from the President." He walked out of the door being held open for him by the security guard.

An uneasy silence fell on the room; stony faces looked to one another but were greeted only by worried shrugs and slow head shaking. After a full two minutes, where nobody spoke, Sir Maurice stood up to stand behind the Prime Minister's chair. Quietly he said, "It is very likely that our civilian advisors, The Chief Constable, as well as the Secretaries for Education, Health, Environment, Work & Pensions and Transport, will be asked to leave upon the Prime Minister's return. Please be ready to do so promptly at his request". The ministers started shuffling away papers and checking pockets. I did the same, as Sir Maurice returned to his seat.

I looked at Maria as she put away her notes and papers. She whispered to me 'I do hope they haven't done anything stupid!" – I assumed by 'them' she meant the Americans.

148

The Prime Minister finally returned. Grim-faced, he stood behind his chair. "The US President has just informed me that two damaged containers with virus-infected compost have been brought ashore in the US. One at Port Newark on the East Coast, and the other at Seattle on the West Coast, neither of which were identified by port authorities as posing a risk. The grass around both ports has become infected." After a short pause, he continued: "Andrea, please would you send everything you have discovered on the virus direct to the President's office. Now, I am afraid I must end this committee meeting now and convene an emergency defence meeting." He looked to Sir Maurice, who nodded. "Those previously asked to leave please do so now." In complete silence, we filed out, Sir Maurice leading the way.

"I thought Sir Maurice would be staying," I said to Maria, as we headed back to the greeting room. She just shrugged and was clearly not happy.

Once the door closed behind us, urgent talking broke out, as the ministers tried to second guess what was going to happen next. Maria was still cursing the Americans, this time to Peter Stubbs. Knowing that Peter and I had been ordered to 'put our heads together,' I felt I had the right to join the conversation, "Why so hard on the Americans – surely they are victims too?" I asked.

"Why?" Questioned Maria, "Maybe it's because we *did* help to crash the Chinese stock market? The Americans asked us to, and we did. They say 'jump' and we ask 'how high?' Now I'd like to bet the Chinese will control the supply of rice, and that the price will rocket. They'll get their money back ten-fold, and still get to build our power stations!"

Peter tapped her on the arm. "Er, Maria, we don't know that." "Oh, don't we? Bloody snakes!" she said as she strutted off.

Andrea came over and asked Peter for the email address she needed, to forward her data to the President's office. He directed her to ask 'Angela' – the blue coffee lady.

"So, Peter, I'm sorry I embarrassed you in there about the flooding and the mud, but I thought it was important."

He sighed. "Oh, not to worry. They are weighty issues indeed, and I shouldn't have overlooked them. There's no need to apologise to this old fool!" He gave me a warm smile, "You did alright in there; you know? I should apologise to *you* for throwing the question straight back at you. However, there's really no need to knock heads any further. I've got a team of engineers on hand. You head off back to that lovely Manor of Arthur's, and tell him I send my very best regards."

I thanked him and turned to leave when he called me back and whispered, "George, don't repeat anything that Maria tells you, I don't think she's got all her facts straight!" He left me with a knowing nod and a strong suspicion that he was lying.

Andrea caught up with me as I turned to go the second time. "Phew! – I'm glad that's over! Apparently, George, we both have to pick up a press pack from Sir Maurice before we leave; they are being printed now. They are a bit disorganised because of this new emergency do-dah going on. They were to have arranged interviews for us, but they're all tied up in there."

I laughed, "*Emergency do-dah!* – I like that. I bet they have a different name for it… Andrea, do you think that they missed the point in there?"

Tilting her head to one side, she asked, "What do you mean?"

"Well, the public, when they get to hear about the cereals, animal feed, no more dairy products, and that we have no control over it, surely they are going to start hoarding food and fighting over it?"

A booming voice over my shoulder startled me, "Absolutely right young man!" The Yorkshire Chief Constable had joined the conversation. "They should have cut all that financial crap the Chancellor droned on and on about, to let me have a turn to speak. We simply don't have the police numbers to deal with what is going to happen. What's left of our army is deployed all over the world. Even if we call up all 25,000 reserves, we'd have barely enough to post three soldiers for each supermarket and distribution centre. I dread to think what's going to happen, especially if they get further distracted by events overseas. As for that lot in there? Probably planning another war, we shouldn't have anything to do with!"

Andrea and I looked at one another, each wanting the other to comment, neither of us wanting to.

The Chief Constable continued, "Sorry! I'm Adrian Parker, and I just lost my audience! I just had to say that to someone who might understand. I'm going to corner Sir Maurice see if we can't get a second Cobra organised to cover the important issues that never even got a mention!"

"Please don't include me!" Andrea said, her hands together as if praying.

"Nor me!" I added quickly.

We had found Sir Maurice before the Chief Constable did. He had our press releases, and apologised for the abrupt termination of the meeting. I asked him how I was supposed to get back, and he pointed to my press pack where I found a 1st Class train ticket to Darlington.

"So this is goodbye," Andrea stated, as we headed for the door to collect our phones, "Though I've got to call a Taxi to Kings Cross, do you want to share?"

I took a deep breath as the warm afternoon air hit. "That's a very good idea! Thanks. I was thinking of having a wander around some of the sights, but I'm just exhausted from all that sitting down!"

"Yes! I feel the same. Must be all that depleted adrenaline." A black cab pulled up and a man in a grey suit departed, "Oh, that's handy," said Andrea, as she waved to the driver, "here's our ride!
... It's certainly been a very draining day. Did you have an early start, George?"

Andrea climbed into the back of the cab, and I followed. "Yes, maybe earlier than necessary – 5 am! - Kings Cross Station, please."

"Wow, I didn't realise that Ingleton is that far?" replied Andria as the taxi pulled away.

"No, well it should have taken five hours but there were problems on the roads, and we diverted to York." I wasn't going to tell her about my stupid attempt to scare the driver. That embarrassing episode seemed so long ago.

We sat in silence for a few minutes. I think we both probably needed a mental break.

Then it occurred to me that I liked this lady; she was very intelligent, and had a wit I shared. But it was unlikely we'd ever see each other again. I tried to get conversation going again: "Where do *you* live Andrea, I don't know much about you?"

"George! Are you asking if I'm single?" She was smiling cheekily, "No ring, look," she waved her left hand, "but I'm not looking for anyone right now. I won't make a good partner for anyone; I completely bury myself in my research. Whenever something like this crops up, I spend whole days, sometimes weeks, in the labs. Only food coaxes me out from time to time! I have a house in Hitchin, that's near Stevenage, but I can't claim to live there very much."

"Oh, I was born in the Lister in Stevenage! And grew up in Letchworth. I know Hitchin well, it's a lovely little town. I wasn't really trying to chat you up, though you are very charming. I just thought that we'll probably never meet again, and that's a shame. Your presence today made that meeting far more bearable."

Andrea smirked, "Thank you. I think you and I are quite alike in some respects. I was just thinking the same thing. My 'friends' are all scientists and university graduates, but, well, they're not 'real' people, and for some reason, I just don't relate, on a personal level. Not with any of them. Odd, because I should be one of them. They get on together socially, but the conversation rarely changes from science, and I need a break from that when I'm out of the lab. Sorry, am I boring you?"

The taxi was pulling up at the station, and I offered payment to the driver and waved away the change.

"No, not at all. I imagine if you put me in a room full of other gardeners that I'd get mighty bored if the subject never changed. But look, Andrea, if this all goes to shit here, and anarchy breaks out; I'd like it very much if you could try to find your way to Ingleton Manor. I'm hoping to start something self-sufficient up there, and you'd be very welcome to join us."

She gave me a long studious look, "Sound's very interesting?" We left the taxi and entered the station. Then together, we stood looking at the large information board. I was hoping that maybe we'd be taking the same train, but the fast train to York and Darlington didn't stop before Peterborough.

"Oh… Different trains, I'm afraid George. So this *is* goodbye."

"Yes, this is ..." I thought of offering a hand to shake? "I'm so glad we got to meet." Instead of putting out a hand I put both out wide inviting a hug. My folder and press pack that had been under my arm, promptly fell to the floor. Andrea laughed as we both stooped to pick it back up.

Then she gave me a really strong squeezing hug, and I dropped the damn folder again! – This time, I just left it on the floor. It was then that I realised just how much taller than me she was. My eyes were level with her neck! She broke the hug and, grinning as she picked up my folder said: "Do you think you might be able to hang on to this all the way to Ingleton, George?!"

"Probability isn't high, is it?"

"No!" She laughed, "Even though there is a mathematical probability! - Goodbye, George." She turned to start walking towards platforms 9 & 10. Then turning back as she walked away she said, "If it does all 'turn to shit' I *will* try to find my way to Ingleton - you can count on it!"

Chapter 6 – Abandoned

I'd slept from somewhere just past Stevenage, not waking again until the train stopped at York. It seemed that I was the only passenger travelling in the 1st class carriage. Probably a good thing, though… I'd woken with a feeling similar to that I remember having as a young boy, on leaving the cinema; a buzzing, hero-like excitement and the urge to tell complete strangers where I had just been, and who I'd met. But, as I thought more about what had occurred at the meeting, the hero- like feeling faded away, to be replaced by a sense of deep disappointment, and then to one of missed opportunity.

The train, now severely delayed due to obstructions on the line between Northallerton and Morpeth, had stopped again, somewhere near Thirsk. The hills were all white, turning to foggy grey as the light faded. In the distance, I could see a dark shadow in the depths of a valley. A valley that had silently succumbed, like so many others, to the invasion of many billions of tiny black flies.

I wondered what life would be like for those living in the villages and hamlets in such valleys. I imagined they'd be forced to seek refuge in their homes, plunged into darkness, by a choking, day- long solar eclipse. I shuddered at the thought and realised that I'd been staring at the same view for many minutes. I looked away from the window and wished the train would quickly move on.

I could see through the carriage door, that the second-class section remained crowded: People were crushed together with many forced to stand for the long journey. A woman was holding both a baby and the hand of an impatient and tugging toddler. I could hear the baby's cries, uncomforted by its mother's attempts to soothe it. I began to feel guilty,

155

sitting there surrounded by empty seats, while so many were uncomfortable just meters away. I felt both embarrassed and somehow disconnected. I began to wish I had not taken my place in the first-class carriage, I felt that I didn't belong there. I began to wonder if I could swap tickets with her – the woman with the baby? I looked behind me and saw a cap, probably belonging to a guard, on a chair at the far end of the carriage. I got up, and after walking between rows of empty seats, found a ticket inspector sitting by the window next to his cap.

He looked up as I approached, "Is there a problem sir? – You have a first-class ticket?"

I produced my ticket, "Yes. I wondered if you would allow that lady and her baby to sit in here. What with her having no seat, the baby becoming distressed, and us not going anywhere?"

He stood up stiffly and squinted to look through the door, and I realised that he was quite an old chap who had probably been napping there. No one had checked my ticket before, "Does she have a first-class ticket?"

"Oh come on! She'd be in here if she had."

He sat back down and folded his arms, "I can't allow passengers with second-class tickets to travel in a first-class compartment," he then yawned dismissively, "I'm sorry: Rules is rules."

I looked back to the door. I could see that a couple of people were now looking through the door, probably wondering why I'd left my seat. "But we're *not* travelling, are we? Can't you sit in the other first-class carriage and just *not* see what happens in here?"

"I'm sorry, no," he replied, "I'm three weeks away from retiring, and I don't want to go out with a disciplinary, thank you very much."

I gave it one more go "That would really matter, would it?" He didn't answer.

Instead of returning to my original seat, I passed him his cap and sat next to him. He took in a deep breath and put on the cap. Then, after about a minute, he checked his watch. "Excuse me," He stood up, and I let him pass. He looked towards the second-class section for a few seconds. Then he said quietly, as if speaking his thoughts rather than talking to me, "I'm going to the other carriage now. I probably won't be back till we pass Dunbar."

He slowly opened the door separating the carriages, and headed towards the back of the train.

I whispered, "Thank you." Without looking back, he gave the smallest of nods as he departed.

I walked towards the front and the other door. I could see hope on the face of the woman with the toddler and baby. I felt I'd achieved more in those few minutes than in all those spent at Whitehall.

I pulled opened the door, those close to it looking at me expectantly as heat and the smell of stale air hit me. "Those without seats can sit in here, but please vacate them before we get to Edinburgh." There were sighs of relief, some questioning looks of disbelief, and a few smiles. People started to file past, allowing the woman with her children and buggy to go first. She mimed a most sincere 'thank you' as she passed. A few others also thanked me, or patted my back, as they went by.

The journey hadn't been a complete waste of time after all. I wondered what Sir Maurice would have thought if he knew what I'd effectively done with his first-class ticket!

There were a few people who remained standing; looking uneasy, they tried to pretend they were unaware of the opportunity to take a seat. Some gave the impression that they were actually quite happy standing for hours on end. I thought they were probably 'prudes'; too scared to break any rules regardless of their situation. The first-class carriage was barely half full, and I took my original seat as the train finally started to move again.

I needed to cadge a lift from Darlington back to Ingleton. I'd usually ask Karen, but she'd be on my case, shaking me like a dog with a rabbit, until I told her where I'd been. Arthur knew where I'd been, and he'd dropped me in it, so I gave him a call. He said he couldn't make it until 7 pm, and the train was due in at 5.15pm. However, we were moving only very slowly and at 6.30 I called again, and he agreed to come out.

It was completely dark by the time I finally got to Darlington, and I was so glad to see the familiar shape of the RAV-4 in the car park. I was not quite so pleased to find Melissa had come along for the ride, and was sitting in the front passenger seat.

"You look tired George, was it a long day?" Arthur turned to greet me as I climbed in the back.

"Thank you for picking me up Arthur. Hello, Mel. Yes, 14 hours ago I set off!"

"Hi, George we are very proud of you!" Melissa said as if not very convinced.

I wondered what Arthur had told her. "Proud of me?

Why?" "Daddy told me where you've been."

Arthur quickly interceded: "She worried it out of me when she realised you were not in the garden today, and is very impressed that you were invited to be shown around the labs at Imperial College, all because of your help with identifying the PCP virus!"

Mel turned around smiling, then as she passed Arthur's view, gave me a very questioning look. She knew me well enough to know I'd have declined such an unlikely invitation. "So was that 'Miss Parker' there then?" There was a distinct note of distaste in her voice that Arthur picked up on immediately. He gave me a concerned look in the rear-view mirror.

Between them, they were starting to make things awkward for me, but I tried to brush it aside and take a pot-shot at Melissa at the same time "Yes, she was; she's a slim, very tall blonde who's *exceptionally* intelligent. We got on really well."

Arthur's second glance in the mirror displayed a wry grin but, not surprisingly, Melissa was less impressed. "Oh, I know the type;" she said turning back, "lanky, all brains and no social skills – yawn!"

I wasn't going to respond to that; my comments had achieved their aims. I just hoped that should Andrea ever call; it wouldn't be Melissa who answered.

"What was it that delayed the train, George?" Arthur asked, "Radio said a whole herd of cows had broken on to the line near Edinburgh."

"I don't know, they only mentioned obstructions on the line." I wanted to tell Arthur all that had gone on, but it would have to wait until the morning. We continued in silence, occasionally slowing for a rabbit or deer, then I fell asleep again, not waking until the car stopped outside the gatehouse and Melissa opened my door.

Thanking them once more, I waved them off and went inside. Suddenly remembering that I'd had an unwanted visitor, I half expected to find a mess with all my drawers turned out. But, apart from the fact that the Pac-Man machine was plugged in, and my laptop had been closed, there was no other indication that anyone had been in.

With Tuesday came heavy rain lashing against my window. There was a cold wind too. Some of the autumn leaves were being blown off the trees early and were tumbling across the mud that was formerly lawn.

Peering through the rain drops on my window, I did wonder if it was worth getting dressed at all. But other jobs could still be done in these conditions; the roses needed pruning, and I had still not found time to half-cut the buddleias that bordered most of the property. I decided to text Karen and asked her if she could take me up to the house as she passed. I could have my chat with Arthur, and then, hopefully, the weather would have improved by the time we had finished.

Karen duly replied and confirmed she'd be with me in 15 minutes. That was when I decided to start a diary, to record all that was happening. I'd have to back-date it and start it from the Friday that Arthur first found the fungus. I pulled out an A4 pad that Peter and I had used to scribble designs on for the East and West Avenues. Folding those pages to the back, I laid it on the bed to remind me to start it later. I was getting cold and needed to get dressed before Karen arrived.

Without warning, my bedroom went dark. Startled, I turned to see a black umbrella shading the morning light, and below it, Melissa's face pressed against the glass trying to peer in. "Bloody Hell!" I yelled, pulling the bedclothes around me, causing the pad to fall on the floor as I violently drew the curtains across. I heard a muffled "Sorry!" from outside, then a few seconds later the doorbell buzzed. I hastily got dressed and angrily opened the door, "What the heck do you think you are doing?!"

Melissa pushed her way in, folding the soaking wet umbrella as she did so. "Sorry, I didn't want to just ring and wake you up if you were still sleeping. Sorry if you were dressing. It was so dark in there, so didn't see anything other than the curtains closing. That made me jump!"

I was sure she was manipulating me; I could hardly just turn her away to plod back through the pouring rain. But I knew that Karen would arrive in less than 15 minutes, and she'd be more than a little suspicious if she were to find Melissa with me first thing in the morning! "Are you on your way to school?"

"What, dressed like this?" She unbuttoned her coat to reveal a nasty brown and yellow striped jumper above jeans with 'designer' cuts across both knees. "School starts again tomorrow."

"Oh, that's *not* a good look! – Well, at least you're not trying to seduce me today!" I immediately regretted saying that.

"No," she said sheepishly, "that's one mistake I'm not going to repeat. That's one of the reasons I'm here - I am just not accepting this 'we can't be friends' nonsense. But I do want an honest chat with you about 'us' – well our feelings – real and honest. No nonsense like 'you went to Imperial College yesterday!' Just a proper talk, so we both understand each other, and you can maybe give me some serious advice too. I genuinely think I need counselling of some sort."

Remembering my decision to try to divert any personal advice requests to Karen, I was about to suggest just that, but she'd be at the door at any moment. So, instead, decided that I'd try to be as honest and upfront with her as possible. "I'm sure you don't need counselling, Mel, and maybe we should find time to talk later. Karen is on her way here now, just to pick me up and drop me off at the house. You'll understand she will take it the wrong way if she finds you here too, first thing in the morning! What was the other reason you came down here?"

Melissa gave me a cheeky grin, knowing she could have some fun with this, but it quickly faded. "OK, I'll wait upstairs. You can show me how to play that big game-box thing, and you get back as quick as you can so we can talk. I mean you can't do much gardening in this, can you?" She pointed through my bedroom to the window where the noise of the rain hadn't subsided. "The other thing was that Daddy wanted you to see these... Mr Government Advisor!" She unfolded a black plastic bag from inside her coat and produced Arthur's papers.

"Ah! Well, I see that didn't stay a secret for very long. You understand why I couldn't say anything until they released, - well released whatever they have."

"Hmmm, I suppose so. I see that 'Miss Parker' *is* a lanky blonde and very plain, no picture of you, though."

"Good! Now off upstairs for some quick Pac-Man training." I led the way, and becoming ever more conscious of the time, I took two steps at a time and plugged the machine in as soon as I got to the top. "It takes a while to get going," I called back as she appeared at the head of the stairs. "I imported this from the USA myself, and had the coin mechanism switched out for one that takes the old 10p's - or two shilling coins - and the transformer, so it runs on 240 volts," Melissa didn't appear to show much interest, but I continued, "that would devalue it, but

162

I've kept the parts and can switch them back should I ever want to sell it."

"I didn't realise you were part nerd!" She said while pretending to yawn.

"You don't understand Mel: This was *the* machine that stimulated a whole new market and the range of classic games that followed!"

"Really? – What am I going to do in ten minutes when this ancient artefact starts to bore me?"

Then we heard the twin beeps from Karen's car. I quickly rattled off the instructions "Clear all the dots to get to the next level, collect fruit when it appears, avoid anything that moves, except the ghosts – get them. Joystick up-down, left and right, Big jar of coins behind the bar. Got to go - see you later!"

"That *was* quick training," she half protested, "don't leave me with this old piece of junk for too long!"

I grabbed the papers and rushed back down the stairs just as the machine started its familiar 'music' – I wished I could stay to guide her and give her some gaming tips, but she'd work it out.

I grabbed my waterproof coat and my gardening 'wet kit.' This was a nylon bag containing waterproof trousers, extra pairs of gloves and socks, a hat and a flask. If Arthur, Karen or Mel were in, and I continued to garden in wet or very cold conditions, I'd only have to leave the flask on the table by the conservatory, and I could rely on someone filling it with nice warming tea!

Karen had Paul with her in the back of the car, and he had a notepad. Karen looked irritated, "He's recording the number of dead animals on the road," explained Karen in a dull and tired tone.

"Oh lovely!" I replied sarcastically. "Morning, Paul."

"I have to group those I can't identify just by size," Paul explained. He passed me his pad. It was exceptionally neat for something he'd written in the back of a car. It was a tally sheet with rows of animals down the side, and condition, and number across the top. Headings included: Alive, Dead, Injured, a semi- circle represented squashed flat, and a complete circle – 'still whole'.

I passed the gruesome document back. "Hmmm… That's very interesting, Paul, but don't show it to Mel – she's squeamish." Then I realised, with it being a wet day, Paul would try to find Mel, and he wouldn't be able to.

"His mother's a bit squeamish too!" announced Karen loudly, "Doesn't stop him reading it out to me. Bad enough I have to see so many poor creatures on the road."

"There was a fox squashed completely flat, but I knew it was a fox from its tail!" Paul announced excitedly, "Mum hit rabbit number 72, but I could see if it was properly flat and she wouldn't go back to see!"

"You see what I mean?" Karen sighed under her breath.

We pulled up in front of the house, and I realised that the rain had turned to drizzle and that the sky was brightening up a little.

"He's back at school tomorrow, so I'll get a bit of a break from his 'inventory of death'. But Bishop Barrington's head teacher wants to speak to me tomorrow, so he'll not be getting the bus, and I'll have to take him to Bishops Auckland."

"Oh… that's a whole lot more road and a whole lot more roadkill to count!" I stated, giving Karen a sympathetic look.

Karen shook her head in frustration. "You know, he actually remembers the ones he'd seen before, and can tell you what was previously on the road that's not even there anymore?" Then Karen added loudly, "Why?!"

Paul spoke up from the back "Because otherwise I could count .the same one twice, and this has to be exactly correct." tapping his notepad insistently.

Karen and I looked at each other as we walked through the arches to the side door. Once Paul was out of sight, running off and calling for Melissa, Karen took my arm and stopped me by the kitchen door. "George?" She whispered, looking me straight in the eye, ever so seriously. "Would you come with us to the school, to see the head teacher?"

I didn't know how to answer. I just stood there with a vague, questioning look. I didn't really want to, because I had other things to catch up with, nor did I think I had the right.

Recognising my confusion, Karen continued: "It's just that, well, I don't want to do everything on my own, and you know Paul really well and can help me to argue my case."

I still didn't answer, I did want to help, I understood why she was asking, but would this be the start of some responsibility towards Paul and Karen? And, did I mind if it was?

"Please," Karen squeezed my arm a little tighter, her eyes watering again. "This is all so new to me, I don't know that I can just cope on my own, especially not if he has to change schools. Paul doesn't like big changes. Please?"

"Yes, of course I will. I'd be proud to." I'd made another one of my snap decisions based purely on my not wanting to see Karen upset again.

"Oh thank you so, so much!" She hugged me and then started to cry on my shoulder.

Arthur appeared at the end of the corridor and, on seeing us, he discreetly turned back.

"We're right by the kitchen, fancy a cuppa?" I didn't get a response "Hey, Karen, look at me."

She released me and stood back, slowly looking up and wiping her eyes "Oh, I'm sorry, that autism diagnosis has screwed up my cosy little world, just when I thought it was improving."

"Hang on" I darted into the kitchen and grabbed some tissues for her. "You know, Karen, I always thought you were as hard as nails. Never saw you cry until Sunday. I think, everyone should sometimes cry, unless they just don't care about anything. You do care for Paul, and it's OK to show it. Now, do you want that tea, more tissues, or should I go find a mop?"

Karen managed a smile. "I'll get the tea 'Doctor Craven', and I'll admit that in private, over the last two years, I've actually done quite a bit of crying. Not because of Paul, mostly over terrible money worries, other things, and maybe a little loneliness too.
Having a shoulder to cry on, it… well… well, it seems to be more of a release. Maybe I'm weird, but it's like the crying is achieving something when you're here. Oh, George, am I bonkers? – I am, aren't I?"

I took her hand and kissed the back of it gently. "I think I understand; you are sharing your pain, and maybe that allows you to feel there's a little less left to burden you? You may consider my shoulder yours to dampen whenever you need. Oh, and I hope you *are* a little bit bonkers, else we just won't get on!" I slowly released her hand.

Karen let out a big sigh and sniffed: "Thank you, especially for agreeing to come with us tomorrow. Don't tell Arthur this, but I was on antidepressants until last week, what with money worries ending and then his very generous offer of accommodation here, well I thought it was the right time to stop. Now this autism thing has thrown me back again. Do you think I should start taking them again?"

"I don't know Karen; I'm simply not qualified to answer that. You'd best talk to your GP. I can tell you that saffron tea is good, though, and we do have some!"

"OK George, I get the hint. You find Arthur. I'll bring it to you when I've made myself a bit more presentable." Then she patted my arm and disappeared into the kitchen.

Arthur was waiting by the library door, "Ah, George. I see you brought the papers back, what do you think of their press release and the news from the States?" He beckoned me into the library.

Following him in I replied, "Haven't had a chance to look at them yet. Karen's going to bring us some tea in a few minutes."

"Ah, good, I've not had a tea yet this morning." He indicated I should sit in one of two grand, old, upright chairs. "Well, to save you reading them, I shall summarise: Apparently, there are people from two separate towns in the US reporting a similar grass fungus. And, God alone knows for what reason, but their homeland security is treating it as a terrorist attack!" Arthur shook his head in disbelief, "The Cobra meeting press report gives both you and Miss Parker a mention as special advisors. They do warn of possible transport disruption caused by both migrating wildlife and possible mudslides and or flooding. They claim to have contingencies for such disruption and predict that by spring, the problems will all be resolved. How does that match what actually went on in the Cabinet Offices yesterday?" He grinned knowingly.

Karen arrived, said good morning to Arthur, and served our tea. I waited for her to leave before answering. I decided that the Official Secrets Act just didn't apply when divulging details to Arthur, and proceeded to tell him everything about the committee meeting and what the Chief Constable and Maria Trellis had said afterwards.

Arthur nodded and tutted from time to time, finally shaking his head when it became apparent the Americans had probably been the catalyst for this crisis. "This is bad news indeed for the Prime Minister. Such a shame that just as we were building bridges with the Chinese, America's distrust of them, and our unfailing willingness to do whatever America wants, is probably going to lead to his resignation. When this gets out – and it *will* – a lot of brown waste will hit the fan. Keeping the fact that the virus will kill cereal crops a secret may keep the public calm for longer, but it won't be long before that breaks too, then they will look even bigger fools."

I started to wonder if even Arthur was missing the point. "Hmmm, I'm not sure the political fallout is the big issue? You know what, Arthur? – I left that committee with a feeling that we, as a country, just don't have the resources available to be able to deal with this: To get food distributed to essential service providers, get sufficient replacement crops to farmers, or maintain order should people hoard or start fighting for what little food remains. They were more concerned with the effects on the economy when I'm not sure there will be an economy left to worry about! What to do about China, and covering their own arses, seemed to have priority over how they are going to feed the population!" I felt myself getting angry, and wished I'd shouted out something about the imminent food crisis before the 'emergency defence' meeting started.

Arthur leant forward and whispered, "So, what do you suggest we do? Considering we do have a few days, prior knowledge, and so an advantage over the rest of the population? Should we start hoarding food here, or would we just become part of the problem? It appears to me that you have formulated some kind of response. George, my dear boy, are you a man-with-a-plan?"

"Well, sort of. I was going to ask if, on Friday, at tea and cakes at eleven, we could all get together and discuss this. I would need you to spend quite a bit of money, while it still has any value, to get us going." I wasn't sure if my ideas had matured enough to be workable yet. "I did get some time to think about the situation and possible solutions to some of the problems on my travels yesterday."

Arthur sat back in his chair and crossed his arms. "Ah, I see. What do you mean by 'while money still has any value?!'"

"Well think about it; everyone will want food, and maybe water too if it gets cut off, but before long the shops won't have any left. The shopkeeper himself won't need money - just food. So, the food itself may well become the only thing of value!"

Arthur didn't look either convinced, nor impressed.

"I can't be sure about this because money has become so ingrained in our culture, but," I continued, "massive food inflation will inevitably follow as stocks run low, and this will also devalue money while it's still in use."

Arthur put his head in his hands, then looked back up and shook his head slowly. "So, if this actually happens, the money I saved up for two years, that Jayne didn't actually want – *nobody* will want?! – Well that will be 'a great leveller' that the leader of the opposition would probably approve of!"

I laughed. "Maybe. But it does have value now, and we'll need to buy storage sheds and a whole lot of other things if I can convince you to agree to this?"

"George, I have a horrible feeling that you are right about what may happen, but you are very wrong to delay a meeting until Friday's tea and cakes. Waiting until then will reduce our advantage, and maybe the ability to obtain some of the things we'll need. Also, Melissa will be at school from tomorrow, and I'd like her to be involved in any discussions. I think you should write down all you think you'll need now, and we'll meet up *this* afternoon, say at three?"

I nodded. Although I wasn't ready to promote my plan, Arthur was right; things could all change very quickly.

Arthur continued, "Where is Melissa by the way? Did she come back up with you and Karen? Just that Paul was looking for her."

"Oh, Melissa wanted to have a go on my Pac-Man machine, and stayed down at the gatehouse."

"Ah, I see. Melissa wanted to play Pac-Man? Hmmm, can I assume Karen doesn't know she was there this morning?"

I looked down at myself "When did I become so completely transparent Arthur? – Yes. Please don't tell her!"

Arthur laughed and tapped the side of his nose. "Not too much gets past me, you know! However, I didn't realise, until last night, that Melissa has added you to her 'hit list'. I thought you dealt with it rather well. Though she could do a lot worse you know, George!" and he winked.

I was surprised by his last comment and chose to take it as

a joke. "Yeah me 29, her 15 - that's just perfect!"

"She's 16 in five days, you know?" he winked again, "But I didn't mean just yet, no, far from it, and I'm afraid she'll come home with some spotty, tattooed oik any day now. I thought she was chasing that tennis chap, though?"

"Yeah… He's not really her 'type', but they are friends."

"Well, George, is there anyone else you'd like at the meeting? Simon Duguid perhaps?"

"I'd like to not involve officials from the village yet, not until we have a more formulated plan. But, do you remember the guy from Ingleton Bury who helped fix the gate for us last year and released the garage door when it jammed?"

"Your friend Richard? – He was here only yesterday! He came asking if the job advert for a gardener was ours?"

"Oh! – I thought he was happy where he was. What did you tell him?"

"I said I'd have to talk to you, and discuss if we still need an additional gardener now we have no lawns. He was quick to point out that something else would soon grow, and that I might not like it! That was apparently not accepted by his current masters, who have laid him off because the majority of their gardens are just lawns. I did think he was maybe a little too old for the job, but I guess he'll see me out!"

"I'd like to have him on board, please? For the meeting, as well as to help with the gardens."

Arthur nodded, "Another mouth to feed you understand?"

"I think he will contribute a lot, and though he sometimes comes across as very negative, he will quickly identify problems with any plans, and is able to offer solutions or alternatives. He's the type of bloke who plays 'devil's advocate' rather than one who just nods and accepts everything blindly."

Arthur nodded. "Well, see if he can join us this afternoon at 3 pm? He has a van I noticed – that could come in handy."

"Yes, while we can fuel it," I added. Petrol vehicles were not going to be a long-term option; that I had already decided.

"Just one more thing before you go, George, I noticed that Karen seemed rather upset earlier. May I enquire if there is anything I can do to help, or should know about?"

"Oh, yes… It's just that Paul is having a few issues at school. Which reminds me, I am very aware that I've not done a great deal of gardening lately, but is it OK to take tomorrow morning off to go Bishops Auckland with Karen and Paul? She's got a meeting with the head and wants me to come along in support."

"Ah, well I'd like those two rose beds sorted, they are looking very shabby now. Could you see to them tomorrow afternoon, when you get back from the school?"

"Thanks, Arthur, yes, that's no problem."

"So, you and Karen; is something going on between you two? The reason I ask, is that you could save Melissa a bus trip in the morning too? If you don't mind her playing gooseberry, that is?"

I grimaced at his question. Here he was allowing me to take the morning off, and now I was going to have to refuse to take his daughter to a school I was travelling to! "Well, Karen and I are not having a 'relationship' as such, it's very early days and kind of complicated, but we might end up together. The problem is we need to discuss, privately, how we are going to approach the meeting with the head teacher. I'm not sure Karen is ready to explain Paul's problems to Melissa yet… Sorry!"

Arthur smiled knowingly, "Ah, not to worry George, she can take the bus as per usual. But you seem a little confused yourself. Don't let your good nature get abused nor allow yourself to become manipulated. All women are endowed with the ability to manage men, effortlessly, and often without them ever being aware of it. Just listen out for 'wants' becoming 'needs' – 'want' is asking you and that's usually OK. When they 'need', especially when accompanied by tears, then stop and think very carefully before replying."

I paused before responding. Although I thought he was being more than a little cynical, he might have a point? I struggled to remember how Karen had worded her request. "Thanks for the advice, Arthur, I will keep that in mind."

On my way out, I looked across the dark brown mud towards the two long rose beds. They did look very sad, and somehow had become the focus of the view now the grass was gone. The rain had stopped. I thought about starting on the rose beds and weighed this against my need to write my list of requirements and prepare for that afternoon's meeting. I decided to go back to my gatehouse. Melissa! – I'd forgotten she was still there and waiting for me.

Just as I was about to hurry back, I heard footsteps behind me. I turned to see Arthur in the doorway. "George, please disregard what I said about women being manipulative. I fear I have become a bitter old man. Karen's a lovely lady, and you should make your *own* choices. I shouldn't be trying to nudge you in another direction, nor influence your decisions, OK?"

I was a little confused, so I just said "Sure, Arthur, no problem."

I then hurried back, hoping Melissa would not be too angry with me for taking so long to return.

On opening my door, I could hear my Pac-Man machine beeping furiously. Melissa was not only still playing it, but judging from the rapidity of the beeps, she had progressed to a very high level. I cocked an ear waiting for the rapidly decreasing scale played when each life is lost, but no such sound came. I discarded my coat and 'wet kit' and crept up the stairs. If she was doing as well as it sounded, she might not appreciate an interruption.

On reaching the top I saw she'd made herself a cup of tea, and found my biscuits. The tea was cold, and the biscuits lay unopened. She had moved one of my bar stools to the machine, and looked almost frozen, staring at the screen as the machine sang, appreciating the player in front of it. The only movement other than the high-paced action on the screen was that from the stubby joystick. But she wasn't gripping it tightly; Melissa was controlling it like a pro, with just thumb and forefinger, perfectly timed and controlled little movements - no panicky jerks.

Somehow a player's senses become super enhanced when playing at such high speeds; they may appear to be entirely focussed and concentrating only on the game, but they somehow also become tuned into their surroundings as if scanning for possible interruptions. Melissa had apparently achieved this state also. As level 201 was cleared, and she waited for the screen to repopulate, she calmly whispered: "Please don't talk to me George, I'm on my last life."

I said nothing, just watched quietly as she raced around the maze, clearing the pellets and timing her taking of the power

174

pellets only when 'Blinky' and 'Clyde' were both very close. I could see she was following the same route around as she did before, and I knew that this strategy would soon fail if she went for the fruit. This she did, and became trapped between the red 'Blinky' and cyan 'Inky' she let out a little scream and tried to pass through Inky undetected, which sometimes works due to a bug in the game, but not so… her last life was finally over. She'd managed a very respectable score of just over 2.3 million, just short of being able to enter her name on the 3-Player, high score table.

"Wow, Mel! – I am *well* impressed! That's an incredible score for your first morning. How did you find *the ancient relic?*"

Mel jumped down from the stool grinning like a cat, and promptly discovered that sitting crossed legged for so long wasn't such a good idea as her left leg gave way and she fell to the floor.

I jumped up and offered her hand. "Ow!" She said as I pulled her up. "I was going to ask if I could try again but maybe not…" She limped around in circles until her leg recovered "Ow – Ow!"

"Oh Mel, I know exactly how that leg feels! Welcome to the painful world of gaming geeks!" I teased.

She was still buzzing from the game-play. "I can't believe I played for so long! It has rubbish 2D graphics, appalling sound, the levels are pretty much all the same, yet it is so playable, and it *doesn't* get boring! Did you see how close I got to putting my name on your high score table?!"

I just sat at the bar and grinned at this new convert to my 1980's classic.

"OK. I admit it – you were right - I'm hooked." She pulled the stool back next to mine at the bar.

"Would you like a fresh cup before we talk?" I asked pointing at her abandoned cup on the bar. "There is going to be an early tea and cakes meeting at 3 pm this afternoon. Arthur wants you to go, and me to invite Richard from Ingleton Bury too. I do need to prepare some notes beforehand. What I'm saying is, that I can't spend too much time chatting with you today."

Mel stopped looking at the Pac-Man machine. "Oh! What is so important that we have our tea and cakes chat advanced by three days?"

"We can still talk, and that's important too. But we are going to discuss what we, at Ingleton Manor, could do to trade with and help the locals survive, if food supplies get very low, or we lose power and water."

Melissa looked interested. "Oh, can I invite Stuart Gilly along? He said something about how this could turn into a global disaster, but I just thought he was being a big drama queen. You actually believe that this grass thingy is that serious?"

"Yes, the more I think about it, the more I'm sure that something as simple as the grass dying is going to dramatically change our lives – possibly end them! – And yes, providing he can be trusted to keep quiet until decisions are made, then please do invite him along."

Melissa pulled her phone out of her pocket "I'll text him – you make the tea!"

While in the kitchen and waiting for the kettle to boil, I phoned Richard. He explained that he'd discovered that the owners of Ingleton Bury were planning to emigrate to Portugal and that the house was for sale. He gladly accepted the assistant gardener post, and also said that he felt honoured to be invited to the meeting. I carefully carried the tea upstairs and found Melissa sitting in one of my two 'cinema' chairs, and playing with the controls. "Did you call Stuart?"

Melissa, finally accepting a very upright position for the chair, replied: "He's not answering, but I left a message. I think he is taking his motorbike test this morning."

I came over to sit in the chair next to her, and swivelled it to face her. Realising that she now appeared to be above me, I raised the back of my chair also. "So Mel, where shall we start?"

Mel thought for a moment before she spoke, "Well there's a few things I'm worried about, but can we get the embarrassing one out of the way first? I've known you for five years and up until now I have always felt I could trust you completely and that you looked out for me as a friend. I kind of always had a crush on you but recognised it as just that – a girly crush."

I thought I knew where this was going and interrupted, "Mel, there's no need to apologise again for Saturday, it wasn't entirely your fault."

Mel snapped, "Please don't interrupt me!" she waited until I nodded in agreement before continuing: "As I was saying, I had a silly girl crush, that you didn't seem to notice. I thought it would pass and that you'd never think of me in that way. So I just tried to ignore it. Then, remember last year, when you took me to see that band Vasey, in Nottingham? Well, you held my hand and stood so close to me."

"Woah! Hang-on Mel: I held your hand because Arthur trusted me not to lose you in the crowd. He didn't want you to go, remember? And we were crushed in there like sardines, we were *all* standing 'so close'. Anyway, I thought you had a thing for their singer; what's-his-name—Vasey?"

"Karl... Karl Vasey," Mel replied dreamily, "he *is* gorgeous, but then I found out he was married and I hoped you'd be jealous of him!"

I laughed, "Me? Jealous of an attractive young man, who is a popular singer-songwriter, and an amazing guitar player? – Never!" I winked at her.

Mel shook her head in bemusement, "Anyway, just recently I thought you were starting to notice me more. Do you remember the day it was raining a bit, and we played that game rolling those apples down the drive into a dustpan and then played that French 'Petanque' game you taught me?"

I remembered the day quite clearly, "Of course, it was only about a month ago; we spent a few hours just having some fun."

"Well, I thought I caught you looking at me a few times, looking at my body. It made me feel attractive and sexy - I liked it. But then, when I hugged you when you let me win, and you *did* let me win, well, then you seemed to pull away, and I thought I'd maybe got it wrong? *Had* I got it wrong?"

This was an embarrassing and delicate question to answer. I decided that the only way to proceed was to answer completely honestly, "Mel, very recently, *not* as long ago as that trip to see Vasey; I noticed that you have matured into a beautiful young woman. I don't recall looking at you in 'that way' on that particular day but will admit, I have done since. I could tell you that it is a natural thing for men to do, but, even if it is; I shouldn't have, and I'm very sorry."

Melissa smiled reassuringly. I think she realised I was also a little embarrassed and was struggling to keep my answers honest.

"So, you looked, and you were attracted. Surely that *is* only natural, isn't it?"

I replied forcefully, "No! ... No, absolutely not. Don't try to excuse me. I mean, yes, I was attracted but, no, I shouldn't have been. You are just fifteen, Mel. I just shouldn't have been looking in the first place. I can't absolutely guarantee I won't be tempted to look again. *That's* why I said, 'we can't be friends.' Now you understand, don't you?"

She shook her head. "I'm sixteen on Thursday, what difference can a few days possibly make? That was the only reason you pushed me away on Saturday, wasn't it?"

Now I shook my head slowly before answering: "No, that's not the only reason. And 'a few days' probably makes the difference between a caution and a prison sentence!"

Melissa crossed her arms angrily, "So why, why did you push me to the floor and run away when we both fancy each other?"

"That's easy to answer Mel; I'm not 16 or even 19 – I am 29! OK, maybe I look young for my age, but I'm *not* your age - that's why. Not because you're unattractive, not because your father is my boss, not because I didn't want to, but because it's just wrong. You showed me I had a weakness and that realisation hit me very suddenly. That's why I pushed you away so hard. I'm sorry, but that's the way it is, and that's the way it *is* going to stay!"

Melissa retorted: "So thirteen years older is freakishly wrong, is it? Well, Daddy was 20 years older than Mummy! What does that make me?"

I had Anticipated this comparison and had rehearsed my answer in my head beforehand. I replied as calmly as I could; "Your father married early in 1990. Jayne was twenty, and your father was then aged thirty-nine. Their, almost twenty-year age difference, may have contributed to their relationship ending after only 13 years. But their relationship, while I'm sure it raised some eyebrows at the time, was acceptable because, at twenty, Jayne wouldn't have been considered a child where a teenager would have been. What does that make you? – Well, their relationship created you! It may have also made you a little confused, but you're still a great kid!"

Melissa didn't appear convinced; "So it's only the opinions of other people that you're really worried about?"

I nodded, "When the majority of other people are likely to think something is wrong, you have to consider they're probably correct. So yes, I am very concerned, especially when I am of the same opinion myself."

Melissa's shoulders dropped a little, indicating that she was starting to accept what I was saying, but she persisted "So if I were 20 and you... you'd be 33 right? Would *that* be OK then?"

"Ask me again in four years!" I winked as I said it, so she'd not take it too seriously.

Mel sighed, "OK. But I'm not waiting four years for anyone. We *are* going to remain friends, though. I can tell from the way you looked after me, when Sandy hit me, that you are a caring friend. And, a caring friend doesn't just abandon you."

I agreed with her sentiments and thought we'd said all we could on the subject. "OK. But let's agree to increase each other's personal space so neither of us... well, you know what I mean!"

She laughed "What, no snogging each other's faces off then?"

"Er… No! Nor forfeits! Now was there really anything else?" I asked, hoping I could get on with planning for that afternoon's meeting.

Melissa nodded slowly, "Yes, I'm a bit scared of a few things. Like who I am, and why I sometimes just do and say things without really thinking first? Then there's Daddy and the Manor. What if Daddy dies? The men in his family have all died young. I can't run everything; I don't even know if I'd want to?" Then, sometimes, I feel like a child, and I'll want to go play with Paul, and other times like an adult and feel that he's just a stupid kid. I think I need counselling or something to help me with all of this."

I wasn't expecting quite so many issues, but none concerned me too much. "Oh, Mel, that's quite a list. I should have taken notes! But most of what you describe is perfectly normal; it's called 'growing up!' I make snap decisions, say things without thinking, I still enjoy playing like a child sometimes, yet at other times, I will dismiss the same activity as childish."

Melissa leant forward, "So even you feel childish sometimes?"

"God, Yes! Adults will rarely refer to themselves as 'childish', but you find me a parent who doesn't get enjoyment out of playing silly games with their children or grandchildren. The law tries to set fixed boundaries; at 16 you suddenly become an adult as far as sex is concerned and at 18 you are old enough to drink, vote and to marry without parental consent. But there is no magical switch at these ages, nor at any other. The transition is slow, the pace varies from person to person, and I don't think the transition is ever fully completed. Your Father is sixty-five and loves watching 'Finding Nemo' – now that's a kid's film!"

Melissa occasionally nodded as I spoke, so I continued, "You say that you don't know who you are? But does anyone? We never stop developing, changing, loving, losing, learning from our mistakes, seeing, hearing or reading things. All able, in small ways, to influence or change who we are, and how we feel. You are an evolving individual, and sometimes you will encounter conflicts that will change your opinions. You're not alone having these feelings of doubt and insecurity. Few people, especially young ones, will have a defined and fixed purpose or outlook. People are fluid; you wouldn't want, or expect, to be the same person in twenty years, as you are now, would you?"

I realised that Melissa's eyes had been slowly dropping, and her slow nodding had ceased.

She was looking a little more confused than when I started. After a while she responded: "Bloody Hell, George, that was deep! 'People are fluid'?" She sighed, "But I guess you are kind of right about us all changing, and you were really just trying to say 'Don't worry about it'?"

I smiled as reassuringly as I could "Yes, but that would have sounded a bit too dismissive, though I did waste a few too many words! However, there is someone who you should go and seek help from..."

Melissa leant forward "Counselling?"

I shook my head, "Not really. But you do need to start talking to your father, rather than arguing with him. He needs to know how you feel about the Manor's future, and he should understand what your concerns are. He is the only one who can help you with your inheritance. I don't know how he deals with everything, especially not the estate's farmers. Try not to think of him as 'out of touch' but more a wise teacher who will want to share all his experiences and knowledge with you."

Melissa looked sad and just stared at the floor.

182

"Hey, Mel, what's the matter?" I leant forward and squeezed her hand then, remembering my own 'rules of personal space', I released her hand and sat back again quickly.

In a very quiet voice, Melissa answered, "I miss Mummy… She was like a bridge between Daddy and me. She sort of translated for us. Daddy said she was like the pivot in a set of scales; she was in the middle understanding both of us and explaining our differences in a way we each understood. Now she has gone, Daddy and I seem further apart. I can't help blaming him for Mummy leaving too. I even imagined that he had killed her!
Though I do know he loved her. But now she's contacted him and is not bothered about me, I am starting to dislike her… and I'm feeling abandoned."

Lady Jayne hadn't given any indication to me that she was unhappy or about to leave, so I had no answers for her, and couldn't just assure her that she'd not been abandoned.

"I understand how you feel, and I can't possibly excuse what your mother has done. But Arthur is the constant in your life, and I'm quite sure he's not suddenly going to die! He is nearly fifty years older than you, so it's almost like you are two generations apart. But now you need to find a way to bridge that gap. You are probably more able than he is, just be patient and accept his views may be dated, but that doesn't necessarily mean they are wrong."

Melissa stood up, walked to the bar, and collected the teas that I'd left there and forgotten. She seemed deep in thought, and I didn't interrupt her. I just followed her slow and deliberate movements. She returned with the teas and handed me one.

"Thank you. Still warm!" I said testing the side of the cup with my hand.

She remained standing and drank down her tea in a few large gulps. Then she put the cup down and headed off at some pace towards the stairs. She called back "Thank you, George, you have been a great help."

I called after her as she started to descend the stairs "Where are you going, Mel?"

"I need to talk to my Daddy - something I've not done for two years." She called back just before my front door slammed shut.

Chapter 7 – A Meeting of Minds

I was still far from ready; pages of notes and a kind of a shopping list were strewn across my kitchen table, along with two cold cups of coffee. I'd just broken up the shopping list and divided it between each different project. I was sure that the original, extremely long list, would scare Arthur off the whole idea.

Armed with my laptop and my many pages of notes, I headed up the drive towards the house. The muddy brown patches either side of the drive reminding me that the problems I thought we faced were real.

The gate clanged shut behind me, and I waited to see who had come in. It was Stuart Gilly. "Good afternoon Lord Gardener" He called out, grinning, as he came closer.

"Good afternoon, Stuart, you look happy!"

"Yes!" He said triumphantly as he caught up with me. We shook hands rather awkwardly, before continuing towards the house.

Still beaming he said, "I just passed my motorbike test!"

"Wow! Congratulations. Do you have your own bike yet?" To me he seemed too tall to be a biker; he was way taller than I was, and I doubted he'd like to be seen in leathers either. Stuart's stride was long and fast, I soon found myself almost jogging to keep up with him.

Stuart looked back realising he was going too quickly. "Sorry! I always walk fast - part of my training, you see. I have yet to convince my Mum that bikes are safe, but she agreed that if I survived a full year on my moped without accident, I could upgrade to a 200cc motorbike."

Remembering my early years on two wheels I was surprised he had 'survived' a whole year without falling off. "You never fell off during the whole of your first year?"

Stuart gave me a shove in the shoulder that caught me off balance, and I stumbled briefly. "Don't be so silly, you! – I fell off three times, but she'll never know!"

"Hmmm, I see, and your trainer, he can't be too impressed either?" I took a step away from him to make it clear I didn't want another shove.

He laughed, "He said that if I break anything, he won't continue to train me, but he will still expect to be paid!" Stuart then became a little more serious; "I *am* going to be more careful, and I'm not going to ride on wet or icy days."

We'd reached the house, and Stuart stopped to admire the topiary box hedges. "Wow those are bigger than I thought! Are any your design?"

I sighed, "No, I'd love to reshape some, that big square one is crying out to be a multi-faceted diamond, but I have strict instructions to keep them exactly as they are. They were designed and shaped in the 1920's by some famous designer and Arthur is very fond of them. As you can see, they are overdue for a trim."

"It's an art form. Must be like being a hairdresser. I'd love to have a go? If this grass thing does turn into some kind of an apocalypse, do you think you'll still be trimming those or will I get a go?!" Stuart joked as ran to one of the topiaries and mimicked the actions of a giant pair of shears up and down the side of it.

I smiled back, "You know, I think Arthur will want them kept in shape regardless. They would be a symbol of normality, and indicate that we are maintaining some kind of stability. Isn't 'apocalypse' a bit strong for what's likely to happen, though? I'm not really sure what the actual definition of 'apocalypse' *is*, do you?"

The main door opened as we approached, and Karen appeared, smiling, to greet us.

"Yeah, maybe that is a bit strong; it means the very final end of the world and all life, it's from the bible I think?" Stuart replied.

"Well, there's a cheery thought! Hello, George, hello Stuart, we've not met, but I've watched you play. I'm Karen and this young man..." Karen looked around behind her, "Well, somewhere around here... You may find my son Paul."

Karen asked Stuart if he preferred tea or coffee, and received the firm answer, that he would only ever drink tap water or unsweetened fruit juice, 'not from concentrate'. Karen nodded in false approval and directed us towards the conservatory, "Richard is here already, but Arthur and Melissa are out walking together! I thought they were coming back about an hour ago, but they set off around the lake for a second time this afternoon!"

Richard stood up as we entered and Karen did the introductions and pointed out Mel and Arthur to Stuart. They were walking back past the formal pond, where 'Melissa's fountain' was splashing away in the centre. We all walked to the rear window to watch them return.

Richard nodded in approval as he scanned the garden "This is a lovely garden, George, even without grass. I didn't get to see out the back when I came to see Arthur yesterday. It must have been tough; you managing all this on your own."

I could only agree: "Yes, it has been very challenging since Peter left. Oh, that reminds me; Peter left us each a beer and a note. I found them in the garage loft on Sunday. If we have time, I'll read it out after the meeting."

Karen had returned with a glass of water for Stuart and, on hearing me mention the note said, "Ah yes, you mentioned that before we went to Appleby and you never got to show it to me. Did I get a beer too?"

Richard gave me a questioning look and, out of sight of Karen, wagged a finger between both of us, asking if we were a couple? Melissa and Arthur came in through the conservatory door as Stuart asked, "Who's Peter?"

I chose to ignore Richard's questioning gesture, as that was a question I couldn't answer myself yet. Aware that Arthur was coming in, I lowered my voice to answer Stuart; "Peter was the head gardener here. He passed away a year last April."

Arthur and Melissa looked content and remained arm-in-arm as they entered. I couldn't remember the last time they both looked happy to be in one another's company. Melissa mouthed, 'Thank you' to me, which Karen saw too. Karen moved closer to me and gave me a slightly questioning look as Arthur welcomed us all, thanked us for coming, and bade us take seats. The round table had been moved in from the patio, it had pots of tea and coffee, mugs and some biscuits on it.

Karen must have been following my gaze "Too short notice for cakes I'm afraid. All your fault George!"

Arthur and Melissa took the two larger, upright chairs, while

Karen, Richard and myself took to the creaking wicker chairs, leaving one seat vacant.

"Sorry Karen, I blame Arthur, he advanced the meeting." I winked at Arthur.

"I'm always happy to correct your many mistakes, my dear boy!" Arthur jibed back. "Well, I think we all know each other, except that I haven't had the privilege of meeting Stuart before, nor has he met the *real* Arthur Quail!" – Arthur put on his glasses just so he could look over them at me.

Stuart, Melissa, Arthur and I laughed while Karen and Richard looked puzzled and shared shrugs.

I smiled back and replied, "Yes, another of my 'many mistakes' was to do Melissa's bidding! Karen and Richard, I'll share the joke with you later. But now we have some more pressing issues to discuss. Where *is* Paul though?"

"Do you really need him here?" Asked Karen.

"Oh yes, he may be pivotal to this venture working! Can you see if he can be found?"

"OK, if you're really sure? Those are his shoes by the window, so I *hope* he's in the house somewhere." She got up and went into the hallway and called out for him. Paul appeared from the library carrying a book, moments later.

Paul quietly took his seat and looked very uncomfortable in his new surroundings.

"What book have you got there Paul?" I asked trying to include him in the group.

Paul didn't say anything but held up the book. It was titled 'Britain at War: Rationing'.

"That's mine," announced Melissa, "I used it for GCSE history, you can have it if you like, Paul?"

Paul meekly nodded his thanks.

I was impressed by his choice: "Rationing is something we may need to consider today Paul! But, if it's OK with you Arthur, I'll start with the potential problems, before suggesting, or asking for possible solutions?"

Arthur waved his open hand, "The floor is yours, George."

I took a brief look at my notes, then decided to pretty much abandon them. I didn't want to appear to either be reading a script, nor making a speech. Taking a deep breath, I began. "I do have to ask you all to keep the following two pieces of information to yourselves for the time being. Only because some of my information comes from sources who, understandably, wish to keep this out of the public domain for as long as possible."

Looking around, I found everyone except Paul was completely focussed on what I was about to reveal. Even Arthur was playing his part, by pretending I'd not already divulged this information. "Firstly, Andrea Parker, heading a team of plant pathologists and biologists, has discovered that the grass virus, 'PCP', *will* infect *all* our cereal crops if it is still active in the environment come spring. I think autumn-sown wheat will be the first to become infected and will alert farmers to the scale of the problem very soon."

"Fuck! Now I realise why you called this meeting so urgently!" Richard interrupted sitting forward in his chair. "So everything in the grass family is going to fail? - Shit!"

Karen coughed loudly, nodded angrily towards Paul,
while raising her eyebrows and glaring at Richard.

"Oh, yes, sorry everyone. I just didn't expect to hear that! Sorry
Paul..." Richard sat back and with thumb and forefinger together
indicated he was zipping his mouth closed.

I continued, "Well I will answer that one question now, but
please then hear me out and ask questions when I've finished."
Everyone except Paul nodded. Paul appeared to be reading his
book. "As far as I know, everything in the grass family; corn, rye,
wheat, maize, barley, etc. will become infected and fail to crop.
The only exceptions are those grasses of the rice varieties, as well
as reeds and bamboo."

Despondent looks were shared, with those of real concern, as I
continued, "Secondly, our police and armed forces are severely
under-resourced and simply do not have the numbers to be able
to ensure food distribution is securely delivered to essential
service providers. Nor will they be able to prevent widespread
looting, or hoarding, once the general public becomes aware
that food supplies are going to be insufficient to meet the
demand."

I glanced back at my notes to see Arthur whispering to Melissa.
I just continued "Sorry to those whom, I know, I am repeating
issues, but none of the following is secret, with some having
been reported in the media already. There will be further
transportation problems; Already we have mass animal
migration, dense clouds of flies and some landslides. We can
expect the animal and fly problem to decrease as winter sets in,
but it may start again when hibernating animals emerge in the
spring when the dormant grass seed germinates and becomes
infected again."

"With heavy rainfall or snow melt, will come flooding and further erosion of railway and road embankments. There is not much that can be done, in the short-term, to prevent this. I predict that our drainage systems will get completely overwhelmed with mud and silt. It has also occurred to me, though not likely to affect us here, that coastal regions with sand dunes are likely to find all the sand held by grasses on the dunes may blow inland."

I turned to Paul. "Paul, does that book tell you if Great Britain is self-sufficient in being able to produce enough food to sustain its population?"

Paul looked up from his book, "Well, this book says that during the 1940's we nearly became food self-sufficient with rationing, but that the population wanted food that we could not produce, and were not completely satisfied with eating only what was seasonal. But I also read other books and looked on the internet. In the 1950's farming land had decreased and the population increased to the point where we were no longer able feed everyone from our farmland. Now we only produce 60% of our food and 90% of that is grasses, or from animals that are fed on grasses, or grass seed."

I had taken a gamble on calling on Paul without warning, but it had certainly paid off. "Thank you, Paul, your research was more detailed than mine!"

Karen patted Paul on the back to a murmur of appreciation from the others.

"So, assuming we don't receive any food imports, and that we have no cereal crops nor animals that feed on them, our farmers will only produce enough to sustain 6% of our population, maybe 10%, because food waste will finally be eliminated. Now, obviously, once farmers become aware of the problems, they will switch to growing root vegetables, cabbage, broccoli, maybe even rice, if it will grow here?"

Paul put his hand up and shouted out the answer "Yes, it can grow here, but it needs lots of water and is very labour intensive, so it is not making money sense."

"Ah, I think you mean 'not economical' but we understand, and you all see why I wanted young Paul here today?"

Karen nodded and smiled as Paul looked back down at his book, clearly embarrassed.

"And, before any of you ask, I did not ask Paul to do *any* research. He's done this, all on his own, after he overheard that we might run out of Weetabix!"

I looked back at my notes. I'd lost my train of thought. "Right, not quite sure where I was? But basically, as a country, we will be very short of food both because of low production and a disrupted transport system. It will be made worse if people hoard or steal food direct from farms or the food distribution network. Historically, whenever there is a product shortage, rapid inflation as well as hoarding will follow."

"Really?" Interrupted Stuart, "has that actually ever happened in this country?"

"I can answer that one," said Richard, "the obvious example to quote would be the dual shortages of petrol and food during the early 70's. The Arab countries imposed an oil embargo on the West for political reasons, then Egypt went to war. By 1974 crude oil barrel prices had increased by 300%, only because the demand was greater than supply. It was much worse at the pumps, those that had any petrol, with prices rising by over 500%. At the same time, there was a Worldwide under-production of food and food prices shot up too. By the end of the year, inflation had reached a record 24%! People started to hoard both food, and even petrol. Good business for makers of jerry cans! The same thing happened with sugar, only there wasn't actually a shortage, that was until housewives started panic-buying the stuff!"

"What's a jerry can?" Asked Paul.

"Old name for a petrol can," I replied, "You see Richard is *very* old, not quite as old as his jokes, mind! But his degree in economics has finally proved useful!"

"Oh, ha-ha! – Mr No-Levels!" Richard replied, grinning at me. For just a few seconds, this friendly banter reminded me of those long evenings spent at the Black Horse with Richard and Peter.
However, the fact that we were discussing an impending disaster scenario brought me back just as rapidly. "Joking apart, Richard makes a good point: There *will be* rapid food inflation. Food will become the one thing everybody wants, and the value of money will soon decay as prices rise and the desire for food exceeds the need for money."

Karen spoke up for the first time. "If you are suggesting that we use the Manor as some giant food store, are you not just accelerating the problem, helping to starve the locals and making us a target for all those less fortunate?"

Melissa joined in, "Yes, and surely if you then start selling it, people will buy it all and leave us with nothing but what you say will be loads of useless money?"

I smiled and nodded in a 'knowing' fashion. "You are both quite right, and that's *not* what I am proposing. This is not a 'for profit' venture; we *would* stock up with some non-perishable

194

foods, but we wouldn't buy this locally. We'd also purchase a range of items that people in Ingleton and the surrounding villages may need; seeds so they can grow some of their own food, maybe petrol, so those further away can get here, and farmers can plough, firewood so they can keep themselves warm, etc."

"Ahem!" Arthur, who was obviously becoming less impressed as the debate went on, finally decided he'd speak out. "Now, George, I do appreciate your generous ideals, but are you seriously suggesting that we just give away, to all and sundry, everything we buy?"

"No!" I laughed, thinking Arthur would already have guessed what I was thinking. "No, we'd barter, exchange, or swap whatever people can produce, find or salvage, for either food or the tools they need to grow their own."

Stuart was looking puzzled, "Sorry, I just don't get it. What are people going to swap?"

I nodded. "OK, let's say: Mrs Boggins knits clothing and Mr Boggins grows tomatoes and peas. The Boggins' have too many potatoes and peas cropping at one time for their own use and they need more wool to continue to make clothes. We take their excess food and clothing and trade it for wool - assuming we will still be able to get any - and other types of food."

Looking around the group, I gauged few were convinced. "We'd need to have lots of trading partners, and all we would be doing is providing a place to trade and an inventory of what we do have and what we, as a community, require. We'd put up notices stating what we get requests for - that we don't have - and invite others to barter these products for those that we do."

I put my head in my hands. Maybe I wasn't conveying my idea in a cohesive manner. "Oh, I'm sorry I'm making a pig's-ear out of this." I took a deep breath and tried again, this time mimicking the methods of a primary school teacher and hoping my, already confused, audience would not start to feel patronised. "Let's say that Mr Baggins doesn't grow anything, nor makes anything, but he still wants food. Mr Farmer needs petrol for his tractor, he has food for us, but we don't have the petrol that he requires to harvest it. Our old friend Mr Boggins is expanding his allotment and wants compost, cabbage and carrot seeds, and we don't have those either. We'd tell Mr Baggins that we will give him food if he can supply any or all of the things that Farmer and Boggins want. Until we convince Baggins to also grow some of his own food, he'd become a scavenger. We'd probably need a lot of scavengers, especially at the beginning."

I looked around for a reaction. Nobody said anything, but each was clearly deep in thought. Hopefully, they were not only beginning to understand, but would now help by offering up suggestions and pointing out pitfalls I'd almost certainly overlooked.

Melissa was the first to speak up. "I think I get it. But communication would be a problem, especially if mobiles, power and the internet all go down. Should we use these to the maximum now, before it all breaks down, or will that cause a panic that will disrupt our own efforts?"

"Excellent! – Good thinking Mel." I wasn't expecting much from Melissa, thinking she'd likely 'poo-poo' the whole idea. "Yes, we need to somehow invite local people here should they run into difficulties over the next few months. Keep it vague. It may confuse them when they first see it, but it will make sense to them when the shops run empty. Use the internet, maybe Facebook while it's still available, but keep it local, we don't want mobs coming in from the cities. How do you think we could advertise both what we require and what is available here should power and the internet fail?"

Melissa sat back in her chair. She looked happy to be able to contribute. "Mail shots, poster points. How about we put posters up on post boxes? Everyone knows where they are. Oh, but what if we don't have any power, how will we print?"

Melissa genuinely impressed me, "Congratulations Mel, you are appointed our head of communications. Post boxes as poster points – brilliant idea! – As for power, I don't know. I fear the national grid will go down. We could run some low power devices like laptops and printers off car batteries. But I was wondering if we couldn't just run things straight off the solar panels that are on the back of the garage?"

"I don't think so," said Arthur, "when the power goes off we have no power, even when the sun is shining."

"They are grid-tied," stated Richard, "that means that they are automatically isolated from the national grid and house if the power is cut."

Stuart cut in, "That's stupid, so many houses with solar panels and they are all turned off just when people need power!"

"They have to be isolated," responded Richard, "if they all pushed power back into the lines, engineers would never be able to switch them off to work on them. Also, the load would exceed the supply, rendering their contribution useless."

"So why can't the power be diverted from the grid to the house when the power is cut?" Arthur asked, directing his question to Richard.

Richard looked puzzled - he'd probably come to the end of his knowledge on the subject. "I'm not too sure, it probably needs stabilising with batteries. Maybe 20 car batteries in series would do it? 20 times 12 volts is 240 volts. We'd need some kind of inverter to change the DC back to AC."

Arthur appeared very interested in this. "We can easily buy car batteries, and there's room in the garage loft for the batteries. Could you set this up, Richard?"

Richard shook his head. "No. It would be dangerous to try, especially when we still have mains power connected. It would need special automatic switches or relays. It's way beyond my abilities, we'd need an experienced solar electrician and probably a whole heap of special tools and accessories. Sorry!"

I was disappointed. I'd really hoped we would be able to utilise the solar panels, and then maybe help others to do the same. "Never mind Richard," I said, "we could still stock up on car batteries and charge them so we can power devices for many months."

Karen was next to express concern, "The kitchen: We will obviously lose the microwave, toaster, mixers, etc. but the stove and grill work on gas, can they be converted to Calor?"

We all looked at each other, but nobody knew the answer. Mel excused herself and ran to her homework room and returned with her notepad. "Got it," she said, "things to research on the internet: Number one: Cookers on Calor gas – question mark."

"Thank you, Mel," said Arthur, "but there is the big old kitchen in the basement? If we could reopen that? It is all wood or coal burning. I remember, as a child, that when that kitchen was in use the whole house seemed warmer!"

Karen, Melissa and I looked at each other in surprise. "I didn't even know there was a basement, other than the wine cellar!" Exclaimed Karen. "Where's the entrance?"

"Nor did I! Oh! ... Is it where you hide the bodies Daddy?!"

Melissa joked. Then looked rather sheepish as her father gave her a stern look and she realised that nobody had laughed. "Sorry Daddy! – So where *is* the entrance?"

"Ah, now that's a bit of a problem," Arthur explained, "after the new gas powered kitchen was opened 'upstairs', in the late 1970's, the old one started to get damp with mozzarella-like fungus growing on the walls and a dank smell began to engulf the whole house. My father decided to seal off the entire below-stairs, leaving only the wine cellar. I can still remember the day I was allowed down there to take a last look around. I was about eighteen, and it was quite an exploration I can tell you!"

Arthur sat back in his chair as he related his recollections of a whole floor that we were all unaware even existed. "As well as the big Kitchen, there is a large cold store room with insulated doors, a laundry room, complete with a huge, scary looking, electric mangle. Now, what else was down there? Ah, yes. The staff quarters, three little rooms under the front of the house, plus the coal and wood store. Also… There was a hatch near the side door where coal was poured straight down into the bunker. I fell down there when I was about six! I was exploring the garden and found the hatch. I had been told to keep away from it, but curiosity got the better of me. I used a large stone to knock the heavy bolts across, and I finally got the big hatch open, holding it high above my head I was too short to be able to get it past upright. It was hefty – very hefty. I leant forward to peer into the dark below and the weight of the hatch increased as I did so. I was unable to step back, I slipped, and the hatch came down hard, pushing me down the steep chute and into the darkness below, the hatch slammed shut as loudly as a gun. I slid down into, what I now know, was coal. I was terrified. I knew I was in trouble, so I just sat there and cried for what seemed like hours."

"What happened?" Asked Melissa, her mouth agape and showing real concern.

I, too, desperately wanted to know how he'd escaped. Looking around the group, I found that everyone's full attention was on Arthur - all willing him to continue.

Arthur smiled, "Well, it was our chauffeur, Peter. He spotted the stone first. Then noticed the hatch bolts were open. He told me later that he was just going to secure the hatch but thought that the stone could have been used to slide the bolts. He opened the hatch and called my name. Suddenly I was blinded by light, and I could only see his silhouette against the sky, way above me. I wasn't sure who it was. I was so scared that it was my Father that I just froze. Then the hatch started to close again. Just as the light became a narrow slit, I called out 'help!' Luckily, Peter heard me, and he went below stairs to get me out. I was in a terrible mess, and in a whole heap of trouble I can tell you!"

Arthur paused clearly enjoying his nostalgic recollections of his childhood. "I think that's it? Oh yes, and the generator and old boiler room full of pipes, cables and metal barrels of diesel. That place was scary too."

"A generator?!" Richard called out, "Is it still there? Does it still work?"

I was still clinging to my idea to use the solar panels, and didn't want for us to become reliant on fuel that would quickly become a scarcity, so I added quickly "I don't want us to have a constant requirement to source diesel."

"No." replied Richard, "That's not what I meant. If it *was* used to power the whole house, it must produce a lot of power. Therefore, we could use it to quickly charge our batteries and then power it down again. We wouldn't need that much diesel. The lighting circuits could easily be isolated and could run on DC from the batteries."

"We'd need to find old tungsten bulbs though, right?" I asked.

"No!" Replied Richard, enthusiastically. "LED and Energy Saving bulbs *will* work on DC. Energy Saving ones may be even dimmer, though."

I had asked Richard to come along for his opinions and ideas and, rather reluctantly, I found myself agreeing with him. "OK, if we can get to the generator, and it still works, we could use that as a backup or battery charging-power source. So, Arthur, where's the entrance, and is the generator still there?"

"Ah, yes. I didn't get to that, did I? Well there were three entrances, including the coal-chute. The chute was capped with concrete just below the top, and a huge Belfast sink dropped into it. That's now the bed to the right of the side door, the one with the little succulents. The biggest entrance had a wide staircase that came up under where we are now." Arthur banged the floor with his stick. "You see, before this conservatory was built, this end of the room didn't come out so far and was the preparation room. About there," he pointed to where the L-shaped room changed direction and ran past the croquet lawn "was a pair of big double doors and beyond them was the original dining room."

"What's a preparation room?" Paul asked.

"Ah, good question young man! The stairs led directly down to the kitchen, you see. The food was brought up to a big table here, where it was dished onto plates before being brought in, through the big doors, to be served. The big doors were kept closed so that room became very hot and helped keep the food warm."

"But what about ice cream?" Paul asked.

"You are a bright lad aren't you!" Arthur patted Paul's shoulder, "Well, cold desserts were often prepared in the cold store then taken to another table in the wine cellar. That, and the cold store, were isolated from the heat of the kitchen by two doors, which were kept closed as much as possible and never opened together. Now the third entrance is probably the only one that can be reopened; that is in the wine cellar, behind the largest rack - opposite where the steps come down. If we *are* to try to get in, that will be the only way." Arthur sat back, then must have remembered that Richard had asked if the generator still there, and if it worked. "As for the generator, well it is huge. I have no clue as to how it got down there - maybe it was taken down in parts? Anyway, there was no way to get it out, so it is definitely still there."

Arthur gave Paul a nudge. "You like your history, don't you Paul?"

Paul nodded, though not very enthusiastically.

Well, the grand sounding 'County of Durham Electric Power Distribution Company Limited' supplied the Manor with mains power soon after the Dunston B power station was built in 1930. Previously to that, we had our very own steam generator! I so wish I had seen, heard, and smelt that working! My grandfather, you see, he was a pioneer of every new scientific development. I bet you didn't know that Ingleton Manor was the first private house in Durham County to have electric light!"

Arthur had gone very 'off topic', but he was such an interesting orator that I felt bad asking him to stop. I looked around our little group and, on seeing that keen interest was shared by all, I allowed him to continue.

"Well, during the war, bombs started to fall, and the power station at Hull was targeted, as was Battersea. That is when my father, fearing power cuts, had the diesel generator installed.

Apparently, it did not see any use at all during the whole of the war! But in the years of austerity between 1945 and 1950, there were many power cuts and so it proved its worth. It was serviced to use during the industrial action and three-day week in the 70's, when we had many power cuts, but it has not been run since then."

I quickly calculated how long ago that was. "So it's been about forty years since it last ran? Surely it will be seized up?"

Richard responded first "A petrol engine would be, but diesel will probably be fine. It's the bearings in the generator part of it that may need freeing up before it is run."

Karen added, "Yes, and as it had just been serviced, that makes it even more likely to work doesn't it?"

"Yes, I guess so." I conceded, "Put 'investigate generator' on the 'to-do' list Mel."

"I already have," replied Melissa, "it's after smash big hole through the floor in the conservatory!"

"No, you do not!" Stated Arthur. "You have my permission to tidily, make a hole in the wall of the cellar, just big enough to crawl through with an extension cable and a lamp. If a bad smell comes up, you can jolly well seal it up again!"

"Bet you want to explore down there don't you Paul? – You're the smallest, so could to crawl through first if you like?" Richard asked Paul.

Karen frowned at him showing her dislike of his idea, but she need not have worried. Paul fiercely shook his head and looked back down at his book.

"Hmmm. Your boy is very wise indeed," Arthur said to Karen. "I shall dig out the plans for the house and see if my father kept any technical details relating to the generator. Excavation will have to wait until the weekend, though - I want to clear the cellar first. Now, one thing that bugs me about this trading scheme of yours, George... We don't really have a lot of spare space on this floor, and I am really not keen on opening up my home to every hungry Tom, Dick and Harriet, from miles around, to go trapesing through it. Do you propose we construct some kind of a barn?"

"No," I answered, "I thought that we — you - could order in a lot of large, secure, sheds that we could construct on either side of the drive between the garages and the fountain? Also, put a porta-cabin by the entrance as an office. Maybe, if we can power them, a refrigerated lorry or a shed insulated from the heat that's dedicated to storage of perishable foods, perhaps even put in some large freezers, again, providing we can power them." I looked at Arthur who was starting to bite his top lip and to Melissa, who was giving me a very doubtful look.

After a few moments, Arthur spoke. "George, you do realise that this is a huge gamble, don't you? On one hand; we have to react quickly while we are still able to acquire assets, and the stock required to get us going. On the other hand; we are presuming that this 'doomsday scenario' isn't going to be averted with food aid from America or Europe. We'd look pretty silly if we built a township of sheds and stocked them with goods nobody needs!" Arthur looked around the room. "If it were not for two things, I'd say absolutely not: Firstly, Maria Trellis called me this morning; she was very thankful for your contribution to the committee meeting and stated that the future does look bleak. She said that any support from Europe was conditional upon the UK preventing this from crossing the Channel. Also, that the US is now saying that they won't be able to help us if they can't contain their own outbreaks. Secondly, there is no grass where you propose to put those sheds, and I'd rather see some colourful sheds on my way down the drive, than acres of muddy field."

I hadn't finished describing my plan, and yet it appeared I was getting approval! I suddenly felt excited, and, despite the seriousness and complexities of the many challenges that lay ahead, I felt positive. I had a real purpose, a mission. However, I did not wish to display any pleasure. "Thank you, Arthur. Without your support, we would not be able to do anything."

Arthur nodded, and half shrugged.

I continued: "The mains water supply will stop if the power fails, and clean water will become second only to food in our priorities. We can't use the water from Langton Beck because it's all run off from fields that will either be nitrogen-rich from fertilisers or animal waste. But there are two natural springs in the hill beyond the lake." I pointed through the window into the dusky light, where the silhouette of the hill was still visible.

"We are going to need an enormous amount of pipe!" Interrupted Melissa, as she reached for her notebook again.

"That field had sheep in it too," stated Arthur, "Will it be safe to drink?"

I'd done some research on the internet, and modifying various methods, had come up with a solution that I thought would best meet our needs. "We'll need more than just some pipe, and yes, Arthur; providing we capture the water as it comes out of the ground and filter it, then it should be okay. What I thought we could do, is temporarily divert the water, while we cut three large steps out of the hill below the largest of the two springs. On each of these steps, we'd have a water butt filled with different filtering materials. The top one would be full of large gravel with cheesecloths on top that we'd need to replace or clean regularly. The second would contain fine gravel. Then the water would pass down into the final one, which would contain more cheese cloths at the bottom and fine sand above."

Richard spoke up "Yes, algae will grow on the pebbles and gravel. The algae will remove any bacteria and nitrates not removed by filtration. But there's another way… Reed beds! These are being used all over the world to filter water, even raw sewerage!"

I had already ruled out reed beds but felt I should explain why: "Yes, reed beds make an excellent natural filter, but they take months to establish, and each litre of water has to pass through many cubic meters of them, very slowly. It takes days to filter."

Richard didn't give up easily and continued to promote his idea: "What if we cut a shallow, meter-wide, track all the way down the hill from the other spring and plant this with reeds? – Yes, it wouldn't be usable until next year, but then it would provide an alternative should there be a problem with the other system, or if demands for water exceed what that alone can produce."

I shook my head. It was going to be hard work installing one system - digging a trench one-meter-wide and about 300meters long was, to me, a project too far.

Arthur spoke. "I think we should build both. If we become responsible for supplying water to a large number of people, a redundant or alternative system would be a wise investment indeed. I can see you are shuddering at the thought of digging out that length of channel George, but we could hire a mini digger to help with both projects and maybe use it to bury the pipe or pipes as they come down to the house, protecting them from animals, frost and summer heat."

I realised that Arthur and Richard were right, and the digger would speed up the building of both systems. I hadn't considered the need to bury the pipe either. I conceded: "Well this is why we have many wise heads together today. You are both absolutely right: we should build both and hire a digger. Paul?"

Paul had looked up from his book as soon as Arthur had mentioned the word 'digger'. "There's a JCB 8030 with a scoop fitted where the tennis courts were."

"Bastards!" Muttered Stuart, before apologising to Paul and shutting up again.

"Richard, that's a job for you. Assuming we can offer cash, Arthur?" I asked.

Arthur was on my wavelength and nodding, replied "If they do the whole job, before Monday, I'll pay £1000 cash. That sound about right?"

Richard, who was now looking less sure of himself, asked, "So, you want me to 'hire' the builders and the digger for a quick cash-in-hand job?"

"Exactly, Richard!" I replied "Much as I'd love to go play with an excavator, most of the work is on the side of a hill, and I'd probably end up rolling it down the hill into the lake! So, would you ask them in the morning? I can't, I'm off to Bishops Auckland, and we need to catch them while they are still on site. Maybe start with an offer of five hundred and offer more if they squirm too much."

Stuart stood up, and moving quietly to the window, he peered out into the failing light.

"Tell them they are welcome to come over and look at the job, measure up, etc.," Arthur added, "Where do you propose we are going to terminate the pipes at the house?"

Still standing by the window, Stuart made a useful observation "That's what I was wondering. Your garden appears to be level all the way from Melissa's fountain to the house. The tap would have to be high enough to put water containers under it. So how about you run it down into the wine cellar to maintain water pressure?"

"Ah, so you're not 'all tennis balls and no brains', Stuart!" Arthur exclaimed, "Be a nice cool place to store the water too. Just so long as we don't flood the place!"

"Who called Stuart 'all tennis balls and no brains'?" Melissa demanded to know. She began looking accusingly between Arthur and myself for the answer. "I invited Stuart here because he has an *exceptional* brain; he's got nine A-star GCSE's! And that's despite the school being reluctant for him to take so much time out for tennis tournaments and training. Also, Stuart predicted that this grass virus would have serious consequences. without any inside information from the government, or some prissy blonde scientist!"

"Meow!" said Karen smiling at me and raising her eyebrows, before a stare from Melissa forced her to meekly mutter, "sorry!"

"It is I who should apologise, my dear," Arthur admitted, "it was made up on-the-spot as it were, I wasn't quoting or repeating anything. Sorry Stuart. Nine A-star GCSE's eh? Well, that Lewis Hamilton chappie claimed his school held him back, yet he almost won the World Championship in his first year!"

Stuart smiled, "No offence taken, though I'm not going to compare myself to Lewis Hamilton - he lives in a different world altogether! There's no need to apologise either, my trainer often calls me much worse than that, I can tell you!"

I needed to get the conversation back on-topic before Richard ploughed in with his detailed knowledge of F1 and more time would be wasted. "Great idea Stuart. Can I ask you to work out the most direct route for the pipes to run to the side of the cellar, so when Richard brings the builders you can show them where they need to channel and trench?"

Stuart nodded, "Sure, but can Arthur help me? I don't know where any other services are buried."

Arthur nodded "Of course, my dear boy, I've got a plan of the grounds showing where the fountain top-up and standpipe water feeds run, also where the cables were laid. Are you able to lay your hands on that surveyor's wheel, George?"

The 'measuring wheel' as I called it was one of those tools that saw very little use. I knew we still had it somewhere, but I couldn't recall where. "Yes, it's probably in the tool shed, or maybe the garage. I'll find it and leave it by the side door tonight. Richard, when you speak to the builder's tomorrow, can you ask them where we could get ourselves a portacabin too?"

"Sure, no problem," Richard replied. Then with a hint of resignation he added, "While I'm here, I will give you 100%."

"What are you saying exactly?" Karen asked.

Richard looked around the group "You are all a lovely bunch of people; I can tell that already. I will do everything I can to help you set up this trading centre thing but, when things kick off and go bad, well then I'm off... Sorry, but we have inherited a large house near Lincoln, and I'll go there; see if I can set up something similar with my sister."

I was deeply disappointed and upset. I'd known Richard for over five years and was looking forward to working together with him on this venture. I said nothing. I didn't know what to say. I felt betrayed.

Karen wasn't so withstrained: "So you're here to poach all our ideas, then you are going off to set up in competition?"

"Oh come on!" Richard said, "Lincoln is 120 miles away so I won't be competing. But if we can find a way to communicate, we can continue to share ideas and solve problems together. Maybe even do some large-scale trading?"

"So, you and your sister have inherited a house? That is very nice," said Arthur, "family is most important. But why are you not down there already?"

Richard smiled, "Well my aunt died and gifted us the house in January, and it was a complete surprise - I'd only ever met the woman once when I was about ten. Anyway, it's a lovely big house just outside Stainton by Lanworth. That's even further from a big population centre than this one! But although shared between my sister and me, we still got lumbered with a huge inheritance tax demand. Neither of us wanted to sell the house, and we managed to offset the tax, agreeing to pay it over three years. We rent the whole house out to students from the agricultural college at Riseholme. The college manages it for us, guarantees payment, and is responsible for insurance, etc. It offers twelve students very comfortable lodgings, at a 'student affordable price' and, in just under three years, will clear our tax debt."

"I see," said, Karen "but if you go there now, what happens

to the students?"

"If this all kicks off, we - my sister, her family and I, will move down there. Some of the students will try to get back to their parents. I am hoping some will stay on because they are exactly the sort of people I'd need to get an agricultural community going. I know you are disappointed George, and I *am* sorry. I will steal some of your ideas for sure, but no way am I going to jeopardise your operation in favour of my own. I'm hoping that there will be groups across the country setting up similar communities and that, at some future date, we will be able to network them all."

Even with his explanation making sense, I remained disappointed and was less eager to provide details of our venture for Richard to take elsewhere. But, he was right, he wasn't competing, and I trusted him to give his all until he left. "OK, Richard, I'll be sorry to see you go. If it doesn't work out for you in Lincolnshire, then I'm sure you'll be welcome back."

"Thank you," Said Richard sincerely, "I'll go down to the tennis courts tomorrow and try to negotiate a deal for the digging and trench work. I'll ask about portacabins too. I was wondering about all the stock control in the sheds, and all that comes in and out. That presents a lot of problems, you know?"

"Yes, I know. Stock control and perishable dates - not that we are going to pay any attention to dates on dried products and tins! We will need to monitor fresh produce, make sure it isn't going to waste. Over time, we will probably have to advise people to switch to growing something else. I can envisage ourselves being overwhelmed with tomatoes, then apples, especially if everyone crops the same things at the same time. That will also apply to the farmers who are used to mass producing just one or two crops. They will have to diversify right from the start."

Richard turned to Arthur, "You own most of the farmland around here, don't you? Can't you just tell them what to grow and maybe tell them to give one of the fields by the lane up for allotments? Those joining our community could each be given a piece of land to increase the variety of produce?"

"Ah, I like the way you're thinking, Richard," replied Arthur, "but, as I was explaining to Melissa only today - I don't own their land anymore. You see, my Father and I decided to give them the land. I still own the farm houses and charge them rent for those, but the farmers were struggling under the old system, which was both unfair and desperately complicated ..."

Arthur sat back in his chair, a sign he was about to tell a long story, "Previously, we took a percentage of their turnover as well as charged rent by the hectare *and* received rent for their houses. There was a lot to manage and administer from here. There was an on-going 'them and us' situation, culminating in 1979, when one of the tenant farmers tried to set fire to the Manor! Luckily, for some reason, Peter was up near the garage late that night and intercepted him and his can of petrol before he got to the door."

Karen was shaking her head "My god, I didn't know any of this, did you Mel?"

"Daddy only told me today. He didn't even call the police!"

I couldn't believe what I was hearing, "What?! – He tried to kill you all and burn down your house, and you let him off?"

Arthur smiled, "Yes! You see, Peter convinced my father, who was rather ill at the time, to find out why this man had been driven to such an extreme action? So instead of calling the police, we locked him in the disused kitchen and called a meeting with all the farmers, the next day, to hear their issues."

Arthur looked very morose and uncomfortable. Melissa took and held his hand as he continued in a quieter than usual voice.

"I was twenty-nine, and my father had just started to prepare me to take over the running of the estate, so I was allowed to sit in with them at that meeting. They were all furious. Most were deep in debt too. Old man Leach told us that Mark Wilson, the Father of the man who came to burn down the Manor, had taken his own life the day before. The eldest of three, Paul Wilson, was younger than I was, and was now responsible for his Mother and two younger siblings. The farm had employed two farm hands, but they had to let them go the previous month."

Arthur was clearly distressed, as was Melissa on hearing the story again. Karen passed them some tissues and Arthur continued. "Well, my Father had heard enough, and at that point, he let Paul Wilson out of the old kitchen to join the meeting. My Father, in front of all of them, cried both with shame and embarrassment. He promised to do what he could to relieve their suffering. I'd never seen my Father cry, he always seemed such a strong, upright and proud man. He never cried again, not even during his last days, when he was in severe pain and dying. You see, my father had become isolated from the lives of the farmers. He wasn't involved in the day-to-day running of the estate. Instead, he employed an estates manager and had little contact with any of those working the farms. This estates manager was on holiday when all this happened and was dismissed upon his return. For not only was he very demanding and unsympathetic to the farmers, but he had not forwarded any of their complaints to my father. Also, he had imposed additional service charges that he was pocketing himself. My Father and I did right by the farmers; the four farms we had were merged into the two that remain, both independent, and profitable. I regard Paul Wilson to be one of my closest friends, and just think; if I hadn't listened to the wise words of Peter Rutherford, I'd have called the police, and he'd have been locked

213

up!"

Melissa squeezed her father's hand, "A good example of a communication failure, and how you can't always trust those you should be able to." Melissa glanced briefly at Richard, "It wasn't your father's fault, Daddy."

I realised that, yet again, we had wandered off topic, but here was an opportunity to read out Peter's final message. I pulled it from my pocket. "I'd like to read you this note from Peter and seek your advice about informing his family about its contents, especially Sandy Rutherford. I found it in a little fridge, with some drinks, in the loft above the garage.

"Ah, that was Peter's little writing den," Arthur added.

"Oh, Peter wrote a gardening journal or something?" I asked, unaware that Peter had written anything.

"No, Peter had a book published; the book describes his family's escape from the Hungarian SS in 1939 and what they found when they revisited their apartment some ten years later. Quite a moving tale about his trying to understand why so many of his own countrymen and friends had turned against them. Called something about bowls of soup and published under his Hungarian name 'Sandorsen'. He did ask if he could write another about his time here as a Chauffeur, but I forbade him. Who'd be interested in what went on here anyway?"

"All of us, probably!" Richard replied, and I nodded in agreement.

I remembered that there were two books on the table by the fridge. Had he left them out for me? I also wondered if Peter had written that second book, despite Arthur's instructions not to? I decided not to mention them, and that I'd remove them to my gatehouse later.

I read out Peter's note. There was surprise registering on everyone's face, except Arthur's, when I got to the part that explained that he knew he was ill. I finished, and nobody spoke for a good few moments as they solemnly digested the contents.

"Do you any of you have the contact details of any of his family?" Richard asked, finally breaking the silence.

Arthur sighed "His daughter - Sandy's mother, moved to Norfolk a couple of years ago. I don't have her address. Sandy's father - they are separated; he still lives in Ingleton with Sandy. However, he and Peter never got on, and Sandy is, how do you say it, Melissa? 'Not exactly on my poke list' or whatever?"

Melissa laughed, "You mean 'friends list' Daddy, not 'poke list'!"

I offered a possible solution; "We could just post the note through their door and hope Sandy, not her father, gets it? We could put our own note with it saying that his ashes can be spread down by the lake… assuming you agree, Arthur?"

Arthur nodded, "Of course and, before you ask; yes, I *was* aware that Peter was unwell. I decided that he'd be better off spending his last days with his family. What I didn't appreciate, at the time, was that his son-in-law didn't like him and that Peter had to travel down to Norfolk for his final days. Luckily, his daughter chose to have the funeral up here because she knew he'd worked here for 57 years and that he loved this area. We chatted at his funeral and were about to share contact details when Sandy butted in and started screaming insults at me."

"So we'd have to ask Sandy for her mother's details? Do you fancy a drink down at the Black Horse, Richard?" I asked.

"Oh, a nice jolly chat with Mad Mick and his crazy bitch? I just can't wait!" Despite his sarcastic comments. Richard nodded and winked. "Well, there will be two of us, and Mick's not going to surprise me with a sneaky punch twice."

I looked at Karen, wondering if she might want to join us, but she politely shook her head before I even asked.

"OK, we'll go down on Thursday evening, maybe leave a poster there if Mel's produced something by then?"

Mel nodded, "I might need some help with the wording, though."

"I'll help you, my dear." Confirmed Arthur.

"More tea anyone?" Karen asked.

I tried to remember what topic had been interrupted this time. As drinks were requested and handed out, I continued, "Richard was asking about stock control and the need to turn-around perishable produce quickly. For this, I think we would need a powered laptop, a database or spreadsheet, and someone who's good at remembering where things are - and who is good at maths - to be our stock controller."

Paul was listening and looked up to find both Karen and I smiling at him encouragingly. "Will I get a barcode scanner?" Paul asked eagerly.

I nodded "Yes, I hadn't thought of that Paul! Maybe a handheld one, if we can find the software to work with it. Although none of our fresh produce will have barcodes, and there is no point pricing anything because we won't be selling it. We'll be swapping it for something else or a service. That's where it's going to get complicated; how are we going to value what we

216

have got? And vary the value of the products as demand increases or decreases? Any ideas?"

The question was greeted with frowns and slow head-shaking. But Paul spoke up "Meals!" he said.

"No dear," said Karen, "we won't be able to cook for everyone."

"No!" Said Paul, "Our new money should be meals or meal tokens they can spend later."

As I thought about it, I realised the potential of this simple idea and I couldn't believe that a twelve-year-old boy had suggested a solution before any of his six elders.

Paul continued because Melissa and Arthur were still giving him questioning looks. "You said that Mr Farmer needs petrol for his tractor, and that is important because Mr Farmer will grow a lot of food." Paul started to rattle away excitedly with one of his long sentences: "So we give Mr Boggins 10 meals' worth of tokens for one Jerry of petrol, and if Mrs Baggins makes a jumper but it's summer and no one needs one and it's going into stock then she would only get one meal token or something like that, and it would take a proper lot of working out, but I can do it! You see we need something fixed to price everything against, like money."

"Bloody Hell!" exclaimed Richard, "Future Chancellor of the Exchequer, here!"

Paul didn't understand, "Is that a bad idea then?" he asked, before looking back down at his book in embarrassment.

"No, definitely not!" I got in quickly, "It is an absolutely brilliant idea, and I think it can work. Ignore Richard, that was one of his 'jokes' that I warned you about."

"Yeah, Sorry Paul," Richard leant over and patted Paul's arm, "it really is a genius idea - the vouchers... People may not want to take all their meals at once, or could use those to trade for other things. Our problem would be stopping anyone copying our vouchers. People desperate for food might try to do that."

"The Quail seal!" Arthur proclaimed, "They'd have a job to copy that. It is a hand press that was used to emboss our family crest onto letterheads and envelopes. I have not used it for several years, but I know exactly where it is. Please excuse me for a second." Arthur got up from his chair and headed out into the hall.

"What is everyone going to do?" Stuart asked.

I didn't understand. "You're asking what *you* can do?"

"No," Replied Stuart, "the people, what are they going to do for entertainment? They won't be spending all their time just getting food, and there will be no TV, newspapers, radio or internet or cinema... The kids too – yeah - what about educating the children?"

"Woah!" I said, "We can't diversify that much. Food and water, a place to trade, charge batteries and maybe to get some tips on growing vegetables. I think that's more than enough for us to handle. We can't build a school, cinema and a tv station!"

Stuart gave me a hard stare. "Don't be sarcastic. Nobody is suggesting we build anything."

Arthur returned with a little wooden box and caught only Stuart's last few words. "Sheds and a portacabin, George. That's all I am granting my permission for. Now, here's the Quail Crest press. Pass me a sheet of paper George."

On receiving a sheet of my notes, Arthur slid the paper into what looked like a big nutcracker and squeezed the handles together.

On removing the paper, a shield-shaped image appeared, embossed into the paper. He passed it around and we each agreed that this complex image including a quail and the Latin words 'humus nostra sustenta' would be very difficult to 'replicate' without the press that created it.

"The Latin means, 'Our lands sustain us', suddenly rather appropriate is it not? The press will have to be kept in a safe place, it is four generations old you know! The vouchers it produces must not be left in the portacabin overnight either. Paul's meal vouchers will become our currency!" said Arthur, as he carefully replaced the press back in its velvet-lined box.

Stuart continued to push his point. "George deliberately misunderstood my question while you were out Arthur. I was asking how we could help to entertain people, especially children. I was going to ask if we could organise a free book exchange and maybe when we are not busy, we could read stories to the children and get them to join in. I wasn't going to suggest we build anything!" Stuart gave me a stare.

Arthur looked at me for a response.

I had been harsh and a little sarcastic. "Sorry, Stuart. You mentioned cinema and TV and I thought your aspirations were bigger than we could manage. How about you, when you're not busy elsewhere, be in charge of entertainment - set up a book, CD and DVD exchange? Maybe that could be the hook to get people here before everything kicks off, and they'd see what else we were doing?"

"So my first poster could advertise these services, not that we are going to be the place to go when the shops are empty?"

Melissa asked.

Arthur answered, "Well, what if we rename ourselves as 'Ingleton Manor Trade and Barter Centre', then advertise the
free book and CD exchange service underneath that? I could sort out a lot of books from here to start it going. But where would you do this? Nobody is to suggest the house nor my library! Or should we hire two portacabins?"

Arthur had apparently already been giving this some thought. So I praised this idea: "Sounds like a good plan. Keep it local, though. Maybe a larger shed, next to the portacabin?

"So, two portacabins ..." Richard stated rather than asked, "then they could go back to back. But what about security, do you have electric fences here? And the gate, it just opens to anyone who presses the button? If we are the only place for miles with food, there will be some people who will just want to take it. I mean I can't see Mad Mick knitting jumpers to exchange for food vouchers!"

"Hmmm, security might become an issue." I agreed, "We can set the gate to not open, but buzz the gatehouse if anyone presses the button. We each have remote controls that can open the gate from about 50 meters away. I'm sure I could wire it so it also buzzes the house, using the intercom cables. But only someone who is in the gatehouse can see who was there, and be close enough to open the gate. Maybe someone in the portacabin could too, if it was put close enough to the gate? We don't have an electric fence, but they are so easy to get through anyway.
Luckily, anyone wanting to get onto the property has to go up the lane, and then they have the beck to cross, and lake to get around. The gate is the only real security risk and even if it remains closed, it can be climbed."

After a few seconds where only blank looks were returned, Melissa spoke up: "What about setting up hidden Wi-Fi cameras? You can get night vision ones. We won't need the internet, just keep it a closed-circuit network. We'd just need enough power to keep a couple of laptops running to screen the images. Some have motion detectors too. Oh, and power for the cameras, oh… and the gate!"

"OK, write that down and research it. Order whatever you need." Arthur replied, "Now, anything else, George?"

I looked at my notes. We seemed to have covered and solved most of the issues, but there were still two outstanding issues. "Almost," I replied, "We need to make it easy, especially for the elderly, to get food and water and charged batteries from here back down to the village. Any suggestions?"

Richard replied, "Wheelbarrows or shopping trollies? Or maybe run my van down, just once a day with water? But what about those from the villages that are further out?"

"Won't you be taking your van with you?" Karen asked coldly.

"Oh, yes. Sorry…" Richard replied, looking rather sheepish.

Arthur chipped in sternly, "We can't be responsible for every aspect; if we are able to supply clean water, then it should be up to those in the villages to organise how to collect and distribute it themselves.

"Good point Arthur, I think we will have enough to do ourselves. Now that leaves just one issue on my list, and that is the complex issue: Sewerage and waste disposal. Again, any suggestions?"

"Ah, water to flush the loo and rubbish collection you

mean?" Arthur asked.

"Yes," I replied, "people can collect rainwater, or get it from Langdon Beck or any number of ponds around here, but will sewerage back-up if the sewerage plant isn't manned, and does anyone know where our sewerage is treated, and how many men work there?"

"Ah, I know exactly where it is my dear boy!" Answered Arthur, "Amazing where duties as an MP take you: It is south-east of Gainford, on the banks of the river Tees, just off the A67." Smiling broadly, he continued, "I also know that it is fully automated and *does* require power. However, if it should get overwhelmed, or the power is off for a long period, it will switch to just removing large solids and grit and, bypassing the settlement and biological processes, will then flow straight into the river. So, in theory, it shouldn't back up! As for the other waste, well they can burn paper and card and compost all food waste. Though I think there will be very little of that over time! As for plastics and glass that can't be reused, we will have to agree to take those to a piece of unused land somewhere."

"There's a great deal of energy in waste plastic, but I don't think we can safely extract it?" Richard said, looking around the group.

"Absolutely not!" Growled Arthur, "we have already fought off an industrial incinerator, we are not now, going to try to build one of our own!"

"I can think of one more thing that incinerators reminded me of," Stuart rather timidly added, almost in a whisper, "what about the dead? What will we do with the bodies?"

Chapter 8 — A Sliding Puzzle

"Argh! ... A throbbing headache!" Upon waking it took a few minutes to realise I was unable to work out what day it was, nor why my head felt that it was full of scorching, sloshing water.

Unbalanced, I instinctively made my way to the cold tap in the kitchen. It screeched as I turned it full on, the sharp sound causing more jarring pain. I stuck my head right under the jet of near-freezing water. As it splashed all over me, I scooped up copious amounts with hands cupped together, and swallowed it down. Finally, I retreated when the cold became too much to bear. I would dry myself off and get dressed before mopping up the kitchen. No… I would take a couple of aspirin, then go back to bed… Sod the kitchen!

I noticed my mobile phone on the kitchen table, next to an empty bottle of red wine. The screen had become a little out of focus, but it confirmed that it was Wednesday 9th September and only 6.05am. I peered through the window that faced the gate. In the dim, early morning light, I noticed an unfamiliar shape. Squinting, I could just make out tiny beads of light reflecting off the many raindrops on Karen's car.

"Oh, God!" I confirmed my recovering memories of that exceptionally long previous evening, by peering back into the bedroom. There was a long bulge along the far side of the bed. I could just see Karen's light-ginger hair on the pillow, and one arm hanging out from under the duvet.

Suddenly I became conscious of my nudity, and remembered that Paul was upstairs. I now recalled Karen laying his sleeping body down on one of my cinema chairs. That was before we retreated downstairs and stupidly opened the bottle of wine that

Karen had taken from the Manor.

Was Karen also naked? I couldn't see any of her clothes. I did remember arguing with her when I let slip that Melissa had also been upstairs that morning, and had played Pac-Man. She'd yelled at me, and I wasn't in any kind of a state to put up a good defensive argument. Oh, no... I'd called her a 'jealous cow' and she actually agreed! Then we'd just started to kiss.

As my memories slowly returned, so my headache became worse. I briefly felt nauseous and headed straight for the bathroom. In an untidy pile by the shower were Karen's clothes. I found myself checking to see if her knickers were there – and they were. I took an aspirin, returned to the bedroom, quietly closed the door, and put on my dressing gown. Sitting on the side of the bed, my delicate head in my hands, I tried to piece together all that had happened the previous evening.

The meeting had gone on for another three hours after Stuart had asked about dead bodies. Richard, Melissa, and Stuart continued to bring up questions, and more and more diverse options and scenario. Coffee and tea were replaced with bottles of wine. We talked about arming ourselves, education, health, keeping fit, Stuart even talked of organising a 'fun day' and what we could do for Christmas. Arthur regularly went off-topic too, and we learned more about his family history, fascinating but mostly irrelevant.

However, it had also been a very productive meeting and exceeded my highest expectations: Melissa researched many things on the internet and answered most of our questions. We'd placed orders for storage sheds, an A-board, Video cameras, Wi- Fi boosters, water butts, gravel, sand, 2Km of 20mm pipe. Also, Calor Gas and heaters, walkie-talkies, car batteries, solar battery chargers, extra wheelbarrows, petrol cans - even a big greenhouse - and many, many other tools and items that we might have difficulties securing during the following months.

Arthur had come up with a new expression as his debit card took a battering: "Two heads are better than one, but six heads cost me 12 arms and legs!"

Paul was first to fall asleep, and Melissa retired at about 11.30, leaving me to take notes. Stuart had been next to falter, and Richard agreed to give him a lift back to Ingleton. Arthur then brought out the brandy, and soon fell asleep himself.

I suggest that Karen was unfit to drive, and that she and Paul should stay in one of the unused bedrooms. She said that they would be cold, and she'd rather not impose on Arthur without his permission. So, she asked if they could camp at the gatehouse. Her driving from the Manor to the gatehouse confirmed she was certainly unable to negotiate public roads, clipping the kerb as she rounded the fountain.

"Oh! My head should hurt, but it doesn't! Morning George, are you OK?"

I turned around to see Karen slowly rising from under the covers and, with a wry smile, she allowed the cover to drop, exposing her breasts "Do you fancy coming back to bed and see if you can stay awake this time?!"

"Morning Karen, you look... Oh, wow! ... You're really beautiful! Oh, tell me I didn't fall asleep last night, did I?"

"Thank you! And yes, you seemed very up for it, but were sound asleep when I returned from the bathroom! You don't look so well now," She pulled back the covers, "are you able to join me for a 'cuddle' now? We've got plenty of time."

She looked stunning. Why she chose to hide such a perfect figure under shapeless and baggy clothing eluded me. Even in my sorry state, she was irresistible. There was no way our relationship could survive if I rejected her naked charms now and no way, headache or not, I was going to miss this opportunity. Without a word, and grinning from ear-to-ear, I slipped out of my dressing gown and joined her under the covers.

At 8.15, we heard first the gate clanging shut, then Paul calling from upstairs. Karen kissed me before getting out of bed and said, "We'd better get him back to my house, into uniform and straight onto the school. The gate closing behind Melissa going for the bus must have woken him."

"Melissa? – Oh, she'd have seen your car!" I stated, as she darted out to grab her clothes from the bathroom.

Karen returned, grinning broadly, "Yes, I think she will have got the message now!" I watched in silence as she hurriedly dressed, unable to hide her glee. Then she quietly opened the door and called back to Paul telling him to quickly come down.

"Good feeling, gone." I said to myself, as I wondered if Karen may have engineered all that had happened? It was she who had suggested that wine could replace the tea and coffee, knowing that Arthur would certainly agree. I also remembered that she insisted I joined Arthur for a brandy, and it was she who had taken the unopened bottle of wine back to the gatehouse. She could have parked her car in the garage, or left it up by the house.

"Hurry up George, I need you to be ready!" Said Karen, interrupting my thoughts as she popped her head briefly around the bedroom door. "What's the matter?" She asked, gauging my solemnness and returning to the room and closing the door. "You're not bailing on me now, are you? You are still going with us to the school?"

226

I managed a smile, trying to dismiss my odious thoughts and convince myself that what had happened had been a lucky happenstance. "Yes, I should go. Sorry, me and red wine – we're not really friends!"

Karen sat on the bed making me feel uncomfortable as I hunted down my clothes. While I'd happily watched her dress, I was less keen that she was now doing the same to me.

"Not jeans," she said as I grabbed a pair from the wardrobe, "something smarter, like what you wore yesterday."

I quietly and quickly obeyed, but her reaction to Melissa having seen her car outside continued to concern me. I had always been honest with her, now she should do the same, "Karen, you seemed to take great pleasure in Mel having seen your car here this morning, was that an accident – leaving your car there?"

Karen's face dropped, she looked deeply disappointed. "You think I planned that? Think about it George - I was hardly in a state to plan that far ahead, was I? Anyway, you said yourself that you were 'very tempted' and now that problem is solved, isn't it? And if you tell me you're upset for Melissa, then I'm going to have to seriously doubt your intentions *and* morals, George!"

"So when did you realise that she would see your car as she left for school?" I probed, ignoring her attack on my morality.

Karen took a deep breath before replying "OK, I am being a little unfair; I can trust you to always be honest with me, and now I'm muddying the waters slightly," she sighed. "I didn't plan the whole thing around Melissa, I wanted you, I need you, George - We need you. I am being completely truthful now; I did plan to spend the night here. After watching you debate last night and how you included Paul, well, I decided that there was a lot more to you than just a gardener and, well, I fancied you! Melissa didn't come into it until we got to the fountain, on the way back I was going to park in the garage, then changed my mind. That's when I hit the kerb, changing direction a bit too late. It was just an opportunity, I was a bit drunk, it wasn't premeditated."

She held out here hand for me to come to her and pleaded with her eyes.

I believed her. Or maybe I just needed to? I desperately didn't want this first sexual encounter to be soured in the same way my very first had been. "OK, I believe you. But this jealousy of Melissa, there's no need for it. I have it completely under control. But if you rub our relationship in her face, you realise that you could lose Paul the only friend he has got?"

Karen sat, silent for a moment, before speaking, "Oh, shit! I hadn't thought of that. I hope she doesn't react badly. Jealousy is a powerful enemy, and I'm afraid I've got buckets of it. Will you accept me, buckets-an'-all?"

I didn't understand how a woman, who didn't 'do love', was still able to be so jealous of another. "Well, I'm not one to say 'no' to a gorgeous pair of buckets! Of course, I accept you – I'm proud and happy that you want me. But… I am not having you arrange *my* wardrobe while *you* continue to hide that gorgeous figure, under drab, loose-fitting clothing yourself! OK?"

Karen stood up, put her arms around me and gave me a long kiss. "Deal," she said, "but now we must get a move on, we're going to be late if there are any problems on the roads."

Paul quietly got into the back of the car, ignoring my "Good morning, Paul." Apparently, he was completely unfazed that we both appeared from the same bedroom, moments before.

"I don't have my school bag," he said as he sat in the back of the car "and I've left my road animal sheet in the library, and I need it."

"Sorry, love - we've only just got enough time to pick up your uniform and school bag from home, we can't go back to the Manor now."

Paul put his hands over his ears. Karen and I looked at each other in both surprise and realisation, neither having previously believed the school when they said he did this.

He sat there with his hands over his ears all the way along Gainford road, as Karen became visibly more upset.

As we turned left, at the end of the road, I saw Melissa still waiting at the bus stop, with two other younger children in uniform. She had seen us too and was waving.

"I think we are going to have to pick her up, Karen?" I said cautiously.

"Bloody Hell!" Muttered Karen, as she indicated and slowed.

"Don't swear, Mummy!" said Paul from the back.

Karen turned angrily to him, "Oh, so you can hear alright with your hands over your ears, can you? – Well now, you can take them down!"

Paul didn't react, he just pressed his hands harder against his ears. I gave him a look of disappointment, hoping that would help. It didn't, he just closed his eyes, too.

"At once!" Ordered Karen, as she brought the car to a stop.

"Hello!" said Melissa opening the rear door and peering in, "Can you give me a lift to the school? The bus hasn't turned up!"

"Sure, hop in," said Karen, hiding her anger well. "No room for your friends, though, I'm afraid."

"Oh, I don't really know them. Thank you. Hands!" she said loudly as she sat down. Paul instantly dropped his hands and Karen, and I shot each other another look of realisation.

"I've brought something for you, Paul!" Melissa produced his 'road animal' sheet from her school bag and Paul's face lit up."

"I'll need a pencil." stated Paul. Melissa had predicted his request too, and was ready to hand him one.

"Thanks again for picking me up," said Melissa, "I was going to knock at the gatehouse as I went past, but I didn't want to disturb you guys."

"That's very considerate," I said, "but we are going to Karen's first to get Paul into uniform, and to pick up his school bag, then we've got a meeting at the school, and Karen and I will want to discuss that before we get there."

"I understand," replied Melissa, "I'll be quiet, and keep Paul occupied."

I could tell Karen was conflicted. Melissa was apparently unconcerned that we had spent the night together, and she had been very thoughtful towards Paul. Maybe she still wanted some kind of reaction, and all she got was pleasantries.

"Would you mind popping in George? Just to help speed things up with Paul?" Karen asked, "I think that bucket may be about to overflow - if you could give me a hand with that?"

"Uh? Oh, yes! No problem, er, I forgot your roof leaked."

I realised that I didn't know exactly where Karen lived, so tried to memorise the route. We turned left just before the Black Horse, and I saw Molly, the Manor's old cook, heading there.

"Does Molly work there now?" I nodded towards the pub as we turned into Springwell.

"Yes," replied Melissa from the back, "That's why the food there is so good... Quail training!" She laughed.

After another turn, we stopped outside a neat little bungalow with a very well kept front garden. "Here we are," said Karen, "Quick, out Paul. I won't lock the car, Mel, will you look out for it? – Thanks."

As Karen unlocked the front door, I said "Nice little place, this, didn't know you were into gardening!"

"I'm not," Karen replied sternly, "the nice old chap opposite does it for me." She shut the door behind us heavily.

"OK, Karen, why are you still trying to wind Melissa up? Why are we playing 'happy families' - all going in together?"

"Paul, quickly put your uniform on. It's all folded at the end of your bed. Everything you are wearing into the wash basket, please. Now hurry!" Karen leaned back against the front door. "Why? – Because I was so close to reaching back and punching her Goodie-Two-Shoes lights out! – That's why!" Karen stood, stiff, still with her back to the front door. She was shaking with fury and pent-up anger.

I shrugged, "Sorry, I don't understand - what did she do?

I thought she was nice and considerate. What did I miss?"

Karen shook her head, "Nice?! – There you go... You really don't get it, do you? First, she'd recognised Paul's hands-on-ears thing before I did, then with just one word from her, he puts them down. He didn't when I asked, did he? oh no! Then wasn't it *nice* of her to remember his damn dead animal sheet, when his mother didn't? And *she's* gonna keep him *nice* and quiet so we can talk, isn't that just so *nice* and understanding of her? Well, I've had just about enough of 'nice', and I've developed a total hatred of the damn word."

I couldn't resist: "That's nice!" I took a step back, expecting her to lash out, but I only received a hard stare. I then asked, "Isn't it more because she didn't react at all to discovering we spent the night together? She just seemed to accept it without even a hint of surprise."

She stood with her arms crossed for a few moments, then she took in a deep breath, followed by a long sigh. Looking at the floor, she rubbed her forehead with one hand. "Do I get to knee you in the balls every time you get to be so bloody right?" She looked up smiling very slightly, "Couldn't she have just been a bit upset, or catty, or sarcastic, or anything except bloody *nice*!?"

I was beginning to wonder what I was letting myself in for, but I wasn't too concerned. Sure that Karen's sudden mood swing and irrational feelings towards Melissa was a temporary hurdle, and that she was over the worst of it, I just smiled at her as she continued to take deep breaths to calm herself down.

Just as Paul appeared from his bedroom, smartly dressed in his new uniform, she whispered, "I'm sorry, George, I'm not really an irrational, crazy, freak-bitch from Hell! Normal Karen has returned and promises to go see her GP about her medication very soon."

"Where is the roof leaking Mummy?" Paul asked as he picked up his school bag.

"Don't worry dear," Karen replied, "George has just fixed that," and she gave me a wink.

Paul swung his bag onto his back and took her hand, then to my surprise, he reached out for my hand too. I didn't take it. It would have been awkward, all of us going through the door with our hands chained together, and I also thought that Melissa would believe that it was false if she noticed.

The onward journey to the school was without further incident: Melissa and Paul quietly chatted in the back, and I divulged to Karen that I felt a little nervous, almost as if I were a naughty child having to see the head teacher. She told me how she had felt the same when she first went there, but that her feelings quickly subsided when she met 'such a nice lady.'

There were far fewer dead animals on the road for Paul to record, but there remained a lot of muddy puddles to negotiate. Almost every vehicle we encountered was covered in mud, splashed up from the wet roads. Windscreens were smeared as wipers failed to cope with the amounts of dirt deposited on them.

The road via Hinton to the A688 had 'road closed' signs across it, so we joined the main road at Staindrop. Here the road was closed west towards Barnard Castle, with many queuing motorists being turned back by police. We joined a slow-moving convoy of muddy vehicles, heading towards Bishop Auckland. "It looks like a scene from a tv news report; mass-migration from a war zone!" I exclaimed.

"Yes," replied Karen, "I imagine we won't be the only ones late for school today. But look at the fields and hills, I never realised that the earth was so many different shades of brown!"

I looked at the landscape, and realised that she was quite right; there were clay-browns, iron-rich red browns, sandy browns, granite-grey browns, chalk-speckled browns and many in between.

"I miss the River Shannon and the folks at Skibbereen, the moorlands and meadows and their Forty Shades of Green," piped up Melissa from the back, "That's from a Johnny Cash song. We did it in English. Only we've got shades of brown."

"Well, even brown has got to be better than Fifty Shades of Grey!" I added.

"Well, when Paul asks," said Karen quietly, "I'll let *you* explain that one, George!"

The usual twenty-minute journey had taken almost an hour. Temporary traffic lights, allowing only single-file traffic to pass a small landslide, had delayed us further as we entered Bishop Auckland.

We turned right at some traffic lights, and I suddenly realised that we had arrived.

"Turn left where the railing ends," said Melissa, "don't go straight on, it takes you right round to the sports centre."

"Yes, I do know," replied Karen coldly, "I do have a child that goes here you know?"

"Yeah, sorry." said Melissa as she leant forward, "Look there's the Head! – Oh, I think the school might be closed."

Karen wound her window down and was, apologetically, informed by the headmistress that, due to so many teachers not managing to get in, the school was closed. Karen reminded her

234

about their meeting and asked if it were possible for it to go ahead, regardless of the school closure? But, apparently, there was no representative from 'SEND' nor the 'SENCO', and so the meeting would have to be rescheduled. However, she did confirm that Paul's place was secure for at least the first term, and that they intended to match his lessons to his 'very special abilities'. She then leant into the car and offered some encouraging words to Paul, and, with some surprise, said 'hello' to Melissa and commented on her very smart attire.

"Well that was an entirely wasted journey," sighed Karen, as we turned around in the carpark.

"Yes," I said, "and we were going to stock up on things while we were here, but we'd need the space in the back and now..."

"Now we are in your way," Melissa correctly finished my sentence. "How about you buy us swimming costumes, with Daddy's card, then you could drop us off at the swimming pool? It's just there." She pointed back down the road. "How do you fancy a whole day swimming Paul?!"

Paul nodded, grinning broadly.

Karen, slightly reluctantly, agreed that Melissa's idea was sound and, providing she kept an eye on Paul and bought him some sensible food during the day, that they could go swimming. "If there are no buses, when you've had enough, give me a call, and I'll come and collect you."

After a quick trip to buy swimming costumes and towels, we dropped off Paul and Melissa at the swimming baths and so began our first shopping trip together, armed with Arthur's Debit Card.

We purchased large quantities of food, including rice and flour, but it wasn't long before I realised just how little we could squeeze onto the back seats and boot of her small Fiat. Two large shopping trolleys full of food was about the limit, and I immediately feared that we'd done little more than a family's weekly shop. We managed to squeeze in screen wash and four petrol cans, before we discovered, at the first filling station, that we were only permitted to fill two of the cans, so had to stop at another on the way back.

Traffic, on the return journey, was a little better; the landslide on the outskirts of Bishop Auckland had been cleared, and the Hinton road was open in the return direction. However, there were two blackened and burnt-out cars, still smoking in a passing point with a single police car in attendance.

Karen slowed as we passed, and stopping, she asked an officer if everyone was OK.

The young officer was white-faced, he solemnly shook his head, "No survivors, we couldn't get to them in time, the fire brigade never made it – a massive accident on the A1 and the train crash at Darlington, you see." Then he received a stern look from his superior and he waved us on.

"Oh shit," said Karen as we continued, "that poor guy looked like he was about to cry. It's starting to happen, isn't it?"

"Yes, I'm afraid it is," I replied, wondering what disasters had occurred on the A1 and at Darlington.

Karen suddenly stopped the car. "I can still smell that smoke. I want those petrol cans out of the car. Now, George!"

"Karen, we're nearly there, we'll be back in five minutes."

"Dump it all, I'm going back for Paul," Karen said.

I laughed, "Don't be silly, we can't just dump all this by the side of the road!" I squeezed her leg in a vain attempt to comfort her.

"Get all that fucking crap out of my car!" Karen yelled, pushing my hand away viciously.

I realised that there was little point in arguing with her, she had been shocked by the accident scene, and I wasn't helping. I struggled to think of a solution. "Karen, it's OK. What if I drive the short way back, dump this lot at my gatehouse and then we'll go straight back for Paul and Melissa?"

Karen, without saying anything, got out of the car. I thought she agreed and that I should drive. But soon realised that she had opened the rear door and had started unloading everything onto the grass verge.

"Wait!" I ordered, with my most authoritative voice, "Arthur won't be at all happy if we abandon this lot. Let me call Richard on his mobile, see if he can come here with his van and offload it all, then you can go back and collect the kids."

Karen froze as I tried to call Richard.

"Stop," she murmured, "I already don't like Richard, I don't want him thinking I'm nuts too."

Richard answered just as she said this.

"Hi, Richard, how'd it go with the builders?" I asked.

"All sweet mate, but really busy right now, can I call you back?" came the reply.

"Sure, no problem. See you later." I replied and ended the

call. "OK, so what *are* we going to do?" I asked.

"Oh, George, I bet you think this is a crap first date, don't you? That accident back there – it scared me. I could smell the bodies you know? – I still can… Fire has always really frightened me.
Can we just leave the petrol? Please?"

"So, we can continue to the Manor and then maybe do a repeat trip – just no petrol?"

"Forgive me? – For being an irrational idiot?" Karen said, with tearing eyes."

"Karen, your weaknesses fuel my strengths," I said earnestly, while at the same time trying to work out if there was any meaning in what I'd just said.

Karen laughed, "Where on Earth did you dig up that shit from, George?"

Together we laughed, and hugged, and I felt closer to Karen in those few mad moments than I ever had before.

We managed three more trips to Bishops Auckland after that, though each time avoiding the Hinton Road. We listened, with great sadness, to the radio as news reports came in on the horrific derailment of a high-speed train near Darlington, and terrible multiple pile-ups and fires on A1 near York, cause by 'fly blindness.' Reporters and the opposition had complained that the government had failed to act to stop the spread of PCP, while in America, they were using crop sprayers to spray weed killer over five-mile-wide strips around where the virus had landed.

Karen calmed down completely as the day went on, not phoning Paul until 4 pm only to find that he and Melissa had managed to catch a bus back after having a great day together. After she had heard this good news, I took the opportunity to ask why she'd said that she didn't like Richard.

"Well, he's got an answer for everything, his jokes are crap, and his buggering off to Lincoln once he's learnt all he can from us! Oh, and he suggested Paul should be the first to crawl into some old dungeon below the house!" Karen answered.

"Oh, well he did also contribute a lot of ideas and posed useful questions himself. I also believe he's achieved some success with the builders today, too. I like him. Can you give him another chance?" I thought that harmony at the Manor was going to be important.

"OK, I promise to review him, and if I still find I don't like him, well, he'll never know. Alright?" Karen smiled at me as we returned from our final trip through the gates of the Manor, only to find Richard, high on a ladder, opposite the gate.

"Thought he was scared of heights? – I think he's installing one of the Wi-Fi cameras. They arrived quickly!" I stated.

On rounding the gatehouse, we encountered a large builders van, towing a trailer with a digger on the back, heading towards us. As it had passed the fountain, we had no option but to reverse back through the gate and a little way up the hill to let it, and the three men in the cab, out.

"They can't have done all the work already, surely?!" I asked, as we passed Richard again. He was now down from the ladder and admiring his work. "I can't see anything!" I called out to him as we passed.

"That's the general idea!" he replied, "We've got three cameras, one covering the gate, one the gatehouse, and the third looking back towards where the portacabin is going. All on different channels, so they will be difficult to jam."

Karen stopped the car. "So the builders have started digging the water steps and trench?"

Richard looked smug, "It cost Arthur a little more than he wanted to spend, but the job's done! They even buried the pipes and drilled holes to take them down into the cellar." Then, probably gauging my slightly worried look, he added, "Don't worry, there are 4 metres of spare pipe at each end of both pipes, and the steps are 20cm deeper than a water butt, and water from that spring isn't washing it all away! It has been diverted around them."

"Wow, I'm impressed. Are the water butts up there already?" I asked.

"No, they haven't arrived, nor the sand and gravel to keep them there. I also need to source the reeds, and the right medium for them to grow in," he replied, "and we forgot to order cheese- cloths."

"What about the portacabins?" Karen asked.

"We got one coming tomorrow - it's a really old one - and a newer one with a toilet, its own lighting, heating and generator coming on Friday. I thought we'd use the older one for the book and CD exchange?"

"You have been very busy," stated Karen, then under her breath she added, "I dislike him slightly less!" and she winked at me.

"Yes, I'm cream-knackered," Richard said, "But, do have a look out the back, before it gets too dark. I think they have done a great job."

The light was fading fast by the time we finally unloaded the car into the spare garage for the fourth time. We went through the house, where Arthur greeted us as we passed the kitchen.

"You must see this." He said as soon as he saw us.

He led us into the conservatory and handed me his big pair of 8x52 binoculars. Through them, even in the poor light, I could see a vast area that had been churned up by the digger, as well as the path of the diverted streams, and the steps where the filtration tanks were to go.

"It is a bloody mess!" Arthur exclaimed, "Please tell me it is what you need? Richard kind of took over. I was not at all sure that is what you wanted?"

I carefully scanned the work before answering, "I'm sorry Arthur, but it appears to be exactly what we need! Sorry, I wasn't here myself today to oversee it, but the new guy, he's done good."

Karen held out her hands for the binoculars, and I passed them to her.

"Ah, I'm so pleased to hear that. I'm only disappointed about one thing today, then." Arthur looked at me again, as if over his glasses.

"Er, OK, you got me! What?" I asked.

"Roses, George - you forgot to prune the roses! What's going to be your excuse tomorrow, eh? Twelve large sheds and a greenhouse to build?" Arthur grinned. "Oh, on a serious note, there is going to be an emergency broadcast tomorrow, all channels and radio at 7, repeated at 9 and 10 pm. Maria gave me the tip-off. Also, earlier in the day, they are going to inform the NFU and farmers directly that the virus is going to affect crops.

I told our farmers this morning, and they took it rather badly, but at least they have a day's head start in ordering replacement crops. The government is under fire for apparently not doing anything - this is their idea of 'doing something'. God knows how they are going to maintain calm, but they will do their best, of that I am sure. Brandy anyone?"

Karen and I both rapidly declined.

"Where's Paul?" Karen asked.

"In Melissa's 'office'. They are all in there trying to get the images from the cameras down by the gate. They are having some problems with the range of the Wi-Fi, or some such."

"We are going to have an early night if you don't mind, Arthur," said Karen, "it's going to be a long day tomorrow and maybe our last chance to find anything of use in the shops."

"Ah, yes." Grinned Arthur, "very wise. Oh, it is Melissa's 16th tomorrow, so a toast and birthday cake here at 5 pm?"

As we left to collect Paul, I whispered to Karen, "Oh, we are having an early night, are we? Your place or mine?"

"Fancy squeezing into a single bed with me?" Karen asked, giving me a peck on the cheek.

"Sounds cosy!" I replied, unable to stop grinning with anticipation.

On entering Melissa's 'office,' we encountered Richard and Melissa arguing over the placement of a 2nd large monitor on her small, and now very crowded, desk. Paul was tapping away at a brand-new laptop, apparently setting it up for Melissa.

"Surely, until it's working, it can just sit on the floor?" Melissa complained.

"It's got two bars on the signal now, it will be working any time now, I can't make adjustments with it sitting on the floor!" Richard replied.

"Not working yet?" I asked.

"No!" Said Richard, frustration beginning to show in his voice.

"Give it a break, and come back with fresh eyes tomorrow," Karen calmly suggested, "You've organised some really great things out the back today, you must be tired."

"Yes," said Melissa, "please sod off, and while you're all out of here I'll find somewhere to put that bloody great monitor and sort this mess out."

"It has to be that big," sighed Richard, "as I've already explained, more than once, it is going to display four live video images, same as the one in the portacabin will. There is no point squeezing four images onto a tiny screen, we'd never see what was going on!"

"Go home, Richard," I said, "as Karen said, you've achieved a lot today. Go sleep off that frustration, it'll probably just work tomorrow."

"We can't," stated Richard, "we are going to the Black Horse, this evening, remember?"

Karen and I looked at each other in dismay. We'd both forgotten that Richard and I had agreed to try to talk to Sandy Rutherford about Peter's note.

"I think that can wait until tomorrow, can't it?" Suggested Karen.

"I don't know," said Richard rather quietly, "Arthur said there is going to be a major announcement tomorrow evening, so this could be our last chance?"

Karen was giving me a pleading look, not wanting me to go, but Peter had been a real friend, and I didn't want to risk losing this opportunity. "Sorry Karen, Richard is right, we can't risk leaving it any longer."

"Then, I'll call Molly," Karen said, "If she's working this evening she can pop into the bar and see who's there. No point going if Sandy's not there."

"Good idea," agreed Richard, "are you joining us if she is there?"

"No, thank you," Karen dismissively replied, "we'll give you a call as soon as I speak to Molly."

"Oh, OK, thanks." said Richard as it dawned on him that Karen was making it clear we would be together later. "How about you Mel? Can I buy you an early birthday drink?"

"No, I don't want another encounter with Mad Mick. Now, can I have some space to sort out *my* office, please?"

"OK, come on Paul, fish fingers and peas today! I hope that will suffice, George?" Karen couldn't resist shooting another look at Melissa but again she wasn't rewarded with even a hint of a reaction. So we all left Melissa to get on with her office reorganisation in peace.

The following morning, Arthur had been buzzing the gatehouse from 7 am, not realising that I wasn't there. He was not at all happy; *a* crane had lifted a very tatty old porta-cabin over the gate and just left it there, blocking the inward opening gates.

Melissa wasn't a happy birthday girl either; she had attempted to climb the gate and, ripping her new skirt in the process, had got herself hung up on it, half way down the other side. Richard had turned up and cut her down, but not before passing comment on her underwear, earning him a probably very deserved slap across the face.

By the time Karen and I got there, we were in a queue behind two delivery vans, a heavy flat-bed lorry with the large sacks of sand and gravel on board, as well as Richard's van.

Melissa was also still on the outside, now wearing Richard's green overalls, and Arthur was yelling at Richard, who had climbed over the gate, probably to escape from Melissa.

I'd never seen Arthur quite so angry, and my attempts to calm things down and suggest solutions were meeting deaf ears.

Finally, Karen, talking through the bars of the gate, appearing like a prisoner, managed to calm him down a little and suggested he go back to the house for a replacement skirt for Melissa, so she could at least get off to school.

We were now left with a huge problem - a puzzle to solve - and I was in my element! – I just love trying to find solutions to practical problems, and this was certainly a challenge on a grand scale.

Richard explained that he had already attempted to use Arthurs RAV-4 to tow the portacabin away from the gate, but it had barely moved before smoke started to pour from the car's clutch.

The sheds and greenhouse would be arriving soon, and both the van delivery drivers were impatient to leave; with or without having made their deliveries. I decided to try use that to our advantage; being in a hurry to get away, I hoped that we could use their muscle. Added to that, they couldn't go anywhere while Karen's car was parked behind them. But it was the flat-bed with its crane, the gravel and sand on board, that would be the key. I needed that driver to agree to help us, and hoped he wasn't either a Health & Safety freak or a jobsworth. After a brief chat with him in his cab, I discovered he was a self-employed driver, and only too happy to help.

Firstly, I got them all to back up to allow Richard to get his van out of the way by reversing it up the lane. Then, using tools and a short ladder from Richard's van, we removed the gate post toppers as Karen carefully climbed over.

With Richard, Karen and myself on the inside and all three delivery drivers, on the outside, we managed to lift off one of the heavy metal gates. After manhandling this out into the lane, we repeated this with the other one. At his point, Arthur returned and, without saying anything, passed Melissa her clothes. She changed in the back of Richard's van, and Arthur walked back to the house after casting some severely disapproving looks at his now dismantled gate and the tatty portacabin still blocking the entrance.

Richard did try to apologise to Melissa when she reappeared from his van, but she just threw his overalls into the hedge and strutted off to school. "Seems I'm not the only one who doesn't like him." said Karen, loudly enough for him to hear clearly.

I could see her words had hurt Richard, and I didn't want this rift to deepen. We needed his help and experience too. I asked Karen if she would be so good as to collect tea and coffee orders to help keep everyone on-side. I also took her car keys so that I could move her car once we'd cleared the drive.

When Karen finally got around to taking Richard's order, I could see them talking for a while. They parted after a brief hug, leaving Richard looking relieved.

We placed packing boxes between the front of the big lorry and the back of the portacabin. Then, using the crane, we lifted the far end of the portacabin allowing trolley jacks and sack barrows to slide under the leading end. Richard, one of the other van drivers, and I, attempted to steer the portacabin around the sharp bend past the gatehouse while the crane now lifted the other end off the drive, and the lorry pushed. It took twenty minutes to slowly manoeuvre it round to where the drive straightened up, and left enough space for the lorry to get in and able to employ the crane to lift and drop the portacabin into its final position.

While it did this I moved Karen's car, and Karen served teas that pacified the two van drivers, who were now finally able to make their deliveries. I couldn't help but laugh when they were delayed yet again on trying to leave, by the first delivery of sheds arriving just as they got back to the gate.

It was a long and hard day, but by the end of it, and with some intermittent help from Stuart, we had repaired the gate and constructed the ten sheds that had arrived. We spacing them as close to one another as we could, while still allowing room for the tractor, pulling its trailer, to navigate between them.

At 4.30 Melissa returned from school and found Richard and I sitting on the floor with our backs to the fountain. I had been showing Richard the hatch cover that hid the fountain's pump and power, suggesting that would be a better place to put the Wi- Fi booster and a backup battery and charger. However, we were both so tired that we'd not got back up again and had taken the opportunity to take a well-deserved rest.

"Here comes Melissa. You'd better apologise for what you said this morning, we have got a birthday cake to share with her in a little while. What *did* you say, exactly?" I asked.

"Oh, yes," Richard grimaced, "well, I was as embarrassed as she was; I found her hanging four foot off the ground, with her skirt hung up behind her head. I had to get real close to cut the material, so I thought I'd just lighten the mood with a bit of silly banter, I said, 'Loving the pink', and 'do you hang around here often?', that's all."

"Hmmm," I whispered, "I think it was the bit about 'the pink' that upset her. Anyway, here she comes, be prepared to grovel - and remember - it's her birthday!"

Melissa was distracted by all the new sheds and the portacabin as she approached, but she stopped in front of us, and we stood up respectfully.

"I see you two are hard at work - putting a few sheds up tiring, was it?" Then she turned to Richard, and, frowning a little, shook her head slowly, "As for you, well, I'm sorry. I overreacted this morning. I'd been hanging there for ages, shouting for George, not knowing he was out, trying to get my mobile out of my bag and dropping it in the process. I'd been there for over ten minutes before you showed up, and I wasn't in the mood for jokes about my knickers, or 'hanging about'!"

Richard and I turned to look at each other, and I said, "I think you've got off lightly, my friend!"

Richard put out a hand to Melissa. "I am the one who should apologise. As I just said to George, I was a bit embarrassed too and was just trying to distract you. Stupid thing to say - I know, and I'm sorry. Really no need for *you* to apologise, Melissa, I got what I deserved. Oh, and happy birthday!"

Melissa refused his handshake and instead used it to yank him in for a hug. "We'll say no more about it. But I did mention it to Daddy, so I'll have a word with him before you come in for cake, OK?" She let Richard free from her embrace. "See you two in about 15 minutes." With that, she walked off towards the house.

Once out of earshot, Richard said, "God, I thought, when she yanked me in I was going to get a knee to the crotch!"

I laughed, "I think that's more Karen's style!"

"Yeah... how long have you two been an item? I kind of fancied her for myself!" Richard grinned.

"It's early days, she's way crazier than I thought, but I mostly like that. Oh, that reminds me - Fancy a quick trip in your van to the other side of Ingle? There might be four 10Ltr cans of petrol still in a hedge!"

Chapter 9 — Dry Ice

After a pleasant late afternoon celebrating Melissa's sixteenth with champagne and birthday cake, Arthur beckoned me to one side and asked if we could meet privately in the library. Karen had tried to follow us, but Arthur had rather firmly insisted she stay with Melissa, Stuart, Paul, and Richard in the conservatory.

Sitting opposite one another in the two upright chairs, Arthur's face became sterner. "George, I was frankly dismayed this morning by the shambles down at the gate." He coughed, "I am trusting you, and you alone, to organise this trading centre venture."

I nodded. I had been expecting some strong feedback after the morning's difficulties.

"You may well nod, but it appears to me that Richard, who has been here barely five minutes, has somehow taken over. You were nowhere to be found, and while Melissa seems to have forgiven him, it was he who had to cut her down, but not before choosing to insult her first!" Arthur cleared his throat again. "So, firstly, I need you to ensure that it is *you* who oversees all the key deliveries and projects, because I am going to hold you personally responsible for their success. You are the project manager, personally accountable to me for any and all failures. Secondly, I need to know if you are not staying at the gatehouse. Oh, finally, if that Richard upsets my daughter once more, he can jolly well pack up and go to straight to Lincolnshire with my boot up his Home Counties! You understand?"

"Yes, all perfectly understood, and agreed." I conceded.

Arthur sat down slowly, "He is a likeable chap, and I saw how well you both worked together today. There's no doubt that you required another pair of hands for you to have assembled those sheds. Just reign him in a little – remind him who's boss. Stuart's a good lad too, but his practical skills need some work. I saw he wasn't being much of a help to you two, so seconded him; I had him unpacking the deliveries in the library today. He managed to barricade himself in as well as lose items under a very untidy mound of packaging! Then it took him half an hour to assemble just one wheelbarrow. He seems to lack basic tool and organisational skills, but they will come with practice. Oh, and he couldn't get the walkie-talkies to work either, he's left them all charging in Melissa's office. He is keen, and I do hope, a quick learner. What is there for him to do tomorrow?"

There were masses of jobs still to do, but finding something for Stuart to do unsupervised had me stumped for a while. Then I remembered his physical strength. "Well, he's keen on physical training, and all that sand and gravel needs barrowing onto the trailer then taking up to the springs. Did the water butts arrive? If so, three of those need to go up and be weighed down, too."

"Yes, nine of them arrived! – Why so many, my dear boy? I thought the filtration system only needed three?"

"I ordered all they had. The water will arrive in the cellar at a constant flow, and we can't have someone stuck down there 24- 7 bottling it, so two down there as a reservoir. That only leaves us with four to collect water from the portacabins, greenhouse, and sheds. Oh, damn!"

Arthur looked puzzled, "What's up?"

"We carefully spaced the sheds out to allow the tractor and trailer to manoeuvre around them, I forgot to allow for the water butts. I'm hoping to source some more, so they each have one. It will stop the whole area getting so muddy, as well as collect a lot of bathing or flushing water." I sighed at the thought of moving those we had constructed that day.

"Hmm," Said Arthur, tapping the side of his head. "Did you allow for the doors being open as the tractor passes?"

"Ah, Yes!" I answered, realising where Arthur was going.

"Well, the butts are no wider than an open door so they will just have to go next to the doors, rather than at the ends of the sheds. All you will have to do is adjust the gutters and do a bit more plumbing. And, maybe, they will make good doorstops too!" Arthur smiled and patted me on the arm. "Come on, let's see if there's any champagne left!"

Very grim faces greeted us on return to the conservatory.

You've run out of cake?" I asked, noting that Paul had disappeared.

"No," Replied Melissa solemnly, "Paul's setting up his database on my laptop. We were talking about all those poor people who lost their lives yesterday at Darlington and York. Richard said that the toll could rise to a hundred with so many having such horrific burns."

"Oh, bloody Hell, Richard! It's Mel's birthday." I said, frustrated that he'd managed to upset Melissa again.

Karen spoke up in his defence, though, "Sorry, I brought up the subject. I caught the headlines earlier - two shocking tragedies in one day and they reminded me of those cars we saw, burnt out, yesterday. I can't stop thinking about those poor families. It's so, so sad."

I thought of the people I'd encountered on the train that

Monday: I hoped that the woman with her baby and toddler had not been travelling again. Then a wave of deeper sadness suddenly engulfed me; because it was far more likely that the kind old ticket inspector would have been on the train, and I remembered that he was just weeks away from retiring.

Just then Paul entered, "The phone was ringing and ringing so I answered it. Andrea Parker, she wants to speak to you." He tugged my arm for me to go to the phone.

"Thank you, Paul, you did the right thing." I gave him a small hug as I passed him, "Excuse me, I should take this…"

"What does *she* want?" Melissa demanded to know.

Karen and I shared a look of curiosity, and some confusion, at her reaction. Then it occurred to me that maybe, Melissa thought that Karen and I were just pretending to be together for her benefit? Whatever it was, I soon discovered, on picking up the receiver, that both Melissa and Karen had followed me into Melissa's office.

"Hello Andrea, how are you?" I asked, trying not to show my two inquisitors too much interest.

"Oh, you are there, George, good." Andrea sounded worried and scared, "I want to ask your advice on something, are you alone? It's very sensitive."

Karen mouthed 'Sensitive?' and frowned as they both leant in to hear better.

"Er, no. Hang on a minute." I pointed at the door and then waved them out, but neither moved an inch. "Out!" I shouted, and pushed them both towards the door. Reluctantly they left, and I closed the door behind them.

"What is it, Andrea?" I asked.

There was a pause before she answered, "I know something, and I'm not sure if I should inform the current government or not? I hate myself for ever getting involved in this, I really do, but they might find out soon anyway. There's bound to be someone in the opposition who will remember the project?" Andrea paused, then seemed to realise that I couldn't have understood what she'd meant. "Project Dry Ice: It was a secret research project commissioned by the last government. I headed it up, and I'm the only member of the team who had access to the results and progress, before the coalition came in and it was buried."

"Project Dry Ice?" I questioned, what did it do, make stage smoke?"

"Don't be flippant!" Andrea angrily replied, "Maybe I'm asking the wrong person. I thought I could trust your independent judgement?"

"Okay, look, I'm sorry. Please do go on." I sat down, after first checking that Karen and Melissa didn't have their ears to the door.

"Alright," she sighed, "In 2005 I accepted an off-campus commission to try to develop a positive-sense single-stranded RNA virus modified from Polymyxa graminis... Oh, sorry! In English: I was tasked to modify an existing root-infecting virus so that it would prevent rice from taking up water. Basically, to do to rice what PCP now does to grass, only with very different methodology."

"Er, so you were secretly commissioned, and funded, to create a virus that would make rice die, and that project was called Dry Ice?" I was still confused; Andrea didn't seem the type of person who would accept such a destructive commission. "Why would you want to get involved in something that could devastate a whole nation's food supply?"

Andrea sighed again, "I was just 20 and had no funding. I got a whole lab, equipment, computers, and the use of 3 undergraduates. Also, they said that the research would ensure that any such virus, naturally-developing, could be defended against if we understood how it might function."

"And *you* believed *that*?!" I asked, not attempting to hide my disbelief.

There was a further pause before Andrea answered, "No, not really. Anyway, after a couple of years, my morality finally kicked in, and I reported that we were failing to produce an effective virus, and used the lab for other research instead. When the government changed, the funding stopped, and Dry Ice was shelved. Then, in April 2010, some kids broke in, trashed all our computers and burnt the paperwork."

"Hmmm, kids, eh? Convenient." I muttered. "But why are you telling me this?"

"Because, I kept a backup memory stick with all the data, and because Dry Ice *was* successful. I do know how to recreate a rice-specific virus, although I denied Dry Ice ever succeeded at the time. I wanted to ask you if you thought it was in the national interest to tell the Prime Minister now, since we know the Chinese almost certainly developed PCP?"

"Fucking Hell, Andrea! I wish I'd not heard any of this. You give this to him, and he'll use it, I'm sure of it. He'll be pressured into using it, tit-for-tat, or the Americans will tell him to. I don't want to be anywhere near a decision that has the potential to kill millions of people! It's just... ah, shit, Andrea! I don't know, I just don't know!"

"I'm sorry George - Welcome to my world. I couldn't think of anyone else who might understand, but I had to tell someone. Someone who wouldn't either use it for profit, or try to make news headlines with it."

My mind had become foggy, it does this when faced with a problem that I don't want to, or am incapable of dealing with. I felt a strong desire to hang up on Andrea and just leave her to deal with a problem that was, after all, almost entirely of her making. But from somewhere an idea began to form. "Andrea, I'll need to speak to Arthur about this, is that OK?"

"If you're sure he'll keep it to himself?" Andrea replied, hesitantly.

"Yes, he's completely trustworthy. I suggest you don't do, or say, anything yet. Let's see what this official announcement is - that may give us a better idea of how the government is likely to react."

"OK, I guess it can wait. Did you know that Jihadists have been deliberately spreading the virus south and to London? Apparently, their websites are encouraging them to spread it to all non-Muslim countries. France has closed the channel tunnel, and all ferry ports, as well as refusing any flights with passengers who have travelled from Britain or America."

"I'd not heard that, no; I've had little time to catch the news. But maybe those nut-jobs spreading it around might be doing us all a favour?" I suggested.

"Yes, like you suggested at Whitehall!" Andrea confirmed, with less fear apparent in her voice. "It's also made everyone aware that this isn't just some Northern issue that is sure to be cured before it gets to their little back gardens. Personally, having watched the spread via infection reporting, it's clear it jumps rivers, even those in flood, as if they are not there."

I agreed, "Birds probably. No doubt seagulls will take it to France and way beyond, including to all Muslim countries. Even China might get infected." The phone fell silent for a few seconds. "Andrea, have you thought any more about coming up here? We *are* building a self-sufficient community and it might be safer for you, especially if anyone starts asking questions about Dry Ice."

"Yes, George, that had crossed my mind but there are a few things that prevent me: Primarily, should I need to recreate the virus, all of which was destroyed, then I'd need full lab facilities. Dry Ice is not something you can knock up on a kitchen table after a quick trip to the pharmacy! Then there's my current research and collaboration with Peta and Cambridge to try to develop an antidote to PCP. Oh, and there's one other thing…"

"Yes?" I asked as the line fell silent again.

Finally, and rather hesitantly, she continued, "Well, I'm going to have to try to be tactful here: You see I like you, George, we got along so effortlessly, but, well, I hope you weren't inviting me up there for anything more? You see, I don't, I'm not… oh, well, the thing is - I just don't fancy you, George. I'm going to use that terrible old line 'You're not my type', and I'm not sure that you didn't invite me thinking we could have a future together as a couple? Or have I misread you completely?"

"Ah," I did feel a little disappointed; with Melissa and Karen now both showing an interest in me, I had foolishly been toying with the idea that I might have suddenly become very attractive to the opposite sex, and that the beautiful Andrea Parker may have also fallen under my spell. However, I wasn't too surprised. This wasn't the first time I'd misinterpreted simple friendliness for attraction. My schoolboy fantasy of building myself a little harem at the Manor would have to be abandoned! Her beauty wasn't the only reason I'd invited her though; Andrea was a scientist who possessed great knowledge and understanding, and she would be an asset to our community. "I see, well though I'm obviously heartbroken," I said in my most sarcastic voice, "I want you here for your brains. Besides, I'm actually in a relationship. Early days, but I think it's going to work."

"Oh, sorry George, I should have trusted your motives. Who's the lucky lady then? What does she do?" Andrea inquired.

I hesitated before answering. Having to explain that Karen was a cleaner was somehow embarrassing. Something I'd not considered before. I had to remind myself, quite forcibly, that I was 'only a gardener!' Also, that Karen certainly wasn't defined by her job title any more than I should be. "Her name's Karen, she's the cleaner at the Manor, and mother to a wonderful autistic boy called Paul."

"Oh, I'm happy for you. I hope I can get to meet them sometime. And, if I do end up there, I'd be glad to help out with the cleaning or cooking, I did both while getting through university." Karen replied. "Anyway, I'm glad we got that cleared up. I've got to go now. Please call me when you and Arthur have had a chance to discuss Dry Ice."

We ended the call, and I returned to the conservatory to find the room empty. I could hear voices from the sitting room and ventured in to find everyone huddled around the big television waiting for the first government emergency announcement. Both Karen and Melissa shot me slightly disapproving looks, which I dismissed by smiling and shaking my head. I stood watching the television, choosing not to take either of the vacant seats next to Karen or Richard.

The television volume had been turned down, and we debated

and speculated on who would present the announcement and what they would say? I read the running news headlines that scrolled across the bottom of the screen: A man had been arrested after pushing infected turf through the rails of Buckingham Palace. The death toll from the rail and road accidents in Yorkshire had reached 101 with 40 remaining seriously injured. The channel tunnel was now closed in both directions. The French, Belgians, and Dutch had closed their borders to anyone travelling from Britain, and an EasyJet flight, very low on fuel, had managed to return to Bournemouth after permission to land at Geneva airport had been refused. All air passengers were being advised to check flight information before travelling to an airport. Diplomats at the Chinese Embassy in London, and Consulate General of the People's Republic of China, had been expelled. This after the expulsion by the Chinese, of American and British ambassadors, and staff from Beijing.

Eventually, the scrolling text started to repeat the grim messages, and I looked up, realising that everyone had stopped talking and were all looking at me with wide smiles on their faces.

"Sorry, my dear boy," said Arthur, "are we boring you?"

The others laughed, and Karen said, "We were all watching your face as you read those headlines."

"Yes," I said, not really impressed that they'd found my expressed concerns funny, "it's all becoming very serious. Sorry for being interested in the possible end of humanity, but this is the first chance I've had to catch up with the news."

Melissa spoke up, "Sorry George, one of the things we had been talking about earlier was how we hide our fears behind humour."

"Ah," cut in Arthur forcefully, "it is about to start." He reached for the remote control, and turned up the volume.

'There follows an emergency message from the Prime Minister' the typical BBC male voice clearly stated.

I took my seat beside Karen, and she snuggled up to me as, in total silence, we listened to the message.

Good evening. Our thoughts today are with those many families who have lost loved ones in Yorkshire. My government has already begun to broadcast a series of public information films with the aim of preventing further loss of life on our roads. We have also implemented speed restrictions on many parts of the rail network where there are similar risks of landslides.

Today, I have to tell you, that Britain faces a crisis that, if not managed correctly, could become a greater challenge than that which we faced together in 1940's. As we did then, the proud people of Great Britain must come together, work together, and succeed together. Everyone will have to resist the temptation to react selfishly and worsen the problems we now face.

Today, I spoke personally to many leading arable farmers, as well as senior representatives from the National Union of Farmers. I had to advise them that the virus responsible for the grass fungus, fly blindness, and landslides, will also infect the majority of our traditional cereal crops.

However, while this does mean our farmers have a very difficult task ahead of them - switching to the many crops that will not be affected - it does not mean there will be significant food shortages during the next 18 months or so. It is for this reason that I have to ask each and every one of you to shop and buy provisions as you usually would. It is important that you do not add additional items to your shopping baskets that may deprive others of the food they require. It is for this reason that I have asked all the key supermarkets to close until 9 am tomorrow. Allowing them time to set up systems to limit the value of food items purchased in any one visit to £150, and to recognise if an individual should attempt to return to the store within five days. The reason we have instigated this is solely because there will be a minority of people who will seek to deprive others of food while they hoard unnecessary quantities for themselves. This selfish behaviour will not be tolerated.

Let me be clear; the security of the food chain, and the management of our significant reserves, is of paramount importance. Your government will be ensuring that food gets to hospitals, to schools and colleges, in fact to all our key workers, as well as to your local stores and homes.

Since the recent discovery of PCP, my government has called two Cobra meetings and has listened carefully to the views of many expert special advisors. We have faced criticism for not reacting against the advice of our experts by spraying weed killer, as the Americans have done, to try to restrict the spread of the virus. Well, I have to report, that those efforts to restrain the virus, in America, have been unsuccessful, as my advisers suggested they would be.

We firmly believe, that the best way to defeat this terrible virus is to exhaust it of its nutrients, to starve it so that it does not reoccur when seeds, already in the soil, start to germinate in the spring. My advisors concur that it is better to distribute this virus across the whole country as fast as possible.
Although temporarily devastating to our lawns and hillsides, we have to take the long-term view.

What my government has also been doing, is securing the food distribution network by working hard with suppliers and the delivery systems to ensure the security of the food supply chain, and our ability to distribute our reserves wisely.

Every government, during times of potential crisis, has to seek help from its proud people by asking them not to over-react. And it is to you that I am making the following requests:

The camera slowly zoomed in on the Prime Minister's face.

Purchase no more food than you would usually. Those who may consider hoarding food for their own use, need to understand this: By acting selfishly, you will create unnecessary shortages for others, and you will be personally responsible for their hardship.

You should continue to go to work, pay taxes, and trust the government to guarantee the security of the food chain. Expect temporary shortages, expect to face a more limited range of products, as those reliant upon wheat and grass become scarce. There are many, many alternative and nutritious crops that we are able to both grow and import that are not related to grass.

Be assured that our top scientists are working around the clock to create an entirely new range of virus-resistant crops, as well as seeking to find an antidote to the virus currently infecting our grasses.

Let me be clear to you all: This is a serious crisis. Together we face a multitude of unique challenges. But I trust and have faith in the proud peoples of England, Scotland and, Wales, to work with us to ensure that these challenges are all met head-on and defeated.

In the coming months, we can expect further transport disruption, and temporary shortages of certain products, until the network is repaired. Our engineers are already working to prevent further embankment erosion; using both traditional engineering methods and seeding with new plants that will bind the soil together in the same way that grass did previously.

I am sorry, there is no quick-fix: There isn't a spray that will either stop the spread of PCP nor eradicate it. And let me make it very clear: This is not the time for party politics, we will not be distracted by negative arguments, nor invalid criticisms. It is the time to work together, to once again show the world that we, the people of Great Britain, can rise to any challenge.

"That was a government emergency broadcast. An extended news programme replaces advertised programmes until 9 pm, when this emergency message will be repeated."

"Hmmm..." Muttered Arthur, as he reached for the remote and muted the volume, "Well he has finally come clean, and was probably wise to compare this with the Blitz: We work together, unselfishly, or we all suffer."

"Oh my God!" Shouted Melissa, with sudden concern "Chocolate! – without milk, there won't be any chocolate!"

"Oh, that is a serious omission indeed," Karen chipped in, without a hint of the sarcasm I expected her to add.

Then Arthur joined in with "What kind of government omits to mention chocolate?"

I looked from one of them to another, and saw only stony, serious faces, and just for a moment I wondered if there was something significant about chocolate that I was missing? But then I saw Richard's nostrils flaring slightly, and I knew he had scripted these ridiculous comments while I had been on the telephone.

"Oh, very amusing, Richard, I guess this was your idea?" Laughter broke out, and Richard nodded, grinning from ear-to-ear. Laughter wasn't something I'd expected after such a serious broadcast, but it was a welcome relief nonetheless.

Chapter 10 – Isolated

My diary entries from Friday 11th September were more like a list of failures and fixes than what I had expected, and indeed hoped for:

Stuart had forgotten to put the cheesecloths in the bottom of the final water butt. Then he decided he'd redirect the water through the system without either telling anyone, nor checking to see if the pipes in the basement were actually connected to anything. The water overwhelmed the first two butts and ran straight into the third, so he succeeded in washing all the sand from that onto the floor in the cellar, before the pipe got completely blocked. I was summoned to talk to Arthur once again and then had to walk to the Black Horse where Stuart, filled with embarrassment and shame, had decided to drink himself into a stupor and needed escorting home.

I did get to speak to Molly, who had called me from the pub, when I went to collect him. She was just as I remembered her from the Manor; happily overweight, with an almost permanent smile, bright red cheeks, and a loud, infectious laugh. She pointed out Stuart, who was slumped over a table in the corner in the partitioned section to the right of the bar. He looked pale and ill.

Molly laughed, "He's not a champion *drinker*, that's for sure! His usual tipple is a glass of water, or, on very special occasions, he might 'splash-out' and have a J-2O. Today he gulped down a pint of Cumberland Ale before ordering a double whisky!"

"What? That's all he's had?" I looked over at his long, limp, body as he struggled to get up and stagger off towards the toilets, with his hand over his mouth.

"No!" yelled Molly, *Not* the kitchen, to your left... Turn left!"
Molly shook her head and laughed "Guess the loos are going to
need a good mopping-up sometime very soon!"

I looked over towards the toilet door, and realised that all the
walls had been painted a pale lime green, "What's with the weird
décor? Are you sure it's not the paint job that's made him ill?"

Molly's grin widened. "Not *my* idea, but Mick absolutely hates it,
so anything that keeps him away... Fancy a bowl of chips,
George? You're way too skinny, you know?"

I looked again towards the toilet.

"Oh, he's gonna be a while yet!" Molly assured me.

"Go on then!" I replied, "and a pint of White Boar too,
please. I've never tried that one."

At the bar of the near empty pub, I enjoyed my beer as we
talked, shared the chips, and reminisced. I discussed our plans
for the Manor, which Molly seemed to dismiss as being 'rather
unnecessary', preferring instead to talk about Lady Jayne's
reappearance. I confirmed the rumours that she had surfaced
again, but only to organise a divorce. Molly seemed to hold no
malice towards Lady Jayne, despite the fact that her sudden
departure had resulted in her losing her job at the Manor. She
said that she was a well-educated and caring lady, who must
have had her reasons. I mentioned Peter's note, but she'd still
not seen either Mick or Sandy, so agreed that she would tell
Sandy that I had a note from her grandfather, and to come and
find me at the Manor.

"Are you on your own today, Molly?" I asked, realising
that neither the Landlord nor his wife seemed to be there.

"Yes, they've had to make a second trip to the cash 'n'

carry. Some big pub chain had cleared them right out when they went on Thursday, and on Friday they'd still not restocked. It's going to be a very limited menu if they don't come back with some stock tonight. Those stupid limits at the supermarkets mean they can no longer fall back on them for supplies.

Then the door opened and a woman entered slowly, "Hello! Er, excuse me?" she said rather timidly, "can you tell me where the waterfalls are?"

"Wrong Ingleton!" Came a chorus from Molly and two old chaps sitting by the fruit machine.

"Oh!" the woman looked puzzled, "Is it far – this other Ingleton?"

Molly gave the woman a warm smile, "I'm sorry, it's about seventy miles away. You're in Durham and the Waterfalls Trail is in the Yorkshire Dales!"

The woman gave a big sigh, "Oh that bloody man and his satnav I told him we were going too far north! Sorry to have bothered you!"

As the door closed, Molly said to the two old chaps, "I think she's the fifth this summer?"

They nodded in agreement.

"Oh, George, you'll never guess what happened to me at Sainsbury's in Tindale?"

I shook my head.

"A bloody 'Facebook anti-hoarding mob' actually challenged *my* usual weekly shop this morning!" Molly winked. "I told them I'd got a husband and six kids to feed! – No bloody mob of self-appointed do-gooders is going to stop me enjoying my food!"

I laughed, "Well, maybe *you* will be knocking at our door soon?"

"Hmmm?" Molly scratched her head as if pretending to be deep in thought, "Well, I'm not sure what I've got to trade with? That is unless you need some lady's clothes? I've got three-year-old size 20 dresses, two-year-old size 22, and soon…" She waved her hand down the one she was wearing and gave me a look that was almost daring me to comment or laugh.

I knew Molly well enough to be able to joke with her, so I nodded thoughtfully and looked over her dress very carefully "Yes, OK. I'll take that one now, if you don't mind. That's got to be worth at least one… yes, one small new potato."

I got a pretend angry glare from Molly before she was distracted by Stuart, who had reappeared from the toilet. Instead of heading back to his seat, he made his way along the bar using one hand as support. "George! I'm so, so, sorry mate! There's sand in the cellar. I'm so sorry - it's all my fault. Arthur is angry, and now I think I've got food poisoning too! – I've just been sick and don't feel well, and I'm sorry about all the sand, and there's water too."

"Food poisoning in the Black Horse! Really?" said Molly. Then, sarcastically; "not alcohol poisoning from the beer and whisky, eh?"

"Come on Stuart, I'll walk you home. Just don't be sick on me! Thanks for the chips Molly, see you again soon, I hope." I pulled Stuart up from his slouched position and guided him to the door.

When I arrived back at the Manor, two large vans loaded with reeds for Richard's alternative water filter system arrived.

Arthur, still not in a good mood, questioned the huge number of plants, and if we still needed a second system 'equally capable of flooding his house?' I still wasn't convinced either but assured him that I would fit automatic float valves to prevent any further flooding.

Melissa and Richard spent the entire weekend - not excavating the cellar to locate the old generator, or planting the reeds - but clearing out all the sand and water from the cellar. They then used mains water pressure to clear the pipe while I worked up by the springs and adjusted the contents and flow rates of the three water butts, so that they were not overwhelmed, and that any excess water would bypass the butts and continue down to the lake.

By Monday lunchtime, we had our first clear water arriving down in the cellar. Reluctantly I had to agree that Richard had been right; we needed a second system. The flow rate was a little more than one litre per hour. Just enough for our own use, but insignificant if we were to supply drinking water to the locals as well.

Arthur listened to my interpretation of what Andrea Parker had divulged about Dry Ice when I caught him alone in the conservatory. He barely reacted at all. He didn't comment on my idea at all either. He just said, when I'd finished, "Tell no one, no one at all." Then he walked off. I guessed he either simply didn't want to be involved, or that he would deal with it and disassociate me from it, and its possible consequences.

Richard spent Tuesday through to Thursday adjusting the slope and route of his reed beds. I had imagined a simple path straight down the hill. Instead, he zig-zagged the stream in terraces, so that the water travelled through about 250 metres of reeds before collecting in a large loft water tank that was plumbed into the second pipe to the cellar. We all helped plant the reeds into the deep, sodden, peat-filled tracks, until Melissa slipped and fell, face-first, into the black mush. Wiping it out of her eyes, she glared at each of us, daring any of us to laugh, before trudging off back to the house. Not surprisingly, she didn't return to the hill that day.

Karen and Paul placed our first posters up on the church notice board, in the Post Office, and on all the post boxes in the area on Friday morning.

Quite excitedly, I expected people to start arriving at the Manor the same day, if not to trade, to find out what we were doing. But no one came until the following Tuesday.

We did get a surprise visit from a Tesco van: The driver had apparently been talking to Richard. He dropped off a whole load of food that was short-dated, in damaged packaging, or dented tins. "I didn't want to see this lot go to waste when I expect people will be glad of it anytime soon," he explained, before asking us to deny he'd ever been. This generous delivery gave Paul a chance to play with his new bar-code scanner. There were a whole lot of new items that he and Karen busied themselves valuing and storing in our new sheds.

Richard had come up with an idea that we could leave the two sheds nearest the gate unsecured, and that these would contain only foodstuffs we had too much of. Therefore, if anyone broke in, they could take that food without doing any damage. We could also monitor them on the hidden cameras, and offer them help if they returned regularly. These two sheds got the nicknames 'Spud and Carrot' because we all felt sure our farmers would over-supply both.

The national news over the same week wasn't as bad as I had predicted: The government had - quite wisely, Arthur said - formed an emergency, cross-party cabinet. Sceptics, of course, claimed that this was to share the blame when everything went wrong, but it did reduce party political squabbling, and resulted in a united message from this unusual coalition. There were endless reports of road closures and delays, as the virus and heavy rain spread throughout the South. However, there were no further major disasters, such as those that had hit Yorkshire so badly.

Social network groups set themselves up as 'hoarder patrols' that reported and shamed those who appeared to be buying excessive quantities of food. There were a few fights and scuffles, but out-of-control panic-buying was limited to a few shops in inner cities and was quickly brought under control.

TV news and radio programmes debated and discussed the issue almost constantly, yet there seemed to be an unusual restraint in their reporting. I felt it was maybe all manipulated to reduce fear and panic? There were experts reciting ever-growing lists of food and drink products that would be affected, and another expert stated that the wheat market alone was worth 95 billion pounds a year. But there were also constant reminders that we wouldn't have benefitted from the next harvests until the following year anyway. Government advisors were always on-hand to report that scientific progress was being made, and that a cure, and replacement crops, would probably be available before any widespread shortages.

The national newspapers were less restrained; they continually reported on the many tens of thousands of cereal-related employees that would soon be out of work, and listed the names of the big casualties, such as Allied Bakeries, Guinness, Weetabix, Kellogg's, Jordan's, Hovis, and McDougall's. Share trading in these and other food-related companies had been suspended on the morning following the Prime Minister's first announcement. But the FTSE 100 and worldwide markets still fell dramatically, as the news circulated, with predictions that the virus would spread to mainland Europe, and on to the vast wheat fields of Russia.

News from America was worse than anyone here had expected, and was used by the British media as an example of the chaos that could happen in the UK if we didn't adhere to the government's directives. American news was an endless stream of reports detailing mass looting, riots, murders, and massacres in food stores. Curfews were imposed and breached. Fires were started and left to burn uncontrollably. Marshall law had been imposed, but the army and police were taking losses against such a heavily-armed general public. The President pleaded and begged for calm, and promised that no one needed to go hungry, but it was too late: The death toll became uncountable, and there were widespread blackouts as the fires in city, after city, raged on. The US-hosted sites including Facebook, Twitter and Google had outages before failing completely. Their internet collapsed, unable to rely solely on European servers for network interconnection across the States.

Arthur seemed to take the news from America very badly. After a week of ever-worsening news, he began to just sit in silence all day, and late into the evening, watching Sky News. Karen said that she had gone to bring him tea, and found him with tears rolling down his face. She came to find me, and suggested we both go and talk to him. However, when we went in, he was standing, and switching off the news. He looked up, grim-faced, and announced, as he got up to leave, "It is all over for that great nation I fear. I simply can't bear to watch any more of that wanton self-destruction. There is not even a glimmer of hope."

Meanwhile and over the following week, we finished plumbing in all the water butts to the sheds and the new greenhouse. The reed beds had been finished, and water was flowing through them, but straight into the lake. Richard had explained that the water would not be safe until the plants had fully established, and that they could take several months. We did manage to measure the flow rate to the hillside tank; a much more

271

impressive 24 Litres per hour.

Under Paul's direction, we continued to fill the sheds. Paul had gone from being very indecisive on what should be stored, and where, to completely dictatorial; every item *had* to be placed in its allocated space. He got very upset, if while he was at school, anyone dared to put things into 'his sheds' without his personal direction. Karen and I both became very impressed and proud of his achievements: Not only was he organising everything - recording expiry dates and calculating values - but he had also gone to Arthur on his own and requested additional racking, so that more could be stored in each shed. Paul also remembered where almost everything was. We would challenge him on where items were stored; for example, where tinned tomatoes were. He was able to state which in which shed and also that they were between the tins of red salmon and kidney beans. It took us a while to realise that his storage system was not based on sweet and savoury, or ingredients and ready to eat; his order was based purely on colour. Karen had mentioned that he judged his food more by appearance than on taste.

On Tuesday, we had our first visitors responding to our posters. Karen and I excitedly rushed down to oversee Paul, who had alerted us to their arrival. Two scruffy-looking teenagers, complete with hoodies and an apparent inability to say anything coherently, had come to exchange some computer games - followed by an old lady in her late nineties who, even with Karen's assistance, took ten minutes to get from the gate to the portacabin. By the time she had arrived, Paul somehow managed to persuade the 'hoodies' to leave what they had brought, despite the fact we had nothing of interest for them. They, clearly unimpressed, just wandered off, muttering between themselves and clutching a bunch of Whitney Houston CD's that Paul had pressed on them. We later found the CD's discarded just outside the gate.

The old lady was exceptionally frail and permanently bowed forward with the curvature of her spine. Karen told Paul to give up his chair for her as she helped her in.

As I knelt before her tiny frame, I saw how her deep blue eyes appeared remarkably young and alert. They penetrated mine as if reading an open book. She quietly asked: "What would you like me to do for you, to receive your food vouchers?"

I smiled warmly, as I struggled with her question, not wishing to portray the fact that I doubted she could be of any help at all. "Can you sew or knit?" I asked hopefully.

She raised her tiny wrinkled hands, and, as they trembled before me, mottled with sunspots and dark purple veins, said: "I'm very much afraid that arthritis no longer permits such pleasures."

I looked at Karen for an answer but found that she had slipped away. The old lady's eyes drew me back, and I noticed a brown cord around her neck. "What's that?" I asked, stalling for time to think.

She gently pulled the cord to reveal an intricately hand-carved, cherry-wood cross, some four inches long. Unusually, it portrayed the nails and bindings of a crucifix, yet there was no figure upon the cross, only the shadow of one. "You are wondering where Jesus is?" The old lady asked, knowingly.

"I was. That's obviously very special to you; it's beautifully crafted. Is it very old?"

"Timeless." She whispered as if divulging a secret.

Then it came to me: "Are you able to pray for us?" I asked. "Every day." She answered with a broad, warm smile. "Paul," I turned to Paul, who was giving me a curious look,

"This lady is to get seven food tokens every week in exchange for prayers." I was sure Paul would question this, or ask how he could account for the trade on his system, but he just nodded and smiled at the old lady, who winked back at him.

Stuart returned, accompanied by his parents, on Saturday afternoon. It was a gloriously sunny day, and a welcome break from the constant cloud cover we had been experiencing. Their arrival at the gate successfully triggered our cameras, and their passage, past our little village of sheds, appeared on screens in the gatehouse, portacabin, and the house, simultaneously. Stuart was still a little shame-faced when I greeted him. I shook hands with his parents, both of whom were very cold and dismissive of me, and my attempts to explain to Stuart that the cellar had all been cleared up, and no harm had been done. Instead, they insisted that they speak to Arthur directly.

I led them to the house, where Arthur was apparently expecting them. He greeted them and welcomed them in. I, apparently not welcome to join them, was left standing outside on the steps. From that vantage point, I surveyed the new structures in the low, yellow, late September light. Yellow, red and orange leaves still fluttered, silently, from the trees - their colours enhanced by the warm light. Long shadows seemed to deepen the three-dimensional look and symmetry of the sheds, while the greenhouse at the back was reflecting light back through them like a searchlight, creating stronger and more jagged shadows that crossed paths with the others. I realised that I no longer noticed that there was no grass. Brown had become the new 'normal' colour for the ground and the surrounding hills.

"Stopped for a rest, have we, George?" Richard had joined me on the steps.

"Yeah, it's been a few weeks since I stopped to look at what we've achieved. I'd hardly have recognised the place if I'd not been here as that lot went up." I sighed, realising that I was now starting to have serious doubts about the whole project. "You know I'm beginning to wonder if any of this is necessary? The general public is putting blind trust in the official announcements. They believe that this is 'a short-term problem that science will have solved by the New Year'. We are not getting the chance to explain to anyone what we are actually attempting to do."

Richard screwed up his face, and shook his head. "This is just the calm before the storm, my friend," he said ominously. "You've heard what's happening across the Atlantic. Well, the
UK won't remain isolated from that forever. I just hope you guys can manage it when it gets here." He looked at me questioningly. "Here, take one of these." He unclipped one of two walkie-talkies from his belt, and handed it to me. "That Stuart is a knob- head! He charged them up OK, then set all eight to different channels - 1 through to 8 - before telling Arthur that they didn't work!"

I laughed as I studied the walkie-talkie. "He's just come back with his parents. Gone to have a moan to Arthur I think?" I pressed the call button on the handset and released it quickly as it made a fierce screech, with it being so close to Richard's.

"Feedback!" stated Richard.

Our handsets then both clicked as Paul's voice crackled from both of them "Hello? Paul in cabin 1 responding. Over."

We laughed, and Richard leant across to turn the volume of mine down before replying "Just testing Paul – thank you!"

Paul replied, "You need to say 'over and out'. Over."

Richard grinned again, "Blood Hell," he muttered, "that kid's a stickler for rules."

I used the excuse to try mine out. "Sorry, Paul. Over and out."
Then "Karen. Two cups of tea to the front steps, please.
Over."

"F-off. Over and out." came Karen's blunt reply.

We both laughed again, before I confirmed that Arthur
hadn't been given a handset yet.

"I've got a question for you, George," Richard said, stroking his
chin as if thinking hard about something. "I've been here over
ten days now, employed as a gardener. Do you think, just
maybe, I should do some gardening? You know, before I leave
for Lincoln?"

I had been harbouring thoughts that Richard, having
discovered how much work was involved setting up a trading
centre, would maybe have reconsidered his plans to leave us.
"Are you still thinking of setting up all over again, down
there?"

Richard smiled and patted me on the arm, "I'll miss you too my
friend, but I've got to do this – for my family. I'm going next
Wednesday, the 23rd. I've been in touch with the students at the
house. Six are very keen to stay, and have begun setting things
up already. My sister and her family are now there, and one of
the students has invited his two siblings to join them too. We
don't have Arthur's big budget, but we do have more bodies and
less to build: We have a large, secure, barn. Plus, an unused
stable block to use as a shop front. We've even got a well in the
courtyard and bee hives! If it all goes shit-shaped here, you'd all
be very welcome to come and join us. We've set up a 100 watt
AM CB-Radio and a 'big twig', so we should still be able to
communicate if the phones go down. Arthur ordered us one
from the States ten days ago, and I hope it gets here before

Wednesday, so that I can set it up."

I was instantly jealous of his set-up. He had the additional manpower; at least eleven adults, where at Ingleton, we'd be left with just three - assuming Stuart was staying - plus an old man, a teenage girl, and Paul. "Wow, that sounds like a better set-up already! A lot of mouths to feed though, and what's a 'big twig'?"

Richard gave me a bemused look. "Do I detect a hint of jealousy, George? But you're right; we'll need to produce more food ourselves, and we don't have the advantage of having two local farmers on-side either. I will go and try to talk to the local farmer. Oh, and a 'big twig' is just the name for the CB aerial. I was into CB, big-time, back in the 80's, I'm embarrassed to admit!"

"I see." I wasn't sure that these CB radios would have the range, but it would be great if we were able to keep in touch. Secretly, I had hoped that his centre would fail and he'd come back with some of the ecology students, but, at the same time, I wished it - and other similar communities around the country - luck. If they prospered, they might eventually trade with one another. For now, I was beginning to feel more and more isolated. Maybe Ingleton was too far away from big towns and cities? Maybe no- one else would come? "There are some unopened boxes in the library," I said, "I think Arthur was waiting for Stuart to return to deal with them - maybe the CB is here already? - But, it's a lovely day, and you did say you wanted to do some gardening!"

Richard looked around and nodded slowly, "Well, there is nothing major left to construct. I picked up another 120 litres of petrol and 40 of diesel this morning. None of the local garages have any jerry-cans left now!"

"Excellent. Well, I guess we are about as ready as we can be, as

277

a trading and bartering centre, so yes… to the garden we must go! Do you want to half-cut the buddleia that's all around the perimeter? Then I could start on the rose bushes at the back. Arthur's been on my case for weeks to prune those."

I'd only just started pruning the second rose bush when my radio crackled, and Karen's voice asked me to meet with Arthur in the conservatory. I acknowledged the request and looked towards the conservatory, where I could just make out Stuart's lanky figure sitting in one of the wicker chairs.

As I arrived, I heard Arthur saying goodbye to Stuart's parents, 'Gordon and Sandra'. I waited in the hallway for him to return.

"Ah, George, there you are. Sorry to tear you away from my roses, yet again, but there are a couple of things I need to discuss with you - Firstly, as I'm sure you know, Karen and Paul are moving into the house next weekend. They are going to take two of the spare rooms on the first floor. I was hoping that, while we still have access to Richard's van, that you could help them move in?" Arthur peered over his glasses at me for a reply.

"Well, yes, I'd already agreed to help. That's no problem at all. Although I think Richard will have gone by then?" I answered. "Maybe we could move some of the big stuff tomorrow?"

"Ah, good man. Yes, check with Karen, would you?" said Arthur, as he took me by the arm and walked me very slowly towards the conservatory. "Now, we are to have another house guest. Stuart's parents are selling up and are moving south. Gordon's brother works for McVities and so is very likely to lose his job soon. They have both found teaching posts down there so they can ensure he can keep up payments on their old family home, or some-such. Anyhow, young Stuart wants to stay here, and as much as his parents are unhappy about it, they have agreed - providing I give him safe lodgings and some kind of employment."

"Well, I'm sure I can find him a lot to do when people start arriving, and I can always do with some muscles to chop and move wood, etc." I agreed.

"Yes, he's a good chap, and Melissa seems to like him. Time to forgive and forget the whole sand-in-the-cellar incident. Now with Melissa and I still rattling about on the top floor, we still have four rooms and possibly the gatehouse going spare?" Arthur stopped walking just before the closed conservatory door.

My heart began to race at the mention of 'my' gatehouse. What did he mean? "But, I'm in the gatehouse, Arthur."

"Well now, here is an opportunity for you, my dear boy. Not wishing to pry - and I have not said a word to Karen, obviously - but there's the second, master bedroom on that floor that you may wish to consider? Well, I'm sure you know what I'm suggesting, don't you George? If you and Karen *are* actually together? Then maybe Stuart, with his lightening reflexes and muscles, could double as our live-in security man down by the gate? Maybe, also, keep him from getting *too close* to young Melissa, He proceeded to give a Monty-Python-like nod, wink and elbow to the side, "if you know what I mean?!"

I wasn't expecting to have to decide if I should move in with Karen so soon. We had been spending most evenings together - either at her bungalow, with Arthur's full knowledge - or at the gatehouse, but we'd not even discussed it properly ourselves. It had been one of those decisions I'd rather make later. Probably much later. And then there was Stuart... I led Arthur back a few steps from the door and whispered, "Arthur, em, well I need to put you straight about Stuart first; he's gay, and Melissa knows it, as do his parents. There's really no reason to worry about him and Melissa getting *too close*."

"What?!" Arthur exclaimed loudly, "Oh, my dear Lord, I do so wish you had informed me of that before I agreed to let him stay here, George, really I do!" Arthur's expression had changed to one of complete disgust, turning away from the conservatory door as if it suddenly repulsed him.

This reaction didn't entirely surprise me; Melissa had said that Arthur still had some prejudices that should have been left in the 1950's. I decided to try to regard his reaction as if it were a joke - thinking that would give him a chance to retract his comments. So I faked a laugh, and said, "That's good acting there Arthur, you would have made a good seventh Python!"

Arthur wasn't going to backtrack, and he angrily and loudly continued, "I'm not joking, George! You let me invite that lanky faggot into my house, and he'll be working with Melissa too. No young schoolgirl should have to associate with deviants like him!"

I tried reasoning, "Not so loud Arthur, he'll hear you. Come on, it's 2015, Arthur. You're not actually saying that, had you known, it would have affected your decision?!"

"Damned right, it would!" Arthur banged his stick heavily on the wooden floor. "I may well be 'behind the times', old-fashioned, outdated, and from a bygone age, but this is *my* house and whilst they can do what they bloody well like elsewhere, in my house, I expect people to live by my standards and beliefs – outdated or not! – I have rights too you know? I will concede only as far as allowing him to live in the gatehouse, but he's not sleeping under my roof or sharing my table. Do you understand?"

I was anxious that Stuart could overhear Arthur's outburst, and resisted my desire to shout back, but instead pulled him further from the door and whispered as loudly as I could "No. I *don't* understand! – He's not contagious!" I was furious, not so much with Arthur and his last-century prejudices, but because he was forcing my hand, and possibly costing me the sanctuary and solitude I enjoyed at the gatehouse. I hadn't formed any kind of a good argument that could dismantle his stone wall of prejudice, so I just turned my back on him and walked away. I really wanted to seek Karen out to vent my anger and frustration, but then I'd have to explain to her that I wasn't decided on moving in with her.

"Where do you think you are going? Come back here this instant! – You do not just walk away from *me*. George!"

I jumped slightly as his stick hit the floor again, even harder than before. I quickened my pace and headed for the front door.
Calling back: "No Arthur. You have a guest to deal with in the conservatory."

I heard Melissa call after me as I hurried down the stone steps. "George, stop. What's he done? I heard the shouting." She stood behind me in the doorway, clearly concerned. She glanced back inside to see if Arthur was pursuing me. "Come on, George," she beckoned me back in, "fancy a coffee? Then you can tell me what's up, in my office."

I could talk to Melissa, I guessed; she'd probably understand my dilemma and knew of her father's prejudices already. "OK, but I don't need any coffee - I'm shaking enough already!"

On seeing Melissa's walkie talkie, I switched mine, then hers, off. I was in no mood to be summoned back to talk to Arthur. We sat in the two swivelling office chairs that now almost filled the little remaining space in front of her crowded desk. I stared gloomily at the screens. One appeared to be a mirror of Paul's spreadsheet. Melissa's laptop was blank and just reflected her face, and the big screen Richard had installed showed four camera images, all frozen, except the one by the gate. That camera was recording Stuart's parents walking out. My gaze fell back to her laptop, and to her reflection, to find that she had done the same, and she poked her tongue out at me as she caught my reflected gaze. She smiled, but appreciating my mood, kept it brief, "So, what were you and Daddy fighting over?" she asked softly.

Exasperated, I huffed before I started, "Well... Arthur agreed that Stuart could stay here." I explained. "He suggested he could move into the gatehouse, as a security guard, allowing me to move in with Karen on the first floor. Anyway... I don't think, well, I'm not sure that I'm ready to move in with Karen so soon - and Stuart as a security guard? – I can't see that working! So anyway... I told him that Stuart was gay."

"You idiot! Why on earth did you do that? – I told you he's stuck in the middle of the last century!" Melissa sat back and crossed her arms, and shook her head in disbelief. "And you don't want to move in with Karen because you can't... You two are just playing at being a couple for my benefit. I'm not stupid, George! Anyone can see there's nothing between you two."

"No, Melissa, I *am* in a relationship with Karen, honestly! It's just that its very early days, and I'm just not ready to make such a major commitment yet. I'm sorry I told your father about Stuart. It was just that he was afraid that you and he would get 'too close' if you were both living under the same roof. That's the only reason I told him - to put his mind at rest."

Melissa shook her head again, "Well, you certainly failed to put his mind at rest! Daddy is scared of what he doesn't understand, or doesn't want to understand; I've argued with him so many times, but he's way too stubborn to change his views now. He is both racist, and homophobic, and will probably take those prejudices with him to the grave. So what has he said? That Stuart has to go?"

I shook my head slowly, "He can stay but only in the gatehouse, and 'not under his roof.' That's assuming Stuart didn't hear him, and still wants to remain at all!"

"Oh, Stuart's more resilient than you'd think. But you, …
You love that little gatehouse, don't you George?" Said Melissa, so quietly that it was almost like a thought.

I was surprised by both her question, and her perception. Slightly puzzled, I nodded gloomily, "Yes, I do: It's my private little bolt-hole and exactly how I like it."

"Well, George, it's time I told you about my secret dream. A dream I've had for years, long before you came here. You see, I've secretly wanted to live in that little house myself! I don't like this big house; I'm not proud of it like Daddy is. I don't buy into this 'ancestral home' nonsense. No, I feel more like Alice-in- Wonderland after taking the pill that made her small: Huge rooms, big furniture, tall walls, wide passageways and little me… lost. After you showed up, my dreams changed – I wanted to snuggle up with you in the gatehouse, all cosy, close, and in love." A single tear trickled slowly down her cheek." She took in a sharp breath and angrily swiped the rogue tear away. "You know why I'm telling you this? It's because if you really felt the same way about Karen, you'd already have moved her in down there, to be close to her all the time. But you don't want to, do you? And I think I know why…" She stared straight into my eyes as if waiting for me to finish her sentence.

This wasn't the conversation I wanted to be having with Melissa. Instead of venting my anger, and maybe finding a solution to Arthur's prejudices, I was being confronted and made to feel guilty about her feelings and those I had buried. She wasn't helping at all. Instead, she was making things worse.

"But Mel, the problem with dreams is that you have to wake up. Just imagine waking up to some old bloke, after having wasted the best years of your life?! Also, I didn't invite Karen into the gatehouse for one simple reason," I stated as forcibly as I could, "Paul… There's no second bedroom for Paul at the gatehouse."

"Crap!" snapped Melissa dismissively, "I'm not going to beg. I know you're never going to change your mind. But I'd have loved you, as an old man, just as much - I'd wake up and be very happy - everyday!" She looked at me earnestly, "Every single day." She paused and then her face hardened as another tear was swiftly dispatched. "And, you? You could easily partition off one end of that huge loft room to make a second bedroom – you just don't want to! Like you don't want to move in here with Karen! You don't care about my feelings, and you deny your own, so you can just get out!" She pointed to the door then shouted: "Get out, and leave me alone, you liar!"

I got up and opened the door, turning back as I left, I said, with genuine sincerity "I'm *really* sorry, Mel, I thought you were over all this, I never meant…"

"Get out!" She hissed, interrupting my lame apology.

Once back out on the main steps, I stood in shocked silence, staring, once again, at the leaves as they fluttered gently from the trees, and at the dark clouds now looming on the horizon. The summer was over. In the distance, I saw Stuart striding away towards the gate. I guessed he was leaving, probably for good.
Richard would be moving away soon, and I suddenly felt that it was the right time for me to go too. I slowly walked back towards the gatehouse. I'd pack up my things and ask Richard to help me get the Pac-Man machine down the stairs and into his van. I was sure he'd be happy to have me in Lincoln.

As I rounded the fountain, I felt dejected and upset - I could see

284

no solutions, only problems. Paul was standing in the doorway of the portacabin. He was waving and calling out in the direction of the gate "Stuart, he's here!"

'Oh God,' I thought to myself, 'Stuart has arrived to move in to the gatehouse already.'

"Why is your walkie-talkie not switched on?" Paul asked as I passed, "Stuart's been looking for you, and so has Mum." I just waved to Paul and smiled weakly. I'd miss Paul. I began to think how Paul would, or maybe wouldn't, manage on his own. He had already said that he didn't want to deal directly with people and thought he'd not be able to answer questions. That would be a challenge for any twelve-year-old, and particularly challenging for Paul. I began to realise I'd be very selfish if I just left Ingleton Manor. I needed to confront Arthur, man-up, and be there for Karen and Paul. As for Melissa? She'd soon get over her feelings for me as I had suppressed those I held for her.

"Hey, George!" Stuart greeted me with an air of happiness about him that I wasn't expecting, "Can we have a chat?"

"Sure," I shrugged, "it's open, I rarely lock it, please go in."

"You don't seem very happy, George?" Stuart inquired, as he looked around and peered into the kitchen.

"No, I'm not overly happy," I said, hoping that Stuart would declare the décor not to his taste, and that 'he couldn't possibly live here!'.

"Hmmm," said Stuart, "Arthur? I had my ear pressed to the door as soon as he kicked off. It wasn't my intention to tell him I was gay – Melissa had pre-warned me not to mention it."

"Oh, I'm so sorry Stuart, this is all my fault. I only told him

285

because he was worried that you and Mel would be at it like bunnies if you were both living in the same house."

Stuart laughed, "Poor Mel, she has the hots for someone else," he raised his eyebrows at me knowingly, "and be warned, she doesn't intend to give up without a fight! Tenacious that one!
But I had a talk with Arthur. I told him that I'm a 'gay virgin' and promised nothing would happen on his property. I also got him to try to put himself in my shoes, and we ended up having a discussion: He brought up the ethics and the Bible, I countered with the Bible and divorce, and we ended up discussing genetics!"

"Wow! I Thought he was completely closed-minded on the subject."

Stuart nodded, "Yes, he admitted that it was something he didn't even want to think about, let alone discuss. I got a sort-of apology, and a feeble shoulder hug that lasted all of half a second! I've not cured him of his prejudice, but maybe improved his understanding a little."

I somehow doubted that Stuart had managed to influence Arthur more than to embarrass him to concede slightly. "So, he said you could stay here in the gatehouse?"

"Oh, that?" Stuart produced a wry grin, and winked, "he didn't take much convincing that I'd make a pretty rubbish doorman! No, I'm staying on the first floor. Arthur chose the room at the far end, it has great views across the beck to the farm as well as across the gardens to the hill. He said you might be glad to hear that I'm not moving into 'your' gatehouse. Karen's probably on the warpath, though, she was clearing the table and overheard Arthur say that you didn't seem too keen on moving in with her. He knew full well she was there!"

I had a feeling that Arthur would do something to 'pay me back' for walking away from him. I knew he hated anyone doing that. "Good feeling, gone!" I muttered "I'm going to lose my little gatehouse, aren't I? One way or another."

Stuart gave me a curious look, then said, "Can I be your gay best- friend?"

I laughed, "I've not had a gay best-friend since I left school, and he hadn't actually come out of the closet yet! Tea? Coffee?"

Stuart shook his head, "Not for me, but a glass of water would be nice? Well, George, I'm probably Melissa's best friend and confidante. She opens up to me and, I can tell you, she's quite confused. She's got it into her head that you and Karen are faking your relationship just for her benefit! Surely you're not - are you?" Stuart tilted his head to one side and raised his eyebrows. Then, when I didn't answer immediately, he then added, "*Are* you?!"

"No Stuart, I've just come from Melissa and had an earful of that nonsense. It was only three weeks ago she was chasing after you, yet she now claims she's had a crush on me for years!" I poured Stuart a glass of water, and we sat either side of the table. I didn't want to have another discussion about Melissa and Karen, but I did need to find a resolution that would close the issue. I couldn't just be pushed along, and continue to leave important decisions 'for another day'.

Stuart sipped his water as if testing it. "Well, you see, she thought you'd make your move, if you saw her, chasing after me."

I sniggered. "What, she was trying to play the jealousy card?"

Stuart cleared his throat rather nervously, "I'm gonna have to come clean: She's not a bad little actress, and a right little schemer; the tennis court thing – she set that up, with just a little help from me. I'm sorry, George."

I was confused, "What? How do you mean, 'she set that up'?"

Stuart sighed, "You were not supposed to agree to impersonate Arthur! She thought you'd refuse, and on seeing me as the competition, you might declare your love for her, there and then. If that didn't work; I was to come up to you and get very angry with her for lying to me about the tennis court. I was supposed to start shouting in her face. We even rehearsed me pushing her over. That was your cue to do the 'knight in shining armour' bit, you know - save her and send me away. Leaving her crying on your shoulder and in need of affectionate comforting. Basically, George... she already knew I was gay!"

"Oh! Bloody Hell! – I never got an inkling that you two had planned all that. You should both get Oscars!" I sat there shaking my head. I went over what had happened that day, looking for the clues that I should have spotted, and finding none. "Oh, she's a bit dangerous, isn't she?"

"Hmm, yes, just a bit. And well, you know what she planned next?" Stuart grinned.

"Yes, I do! I didn't realise you were in on that, too?" I was starting to get a little uncomfortable in Stuart's company now, realising he and Melissa had been in cahoots.

"Oh, no!" Stuart was now shaking his head furiously, "*That* was so *not* my idea and didn't get my blessing or encouragement, I promise you, George, honestly! I'll tell you what, though, she was extremely embarrassed after you volleyed away her near naked advances! But, you know, even Arthur has some doubts about you and Karen actually being together. He said you don't seem to act like a couple."

"It's just early days. It kind of just snuck up on me. We were
friends, have been for years, then she suggested getting together,
more for practical reasons really. She said she doesn't really 'do
love.' Then, well, she did sort of trick me into bed with her. It
had nothing to do with Melissa, though. I'd never play games
like that. And now, Karen and I, well, Karen and I are ..."

"I know," Stuart interrupted my indecisive sentence, "Women
float your boat, then you realise they're steering it too, right?"

"Yeah! That's a good analogy, Stuart! I think they might
control the damn wind direction, and the currents too!"

"Do you love her?" Stuart asked flatly.

"Yeah, actually, I think I do! Maybe I need a shove to get me to
go anywhere? I was just clinging to this gatehouse because it's
comfortable. But it's not so important, not really. Karen's a
beautiful woman underneath that drab clothing, and she's kind
and caring too. I should be more appreciative that she wants me
to be with her. I should show her some affection, even if she's
not able to reciprocate."

"And Mel?" Stuart asked with equal seriousness.

"She's just too young. If I were five years younger, or better still,
she was five years older... I do feel for her - I am fond of her,
and I don't want to lose her as a friend. We just had all this out,
well, we sort of did. Now she's upset again, and furious with me
too."

"George, you didn't really answer my question. Mel is convinced
that you feel just as strongly for her. If you do, then why are you
so hung up on the numbers? What's five years here or there,

versus happiness? Does it make a difference to you, or are you just worried about what other people would say, or think?"

I sighed again, "Oh, Stuart. I've had this same conversation with Mel. I admit some feelings for her built up without me realising it, and she has indeed become very attractive, but my feelings are not as strong as those that Mel seems to have, and I still think of her as a child most of the time. Yes, I am worried about the numbers, a lot of people would consider it wrong - most people - and, as I said to Mel, if most people think something is wrong, then it probably is! Mel made it difficult for me to let her down gently, and I'm sorry she's upset. But you, Stuart, you have just helped me make up my mind: I'm going to ask her - Karen - to move in here if Arthur lets me build a second bedroom upstairs. Or, I'll move in with her at the Manor if she thinks this place is too small." I felt better about myself. I'd finally made a decision and would accept whatever option Karen preferred.

Stuart smiled, "Well, I'm glad if I helped. Just one last word of caution, though: Mel has her eye on this place. She's always felt depressed by the size of the Manor, and has often talked of asking Arthur if she could make this *her* home. It would probably be a double kick in her guts if you and Karen set up home here."

I looked at Stuart, and I could see his concern for his true friend. I looked around sadly, "Yeah, you're right." I sighed, "Oh, goodbye gatehouse!"

"Sorry, George!" Stuart said, "Though I don't think she should move down here on her own. Not yet anyway. Not until this grass virus thing is over."

I agreed. I spent the remainder of the afternoon helping Stuart move his belongings from Ingleton to the first floor using Richard's van. I didn't see Karen or Arthur as we went back and forth, but on my last trip back, I realised that the portacabin was closed, and Karen's car had gone. I needed to clear the air with Arthur, especially if I was going to be moving in, and I also needed to talk to Karen, if only to arrange to move her and Paul's belongings the following day.

I had just decided to walk to Karen's bungalow when Richard appeared with his hand out for his van keys. "I hope you've finished with it?" he asked.

"Er, yes, sorry! But is it still OK to use it tomorrow, to move Karen's stuff?"

Richard frowned slightly "Ah, well *I'm* helping her move tomorrow - she asked me before she left. I told her I'm departing on Wednesday. I also got the impression you two have had some sort of an argument?"

"Oh, OK. We didn't argue, not really - other people kind of had a row on our behalf! I still need to speak to her. Can you drop me off at her bungalow after, it's only...?"

"Yes," interrupted Richard, "I know where it is. Can I drop you off opposite the Black Horse?"

As Richard dropped me off, I noticed chalkboards outside the pub stating 'Restaurant closed Sunday.' I guessed the cash 'n' carry was still out of stock. I wondered if this was due to the transport problems that now plagued London and the rest of the South, or if food supplies were already starting to run short?

Karen opened the door and coldly stood in the doorway, her arms folded with a stern look that was not at all welcoming. "Yes?" She asked, as if I were a stranger or cold caller.

"Evening Karen, may I come in? I know, I've been selfish and inconsiderate, and I want to make things right. Can we talk?"

She turned and walked straight into her little kitchen, leaving the door open, I followed her in and watched as she poured steaming hot baked beans onto two pieces of honey-brown toast. "Paul! - Come and get your tea." She called out.

Paul appeared in the doorway, gave me a blank look, and took his plate into his bedroom. "Not in there!" Karen yelled. Paul turned around and took his food into the sitting room. "Well?" She asked, "Explain why you chose to tell Arthur you didn't want to be with us before you told me?" Karen continued to busy herself in the kitchen, noisily packing piles of plates, pans, cutlery and cups into boxes that were all over the floor.

There was nowhere to sit, and I felt uncomfortable standing in her way as she busied around without casting me even a single glance.

"You're not going to need any of those at the Manor, are you?" I pointed to the boxes. "Can I help load them?"

"Charity shop. I can't leave anything here, and no, I'll be quite alright on my own."

"I hear you and Paul are moving into the first floor, and that Richard's helping you move tomorrow? I asked if I could borrow his van to do the same."

Karen didn't respond.

"I wanted to help you move, but I guess he got to ask first? And, Karen, I wanted to talk to you about the move."

Without looking up from the box she was packing, she said,

very matter-of-factly, "Well someone switched their walkie-talkie off and left their mobile phone here." She pointed to her bedroom. "Collect it as you leave."

I went and took my phone from the unusually uncluttered little bedside table. I sat on the edge of the bed, and for a few seconds I considered just leaving without even a saying 'goodbye', but that wouldn't have solved anything, and I did take a little comfort in the fact that Karen was angry with me; maybe she did 'do love' after all? I caught her glancing around. Maybe she was trying to see if I was leaving or not?

Just then Paul returned with his empty plate. "Can I have some more, please, Mum?"

"More? No!" Snapped Karen, "I need to pack all this away. I haven't got time as it is."

Paul stood holding his plate out a little like Oliver Twist. "But Mum, I'm still hungry because of yesterday."

I got up and stood in the doorway, "Looks like you could do with an extra pair of hands?" I asked quietly.

"What happened yesterday that makes you hungry today?" Karen asked Paul, snatching his plate away from him, causing his fork to clatter to the floor.

Paul meekly picked up his fork and handed it to his Mum. "School dinners… They were only doing small portions. I got pushed to the back of the queue again, and there was only gravy and a few peas left, and I hate green food."

Karen and I shot each other serious looks. "Why didn't you tell me this before, Paul?" She knelt down to him and pulled him in for a hug, "Of course you can have some more. But you should have told me yesterday. Hell, the damned school should have told me!"

"Sorry Mum, there's a letter in my bag," Paul pointed to his school bag.

"OK, Paul, I'll get it," she let him go, "you go play in your bedroom, and I'll call you when it's ready."

Karen looked at me as Paul pushed passed, "It really has started, hasn't it?"

I sighed, "Maybe? The Black Horse is having trouble getting food in, and they aren't serving any tomorrow. It could be just a temporary distribution problem, but I guess some large establishments have got greedy and stocked up."

Karen shook her head, "And here's me, running my cupboards low because I'm about to move!" She opened two large cupboards to show that were each almost empty.

"Don't worry," I said, "I know where there's a shed load! Listen, Karen: Arthur and I had an argument about Stuart, and I just walked away from him. Then, straight after, I had Melissa yelling at me. That's why I switched off the walkie-talkie - not to cut you off. I did *not* say to Arthur that I didn't want to move in with you! I just didn't want to assume you would want me to – we hadn't discussed it yet. So, can we talk about it now?"

Karen put some more bread in the toaster while she considered what I had said, "What were you arguing with Melissa about? I don't like the way she's still always creeping around you."

I smiled, closed my eyes and slowly shook my head before answering, "Oh, Melissa... Yes, well she got it into her ditzy little head that you and I were faking our relationship. In her

294

defence, even Arthur has his doubts. And she did, quite correctly, determine that I was reluctant to leave the gatehouse because I do love my own space down there."

Karen called Paul to take his second plate of food. This time, meatballs and toast. She then beckoned me to follow her into her bedroom, and closed the door. Karen sat in her little chair by her dresser, and I sat on the edge of her bed. She looked tired, and she yawned before speaking, "Maybe we have been too wrapped up in having sex and planning for the world's end rather than talking about where we should live? So, George, I'm asking you now: Do you want to move in with me and Paul at the Manor - and undoubtedly upset your little 'personal assistant'- or do you want to stay in the little house you love, and we'll go back to being 'just good friends'? I've told you before: I don't think I'm wired-up to do the 'love thing' so I won't be upset if you choose to stay put. There isn't a 'third way' as far as I know, is there?"

I wondered about suggesting building a new bedroom in the gatehouse, but Stuart was right - that would be unfair on Melissa. "No, there's no third way," I replied.

Living at the Manor didn't appeal to me at all; I had never really felt comfortable there. It wasn't just that it was Arthur's house - after all, he also owned the gatehouse. Maybe, I was a little like Melissa - the Manor was just too big for me, too tidy, grand and imposing. I started to wonder if maybe the house didn't like me, when Karen coughed loudly. I looked up to see her now sitting with her arms folded again.

"You appear confused," she stated.

"I'm just working things out - Arthur said, assuming he hasn't retracted the offer that is; that we could take the second master bedroom. It's in the middle of the first floor. You know it?"

Karen unfolded her arms and leant towards me, her eyes a little wider, "Of course, I know it. I used to clean it every week! Go on …"

It was time, I had to tell her, I couldn't put this off any longer, "Karen, please, I'd very much like it if you would allow me to move in with you at the Manor and share that room with you?"

Karen's face lit up, and she leant further forward and took my hands in hers. "Of course! And, George, I really do appreciate you giving up your man-pad. I'd rather live here in this little bungalow than in the Manor, and if it weren't for the small matter of the rent, we'd be staying right here! How about, long term, when all this grass shit is over, we look for somewhere more cosy. Something less 'Lord and Lady' and more," she paused, thinking... "More – 'Mum and Dad'?"

I gave her a kiss, and then laughed "So tomorrow we move in, and today we plan to move out again!"

Chapter 11 – Underworlds

'Wednesday the 23rd of September: Raining hard. Richard leaves today. Last night at gatehouse with Karen and Paul.'

Odd that's all I wrote for that day's entry. Maybe I was just too tired and relying on my memory to fill in the gaps, or was I just worried that my diary could fall into the wrong hands?

It certainly *was* raining hard: There had been a violent storm overnight that had brought Paul down from his reclined chair three times. This slightly spoiling our planned romantic and cosy, last night together in the single bed, at the gatehouse. I'd tried to compensate by making Karen a simple breakfast in bed. I was returning to the bedroom, to ask how she liked her eggs, when I heard Karen talking on her phone. Curiosity got the better of me; I stopped by the part-opened door listening to her side of an unusually hushed, yet forceful conversation.

"No, listen - I've already told you; I really don't need it anymore..."

"No! Nice of you to offer but we've actually already moved everything out ..."

"I do have friends, you know."

"None of your damned business!"

Karen then sighed deeply, "Yes, it does end on Saturday, but I've already told you, I've ..."

"Excuse me! I do *not* need to tell you where we're going, and don't you dare talk to me about *your* rights. It was a very twisted arrangement in the first place, and though I am grateful to you, you had your own dark motives. It's been another constant reminder, and it's time it stopped."

"No! Goodbye, and *don't* make me change my number!"

I stood outside the door for a second, then crept away silently, realising the toast was still on, and that the decision about the eggs had been made for her. As I prepared her breakfast, I became a little worried that there were parts of Karen's life that she kept secret, and may never share with me. I first assumed that the person on the phone must have been Paul's father. All I knew about him was that Karen had, point blank, refused to talk about him, and had warned me, soon after we first met, not to ever ask about him, or ever bring him up in conversation. Then I briefly questioned if poverty had sucked her into some kind of prostitution? I had previously wondered how she could afford the rent on her bungalow. I quickly dismissed that idea; that just wasn't Karen - *my* Karen.

It was still raining hard when Richard arrived, with his van packed with all his belongings. We had agreed to meet up for our last coffee together at the gatehouse rather than at the Manor.
This was because Melissa was barely speaking to either of us, and Arthur was still acting coldly towards me; though he had offered a brief half-apology, before demanding that I agree never to walk out on him mid-argument again.

The forecast was for more rain throughout the day, followed by warnings of fresh landslips, muddy and flooded roads. I had suggested to Richard that he stay a further day, but he explained that he had handed back his key and therefore was committed to moving. He'd spent most of the previous day setting up the CB radio, with its big aerial mounted on the garage roof, after Arthur had flatly refused permission for it to go on the main roof. Richard spent hours trying to contact his family in Lincoln, before finally phoning them, only to discover that their set-up had been switched off. Once it was on, communication was established, and the best channel selected. The quality was reasonable, and a daily check-in was arranged.

The big topic of discussion over coffee was the likely reasons for the school and the Black Horse still not being able to secure food supplies. Television news over the weekend had reported that there were some rural areas where schools, restaurants, colleges, hospitals, and care homes, etc. had been temporarily unable to provide meals. The official line was that this was purely a short-term distribution problem, affecting only some remote areas. However, the public from all around the country sent in emails and texts, complaining that their regions had also been affected and that some shops and supermarkets were also running out of more general food products, not just the dairy products that became scarce, everywhere, almost immediately.

Richard was nursing a conspiracy theory: He said that, because the social networking groups were, reportedly, doing a great job of policing the supermarkets and preventing hoarding, that either the government themselves were diverting reserves for the military, or the supermarket chains were deliberately withholding stocks so they could increase prices. Karen and I disagreed, and offered the more likely explanation that people were hoarding and avoiding the self-appointed 'Facebook police' by simply visiting several different supermarkets, or returning to the same one in their partner's car.

Paul didn't care. After three days of taking in packed lunches, the school had closed after teaching staff walked out in sympathy with the canteen staff, who had been laid off without pay. He was much happier recording and storing away the food and materials that Arthur was ordering in from each of the supermarkets anyway. But, even Paul had suggested that we might have become part of the problem, by receiving four home deliveries every week as well as Arthur and Karen buying food and supplies from as far away as Carlisle and Newcastle twice every week.

As the rain pelted against the window, I noticed that Richard was fidgety, and was regularly looking out of the window, impatient for some change in the weather.

Karen noticed this too, "Hey, Richard, this weather's not likely to get any better today, and the roads will be a real mess of mud, floods, and landslides. You could stay here tonight? The bed, the furniture, and everything in the kitchen, is staying."

Richard looked as gloomy at the weather and slowly shook his head. "I just really want to get to Lincoln, there's so much to do there. Now the CB's set up here, and all that damned buddleia has been cut, I need a new project, and at Lincoln there are many. I'm itching to get started."

I found myself looking out of the window, as the wind whipped up the rain and crashed it into the rapidly misting windows. Then I realised there was a still-to-do project that should fire Richard's interest, and might prevent him from making such a dangerous journey. "I have a project for us, Richard: The excavation of the cellar and assessment of that old diesel generator!"

Richard looked up as a grin spread across his face, and he stood up quickly, "Yes, let's do it! – I'll stay one more day, and we *will* get that generator working, *and* wired to charge up all those car batteries! Maybe even wire them up so they can be switched to power the Manor's lights should the mains be cut off. I saw a sledgehammer in the garage." He looked at us, all wide-eyed, and said, "Come on – let's get to it!" He grabbed his coat and waited by the door. "Oh, sorry, I can't give either of you a lift, my van's full! I'll see you up there." With that said, he hurried out through the rain to his van, which was soon speeding up the drive.

"Wow," said Karen, "it's 'all or nothing' with Richard, isn't it?!"

"Yes," I agreed, "he does love a project! I just hope Arthur doesn't perceive that he is running the show, even though he probably will be - I got a lecture from Arthur about that after that 'debacle' at the gate!"

Karen looked a little more serious, "Well, you'd better hurry on down there. You did tell Arthur we'd be taking the second master bedroom, didn't you?"

I hadn't. "Oh, no! ... I thought you had! I'll tell him before he goes to Darlington. He's got to collect some papers and sign something at his solicitors today."

"OK, I'm going to change before I go to the house, into something I think you'll like! I'll do tea at twelve, or sooner if Arthur gets back."

Almost as soon as I got in through the door, I heard a dull thump emanating from the cellar. 'Bloody Hell, he's started already!' I hurriedly took off my wet coat and headed for the cellar. The door was open, and an unusually bright light was shining up from it. As I descended the steep steps I was surprised to see Richard, not wielding the heavy hammer, but redirecting the beam of an arc light on a stand that was brightly illuminating the usually gloomy space. Arthur was giving him instructions from the foot of the steps, and Stuart was about to swing the hammer for the second blow.

"Ah, there you are, George. I wondered if you were going to show yourself today. Now, have you and the lovely Karen sorted out where you are staying yet?"

I replied quickly, and with much thankfulness, "Oh, yes! We'd very much like to take you up on your kind offer of the second master bedroom. Sorry, we should have told you earlier."

Arthur nodded. "Yes, well, someone should have told me by now." He proceeded to stare at me accusingly, before breaking into a smile and adding, "Only kidding, George! I do appreciate that wasn't a decision to rush into. Now come on Stuart, put your back into it this time."

Stuart pulled back the heavy hammer once more and let it fall back, where it hit a brick at the very bottom of the wall. Again, there was a dull thud, and a small amount of dust, but no sign of any real damage to the wall. Richard was shaking his head and shot me a pleading look.

After two more unsuccessful attempts, I suggested that Richard should have a go. After a nod from Arthur, he took the sledgehammer from Stuart, swung in right back, and smashed it into the bricks, this time, higher up the wall, and with all his weight behind it. A group of four bricks broke away and disappeared into the abyss beyond, leaving a dark hole, and a cloud of dust that sparkled in the bright yellow light. Richard immediately swung again, and more bricks crashed to the ground.

"Wait up!" Ordered Arthur urgently. "Now, before you make too much dust, get some face-masks on. I'll mark out how much you can knock out, so you can safely get through without giving us a huge job repairing it, should you find the generator is inoperable. And, George, I'm leaving you in charge - understand? If there's a bad smell, you'll either have to abandon the idea, or find a way of stopping it getting up to the house."

"Yes boss." I replied, noting that both Richard and Stuart were mimicking his finger-pointing behind his back.

On returning from the shed with extension cables, goggles and face-masks, I stopped by the portacabin, where Paul was looking bored and was playing games on his laptop. I wondered if Karen's assumption that Paul wouldn't want to explore the rooms below the house was more based on *her* not wanting him to, than any fears he had himself? I know, as a kid of his age, I'd have jumped at the chance. However, Paul offered no explanation and shook his head very firmly when I asked him if he'd like to come exploring with us.

When I got back to the house, Karen, Melissa, and Arthur were talking together in the hallway. Arthur, in his big green raincoat, acknowledged my return with a simple nod, before passing me and heading out of the house. It was then that I noticed what Karen was wearing, and how it contrasted so dramatically with Melissa's attire. It was almost as if they had switched outfits; Karen was wearing tight, figure hugging, jeans that showed off her long legs and pert bum, above which was an equally snug-fitting, deep red jumper that highlighted every contour of her ample breasts. Next to her, Melissa looked uncomfortable - in baggy, old, stone-washed jeans and a denim jacket over a dark shirt. It wasn't a good look, but it did indicate, to me, that she also wanted to explore the basement rooms - so we'd be working together - and that might be awkward.

Karen must have been following my eyes, "You approve?" she asked, before turning on the spot, then stopping to eye Melissa up and down, as if examining something she'd trodden in.

I didn't want to upset Melissa, but to suggest that Karen's first public appearance in figure-hugging clothes wasn't alluring would be equally unjustified, and, quite selfishly, I wanted to encourage this new look. "Wow, yes, I love the outfit – very sexy! and Melissa, you look suitably dressed for excavation duties, below stairs."

Karen's smile quickly evaporated, "You don't need her down

there do you? There's already you, Stuart, and Richard. Won't she just get in the way?"

Melissa ignored her. She just took a pair of goggles and a face-mask out of my hands and said: "Oh, look... *four* pairs of goggles!" She then headed down the cellar steps, calling out loudly, "Morning, Stuart. Oh, hi Richard! You're looking good today!"

I couldn't help but quietly laugh, even Karen's stern expression weakened, and she managed a wry grin, "She's really going to flirt with Richard to make you jealous? – She'll give the poor old sod a heart attack!"

Arthur had marked out a square on the wall, just three bricks wide and eight high, with chalk. Richard and Stuart were following the lines with hammers and screwdrivers weakening the mortar. Melissa was kneeling next to Richard with one arm around him, and was holding his screwdriver as he hit it, and he clearly wasn't happy about it. "Sorry Mel, but you're slowing me down, I'm not really happy whacking it while you're holding it. I'm scared I might hit your hand."

"Oh, don't worry, I'm sure you'll kiss it better." She replied, pushing up to him and putting him off balance.

Richard stood up suddenly, and held out his hand to Melissa, who was left still kneeling. "So, you fancy a bit of Richard do you, Mel?" She smiled and took his hand while shooting me a smug glance as she allowed him to pull her up. Then, as Stuart and I looked on in amazement, he pulled her up and in close and tight. As her smile quickly faded and was replaced by a look of alarm, he said, with his face inches from hers, "Right, your dad's out, let's go upstairs now and I'll give you a proper good shagging!" He then planted a heavy kiss on her lips before pulling her towards the steps. Melissa shrieked and pulled away, resulting in her falling back against the wall.

"No?!" continued Richard, "Then don't flirt with what you're too young to handle!" He then smiled warmly at her, "Come on," again he offered a hand to help her up.

She reluctantly took his hand and gave him a defeated look before muttering, 'Sorry. I was only messing with you."

"Yeah, I know you were. But you really shouldn't play with fire! Now do you think you could find us a couple of those big gardening buckets to put all these bricks in? They're in the gardening shed."

"Sure, I know where they are." She gave him a pat on the arm as she passed, and ascended the steps to find the buckets while being careful not to catch my eye.

I grinned and whispered in Richard's ear, "Well done! … But what if she'd have said, 'OK,' and gone with you?"

Richard gave me a very blank look and said very matter-of-factly, "Then I'd have shagged her."

I wasn't sure if he was serious or not, so I responded with a beaming smile as if appreciating his joke, but his expression didn't change at all as he returned to the wall to chip away at the mortar.

Stuart caught my eye and just shrugged before we continued to remove the marked bricks and clear them to one side.

We all stood around looking at the very uninviting black hole. I peered in and sniffed. There was a strange smell that I didn't recognise, but it wasn't damp, it was slightly sweet with a hint of soap mixed in with the brick dust.

305

Melissa appeared with the two buckets Richard had requested, "Scared of the dark are we, boys?" She dropped the buckets by the hole, peered in, then, without hesitation, crawled through into the darkness beyond. "God, it's so dark in here, I can't see anything," she called back, as she stood up and took a few tentative steps.

"Hang on," I called in after her, "I'll just put the extension cable on the lamp and pass it through. Don't go any further; you might trip on something."

"That light's really hot," warned Richard, "You'd be better off with a low-energy lamp that she can't burn herself on."

"I don't care what it is, just hurry up!" Melissa's voice had lost some of its confidence and bravado. "Come on; it's dark in here!"

"Hang on Mel; I'm just going to grab the lamp from the hallway and take its shade off – only be a minute."

"Hurry up; there are cobwebs in here, and that means spiders!" Melissa said urgently, her calm evaporating.

When I got back down the stairs with the rather heavy ornate lamp, Melissa was crawling back through the hole into the cellar. "You were bloody ages!" She exclaimed, her face white with fear, "and it's creepy in there."

I offered the light to Stuart, but he'd seen Melissa's face and waved it away.

"You go ahead with the lamp; I'll follow with the spare extension cables and some tools." Richard commanded, "One of you can follow if you want to, but one must stay here in case we pull the plug out."

306

For a second, I considered countermanding his instructions. Arthur had made it clear that he didn't want Richard to run this project. However, I had to accept that he was older, wiser, and had the ability to predict problems I'd probably not have thought of, so I just nodded.

"I'll stay here," offered Stuart, promptly, "I can rewire the plug if you pull the wire right out and reset the fuse if it blows."

"You don't even know where the fuse box is!"
Exclaimed Melissa indignantly.

"Yes, I do. Your Father showed me this morning, and he gave me this, too." He waved an electrical test screwdriver in Melissa's face.

She snatched it from him, "We'll be needing that for the generator. I'll go with you two, but I'm going to get a torch first." With that, she hurried back up the stairs and almost ran into Karen, who appeared at the top.

"Oops! Someone's in a hurry!" She said as she side-stepped Melissa. "Oh, so that's what happened to the rest of the table lamp. You be careful with that, it looks expensive. Now, has anybody remembered their walkie-talkies today?"

I hadn't got mine, it was in my coat pocket upstairs, so I shook my head. Richard shrugged, "I gave mine back yesterday."

Stuart produced his and checked it was on. "I've got mine - not heard a peep from it, though. Probably no signal down here."

"Hmmm..." Karen said, doubting him, "Well, Paul's been calling, and as none of you answered, I had to agree to something on my own: We had a young couple come, and they were asking about how to get food. He's ex-Navy, currently unemployed, and was looking for a job in communications. She knows Paul and Melissa because she was a cook at the school. I got chatting to them about what they could offer us. She makes scented candles, but I said we have already bought loads of candles. But, it turns out they first met when working on a farm. So, I suggested that they go and talk to Paul Wilson and Mr Leach, and see if either could use them as farm hands. They seemed keen on that, and so, if it works out, then we'd supply them with the food tokens, six per day. What do you think?" Karen asked, obviously happy with her proposition.

"Six tokens?" Richard questioned, "I thought we'd agreed on a daily maximum of two per day, per person, for labouring work?"

Melissa returned with a bright yellow torch and looked suspiciously at Karen for an answer.

"Oh, sorry, I forgot to say, they have a six-year-old boy. They suggested, after looking around the portacabins, that the old one that's failing as a games and book exchange could be used as a crèche." Looking around at our doubtful faces, she added: "Well, they can't take him with them to the farms, can they?"

"And who would run this crèche?" Melissa asked coldly, "Nobody suggest me, because I'm not doing it!"

Richard had responded before I got a chance to comment, "It's a bit early to declare that the exchange thing isn't working - we've only had two lots of visitors - but maybe it could double as a crèche if we can find a couple of other mothers willing to run it."

"Sexist!" Said both Karen and Melissa together. They then shared a rare warm smile.

"I'll volunteer!" said Stuart, "I used to love helping my mother in school. As long as I can have a desk in there, so I can organise entertainment and design posters."

Karen looked at me for reaction.

I wasn't too keen on the idea of a lot of kids running around. "We'll need porta-loos or something down there. Paul's been using the toilet in the gatehouse, but we can't have a load of kids trooping in there, plus it's a bit too far away, and very near the gate."

"Have a word with Arthur," chipped in Richard, "he's still in a generous mood. You'll have to consider any ideas that visitors suggest, and the crèche is quite a good one. You'll just have to watch how many non-productive mouths you have to feed, and that will have to include any young kids, and those looking after them."

Richard was right; we could all too easily create a social care society that was not sufficiently productive. "We started this with absolutely no idea of the ratio of food producers to other workers and children." I stated, "But I'll ask him about porta-loos. Also, it could be a good idea if we taught the kids how to grow and tend to crops? Anyway, good decisions, Karen; and we'll have to remember to leave a walkie-talkie at the top of the steps so we can hear you while we're working down here."

"Oh, one more thing, "Karen said, as she started to climb back up the steps, "They are living in Bishop Auckland at the moment and don't want to travel that far, not with the roads as they are now - it took them two hours this morning. Does anyone know of a house to let, or empty property close by? I suggested my old bungalow, but the rent's high and it's a bit too small."

Richard answered immediately, "I'm fairly sure that the Bury is empty; they were in a hurry to move out, and I seriously doubt they managed to sell it."

"Wow, that's certainly big enough, but surely it's going to be all locked up and alarmed?" Karen asked, "I did a short spell of cleaning there before I came here, and they've got a pretty advanced alarm system."

"Yeah, they do... But, I've still got a key," beamed Richard, "*and I know the code for the alarm!*" On seeing doubtful and scornful looks from his, less than impressed audience, he attempted to justify his statements: "Look at it this way, they are out of the country. This new family can act as house-sitters, and probably prevent it from getting looted, or burnt down. You could place a lot of people there, and it's just 10 minutes' walk away?"

"It does make sense, actually," agreed Karen, "In fact, it might be the perfect place for the crèche or even a school? But please, Richard, can you check it is empty, and that the alarm code hasn't been changed before you go tomorrow?"

"I will. You can count on it." Richard assured her, "Now, who's game for finding this generator?"

Surprisingly, it was Melissa who took the lamp from me and, after switching it on, was the first to climb back in through the hole.

Stuart stayed behind, and Richard and I followed her with the second extension cable. Once inside, we found ourselves in a narrow room with plain white walls. Dark grey tangles of cobwebs were drooping from the corners and a fluorescent light fitting that was missing its tube. There was just a solitary door ahead of us, with a sign saying, simply, 'Cool Room – Keep Closed'. I guessed this was where Arthur had said the cold desserts were kept cool, before being served upstairs.

Melissa opened the second door easily. "Strange door," she said, "it's really light, and has silver foil on both sides!"

Beyond that was a long corridor, with three equally-spaced doors on the left, and an odd one at the far end. These, I worked out, were under the front of the house, and so the two on the right must be under the back. Melissa pushed open the first door on the left, "Oh, look! It's a tiny little bedroom!"

On peering in, I found it hard to believe that this was the same building; the rooms upstairs had wide, heavy wooden doors, and high ceilings with ornate cornices and light fittings. By contrast, this room had a narrow basic door, was compact, with very low ceilings and only a single narrow little basement window at ceiling level. The room still had a small, single bed with a nasty looking mattress, black with mildew. There was a wooden rail for hanging clothes, a single picture hook, and a three-drawer unit that was white with mould. The room smelt heavy with moisture, and a spore-ridden dampness. There were dark green and black stains on the walls below the window, and the wallpaper had all peeled off and was laying in dark curls all around the edges of the room. "Come on out, Mel, we need to keep this door shut - that room stinks!"

Melissa took a final look around and closed the door. Richard had already peered in the second room, "Another bedroom, damper still!" He started to close the door, but Melissa put her foot in the door, and insisted that she looked in too, "This is my house you know, Richard! – Ew, that does stink!" She shut the door quickly.

The last bedroom was much the same, only this one was completely unaffected by damp and was wider, boasting two little slit windows and a plain wooden wardrobe. Here, a patterned wallpaper was still attached to the wall, and someone had penned 'Kerry Anne Clarke 1889-1911' on the wallpaper by the door. Above this were earlier names and dates, but they were no longer legible. "Why is this room bigger, and has a five-drawer unit and a wardrobe?" Melissa asked.

"I don't know; maybe it belonged to the housekeeper or butler? Did you have a butler?" Richard asked Melissa.

"No! Well, no, I don't think so? There was a Chauffer - but that was probably only because my grandad didn't like to drive - and the Chauffer lived in the gatehouse. Look, that's a bell board." Melissa pointed to a wooden plaque above the door that had three big springs with bells on the end. The cables that operated the bells were all detached.

I looked around for a replacement and found I was standing right in front of it; a wooden box, complete with a black metal plate, that read; 'Western Electric Intercom'. "That's similar to the one in the gatehouse," I said, "only this one has a red talk button, and electric bell on the top." It also had a Bakelite earpiece that hung on a hook on the side, rather than a loudspeaker. The fluted mouthpiece had been broken, and the brown wire leading from it was frayed, with some of the copper cables inside exposed. I pressed the red button, but nothing appeared to happen.

We then crossed the corridor and peered into the other two larger rooms. Thankfully, these were not damp because neither of them had doors. One had a long table, some metal tubs, a huge, menacing looking electric mangle, and a row of large stone sinks along the wall. "Washroom." Richard stated, apparently unimpressed.

The other room's use remained a mystery; it had some shelving along one side, but other than that it was empty. We took a few guesses at what it was for, with 'ironing room' being the most likely, but it was a very large space for that single task.

Now we were just left with just the odd little door at the far left, and the door at the end of the corridor. I was beginning to wonder how much room was left for the kitchen, pantry, and generator room. Just as we got to the little door, the cable went taut and the light Melissa was carrying went out, plunging us into total darkness.

"Shit!" said Melissa, "Someone take this light from me so I can unclip the torch." I groped my way towards her in the darkness, and finding the cable first, followed it to her.

"Who's that?" she asked nervously.

"It's only me," I replied, as Richard laughed.

"OK, I've got the lamp, so you can let go now." I briefly felt her hand stroke mine as she let go. She felt warm in the cold room, but I pulled away quickly.

I could hear her fumbling as she tried to unclip the torch and finally switched it on. The weak, yellow beam illuminating the final door with a ripple pattern.

"That torch is a bit crap." Richard stated flatly.

"Yeah?" replied Melissa, "What torch have you got to offer?"

"Fair point. Sorry, Mel." Richard conceded, "Shine it back along the cable; I think it unplugged from the second extension reel, or else Stuart would have reconnected it by now."

Richard was right; after adding our final extension reel, we soon had our decent light back and opened the small door on the left. The light seemed to fade out as Melissa walked in. The smell gave it away for me, bringing back memories of my childhood in a house with a coal fire.

"It's all black, and it smells." Melissa said with disdain.

I peered in, and recalling Arthur's story of falling through the hatch, I involuntarily shuddered. The slope down the far wall was desperately steep, and the confined space was cramped and dark. "That's where your Father fell in when he was a child." I said, pointing up to the top of the slope.

We all stood there in silence for several minutes, each of us trying to imagine how Arthur must have felt. Melissa took my arm and squeezed it. I didn't pull away; I could tell that the scene was intensely emotional for her.

"So, if it wasn't for Peter..." Melissa finally broke the silence, "he could have died down here... all alone."

I shuddered again and suggested we move on to the final door.

I'd lost all sense of where we were below the house. I had thought that we must be near the end by now. I was very surprised when, on opening the final door, a huge, white tiled room was spread out before us.

"Wow!" said Richard, "That's a massive kitchen, and look at those stairs!" He pointed to stairs that ran up from the middle of the kitchen to the ceiling, where it was now blocked off.

Some of the stoves and fittings had been removed, but two long, wrought iron Agas ran along the far wall. "I guess they removed everything they could get up the stairs," I stated.

Richard and I both jumped, and turned, as we heard the noise of a heavy sliding door opening to our left. Melissa was using all her might to drag the floor-to-ceiling door and was exposing a dark, cavernous, space beyond as she did so. To our amazement, she had uncovered a brick-walled tunnel some three meters wide and at least thirty meters long. I approached with the lamp, and again, this space seemed to absorb all the light without illuminating anything other than the side walls closest to the light.

"This must be it!" exclaimed Melissa, as she pushed the door wide open.

The three of us ventured in and were struck by the cold. We walked slowly, being careful not to trip on the odd bits of wood and brick that were strewn across the sandy floor. We passed two black oil drums, one of which had a large brown funnel resting on it. Ahead, in the gloom, we could see a menacing, black, mechanical shape looming.

"It's a giant sleeping beast." whispered Richard, as if he was frightened of waking it. "We'll need more light here. Look at those old fuse boards, and heavy duty pull-switches!" He pointed to a board on the wall that looked a little like they belonged on the set of an early Frankenstein film.

I was beginning to wish we'd not found it. The generator was a monster of a machine, resting on six railway sleepers, with pipes and wires crawling all over it. I wasn't sure I wanted it to run; I was scared of the noise and vibration it would create in that confined space.

I noted that even Richard was wary as he cautiously traced the path of the wires and pipes. "The exhaust gases go up that pipe. Do you know where it comes out, and if it's been blocked?" he asked.

I looked back into the kitchen and noted where the stairs went up. That was the only reference point I had with the house above. I paced out the distance from there to the far end of the tunnel, where the pipe disappeared through the brick roof. "Wow, that's well over forty meters, so this tunnel was added after the kitchen was built and must run under the kitchen garden towards the garage."

"Well, there's a wide black pipe like that, I thought it was a water downpipe, that comes out of the floor and up into the loft under the first garage," said Melissa, "could that be it?"

"Might well be." said Richard, "We'll have to get Stuart to go and bang on it."

"Why did they dig such a big tunnel?" Melissa asked.

"Well, I guess it was to stop the noise getting back to the house?" Richard offered.

"It was probably dug out this big, and long, because originally there was a steam generator here. Remember your father said it was steam before diesel?" I reminded them.

"That would have been Fred Dibnah's wet-dream of a machine." said Richard, "You think this is big and complicated?! I'm gonna need that arc lamp down here, and work out if those switches still isolate the house from the mains, and if the generator's output can still replace it?"

"Look! Tools and instruction sheets!" Melissa exclaimed as she pulled out a drawer from an old unit I'd not even noticed.

"Mel, you're a star!" said Richard, as he took the folder of paperwork. "I'll need a cuppa to read these over. How about we find some daylight and hot tea?"

It was midday before we finished our tea, and Richard was

happy he knew how to get the generator started, and that he could safely isolate the house from the mains supply. The arc light was carried into the tunnel, and we found a better second light in one of the bedrooms. Armed with these, and the torch, Richard spent the next four hours working - mostly on his own - on the generator. Stuart had confirmed that the black pipe exited the roof at the back of the garage was that from the generator, but that it had a bird's nest on the top of it.

At 5.15pm Arthur returned, huffing and puffing about his day spent sitting in traffic jams, and how he thought that all of the road clearing and flood prevention was happening in the South, with 'not a workman to be seen north of Darlington.' He'd just sat down with a cup of tea, in front of the television in the study, and had asked me how the excavations had gone when the power suddenly went out.

"Ah, now… is that a power cut, or has someone got the generator working on their own?" Arthur asked.

I thought he would realise that I'd left Richard in charge again, because the generator was beyond my technical abilities, and that it scared me a bit too. "Let's give it a couple of minutes," I said, hoping that Richard would either reconnect the mains or the working generator soon. "I'm sorry, but I did leave it to him; I was rather overwhelmed by the complexity of it, to be honest. Stuart helped to get all of the car batteries down there, and all I did was clear a bird's nests from the top of the exhaust, wire the batteries together, and take him some tea. The rest of the day I've spent moving my stuff in from the gatehouse."

Just then, the lights flickered on dimly. Then we heard a distant and subterranean noise as the lights brightened, and finally, the television came back on as the noise increased.

"It is far noisier than I remember it, "said Arthur, "but the old boy has done good, and much quicker than I imagined.

317

I too was worried about the noise, "I think the big sliding door separating the old kitchen from the tunnel is probably still open, maybe it'll be quieter when that's shut?"

"Oh yes," agreed Arthur, "that will be it. But go tell him to switch it off. I've just remembered another issue we need to sort out."

"Oh, what's that?" I asked.

"Ah, well, we left the exhaust pipe fitted, but, when it was running, with that door shut, there was an issue with a lack of oxygen and heat build-up in the tunnel. To resolve this, a ventilation shaft was installed, but it has since been filled in. You're going to have to dig it open again and refit a couple of fans - one that takes fresh air in, and the other that takes the hot out. All the bits; the fans, pipes and whatnots, are in the garage loft underneath all those compost bags. The pipes surfaced behind the garage, where you'll find a power point for the fans. It is not easy to get to, I'm afraid, but it was marked with a flagstone in case we ever needed to excavate it again."

"OK," I said, not looking forward to the job because the space directly behind the garage was narrow, overgrown, and fell steeply away into a deep drainage ditch. "Do you know why it was filled in?"

"Ah, yes..." nodded Arthur slowly, "It was thought that water might start getting in through it, and was contributing to that terrible smell. I take it that has gone?"

"Yes, in fact, the kitchen end and tunnel where the generator is, is all quite dry. Just two of the little bedrooms are damp and smelly, and we've left them closed." I explained.

"I suppose they will have to be dealt with at some time, we don't want rising damp appearing up here! Ah, yes," Arthur tapped the side of his head, "I had a thought while I was out; somewhere down there is a string of lamps that the engineers rigged up. They can be hung from hooks in the ceiling all the way from the kitchen to the first cold room door. Save you carrying lights, or using torches. See if you can't set them up, would you, George?"

"OK," I replied, "I'll go take a look for them now, and I'll tell Richard to switch it off, too."

I found Melissa's torch on the floor of the cellar, by the hole in the wall. I noticed that Richard had knocked a few more bricks out, making getting through to the cold room a lot easier. On opening the insulated door, I was surprised to be greeted by a well-lit passageway. Bare bulbs were hanging from the ceiling in a chain - like fairground lights - clearly illuminating the corridor, with its many cobwebs, all the way to the kitchen. As I approached, the noise from the generator increased, and, for an inexplicable reason, I felt my heart rate rise the closer I got. I can't really explain why; I simply love motor racing, including drag racing. Standing close to even a rocket car, revving, up fills me only with excitement, not fear. As the noise increased, I was reminded of the time my father took me down into a noisy generator room at his work. That had stone steps into a confined space that was full of heat and screaming machines. I remember hating it and pulling him back to the steps. Maybe that was the source of the irrational fear that I was experiencing?

The tunnel door was wide open, and both the arc light and the table lamp were on, so the tunnel was well lit. Richard had brought a ladder in from the garage, probably so he could reach over the large machine that was now filling the air with noise, heat, and constant vibration. Richard hadn't noticed me as I came in, as he was busy writing labels for the switches on the wall. I cautiously walked right up to the machine. I knew I'd

319

have to overcome my fear of it; I would almost certainly be the one who'd have to start and maintain it once Richard left. Thankfully, the brighter light in the tunnel had already caused my fear to subside somewhat.

"Hello!" shouted Richard over the machine, "Noisy bastard, isn't it?! – I had to increase the revs to power the whole house!"

"Turn it off!" I yelled.

"What?!" he said, cupping his ear.

I drew my finger across my throat and yelled again "Off! Turn it OFF!"

Richard nodded, and reversed the position of the two big switches, causing the lights to flicker briefly off. He then leant over to my side of the machine and pressed a small round red button. The huge machine shuddered and stuttered before finally falling silent and still.

"God, it's nice when it stops!" exclaimed Richard, who was filthy with oil, sweat and brick dust.

"Hot bath and a cuppa?"

Richard grinned, "Oh, yes, I've certainly earned that today!"

Before we left the cooling machine, Richard showed me how to fuel it, start it, and set the revs to register the required amperage to supply either the whole house, or a lower setting to power the inverter that could charge the row of 12 pairs of two car batteries that ran along the wall at the very back of the tunnel. "Now, they," he pointed at the batteries, "will only do the lighting," he warned, "so if the mains fails, you either use the generator all the time to power everything, and risk running out of diesel, or you just use it to charge up the batteries and power only the lights.

Just manually trip the fuses for the three ring mains in the fuse box upstairs. I don't know if the heating pump will still work, probably not. I can't find a fuse for the original lighting and sockets in the old kitchen; I think they were disconnected before that new consumer unit was fitted."

As we walked back, I explained about the need for ventilation and expressed my gratitude for all he'd achieved. I also related Arthur's sorry tales of problems on the road, so as to reinforce that his decision to stay an extra day was the right one. "We'll miss you, Richard. I know you've not been here long, but we've kind-of come to rely on you."

Richard chuckled, "Well I'm not sure Melissa will miss me - she's going to give you and Karen trouble, that one! But remember, I'm just a click away on the CB, and will always be willing to share ideas and knowledge. And, if it wasn't for you, George, and your trading centre plan here, there'd never have been a second centre in Lincolnshire - although I'd probably still have moved down there."

Arthur met us at the top of the stairs, "Well done, Richard, you have proved, beyond doubt, that George was right to recommend you. I hear you have stayed an extra day to sort the generator out, and that George would have been unable to get it going without your help?"

Richard looked a little embarrassed. "Well, I'm sure he'd have got it going eventually, and Mel found the maintenance guide and wiring diagrams for it; which really helped. And, yes, I'm going to take a shower, then head off, first thing tomorrow."

"Well, thank you again, old chap. I hope this might help you get your venture in Lincoln off to a good start." Arthur handed

Richard a thick, unsealed envelope.

"What's this?" Richard asked as he peered in, "Oh, my God! I can't take this, Arthur!" Richard attempted to hand it back.

However, Arthur stood with his hands firmly behind him. "Don't make a fuss, please, Richard. Just take it, use it well, and promise to keep in touch."

"I will, I promise. I'd give you a hug, but I'm rather oily!"

"Ah, well, I do not really 'do' hugs, Richard, but I am

always
happy to shake a hard worker's hands, no matter how dirty." He extended his and they shook hands firmly. "Good luck! Now I'll leave you to say your goodbyes to George."

We stood grinning at each other for a second, before embracing in a hug. Neither of us had any new words, and I could see Richard's eyes were already looking glassy, so I said simply; "Go on, sod off you dirty bastard!"

He laughed, and he departed, leaving me wondering if I'd ever see him again?

Arthur popped his head back around the study door, "When you've cleaned up a bit, I've got some news to share with you. I'll wait in here. Not for Karen or Melissa's ears, though."

"OK," I replied, and set off, first towards the front door, and the gatehouse, then correcting myself, headed for the stairs and my new residence.

I could hear Karen vacuuming on the top floor as I entered our new room, and was surprised to find Melissa in there, now dressed in her 'PA's' outfit. My sudden appearance made her jump, and she appeared briefly nervous as I surveyed the mess of Karen's belongings that were still strewn untidily on the bed. "What are you up to now, Mel?" I asked directly.

"Flowers: I wanted to surprise you both by welcoming you here with flowers - look." She pointed at the large mirrored dressing table, which was now almost completely engulfed by a ceramic pitcher overflowing with flowers from the garden and meadow.

"Wow!" Was all I could say. I saw a card had been placed in front of the pitcher and hurried over to read it, still doubting her and assuming they were actually from Arthur. The card read, 'My dearest friends, Karen & Richard. Welcome to Ingleton Manor, I hope your stay here is long and happy. Mel x x'

I was taken aback by the note, yet remained slightly suspicious. "Wow, these are gorgeous, Mel. Thank you, this is …"

Mel had followed me and stood beside me. Together we looked at the flowers and each other in the mirror. She appeared very calm and maybe just a little sad. "This is… very unexpected?" she asked flatly.

"Yes, that's the word! No, actually no, that's not it… It's both very understanding of you, as well as a kind and thoughtful gesture." I smiled, still questioning my choice of words and her motives.

"Well, I went down to talk to Richard this afternoon, just to apologise for what I did this morning. Eventually, we got chatting, and I opened up to him a bit. He said that if I set about messing up your relationship with Karen, then you'd probably never forgive me, and I'd lose you as a friend too. So, this is not

323

me saying, 'I'm suddenly over you,' but I'm admitting defeat: The more 'suitable' woman won, and - damn it - she's actually very pretty too! I'd really never noticed until today. But, if I'm still single… No, forget it. This," she pointed at the flowers, "is really my way of saying sorry to Karen for being a bit of a bitch, and to you for all my silliness, and the embarrassment I caused you, and myself!"

"Thank you, Melissa!" We both spun around to see Karen in standing in the doorway behind us, with her hands on her hips.

"I was a little worried when I first looked in and saw you two standing next to each other in front of the bedroom mirror! – Oh, what lovely flowers!" Karen hurried across the room and read the note, as Melissa and I quickly moved apart.

"Mel was just saying…" I said, hastily trying to offer an explanation.

"I know, don't worry, I heard everything. That's really nice and very mature of you Mel. Oh, sorry… That sounded so patronising. No, it was a very adult solution to what must have been a very difficult situation."

Melissa nodded sheepishly, clearly embarrassed, knowing that Karen now also knew how she felt.

"Now," announced Karen definitively, "let's move on, forget everything that's been said or done, and you and me, Mel, are going out for a drink, so that this filthy man can get himself cleaned up, and then sort this bedroom out."

Mel hesitated for a second, then nodded and smiled, "Yes, that would be nice. Just let me get changed, maybe we'll pull a nice pair of men – clean ones preferably!" She winked at Karen, and her happy smile returned as she almost skipped away to change.

"Phew!" I said as I sat back heavily on the bed, "I'm so glad that's sorted and everyone's happy."

"Get off the clean sheets!" Karen ordered, "And get in there." She pointed to the bathroom. "I'll still be keeping an eye on her, and don't you be giving her any of your 'mixed messages' either, George!"

"No, I won't. I'll be extra careful. Now, Karen, is there anything *you* need to tell *me*?" I remembered her phone conversation of that morning.

"No? What do you mean?" Karen asked, looking puzzled.

"Well it's just, as Melissa had cleared the air, I wondered if there was anything you need to tell me before we shack up together."

"No. I'll see you later, George." She replied dismissively, before leaving and calling out for Melissa, obviously in a bit of a huff and with no kiss goodbye.

Remembering that Arthur was waiting for me, I hurriedly took a bath and changed.

"Ah, George, I'd like to offer you a cup of tea, but either Melissa and Karen have gone out together," Arthur grinned, "or these damn walkie-talkies aren't working?"

"Well, Arthur, unlikely as it may seem, they *have* gone out for a drink together!"

"Oh! And Stuart and Paul, where are they?" he asked.

"Stuart has gone to say goodbye to his parents, and I passed Paul going upstairs as I came down." I answered, wondering why he needed to know where everyone was?

"Good," said Arthur, "please sit down. We need to have a talk about Dry Ice; I wasn't stuck in traffic *all* day, you see. After signing off the decree nisi, I met up with Maria Trellis in York, found a secure restaurant, and filled her in about Dry Ice." He paused for a reaction.

"Oh, I'd forgotten about that. I thought you'd decided not to mention it?" I had hoped that it would just go away, and I'd hear no more of it.

"Well. It's all gone a bit 'cloak and dagger' I'm afraid: I called Maria yesterday afternoon; she explained that Andrea Parker had disappeared from the South Kensington Campus at Imperial College, yesterday morning just after she arrived. CCTV shows her being pushed into the back of a dark Nissan by an overweight black man. Sound familiar?"

"Oh, Shit - yes. Well, at least, it's *our* government that's got her, then?" I asked.

"Hmm… Well, that depends on how you define 'our government'. Remember, we now have a cross-party cabinet that probably includes someone who has remembered Dry Ice. Anyway, that's no longer the issue, because somehow she got away or, at least, Maria thinks she has. The Nissan was found, crashed into a tree, near Henlow in Bedfordshire. Apparently, a victim of the black flies that are bedevilling the Home Counties. Only thing is; why were they anywhere near Henlow?!"

"So, what's happened? Was nobody in the car? Any blood?" I asked, becoming worried for Andrea's welfare.

"As far as Maria knows, the Nissan was empty and clean. Maria believes that she made too many enquiries and that someone noticed; suddenly she was taken out of the loop and a curtain of

governmental denial descended. Maria suggested that they may
have been trying to cut across to the A1 - it was closed, North of
London, because the Hatfield tunnel is still flooded. If so, she
may have been heading here, or possibly to her house?"

"She didn't divulge that to anyone else, I hope?" I asked,
regretting the question immediately.

Arthur shook his head slowly, "She's not stupid - but she *is*
worried. She had no knowledge of the Dry Ice project and was
appalled to learn of it. The spooks had some kind of a tip-off,
they discovered that Maria and Miss Parker had spoken, and that
she was enquiring after Andrea's whereabouts following her
abduction. Maria fears she could be 'picked up' next. So, I've
brought her here; I dropped her off at the gatehouse so I can
brief you in private, before bringing her up to the house. Also, I
needed to check that you'd not had any odd calls or visitors
today?"

I shook my head, "No odd visitors or calls, but Arthur: Richard
is in the gatehouse - just for the night. He gave his key back to
his landlord, this morning - so I said, as he was working an
extra day for us here, that he could stay there tonight!"

"Bugger!" Said Arthur, standing up angrily. "You have got to
start clearing things with me first, George!" He headed for the
door, and I followed.

"Sorry, I had no idea ..." I spluttered.

"No, no, of course, you didn't. You'd better go down there.
Send her up here and button up Richard's mouth. He's *not* seen
her! Understand?"

"Perfectly." I said, as I grabbed my coat on the way out. It was
still lightly drizzling as the light faded, and I walked briskly down
to the gatehouse.

Maria Trellis is a middle-aged woman with, probably dyed, chin-length, 80's style, layered blonde hair. She looked up from her cup of tea on the kitchen table slightly nervously. Twiddling her pearl necklace, her smile was weak and questioning. She reminded me of those Hollywood actresses who are very well spoken, with a perfect figure and posture, but who try too hard to maintain a youthful appearance by simply applying additional layers of makeup. I wondered if she was, in fact, Dame Trellis? That had a familiar ring to it, and the title suited her even if she'd not earned it. She clearly recognised me as I looked around for Richard.

She stood up, "Hello, George, nice to see you again. Richard's in the bathroom - I rather surprised him in there, I'm afraid!"

"Hello, Maria. Arthur told me about Andrea. It's safe for you to go up to the Manor, we've had no unusual visitors or phone calls today, but Arthur wants me to tell Richard that he's *not* seen you before we go up."

"Oh, I've dealt with him, don't worry," she responded firmly, "let's go now," she said urgently, as she collected her blue coat off the table.

I suddenly felt enormous concern for Richard; how has she 'dealt with him'?

I went straight to the bathroom door and called in.
"Richard, Richard! Are you OK?"

"Jesus! No chance I can have my bath in peace *here*, is there?" came back the reply.

"Oh, sorry mate. I'm just taking Maria up to the house. Have a safe trip tomorrow." I turned back to Maria, who was frowning at me and shaking her head.

"I dread to think what you thought I'd done, George!" Then her smile returned, and she winked. "Too many spy books in Arthur's library, eh, George?"

"Maybe so, but you look worried yourself. Anyway, I'm sorry, it's just that with what's happened to Andrea, and my earlier interrogation by Susannah Coburn, I've kind of lost my trust in anything 'Government'.

"Likewise." she said, "We'll have a slow walk up to the house - because you and I need a little chat, I think, George."

It had finally stopped raining, but the drive still glistened with droplets of water, and the sky remained a solid grey. In the distance, I could hear the roar of a powerful motorbike climbing the hill towards the old mill, beyond Gainford road.

Maria took my arm as we walked, probably to control my pace, "So, I believe Andrea has been in touch with you since she first described Dry Ice to you?"

"No, she hasn't," I replied firmly.

"Oh, really? Well, of course, officially, Dry Ice doesn't exist," Maria continued, "All I have is third-hand from Andrea via you, and then Arthur." She paused, noting my reluctance to elaborate. "Look, George, you have got to trust me; Arthur does, and I am extremely concerned about the whereabouts of Andrea, and what could happen if that memory card of hers fall into the wrong hands."

"Memory stick," I corrected, "Andrea said that the data was on a memory stick. And, no, she really hasn't contacted me." I stopped walking by the fountain and sat on the cold surround, facing the house, the sound of the water drowning out the noise of the distant motorbike. "Can I ask *you* a few questions, Maria?"

"OK, George. Trust is a two-way thing. I'll answer as honestly as I am able." She looked disdainfully at the stone surround but still chose to sit next to me, despite the stone still being a little damp.

"Who sent Nigel to pick up Andrea? And where is he now? Oh, and was that Coburn woman in the car too?"

"Good questions, George," came Maria's patronising reply, "well, Susannah Coburn wasn't in the car. I cornered her at Westminster, soon after I heard that Imperial College had reported Andrea's abduction. Coburn claimed that Andrea had accepted 'an invitation' to return to Westminster, to update the cabinet on her research to create a counter-virus to PCP. As for Nigel; we really don't know? His mobile phone followed the track of the Nissan and was found, smashed, a little further down the road towards Henlow. All we do know for sure, is that they stopped for petrol at Edbury Street. CCTV doesn't show the stationary car, but it does speed out unusually fast. The dark windows obstruct any chance to see who was driving. But it was Nigel who paid for the petrol at the pump."

"So, she got away when they stopped for petrol?" I asked.

"Possibly, but that would mean that either Nigel forgot to lock her in, and that's unlikely, or Andrea found the button that opens the glass partition and she squeezed over to the front, either finding the key in the ignition or making a run for it on foot."

"Why hasn't Nigel reported in?" I asked, now hoping that Andrea had got away in the Nissan, and was unhurt in the crash.

"Well, "Maria considered for a second, "assuming he wasn't in the Nissan; he has lost both his phone and his passenger. He would do whatever he could to re-acquire his asset. Probably steal another vehicle, and give chase."

"Oh, so she's not out of danger?" I said, wondering where she might go.

"Well, no," Maria's tone became less sympathetic, "but, she did, as I understand it, accept this 'unholy commission', knowing full well that it was clandestine and potentially devastating to the populations of so many countries that rely on rice. It's not just China that would be affected if Dry Ice is released, you realise? It may well have diverted attention from the fact that no weapons of mass destruction were being found in Iraq, but the consequences would have been globally disastrous. If it were ever traced back to the UK, both she, her team, and all those in power would be facing a lifetime behind bars!"

She was right; I hadn't thought of it like that, but I still tried to fight her corner, "She was young, and used by the government, and if she'd refused, someone else would have done it. Anyway, as it seems the Chinese have done it to *us* now, then maybe having it would have been a deterrent?"

Maria sighed, "George, I do quite like you; I'm quite sure you're a great gardener, but as a political analyst, you suck! And your judgement, I fear, has been swayed by a pretty face atop a pair of long legs. Now, Arthur said you had thought of a possible solution, or use, for Dry Ice? I'm beginning to think that maybe I don't want to hear it, especially if it involves recreating the Dry Ice virus?"

I felt insulted and intellectually inferior. Maybe I shouldn't have any sympathy for Andrea. I wondered if I'd feel the same way if it had been a geeky young man who had developed Dry Ice? I

had to admit to myself - I probably wouldn't. As for my idea, I had lost confidence in it but would offer it anyway, "OK, I admit
- I'm a 'fish out of water' and it's not my field of expertise, so my idea is probably hogwash and unworkable, but, if you still want to hear it ...?"

"Go on. Sorry, George, I was a bit harsh." She squeezed my hand encouragingly.

I thought a little before offering my idea, "Well, I assume China, as the top producer, is now controlling the price of rice and is effectively blackmailing most of the rest of the world?"

"Yes," acknowledged Maria, "rice has rocketed in price in the same way hay has, by weight, it may even cost as much as coffee if it continues."

"But the American market has collapsed because everything over there looks like it's gone to shit?" I asked.

"Possibly ..." Maria answered doubtfully, "there is so little news coming out of the States now that no one really knows what's going on. Satellite images show fires burning in cities from coast to coast. But it's a complete communication nightmare: GCHQ has gone back to monitoring their radio, rather than internet traffic."

"We spy on the Americans?!" I turned to look at her in surprise.

"I will deny ever saying that." Maria replied with a sly grin.

"Well, if you had access to the data on that memory stick, could you, without the rest of the government necessarily knowing, send a copy to the right people in China? Along with a message that says 'we require x-million tonnes of rice per month, or we will distribute this.'?" They will know from the test results that we have produced it and that it works. They would have no reason to think we don't actually still have it. And, anyway, we wouldn't want to use it - well, I hope we wouldn't!"

Maria looked at the ground and closed her eyes. She appeared to be deep in thought. Then she opened her eyes and took a deep breath, "George, I think I can trust a man who would be able to both translate a message, similar to that you suggest, and who will know the right person in China to send it to. The big flaw in your plan is that we don't have that damned memory stick. Another is that we'd be handing them the instructions for another weapon. While they'd unlikely develop it, they would immediately be able to start research on how to counter it."

A bright light suddenly hit part of the front of the house, and a wobbling shadow of the fountain appeared on it. This was accompanied by the roar of a motorbike tearing up the drive behind us, and heading for the house. Instinctively I peered around the fountain to see who it might be, but Maria tugged me back, so I'd not be seen.

The noise increased as it got closer, but then the revs dropped as the bike slowed to navigate around the fountain. As soon as it did so, its headlamp was switched off. I could not make out who was on the bike, but I judged by the size of the rider that it was likely to be Nigel. I found myself gripping Maria's arm. I felt my heart thumping, and a feeling of nausea accompany my fear.

The bike engine stopped and it free-wheeled onto the gravel, but it was too far away and dark to see any details.

As I reached for my walkie-talkie, Maria asked urgently, "Who is in the house?"

"Er, just Arthur I think, oh, and Karen's son Paul - he's only twelve!" I pressed the talk button, "Anyone in the house. Urgent! You have unwanted visitors at the main door. Do not answer the door, I repeat, do not..."

Maria pushed me hard and pointed, "Too late, the door is opening - look!"

A crack of yellow light had appeared and widened. Against this slit of light appeared Paul's tiny silhouette.

"Shut the door!" I screamed into both the walkie-talkie and towards the house. Paul's silhouette was suddenly dwarfed by a much larger shape, climbing the steps. I started to run for the door. Maria tried to grab my arm, but I slipped out of her grip, her actions only succeeding in making me stumble briefly. "Paul!" I yelled again. I could see more movement in front of the door. It appeared that two shapes were moving on the steps and into the house. I ran past the motorbike and jumped over crash helmets laying on the ground behind it. The door started to close, and I screamed again, "Paul!" Someone had heard; the door was opening again, just a little, and a head peered out. Too small to be Nigel's and too high up the door to be Paul's. Panting, I ran up the steps, fully ready to barge the door to prevent it from being closed. I charged - and found myself screaming like a banshee and hoping my momentum would be enough to knock Nigel to the ground. I had no plan beyond that. I remembered briefly comparing my rash actions with those of a Japanese Kamikaze pilot, thinking that this was doomed to fail. But the woman - yes, it was a woman - holding the door open, she opened it further and side-stepped me as I charged, head first into the bulk that was Nigel.

Nigel wasn't about to be floored by a skinny gardener who's screaming had given him plenty of warning: He grabbed me and turned his body as I struck him, effectively using my own momentum to fling me, hard, into the wall. My forehead was the first thing to hit, then the rest of my body, winding me and rendering me completely useless.

As I lay on the floor trying to take a breath and doubled up in pain, I heard a voice I recognised.

"George! Are you crazy? You are OK?" Andrea was kneeling in front of me, her face filled with both concern and bewilderment.

"Brave." stated Nigel, in a deep, and completely unflustered voice, "Stupid, but brave."

Then as I managed to take my first breath, I heard Arthur's voice, "What the blazes is going on in here? Who in Heaven are you, and where the blazes is Maria?"

I just pointed towards the door. I still couldn't speak.

Andrea briefly introduced herself to Arthur before introducing Nigel as 'her saviour.' Arthur pointed towards the sitting room, and I found myself being carried in there by Nigel and dropped rather heavily on the settee, while Andrea went out, calling for Maria.

As soon as I could, and while still very confused, I sat up and felt my head. It was hot, and a bump had already come up.

Arthur handed me a Brandy, "That's going to bruise," he stated, "here, have this, and I'll find some arnica."

"Wait, Arthur. What's going on? Where did Paul go? Why are both Andrea and Nigel here? - I don't understand."

Arthur smiled and shrugged "Join the club, young fellow! Though, I think young Paul ran off up the stairs when he heard you screaming like an idiot."

As Arthur returned with his herbal remedy for bruises, so did Maria. She came in, with Andrea, who was now looking completely calm. Maria glanced at me and shook her head, disapprovingly, before going up to Nigel and shaking his hand. "Thank you, Nigel, I'm so glad that Coburn woman's orders were countermanded. The PM's gone up in my estimation considerably today!"

"Please, will somebody tell me what's going on?" I asked.

Maria answered, "Sorry George, and Arthur, too, this must all seem very odd, and I've only just got my head around it myself. Nigel had been sent to collect Andrea - that bloody Coburn woman must have had my phone tapped, or my office bugged. She's always been one I didn't trust. She comes with the Home Office, you see? She has effectively worked for both parties. She has some very dodgy friends - sometimes useful, sometimes not. Anyway, someone else must have leaked the details of Dry Ice - the data stick, and Coburn's plan to *acquire* both Andrea and the data - to the Prime Minister.

The PM contacted Nigel directly, told him to make sure he was seen on CCTV abducting Andrea, but then to fake her escape. It was Nigel's own idea to bring her here by bike after crashing the car in a fly-blizzard. The bike has no front plate, you see, and he covered the rear in mud. Besides, they were looking for one, or maybe two people in a car."

"I see," said Arthur, "so now what? Does the PM know you are here?"

Nigel shook his head.

"Don't say much do you, old boy?" Arthur said to Nigel, who said nothing - his expression remaining a stern blank.

"We'll leave it like that for now," stated Maria, "you have had a hard day I expect, Andrea?"

"Yes," Andrea replied, "I'm no fan of being abducted and motorcycle helmets do nothing for a girl's hair! I'd love to be able to take a shower. Oh, and will I still be able to stay here? At least for now?"

"Still? Oh, well yes, this house is certainly filling up, isn't it?" Arthur said, directing his comment towards me with a raised eyebrow.

"Er, yes," I replied, "there's still one room free on the first floor, far end, right at the top of the stairs. I'll see if I can make the bed up for you. I guess Maria is staying, and Nigel too?"

I could tell that Arthur was hiding the fact that he was appalled at the idea of a huge black man staying under his roof, but he was wise enough to not allow his feelings to show. "Ah, Nigel, good man. Yes, well, while you are here, you'd be perfect for our gatehouse security man. But there is another chap there tonight, so, er, just for the one night, you could take a room on the top floor, as can you, Maria?"

Nigel gave Arthur a bit of a stare before nodding once more.

I sorted out the three bedrooms - running endlessly up and down the stairs finding bedding and pillows - and finally returned to our room, ready to fall onto the soft double bed and just go straight to sleep. But on opening the door, I remembered I'd promised to put all the piles of our belongings away and that I'd better go to check on Paul. This 'living together' hadn't got off to a great start, and I wondered what stories Melissa and Karen had been sharing while I nursed my bruises, played housekeeper, and tidied away Karen's many belongings.

Chapter 12 — Establishing Some Order

During the following couple of days, life at the Manor became problematic; tempers were tested, and we failed to communicate with either each other or the villagers we were trying to help. We did not make a good first impression.

Firstly, Andrea, Maria, and Nigel seemed to think that they could treat the house like a hotel; poor Karen was expected to make meals, whenever requested, produce tea on demand, and generally tidy up after them. Then we had our first few groups of people arrive responding either to our posters or Melissa's Facebook page. But, no one seemed to be available to deal with them except Paul. Maria had started to treat me like her own personal dogsbody, assuming her 'governmental needs' had priority over those arriving at the portacabin, whereas Paul was refusing to engage in conversation with any of those making enquiries. He became rapidly overwhelmed, and just sat in front of our first visitors with his eyes tightly shut and his hands over his ears.

It all came to a head shortly after Maria Trellis secured a walkie-talkie for herself. She used this solely as a means by which she could issue commands without leaving her room. She used it to tell Karen to clear away the plates she'd taken to her room, change her bed 'because she likes it changed daily', and make both her and Nigel another cup of tea. After another one of these demanding requests; Karen decided to pay Maria a visit in her room on the top floor. Apparently, she'd said in a very subservient voice, 'You called, me-lady?' Then, before Maria could even respond she screamed, at the top of her voice, 'Why don't you fuck off back to London and take your fucking entourage of lazy bastards with you?!' She then, while Maria was still agape, picked up her dirty plates and threw them at her, before storming off to our room and slamming the door loudly.

All of this was overheard by Arthur, who'd been trying to take a nap in his bedroom next door.

"Karen was not happy," Arthur related to me after I returned from the Post Office for Maria, "I think I had better call another meeting and get some things sorted. Would you gather all the troops in the drawing room at 3 pm? Melissa and I will make the tea. In the meantime, go to Karen, she is still in your room. Take a pot of tea and your best listening ears! Oh, and Melissa is knocking up a 'closed until Monday' poster. Can you attach it to the gate and disable the press-to-open option?"

I wanted to ensure Arthur knew I wasn't happy about Maria's assumptions either, "Yes, and can I also put in a request that I'm not Maria's personal secretary, and that I'd rather be helping Paul, or doing gardening, or *anything* else!"

"Ah, yes, I'd noticed she was bossing you about too. Did Richard remember to check out the Bury on his way out on Thursday?"

"Oh, yes! Sorry, I forgot to mention; we spoke on the CB at twelve, as arranged; he said the code to their alarm is 01325, and that the place is completely deserted - with two empty fridges and freezers."

"Their alarm code is our dialling code! – We'll have no problem remembering that!" Arthur exclaimed, "Thanks, George."

I found Melissa's office door closed, so I knocked before entering. Melissa was fighting with the printer and cursing it as she did so.

"Problems." I stated, rather than asked.

"That bloody woman's been sending endless documents to my

printer, and then she tells me to run them up to her! After three trips up those stairs, I turned off my walkie-talkie." She turned to me, looking exasperated, "I'm fed up with her, and now the printer's jammed up - probably with that special paper she had you get - and you know what she did then? She only radioed Nigel to come up from the gatehouse, just to tell me to hurry up with her sodding printouts!"

"Hmm..." I tried to sympathise without showing too much concern - Karen's reminder not to give Melissa 'mixed messages' still fresh in my mind, "I think she's used to having staff on-hand, and we are just not up to her demanding standards! Well, you're not alone Mel, she's pissed me off a bit, and Karen - a lot! Did you manage to print the 'closed' poster, Arthur asked for?"

"She's like," she paused, "frightfully demanding alright! The poster's in the damn print queue. I just can't get anything to print now, and I'm really getting pissed off with that too. I'm sure it's that posh paper that you bought for her."

"Sit down, and let's see if I can get it going again," I could see the toner drum wasn't lying flat and on removing it found a concertinaed piece of paper jammed underneath, covered in black toner dust. After some jiggling and tugging, it came out in three separate torn strips. I held the tatty paper up to Melissa, then, as if placing them on a silver tray held aloft, I dropped them into my upheld hand, "Shall I just run this up to Madam, directly?"
"Oh, no, Jeeves…," came Melissa's reply, "do let me do it. I know just where to place it!" Melissa grinned back, "…with the tray."

"Ew!" I said looking at my hand with distaste and quickly hiding it behind my back.
On replacing the toner cartridge and reloading it with our usual

paper, I closed the printer and waited. Before long it whirred then clunked for a while, before it began to print again, finally ejecting Maria's letters and the poster.

I started to look at some of Maria's pages, but Melissa snatched them from me, "No! We are not to look at them – 'she who must be obeyed' said so. They are all very boring anyway!" She chuckled.

"Well I'm glad I've cheered you up a bit, and I'm hoping Arthur is going to sort our new 'hierarchical' problems this afternoon. Now, I must put this up," I waved the poster, "and set the gate to 'piss off' mode before I see if I can do anything about Karen's mood."

"I'll put the poster up and set the gate if you like?" Melissa said, "I heard Karen shouting all the way down here, and have never known her to blow her top like that before! I think she needs you *now*. You could tell that woman her printing is down here on the printer if you like?"

"Yes, thank you, that's very kind of you, Mel. I suppose, as I'm going up anyway, I could bring Maria's sheets up to her? – show some willing?"

"Don't you dare!" replied Melissa, sternly.

I found the door locked when I went to our room armed with a cup of tea. Knocking quietly, I whispered "Karen, it's only me and I come *with* tea!"

After a few seconds, I heard the door unlock, but it didn't open. Cautiously, I entered, to find Karen busying herself sorting out drawers, her back to me. "You made right a mess of putting everything away the other night," she said coldly, "I'll have to do it all again myself."

"Sorry," I muttered.

"And, don't tell me that you were busy making up beds and chatting to Arthur, because, believe me, you don't know what 'busy' is until you've spent a couple of days with your good friend Maria."

"Sounds like a line from West Side Story! Is she the craziest girl on the block?" I joked, hoping to calm her mood.

"You'll know her as soon as I've killed her!" she sung back, turning to me and smiling weakly, "I didn't know you liked musicals, George - should I be worried?"

"Well, I saw you had the DVD… Oh! You've been crying." Her temporary smile was not hiding her slightly bloodshot eyes, or the pale streaks below them. "We are… well, Arthur is; going to be holding a meeting this afternoon to straighten out our new arrivals. Get them to appreciate that this isn't a hotel and that we're not all at their beck and call."

"I've not been crying because of that stuck-up cow! Well, not directly. It was because I couldn't get to help Paul and the fact that Paul wasn't able to speak to our first visitors. Stuart was AWOL, Arthur isn't very well and was trying to nap, and you were running around for Maria and had gone out of radio range for the second time this morning."

"Yes, sorry: She had me go down to the Post Office, again to post mail, and buy more envelopes and stamps. Before that, I had to go to Darlington for printing paper, 'two reams - and none of that inferior stuff you use!', Well her super-duper paper succeeded in jamming up the printer! So, I've reloaded it with our usual 'inferior' stuff!"

Karen was slowly shaking her head, "You avoided the issue, George."

I thought for a second, "Yes, sorry," I had forgotten Paul and the problems he was having, "I will also make it clear at the meeting that Paul should not be left alone to deal with visitors."

"Oh, I see: tell everyone he has autism and isn't able to cope like a *normal* child?" Karen asked accusingly, "That'll sure boost his confidence!"

"No," I replied forcefully, "but maybe remind some of them that he is just twelve-years-old, and it's too much to expect from *any* child of his age. We are damn lucky he is so good at using that software, and linking it to his spreadsheet, and remembers where everything is!" We'd have really struggled to get this far without him, and the meal tokens – they were his idea, remember?"

"Yes, I suppose you're right. It's just, well, apparently, he froze up and wasn't even saying 'hello'. But, if you can make sure someone is always there with him, then he'll be okay. Paul did say he'd be OK telling, or showing, people where things are. He just can't explain our whole system, field other questions, and certainly not discuss what they could offer us if they don't bring in goods for exchange. Actually, do you know what?"

I shook my head and shrugged.

"I'd find it difficult myself! We should have never left him there on his own, I just thought that he liked it down there. Now, is that tea for me?" Karen pointed to the cup still in my hand.

I had almost forgotten the tea, "Oh, yes. I hope it's still warm."

She took the tea and smiled a little, before sitting down on the tiny chair in front of the dressing table.

I had been thinking about Paul in the portacabin, "I believe he does like it down there. For two reasons, he's got his computer, and well, he's on his own."

Karen, who was about to take a sip of tea, returned the cup to her lap. "What do you mean?"

Well, I'm sure you've noticed? If he's in a room with other people, he'll be in the far corner playing with something or looking out of the window. When the weather is good, he doesn't play in the house where we are; he goes down to the beck or the lake. He always tries to take his plate of food away from where people are talking. What I'm saying isn't that he doesn't like us, it's just that he doesn't always understand conversations or doesn't feel confident enough to join in, so he avoids them. You must have seen how if it's just you or I talking with him, he's more or less OK, but as soon as someone else joins in, or even enters the room, his expression changes and he'll start tugging to go or just quietly sneaks away?"

"You're not telling me anything I don't know, George," Karen replied, "Are you saying we shouldn't send someone down there?"

"Well, no, rather the opposite," I replied, trying to be tactful and not condescending, "Paul *does* like it down there, and so hopefully, he'll stay *despite* having someone else with him. He might then slowly get used to being around more people, even if he doesn't directly interact with them? He's going to have to stay while we explain what we are doing and what they need from us. Maybe he'll eventually get more involved himself?"

"Hmmm, possibly? Maybe start with Melissa? But, he's never been easy to predict, though he *is* proud of his contributions so far." She took a sip of tea and screwed up her face a little, "It's a

344

bit cold George, but that's not your fault, it was a nice thought."
She put the cup down on the dressing table, and I noticed that
the flowers had gone. "It's not been such a great start has it,
George?" she stated gloomily, "You and me, together here, nor
the fact that some of our very first visitors have walked away
thinking were a bunch of weirdos who hide in sheds and are
fronted by a mute child!"

I laughed at her exaggerated description, "Well, it can only
get better!" I said, looking around the room for the flowers.

Karen left her tea, and the little dressing table chair, to sit next
to me on the edge of the bed, before asking, "Would Arthur
mind if I don't attend this meeting? I'm not sure I won't find
something heavier to throw at Maria, and maybe I'll improve my
aim this time!"

"Leave her in an advanced state of shock?" I replied.

"Oh, you know *all* the lyrics! - Now I *am* worried! Are
you secretly batting for the other side along with Stuart?"
She grinned.

"Hmmm, no. But it's nice to find we have something in
common, and I know all the words because we
performed 'Craven-Side Story' a very milky spoof of it, at
school."

"Oh, I wonder who could have written that? Mr George
Craven?" She gave me a jab in the ribs.

"Well, at school my nickname was 'The Milky Bra Kid," I
chose to go along with it - rather than get upset." I explained -
memories of my school days distracting me from my search for
the missing flowers.

"Oh, did you wear a bra?" she asked gave me a flirty look.

I laughed, "Yes, in 'Craven-Side Story' I *did* - a cream coloured one - on the *outside* of my shirt!"

"OMG, George, you have no shame! Wish I'd known you back then."

"Ah! That's sweet. I wish I'd met you then, too." I gave her a squeeze.

"Yes, then I'd have called you 'Dale'." she said smugly.

"Hmmm... Well, if we do marry and we have a boy...?" I winked and stuck my tongue in my cheek.

"Oh my God, I'd be 'Karen Olive Craven'! That's it – we can't possibly ever get married!"

"I'm glad you've cheered up, KOC!" I laughed. "Listen, don't worry too much about Paul, or Maria. We'll get everything sorted and, no, you don't need to go to the meeting - although you could join us after about half an hour when certain people have been put in their place? We always appreciate your contribution."

"I was thinking of listening at the door!" she held her finger to her mouth. "I tell you what - if it's going well I will make an appearance, see if I can gracefully accept a few apologies."

"Great! Oh, how did it go with Mel the other night? You were back very late." Karen hadn't mentioned their night out, nor had Melissa, and my curiosity had been rising.

"Oh, fine!" replied Karen, with more than a slight twinkle in her eye, "Just 'girl talk' you know: All very secret and said while slightly intoxicated... Well *one* of us was anyway! Obviously, I shan't be going into any details as, us girls, we like to keep things between ourselves - especially matters of the heart!"

"Oh, well as long as you two are still friends." I said, pretending I wasn't interested. "I'd better get on; I need to find where Stuart has got to, and dig out that ventilation for the generator." I gave Karen a quick kiss and started to leave.

"Before you go," Karen pulled me back, "I just thought I'd let you know; Andrea has barely put her head outside her door since she arrived. I did knock for her, twice, but both times she just said she was busy. Is she alright? I'm still not sure why she and that Nigel came to be here?"

I gave Karen a sketchy outline of the reason, without mentioning Dry Ice or the memory stick. I'm not sure Karen was much wiser when I finished and made a move to go again. "I will just look in on her and check she's OK."

I checked Karen's expression for any adverse reaction, but she just nodded in agreement, although I thought I saw just a hint of mischievousness in her expression, almost as if she were about to tell a joke.

Just as I was closing the door, I heard Karen giggle before she called out, "Oh, George, if you ever have some spare time; I wouldn't mind playing a little game of croquet with you someday
- Melissa's rules!"

"Shit!" I said under my breath as I walked away, realising which one of them had been confessing while under the influence of alcohol. But, at least Karen wasn't angry about it, nor seemed to hold any malice towards Melissa.

Andrea was still in her room and agreed to open the door, only after I promised that I was alone. I opened the door to find

347

her sitting in front of her dressing table mirror looking drawn and pale. On her chest of drawers, were the missing flowers minus the card.

"Hey, what's up. Are you not well?" I asked.

She just sat there, twiddling a pendant that hung from her neck on a silver chain with one hand, while playing with her hair with the other.

"Maria gave you a hard time?" I tried again, assuming Maria may have repeated what she'd told me about her actions. "She's not very understanding that one!"

Still, she didn't say anything, but she did look in the mirror to check if the door was closed. I went back and closed it quietly then sat down on the bed behind her.

Slowly she turned and whispered right into my ear, "Could Maria or anyone else have bugged this room?"

Normally I'd have thought the question daft and would have laughed it off, but with Maria and Nigel in the vicinity, I could no longer be so sure. So I shrugged and said, "Have you seen the gardens here? There's a lovely walk around the lake and a great view from the top of the hill beyond. Come on; you look like you could do with some fresh air."

Without saying anything, she stood up, towering above me, before picking up her coat. I got up and followed her to the door where she waited with her hand on the door knob for several seconds before opening it, hesitantly peering down the corridor before finally leaving the room.

Maria was coming down the stairs from the second floor just as we reached the stairs to go down ourselves. Following Andrea,

I saw her tense up, but she carried on without catching Maria's stare.

"Not remembered where you might have 'lost' it yet, Andrea?" Maria asked sternly, as we passed.

Andrea just quickened her pace down the stairs and shook her head firmly as I followed. I began to wonder if Andrea may have been right about her room being bugged?

Maria followed us down and muttered something about having to collect her own printouts while everyone sat about with nothing to do. I did not rise to the argument, nor was I convinced that this was the reason she had suddenly appeared on the stairs.

As we headed towards the conservatory, I just caught a glimpse of Maria in a reflection in the conservatory windows. She had stopped in the hallway and was watching us leave with her arms tightly folded.

"Though here," I ushered, indicating the door that leads onto the croquet lawn and out into the rear garden, "head straight for Melissa's fountain, the noise from the splashing water will prevent anyone from eavesdropping."

I looked back at the house, scanning the windows for movement. Karen was looking out of our window and just waved. Clearly, she no longer viewed Andrea as competition or, after her little chat with Melissa, realised she could trust me, and that felt good. I smiled and waved back.

"Who's that?" Andrea asked, obviously concerned, but not wishing to look back herself.

"It's Karen, just waving us off. She told me you'd hardly

left your room since you got here."

"How long has Karen been here?" Andrea asked.

I laughed, "Karen's been here longer than me, she's a local lass; born in Summerhouse, just down the road. You may have heard her yelling at Maria earlier?"

We were nearly at the fountain when Andrea appeared to try to change the subject, "That's a lovely fountain. The little girl with the watering can, she represents Melissa as a child?"

She pointed to the stone statue of a little girl, twirling around holding a watering can, which was cleverly spraying out the water at an angle as if *was* being spun.

"Yes. My design that is!" I said with some pride, "Arthur and Lady Jayne wanted to buy or commission a statue or water feature to celebrate their first child. They couldn't find anything they both liked, so for years it was a raised pond with an empty plinth in the middle. One morning, I had an idea and sketched that." I pointed at the statue. Peter thought they'd like it, so he showed the drawing to Jayne and Arthur, who both loved it.
Cost a packet to have made and took almost a year, but everyone loves it. Well, everyone except Melissa! She doesn't like the way her skirt is flying out and says that her legs were never that chubby!"

"It's nice. Melissa should be proud to have something like that in her honour." Then she murmured, "Someone told Maria Trellis about Dry Ice and the memory stick. Now she wants the data."

I replied in an equally quiet voice, despite the distance from the house and the splashing from the fountain, "Let's keep walking towards the lake." We continued to the point where the lawn ended, and the meadow began. Here there were still some green plants including thistles, red clover, nettles, and cow parsley. I scanned the growth carefully, looking for any signs of a surviving grass variety, but there were none. The path drops down about one meter to the rocky edge of the water. It was here, just out of sight of the house, that we continued to discuss Dry Ice and her memory stick.

"I take it that you told Maria that you'd lost the data. Have you?" I asked as I used smaller rocks in the shallows of the water as stepping stones to reach a large flat, grey granite rock that I often sat on to watch the sunset over the water and hill beyond.

On looking back to see if Andrea would follow, I saw her kick off her shoes before carefully picking out a route towards the big rock. "I hope I don't fall in, I have no change of clothes here you know!" Eventually, she sat down next to me. "It's a beautiful view, even without the grass." she exclaimed as she shifted her weight to make herself more comfortable. "I said I had lost it when Nigel picked me up, but she doesn't believe me. The cow went through my clothes, on the end of my bed, on Thursday night. She actually said, 'I don't care if you're not asleep' while she searched. But she's government, and I don't trust her."

I tried to reassure her, "Well, Arthur trusts her, and he's known her for years. He was an MP up here years ago, you see. She intends to send the data to the Chinese in exchange for large quantities of rice. She's *not* going to recreate the virus and use it." I decided it was better not to say that it was my idea.

Andrea shook her head, "I trusted you; you trust Arthur, he trusts Maria, and she trusts who else? Don't get me wrong; I'm the last person who should be taking the moral high ground, but what she intends to do is try to blackmail the Chinese: Give

351

us rice or we send a virus that might wipe you out. Well, once they have the data, they will be able to develop an antidote, and what then?"

Although I didn't like Maria, I felt that our short-term need for rice outweighed the risks, so I found myself fighting her corner; "Well it could buy enough time to develop something ourselves - or maybe some grasses are immune and would have repopulated naturally by then? And, she is a close friend with the PM, and it was *he* who instructed Nigel not to bring you in to face Coburn and her gang of friends, some of whom probably tasked you to create the rice virus in the first place."

She began playing with her silver pendant again while she stared blankly at the water. "Maybe you're right," she said softly, "but what if someone in her office is also working for the other side? Don't forget we have a cross-party cabinet at the moment, who knows who is brown-nosing who, now? Remember all those groups of rude arseholes in that room at the Cabinet Offices? – how many of those would you trust with this?" She held out her little pendant in front of her.

"Wow! Is it in there? I thought it was a USB stick, something a lot bigger than that?" I took a closer look at the slim, upright, rather crudely made, silver plaque with four, tiny, hieroglyphic symbols pressed into it.

Andrea began to run the fine chain through the loop, "It *was* on a USB stick, but I transferred it to a Micro-SD card. This," she waved the pendant, "was a present my ex-boyfriend gave me after he went to Egypt with his *mates*. It's made from a pressed tube of silver, so it's hollow." She found the clasp and detached the chain from the pendant "The card just fitted inside. We'll probably have to destroy the pendant to get it out, but I don't care. He never cared, he didn't even bother to find out what the symbols mean." Without warning, she passed the pendant to me as she slid off the rock. "George, I am going to trust *you* with it."

I turned and watched as she delicately tiptoed her way back to
the safety of the shore, then back to my hand and the pendant I
found myself entrusted with. I could just see the tiny black card
inside the bottom of the pendant. "You want me to have it?!
Why?"

As Andrea replaced her shoes, on the shore, she said flatly, "Oh,
I think I've done enough already. Sorry, George, but I won't ever
criticise your decision, whatever and whenever you make it, nor
the consequences." She started to climb the path up to the
meadow leaving me staring at the pendant as my heart again began
to thump rapidly in my ears.

I don't remember thinking about it for very long; at some
point, I think I must have decided that the card, or at least the
data on it, was potentially globally toxic. What I do remember
well, and something I'll never forget, is the insignificant little
splash and tiny ripples it caused as it hit the water, some five
meters away from my rock. The feeling of relief was powerful
and overwhelmed me the instant it disappeared below the
surface. 'Sorted!' I said under my breath.

I had to run to catch up with Andrea, who had got almost as
far as Melissa's fountain by the time I got up through the
meadow. "Wet Ice!" I whispered, as I finally caught up with her.

She stopped, turned and smiled, "I so hoped you'd do that."
She said quietly, as she continued more slowly, allowing me to
catch my breath, "I *was* right to trust you. They won't ever find
it will they?"

"No. I'll tell Maria that I threw it in Langdon Beck, which is in
flood at the moment. I'll take any flack, and they can search
there for years if they want to! Now, would you like me to ask
Arthur if you can borrow his car, after this meeting, so you can

get yourself some more clothes?"

"Er, OK. But I've only got my personal credit cards, and I'm worried I'll be traced if I use them. Oh, and what meeting?"

"Oh, yes, the meeting is really to reign Maria in, but everyone staying here, including you, is going to have to help out in some way, just like the villagers: No free food tokens! Arthur has loaded me up with cash for the Trading Centre; I can give you some of that for your clothes."

We crossed the damp mud flat that had been the croquet lawn. I could see Arthur and Melissa in the conservatory, starting to arrange chairs brought in from the drawing room and library into a circle.

"I'll help in any way I can," said Andrea as we approached, "I'm a fair cook, or I could help you in the garden, or with anything really."

"That's great; I'll let you tell Arthur when the time is right." I held the door open, and we entered.

"Ah, George and our elusive, and may I say, very beautiful new guest, Andrea! How are you finding your room, my dear?" Arthur said with an unusually broad and welcoming smile.

"Hello, Arthur," Andrea strode over to him and put out her hand, "I'm sorry, we never got properly introduced, and I've been feeling a little under-the-weather since I arrived. But I'm better now and ready to repay you for your kind offer of the, exceptionally fine room by offering my assistance wherever it may be required."

Arthur's smile widened further as he shook her hand

vigorously. "Well, I am honoured to have both Craven and Parker here together, I am not so sure we really needed the poly-wotsit too, though, eh?"

Andrea laughed, "I think I preferred it when people called it 'Northern Grass Fungus', now I know what it's doing, I certainly wouldn't have been so keen to put my name to it."

"Nor me." I added, "Arthur, Andrea's not got a change of clothes here, can she borrow the car after the meeting and go to Darlington, see what's still open?"

"I can do better that," he turned to Andrea, "I will drive you there, my dear. It occurred to me that sturdy shoes and boots are going to be something people will need, especially with all this mud and people growing their own food; so, I am going to stock up. I would be most honoured if you'd accompany me? May have to be in the morning; some of our meetings do drag on a bit, especially if Karen finds her way to the wine cellar at some point!"

Andrea nodded happily and thanked him, "I'll go and help with the beverages. Oh, and 'thank you' for the lovely flowers."

"Oh, yes," Arthur looked puzzled, "Would you be a dear and gather up any cups from the bedrooms?" Arthur asked, "We seem to be missing quite a few."

"Does Karen know you two went off for a cosy walk together?" Melissa asked, as soon as Andrea was out of sight.

"Yes," I replied flatly. "Do you know where Stuart is today? I need to track him down for this meeting."

"Ah," said Arthur, "the young lad has been a little homesick; he went off for a long walk to consider if he stays here or heads

South to be with his parents. He is back, has decided to stay. He is in the portacabin helping Paul record and store our last home delivery. Tesco has also discontinued their home delivery service, so we're pretty much on our own now."

Melissa chipped in again, "All the shelves at the Co-op in Barny were empty yesterday, and people there were talking about moving south. Apparently, there is still plenty of food in the south. Oh, and you know what?" She looked exasperated, "I spent ages getting the Ingleton Manor Trading Centre Facebook page up and looking good - the wording took ages - and this afternoon the whole site has just gone! The UK one, not just the American hosted site. Only got about 30 'likes' before it all just went!"

"Hmmm, Google search wasn't working properly either, it just brought up a page of broken links. It appears to have started," stated Arthur, "so we need to get organised and make the most of the services that are still operating. Did young Paul manage to host a copy of your page, Melissa?"

"Yes, and he Tweeted its address, but Paul said that very few people were looking at it. And that it takes days to appear in search engines, and by then, none of those will be working! We may be left with just our posters and word-of-mouth soon."

"Evening all!" We all turned to the door where Stuart and a skinny, stern looking man, in a police uniform, had entered the room together.

"Ah, Simon, I am so glad you came," proclaimed Arthur, "I believe we are nearly all here. George, this is Simon Duguid, our local Bobby and Parish Councillor. Now, George, would you please round up Maria, and see if Karen is ready to join us too? Then we can get started. Please take a seat, Simon. Mel, please bring in the refreshments. I'm afraid we have only powdered milk for the tea and coffee."

Melissa and I left together and, just as I got to the stairs, Melissa whispered, "Let Karen know that Simon Duguid is here, she's not a fan! He came into the Black Horse and she sunk deep into her seat until he left. I don't know what her problem with him is; she wouldn't say, but she's certainly not happy to be in his company."

"OK, Mel, thanks. That's considerate of you. You and Karen, you're OK now? You two had a good few drinks and a chat, I hear?" I probed, wondering if Melissa remembered much about their night out.

"Oh, yes, we're fine," Melissa produced a coy smile, "no secrets between us girls, and no little man is going to break our friendship. I've known Karen since I was a toddler. We just hit a bump in the road. Oh, and Karen said: 'she's quite capable of steam-rolling over the cause of the bump if it reappears'," She then gave me a very knowing, almost accusing look and glanced down at my trousers, "So, be warned!"

"Right, OK…" I said as I headed up the stairs, "see you in a minute." I wondered if Melissa had misinterpreted Karen's threat wasn't she actually threatening her? When I entered our room, Karen was standing and nervously wringing her hands, "Oh, George, I don't know if I should go straight down to this meeting or not? I don't want to appear scared of Maria, but I am a bit, and I did throw plates at her, and that wasn't very mature of me was it?"

Wondering what issue Karen had with our local, part-time, Police Officer, I asked; "Well if I tell you that Simon Duguid is here for the meeting, would that influence your decision?"

"No," she said bluntly, "it wouldn't, and I don't know what you mean by that?" She looked directly at me. "Explain yourself? Do you think I've been in trouble with the police?"

I wish I'd not asked, as she had reversed my attempted inquisition with what seemed like practised ease. "Oh, well I just thought you didn't think highly of him. You didn't want to go to his house when the black Nissan was following us."

Karen shook her head, "Don't try to be clever, George, it doesn't suit you. It didn't occur to you that I considered Simon too old to be able to help and that he lives at the end of Manor Close, which is a cul-de-sac? What would we do if it followed us up there? Hide in the school? Endanger the primary school kids too?" She shook her head and muttered, "Idiot!"

"Oh, OK. Sorry!" I realised that I just been insulted, and yet, somehow, *I* was apologising, "So you're coming straight down for the meeting then?"

"Yes, alright! I'll be there in a minute." There was some anger and resignation in her voice. She obviously didn't want to go, and I became convinced she *was* hiding something. Her insults were merely a diversionary tactic. But I also decided, that it was probably better, not to pursue the issue any further.

"Right, I'll just go up and get Maria, I'll see you there." I headed out.

"George?" Karen called out after me.

I popped my head back around the door.

"I'm sorry. You're not an idiot. I was just still a bit angry about Maria. When you've sent her down, would you please come back so that we can go down together?"

358

"I'd be honoured." I said, as I blew her a kiss.

Andrea passed me on the stairs carrying a pile of cups, "Has anyone told Maria about this meeting?" She whispered as we passed.

"No, I'm just about to." I said, "This could be fun!"

It wasn't fun:

I knocked on her door, and called "Maria, are you there?" The door opened a crack, she grabbed my arm tightly and yanked me in; I banged my head on the door as I went through, and she tripped me so I fell forwards. Thankfully, my already sore head was cushioned by the end of her bed. She stood behind me, her arm around my neck, and her knee pressed hard into my back, pinning me down, while bending my spine backwards. "Bloody Hell! What the fuck?" I protested, frightened even to try to move in case that resulted in her further increasing the pressure on my spine.

"Shut up and answer this one simple question." She pushed her knee harder into my back, the pressure now completely immobilised me as the pain increased. "You lie to me…," she hissed, "I'll make you wheelchair-fodder! Now, where's that memory stick? I know one of you has it."

I couldn't bear the pain. It felt like she may have already broken my back. "I threw it in Landon Beck. It's gone." I blurted out, "You can't have it. I'm sorry! Please let me up. Please! I'm sorry! I was going to tell you," I begged, on the verge of tears.

She released me, and the pain stopped. I slowly drew my legs up towards the bed to test my back and then just gently fell forwards so that I was left kneeling at the end of her bed as if in prayer.

"That was *not* your decision to make," Maria stated with no emotion, "is there any chance it could be recovered?"

"No, the Beck is in flood and thick with muddy water, it's gone."

"Good. Come on, let me help you up." She put her hands under my arms and helped me rise. My back ached but seemed undamaged. "George, have you ever lit a giant firework and stood right over it as the fuse burned down?"

"No?" I replied, both indignantly and confused by her question. I straightened up, and turned to face her, stretching my back cautiously.

"You surprise me," she smiled knowingly, and shook her head, "you attacked Nigel, who could eliminate you in his sleep, and then you steal and destroy critical government data. You are very lucky to be alive. It's a good thing I had decided against your ill-conceived idea to blackmail the Chinese. I had intended to oversee its destruction personally." She pushed me back onto the bed, "Now we just need to get a few things straight, don't we George?" She leant over me, preventing me from sitting upright, her face uncomfortably close to my own.

I nodded, wondering how a woman in her mid-sixties was able to overpower me with such ease?

"You know absolutely nothing about Dry Ice, nor Andrea's work on it. You have never seen or heard of it - or the memory stick. You never talk to *anyone* about it, *anyone at all*. There could be severe consequences for you, and Andrea, if you ever do. Do you *completely* understand me, George?"

"Yes, absolutely." I said earnestly.

"Now, what had you come to see me about?" She

asked, standing back and allowing me to sit up.

"Arthur has called a meeting in the conservatory to sort a few things out, er, Arthur wants you to go." I said timidly.

"Oh, is that so?" Maria smiled, and straightened her out her long black jacket, "then I had better attend, shouldn't I? Now, I'll need a few moments, so off you go. Oh, and George, do slow down a bit; think carefully *before* you act and try to learn to recognise who your friends really are ..." She gave me a knowing nod as I left, leaving me feeling embarrassed, slightly battered, and a little confused.

"You were a while up there. What was that heavy thump? She had you moving her furniture around?" Karen asked as I returned to collect her.

"Yeah, something like that," I said, "come on, let's get down there before Maria does."

"Good idea, has anyone told Paul or isn't he needed?" Karen asked as we descended the stairs.

Her question was answered before we got to the bottom; We heard a deep, booming laugh, together with high pitched giggles. Paul and Nigel were coming in through the front door. Nigel was ducking because he had Paul on his shoulders - Paul was holding his laptop in front of Nigel's face and giving him instructions on where to go and when to duck.

"Paul!" Said Karen sternly, "that's a very silly game to be playing! What if you dropped your laptop or hit your head?"

I squeezed her Karen's arm gently and whispered: "He's made a new friend, let him be!"

"You're not his…" Karen stopped herself, "Sorry! You're right," she whispered back, "odd that he chooses to be friends with someone who hardly ever speaks!"

Nigel let Paul slide off over his head, very carefully, and nodded sheepishly to Karen. Paul put out his hand, Nigel took it, and together they walked into the conservatory, where they sat down together, cross-legged by the window, under the large fig-leafed palm that arched over them both from its giant yellow pot.

"Ah, George and Karen, good to see you both," Arthur welcomed us, and directed us towards the few remaining empty chairs, "Maria is coming down I hope? Oh, this is Pat Wilson, I think you have met, George?" A wind-worn man in scruffy jeans and rather tatty green fleece stood up and put a rough, workman's hand out for me to shake.

"Yes, we have sort of met, we often say 'hello' to each other over the boundary or in the lane. You farm the eastern fields and look after our new meadows, and graze your sheep on the hill, don't you?"

"Ay, that I do, or I did. From here as far as Killerby's. But it's not been rewardin' just as lately. Sellin' off cattle and most of ma sheep, for close as a half-farthin'. Like as not I'll be in luck to not be going south, as are most folks round hereabouts. I hopes you 'as answers, whereas I sees few likely as to work?"

Melissa leant across to me and whispered. "Should I translate?"

"No, I've been hereabouts so long as to know what you folks is a sayin' - well most of it." I whispered back, attempting to imitate Pat's accent.

Arthur shot us both a warning look before he answered Pat. "Well, as I mentioned before, we hope to be able to assist you to continue to farm so you can supply us with food. Later we

362

will discuss what you will be requiring. We'll start with what Simon has to say. He is only able to stay here a short while before reporting back to a meeting that is being held in the community centre."

"Ingleton has a community centre?" I asked, having never encountered it before.

Karen replied, "Yes, it's down a little track past the church, it's not much to…"

"Hello, everyone," Maria interrupted, "for those who don't recognise me - I am Maria Trellis, Secretary of State for the Environment, Food and Rural Affairs." Maria entered walking and talking as she did so, "Now before we start, I think my walkie-talkie battery may need recharging, it doesn't seem to be working." She pressed her call button, and at least two other sets screeched with feedback. "Oh," she said looking accusingly around the group, "I see!" She took the remaining seat between Pat Wilson and Simon Duguid, "If you agree. I think I should chair the meeting, Arthur?"

"Ah, nice of you to offer Maria," Arthur stood up, "and I do respect your abilities in such matters, but I have a specific agenda to get through, and I didn't make legible notes that I can share." Arthur continued before Maria could protest, "Simon has just come from a meeting that some of the villagers are holding in the community centre. Apparently, they are not very happy with us and think we should just hand over our food supplies. Simon, would you explain exactly what is going on?" Arthur sat down.

Simon took his hat off and placed it on his chair. He nodded to Karen and Pat as he looked around the room a little nervously. "Good afternoon, whilst I *am* in uniform, I am not here in an official police capacity." He began to pace around the room, not directly talking to anyone, and appearing to avoid any eye contact. "Some of the folk in Ingleton, as well as some from other parts of the parish, have asked me to express their concerns about the hoarding of food that's apparently been going on here? They got some idea that you are selling it or bartering maybe, but they are not clear, and those who visited you this morning returned none-the-wiser. Some are demanding that you hand over all you have stored here. They do not have any legal entitlement to your produce, and I did make that clear to them. What I want to achieve is an understanding of your intentions, and then I can report back to try and diffuse this tension that's been building since the local stores ran out of food."

I stood up, almost without thinking. "Can I try to answer those concerns?" I had been worried that people would notice our many deliveries, and more frequent shopping trips, and our posters and the short-lived Facebook page never fully explained what we were trying to do."

Arthur nodded, and Simon shrugged, sat down, and began playing with his hat, rolling it round and round between his knees before adding, "You do need to know that they feel you are out to take possession of all their worldly goods in exchange for food, and they have little trust. Some, inspired somewhat by Mick and Sandra, were talking about coming up here mob-handed and just taking what they wanted. You'll need to offer them something, assure them you are not trying to profit from this crisis."

I thanked Simon for being so upfront, then began to explain how we hoped our system should work, and accepted that we'd not made the best of starts. I asked Pat to confirm that he'd be happy to plough large allotments into the field the other side of the lane. I explained that people of the village would have free use of these allotments, could use our services to exchange food they had grown themselves, and that we had good stocks of vegetable seeds and tools which we would also supply free of charge.

I quoted many examples of possible trades and fielded some questions, mostly from Pat and Simon.

Pat explained that he'd not previously grown many of the new crops he had purchased seed for, and, because of that, he'd need more workers to help harvest and clean his produce.

I gave the example of sending someone, who had no service to offer us, scavenging for petrol or diesel to keep the farms working. Pat agreed and said that fuel was likely to be the biggest problem the farms faced, especially if the power was cut at the pumps. It was then that Maria made her first useful contribution: "May I interrupt? Pat, it is Pat, isn't it?" Maria waited for Pat to nod suspiciously. It appeared to me that Pat already knew of Maria and, judging by his expression since she came in, didn't like her at all.

"You require petrol and diesel to keep your farm going? Would a tanker of each suffice for a whole year?" There was a slight gasp of surprise from Simon, and everyone looked to Maria for further explanation.

"You look doubtful, Mr Wilson?" Maria stated, "Well, Pat, I have been in discussion with the PM, and he has accepted *my* proposal that farms must be prioritised, along with fishing boats, hospitals and those distributing food, for fuel. I need to make just one call, and it will be delivered. All you will have to do is provide the drivers with a lift back to Darlington, and allow any passing military or police personnel to top up should they need it. Now, would one tanker of each suffice for twelve months?"

Pat Wilson leant forward in his chair. "You serious? Three thousand gallon tankers? That'd be doin' me an' Leach's farm for two years, likely has it!"

Maria smiled, "No, they each hold 37,000 litres, I think that's more like 8000 gallons. Shall I organise it?" she said triumphantly, "You are able to hide the tankers from prying eyes at your farm?"

Pat frowned, "No. Probably never get tankers that big up the lane neither, but Jerry Leach, he's got good access, 'an 'as three dutch barns as serves no good use mostly."

"That's settled then, tell him to expect them tomorrow." Maria said, "And, now we are on the subject of tomorrow, I'm needed in London, so I'll be leaving you in the morning. I really can't function properly here without my staff."

Karen, Melissa and Andrea glanced at one another in silent approval.

"Oh," said Arthur, "sorry to see you go so soon, but is it wise for you to head back now?"

Maria sighed deeply, "Things aren't going to plan - the cross-party cabinet was disbanded this morning - too much blame, party-politics and in-fighting. Much of it concerning why the leader of the opposition hadn't been included, and only those in his party who opposed him were. It seems the PM couldn't bear to miss a trick, but this one has backfired rather badly. Now, he faces calls for a vote of no confidence." Maria looked around, maybe expecting to see concerned faces? "The US president and the French… Oh, did you know there are confirmed outbreaks of PCP in France, the Netherlands and Belgium? Well, anyway, America is on the verge of declaring war on China, this despite the fact that it's already at war with most of his own people. The French have agreed to support them militarily and for once we have said, 'not this time!' That's caused some international fury too! Added to that, hundreds of thousands of people are crowding into London and the Southern Counties, thinking all the food is somehow being kept there! This is only adding to our distribution problems." Maria sighed again, "I just can't stay up here, lovely though the thought is, I'm not one for running and hiding," she shot me a look, "no, Maria Trellis is happier in the thick of it."

"My God," Simon said, "is any of that confidential, or can I report that back to those waiting in the community centre?"

"It'll all be in the media by tomorrow," Maria said quietly, "but would you make it clear to them, that heading south *isn't* the answer? Also, tell them that we've set up roadblocks on all major routes. Turning people away isn't something we should be wasting our resources on right now!" Then, while repeatedly pointing her finger at Simon, she added, "And you can tell those doubters in the village, that Ingleton Manor has the full support of a government minister. However, please don't say 'you have support from the government.' Bartering is not something the revenue is ever going to encourage!"

"Virtually untaxable!" Arthur added, grinning broadly.

Stuart spoke up for the first time, "I'll get you some print-outs from our website, they'll help to explain what we want people to do in exchange for food."

Simon thanked Stuart and said his 'goodbyes' before heading out. But before he did, he tapped me on the arm, "May I have a private word with you please, Mr Craven?"

"Um, yes," I said, as he picked up his hat and we headed for the hallway where we stopped, "what's up?"

For a police officer, Simon Duguid looked decidedly guilty, and he led me a little further from the door before he spoke in a near whisper, "It's my son, Mick. I overheard him talking on the

367

phone to some of his mates. It seems he intends to release the inmates from Startforth - the young offender's place near Barney. Some of his old mates reside there already. Listen, George, this may not come to anything, but he's got this crazy idea that he's going to lead this crowd as 'road pirates', taking food and supplies from anyone that can't put up a fight."

"I see. Do you think he's a strong enough character to be able to maintain control of those from Startforth?" I asked, doubting very much he'd be the strongest or smartest of those he'd try to release.

"Well, I don't know, but policing around here's gonna be non-existent soon, so you'll be on your own against him, or whoever else tries to come here." He coughed, and whispered even more quietly, "the pub and this place are his first targets. So be warned, that Nigel guy may not be able to hold them all off."

"OK, thanks for the heads-up. I appreciate that's it's not easy for you to be warning us about your own son's intentions." I patted Simon on the arm.

"It's partly my doing... I saved him from the due course of the law many times. In hindsight, I should have had him locked up thirteen years ago. Maybe he'd have been rehabilitated and be a different man by now?" Simon shook my hand. "Good luck."

As he left I wondered what Mick could have done that deserved a prison sentence? I thought he was just a persistent petty criminal and general nuisance. But Simon's tip-off was valuable information, and we could at least prepare for his arrival.

When I returned, Maria was explaining to Andrea that it would be better for her to stay at the Manor and that Nigel should stay too, "Nigel, you don't work for Susannah anymore. You take orders directly from me or the PM. Stay off the grid, and report to Arthur, here. Your job is to protect this community, watch the cameras and keep an eye out for thieves, you understand?"

Nigel nodded, "Report to Arthur."

Maria's phone then rang and, looking gravely at the caller ID, she then excused herself too.

"Daddy?" Melissa spoke up, "Have you seen all the small ads in the Westmoreland Gazette?"

"Er, no, my dear. What's being advertised?" Arthur answered distantly as if he'd just been given terrible news.

"Not for sale, they're completely free!" Melissa continued, "They can go to anyone who can provide a good home and feed." Then her voice switched to her familiar pleading tone one she reserved just for her Father, "You did say I could have one, and now they are being given away, maybe we should take a few?"

"Ah, my dear, do stop talking in riddles. What is it you want?" Arthur said, peering over his glasses.

"Horses," said Karen, "their owners can't afford the price of hay or feed, and there's no grass. There must be twenty or so being offered. They say things like; 'want to be able to visit 'Cassie,' will groom and muck out for free'. It's so sad."

"Yes," added Melissa, "the owners are getting desperate now. The price of hay has gone up so much, and few farms have any left. There probably won't be any next autumn. Please Daddy, can we take just a few?"

Arthur looked at me with a questioning expression, "George,

369

can *we* feed them, make use of them and house them? We certainly can't have them cantering around and churning up my garden!"

"I don't know that we can feed them?" I shrugged, "Pat, have you got any hay left? And what about stables?"

Stuart answered before Pat could, "They have stomachs that have evolved to eat grass. They'll eat a few carrots and apples, but they are not good for them. They are grazing animals really, and they are going to need grass in the spring – but there just isn't going to be any."

Melissa gave Stuart an angry stare and hissed "Thanks, Stuart!"

Pat coughed before speaking, "Lad's near as be right… But I do 'as a barn fulla hay. I could have been sellin' it for close as seventy pounds a bale! Three pound was best I'd a got before your damn PCP arrived," Pat waved his finger at Andrea and me, "but Arthur said that money wouldn't count as for much soon, and folks were thieving it right from the field. That's why sign on the gate says 'No Hay'." Pat sat back and spoke directly to Melissa, who was now looking more hopeful, "A horse'll eat legumes," Pat continued, "such as clover, cow parsley and alfalfa, which is all growing well on the far side of the hill and down as far as Langdon Beck. If you spread hay around there, so horses eat a mix, then come spring, we might keep them from getting colic. They'll always need the hay though for the cellulose, see?
For every year, there's no grass, we'll still need hay. Run out of hay and all we got is horse meat. You understands, me dear?"

Melissa nodded, "What about stables?"

Pat laughed, "I'd keep 'em out as nature intended, but there's the milking sheds that serves as no good purpose now. But," he pointed a finger at Melissa, "two things; I'm not bringing 'em in, nor is I muckin' 'em out. Then you're gonna have to decide on how many... Six, and maybe there's enough hay for two years - keep three, and they'll live for four. Understand, my dear?"

Melissa looked at Andrea, "Do you think we'll have grass back again in two years, Andrea?"

Andrea spoke quietly. I'd noticed that she had clearly been very interested in this new topic. "I can't guarantee grasses will ever come back. If they don't, then many species may become extinct, including horses and cows. Small numbers of sheep will survive, living on just weeds." Realising she'd not answered the question, Andrea quickly continued; "I seriously doubt we'll have any widespread coverage of grass for at least three years, probably be longer... sorry!"

"So, we could offer to keep just three, if the owners will look after them, but we just can't promise to be able to keep them alive indefinitely?" Melissa asked, her eyes pleading.

Stuart spoke again, "The horses could prove useful; give the kids rides, pull small carts, and maybe we could use them to get about too."

"Can I leave you two to organise that?" Arthur looked to Melissa and Stuart, who both nodded excitedly in agreement, "Do not make the owners any promises, make it clear they are looking after them, and if they want food for themselves then they can work here or on the farms. Keeping horses does not entitle them to free food!"

Melissa yanked Stuart to his feet, "Come on! – Let's get choosing. My friend Claire owns a horse, let's see if she's advertising?"

Stuart looked to Arthur for permission to leave, and Arthur nodded, "I think we've covered everything. Come on Andrea, let's see if Darlington is still open for business."

Chapter 13 – Long Day?

Saturday: 5th December:

'It's not working. We will run out of food before Christmas, and there's absolutely nothing I can do about it. Today I must tell Arthur that I can't put this off any longer: I have failed.'

I underlined the final three words and threw down my pen before returning my despondent gaze to the window. It was 8am, drizzling, and winter's gloom outside did nothing to enhance my mood. Karen, who was sitting next to me on the bed, gave me a hug. I'd not been sleeping well for a while, and had been woken at 6.30 by the thunderous report of a shotgun. I'd got up, and my pacing of the room had woken Karen just before 7am.

"You did your best, George - you know you did." Karen kissed my cheek, "And, it wasn't *you* who failed... *we* failed: all of us - this whole community, all trying hard but failing for so many reasons, mostly beyond our control. Arthur *will* understand, and you have succeeded in bringing over two hundred people together and *have* kept them all fed for the last ten weeks."

I sighed, feeling completely drained and depressed. I had realised by mid-October that the population that had remained in Ingleton, Staindrop, and the surrounding villages were mostly elderly. Fortunately, they did include a large number of very keen gardeners who had snapped up the 12 allotments Pat had ploughed, and the additional 18 he ploughed at their request. They worked hard, fertilising and preparing these plots, but little could be grown quickly in the cold, wet, and short days at that end of the year, with most planning to sow in the spring.

Our stocks of food were becoming depleted, and we had only had enough for about one more week. The trickle of radishes, turnips, onions, winter rocket and bitter-tasting winter lettuce, that was being harvested, could never sustain the 240 people who had now put their trust in us to keep them fed.

What was worse, was that these people had become our friends. We had discussed with each of them what they could offer us. Everyone had a story to tell that explained an ability or attribute gained during their lifetimes. Initially, some just offered advice and left. But many returned, having become prolific scavengers or having discovered that they had practical skills that we, or someone in our new community, needed.

Two young guys in particular, worked incredibly hard and earned much respect: Phillip and Jason were friends who previously worked together in an electrical store. They provided and fitted lighting and twelve-volt power sockets that would run off car batteries in at least two rooms, in over 40 houses in Ingleton as well in as our portacabin and the community centre.

Intermittent power cuts had started on the 10th October, and the power went off permanently during the night of the 31st, cutting us off from the ever more depressing and intermittent TV news reports.

Without anyone asking, a team of elderly men, working from their garden sheds, built a sturdy little cart that could be pulled by hand, or by a horse. They proudly presented the cart to us, as a means to carry our charged batteries to the village and flat ones back to the Manor for recharging. Thankfully, Phillip and Jason also realised the effort involved in hauling batteries up from the generator tunnel, through the house, to the cart, was a tiring problem for us. They ran cables up through the ventilation shaft, into the garage, so that batteries could be charged and collected directly from there.

Our new, and very willing, community helped us accumulate masses of clothing, tools and even bicycles. The book and DVD exchange portacabin was also busy, and bulging with stock. Retired teachers were educating the children at Ingleton Bury, where Stuart enthusiastically entertained them by organising games, sports, and other recreational activities including horse riding, and of course, tennis. The lawns at the Bury were divided into little plots where the children themselves grew and tended their own plants.

"If we only had better stocks of food before we started, enough to last us until January, then maybe we could have kept everyone fed," I told Karen, probably for the fifth or sixth time that morning.

The forty or so younger people, including the girls who's horses we had saved, had helped our two farmers plant carrots, winter squash, broccoli, sprouts, leeks and kale, but none of this was ready to harvest yet. Peas and beans were growing well on some of the allotments, but again, they were not going to be ready to harvest for several more weeks.

Paul had started to devalue the worth of many of the items and services people were providing, to try to limit the number of food tokens being given out. We also reduced the amount of food that we would exchange for a token. But this wonderful new community - that was united in trying so hard - needed food every day. We were producing and scavenging less than 25% of their daily needs. I had completely underestimated the number of people we would be serving, and this population was slowly increasing, as some of those who had gone south returned, with terrible stories of flooding, riots, fighting, road piracy, starvation, and contaminated water.

"We should have authorised the looting of the empty houses

before Mad Mick and his mob cleared them all out," I said despondently, "he went off to Barnard Castle with a truckload of food from here."

Karen kissed me again, "Don't beat yourself up. Hindsight is a useless ability at the best of times. Let's tell Arthur just how bad it is. Maybe get Simon Duguid to organise another meeting in the community centre and knock our heads together for ideas. Be honest, and tell everyone the scale of the problem. They must already be aware we are running very low. Maybe someone will come up with a great new idea, or know of a little shop somewhere, that's not been looted? Hey, tomorrow you could be writing a diary entry that says 'fresh hope!'" Karen's smile wasn't convincing, and her eyes could not hide the despair that I was feeding them. "Come on, George, let's go down together."

As we got to the bottom of the stairs, we could hear raised voices from the conservatory. Arthur was pacing about waving his stick. Simon Duguid was there in a uniform that appeared to have been pelted with eggs, and both Phillip and Jason were talking in a very animated fashion, while Melissa was sitting with her arms crossed, angrily.

"Bloody Pikeys, that's all we need!" Shouted Arthur, banging his stick on the ground and ignoring Melissa's hard stare and protests that they were not 'Pikeys' but 'Travellers.'

"We'll all go down there together, George, Nigel, Stuart. Get everyone we can and just push them off!" Jason stated excitedly, getting a nod of agreement only from Phillip.

"Morning everyone!" Announced Karen loudly, "So do I gather we have Travellers nearby?"

"Morning, Karen," said Simon Duguid, sheepishly, "yes, they arrived sometime yesterday evening. They are camped by the swings in the far corner of the cricket ground - the field behind the community centre. I asked them to move on, and they did this!" He pointed at his uniform, still slimy with splattered eggs, "then threatened to set their damned dogs on me!"

"Pikeys; they have no respect for anyone. They will rob us blind and leave behind a stinking mess, you just wait and see!" Arthur added.

"You can't *know* that Daddy," Melissa protested, "and we can't go down there and start a fight. We should try to talk with them!"

"Well, that's clearly not going to work!" Simon replied, indicating, again, the state of his tunic and trousers.

I thought I'd better enter the conversation and try to calm things down a bit, "Morning everyone, nice to see so many here so early. So, maybe our lights have attracted these people? And Simon, you didn't try talking to them, did you? You alone - in uniform - just told them to go away?"

"Yes, I did! They have absolutely no right to bring any vehicles onto that land, and as for livestock… Have they no respect for bylaws?" Simon continued to wipe his tunic with a cloth Karen had found for him.

"What livestock?" I asked.

Karen whispered, "I think Simon is wearing a clue!"

"Chickens," said Phillip, "they have penned them in the kiddies play area - must be twenty or more."

I smiled, "Right, so they have eggs and so must have a need for corn. Pat's got seed corn he can't plant, and that we have been unable to mill, so maybe we can do some trading? I'm sure they are not here for a fight, and maybe they need food just as much as we do?"

"They've also got a tatty old refrigerated van that they seem to be having trouble with – parts everywhere," Phillip added.

"Which they would have stolen no doubt!" Arthur said firmly, before sitting down heavily and crossing his arms, "I suggest you keep well away from them George; they are nothing but trouble: That, I can assure you."

"Maybe so," I agreed, "but this could be an opportunity to do some trading? Big Fridge at Langdon moved south weeks ago. They have hidden one of their refrigerated trailers and a mobile canteen behind their buildings. If these Travellers have a refrigerated van, it stands to reason they have access to fresh food. Who's up for borrowing that refrigerated trailer, and paying them a visit with that, and a big bag of corn?"

"Foolhardy!" stated Arthur, "they will take the trailer and corn, and then beat you to a pulp!"

Karen gave me a concerned look, "Arthur might be right, why not, at least, take Nigel with you?"

"I'm not sure. Maybe he could drive the van, and stay in it, only come out if it looks like I'm in trouble?" I suggested, the fear shared by Arthur and now Karen, had started to rub off on me. "There's something else I need to tell you all," I felt Karen squeeze my arm in support, "the trading centre, it's just not collecting or growing enough food. Unless something changes, we have probably only got one week's worth of food remaining. We are still three to four weeks away from being able to start harvesting what the farms are growing. We are even running low of potatoes, and there won't be another crop of those until next June."

378

"I know." said Arthur, "Young Paul and I were discussing the numbers and stock levels yesterday. I spoke to Richard in Lincolnshire yesterday too. They are faring much better and have an excess of fresh food already. Their population is only 42, and they nearly all contribute to their own food stores. However, they are desperate for tools, boots, gardening gloves and seasoned firewood. So we are going to try to organise an exchange. Due to the road piracy and flooding, Richard is going to try and find a safe place and route to trade. He's got himself one of those drones and is going to see if it can be flown ahead to warn of trouble. Richard is very concerned that our population is just too big, but he has no palatable suggestions of how to reduce it."

I was surprised that Arthur already appreciated the seriousness of our situation, and also by the apparent lack of concern shown by the others in the room. "We know lorries are getting attacked on the main roads; maybe we would be better off using a small convoy of vans and cars to get through?" I asked, "strength in numbers. The Travellers must have made it here from somewhere, and their numbers must have been enough to stop the pirates. Another reason I've got to go and try to talk with them. I'm going to get Nigel, then see if we can get that refrigerated trailer going at Langdon before they find it for themselves!"

"Please take care, George!" Karen said as I headed for the door, her eyes displaying such real concern that I returned to give her a kiss, and whispered, "I'm going to be very careful, I promise."

Nigel had managed to acquire another black Nissan that he had found abandoned, with an empty fuel tank, near Stainton, and luckily, this one had a tow bar. We looked at the trailer, and the long chain that secured it to a concrete post via a heavy and slightly rusty old padlock.

"We'll need a monster pair of bolt cutters to get through that! Anything useful in the back of the car?" I asked as Nigel picked up the chain.

Nigel shrugged and left me searching a dirty and part-shredded plastic bag that was the closest thing there was to a toolbox. The best I could find was a small junior hacksaw with a dull blade. I guessed it would take ages attempting to cut through the chain with that, but I turned to offer it to Nigel as our only option.

However, he was already pulling the trailer towards the back of the Nissan. The chain lay like a dead snake on the gravel - its padlock agape and parted from its body. I gave Nigel a questioning look, and he gave me a great big toothy smile and then laughed as he took the hacksaw I still held out for him. "Picked the lock." he said simply, and, still grinning broadly, he tossed the hacksaw into the back of the Nissan.

"You're a man of few words, but many hidden talents, Nigel!"

Nigel said nothing more as he attached the trailer to the Nissan and connected it up.

I got back in too, and checked the sack of corn hadn't fallen off the rear seat. "We can get to their camp either down the narrow track past the church or via Nursery End to the cricket club just off Gainford Road." I said to Nigel.

Nigel just nodded, he always just seemed to know where he was going, and I suspected that he'd already scouted out the park that morning. He turned into Nursery End and then left again to the cricket club, where quite a gathering of locals had formed by the side of the clubhouse. Nigel stopped just past the group, some of whom held gardening forks and hoes. I scanned the group and counted fifteen people. Most I recognised as regular visitors to the Manor or the allotments. Amongst them, I also spotted a familiar face from the past, his grey beard and green flat cap giving him away. Broken over his arm he carried his shotgun. I got out of the van to murmurs of 'about time' and 'where's the rest of ya?'

Ignoring them, I headed straight to James Granger, who had separated himself from the rest of the mob and was looking at our trailer with some interest.

"Nice to be seeing you again, George, so what's with the fridge on wheels? Trojan 'orse, full of more, such as the big fella?" he nodded towards Nigel, "Or you planning on givin' 'em a cold reception by throwing ice cubes at these 'ere Pikeys?"

"James! Where have you been hiding?" we hugged briefly. "I was expecting you to be one of our first visitors at the Manor. I assumed for sure you'd be supplying us with rabbits, pheasants and maybe the odd deer?"

"Was my intention, but I was watching you, and I sees you have way too many folks for the countryside 'ere-abouts to keep fed. There be few rabbits and even less deer anyhow. I've been gathering mushroom, berries, taking the odd pigeon and partridge, enough for a few, but I can't be doing so for such as many folks as you were taking on." He then smiled. "I 'as been round-about though, early morning I shoot the odd rabbit and a few rats to keep 'em off your allotments."

"Thanks. Arthur has asked after you from time-to-time, I'll tell him you're still with the living, and looking well."

James screwed up his face, "I suppose he was right to be getting rid of me? I soon found there were no estates as needed a gamekeeper this side of the border and like-as-not, none will be needin' such services since all the grass has gone. So, I've been working as pest controller mostly."

The little mob had gathered around us in a circle as we spoke and were becoming impatient, muttering between themselves, and goading one another to speak out.

"Where's Arthur?" one called out, "Did you hear what they did to Duguid? – Shame on them," another said.

"You gonna have to say something, George," James whispered, "these folk, they aren't fit for any kind of a fight, and I'm as happy to as leave 'em be. They'll move on in time, like as not."

I walked past the clubhouse and looked across the weed-free and grassless cricket pitch, to the park in the far corner. I soon realised that I was the only one of this 'mob' who had come this far, and dared to show their face - the others remained hidden behind the clubhouse. Yet, their 'foe' was way in the distance, in the far corner of the field. I could just make out a variety of big cars - Range Rover, Jeeps and a big old Corvette. Among these were some modern caravans, three campervans, a flatbed truck, and the refrigerated van that appeared to be in pieces with darkly dressed figures moving around it. There was a small fire with grey-white smoke rising almost straight up into the windless sky. I could hear the barking of dogs and see washing hanging motionless on lines that must have been strung between the caravans.

I turned back to find James had joined me and was hiding his gun behind his back. The rest had formed a queue, two abreast, almost as if they were a rag-tag army willing to follow us into battle. However, many of their faces clearly showed nothing but fear and reluctance.

"Assuming there be two people per van, then there's maybe only thirty people yonder," James said, "you and Dad's Army 'ere, you gonna attack?" he grinned.

"I'm not here for a fight," I announced loudly and clearly, "I just want to see if we can do some trading. We are desperately low on food, and there is a possibility these Travellers might be able to help us. Marching on them with garden forks because they have camped on an unusable cricket pitch is pointless. What are you defending? A field of mud?"

I think I could see the relief on some of the villager's faces, but there was a gaggle of people who continued to speak out against the mess they would leave and the thieving that they would all be suffering. "What if they'd camped out in the Manor gardens, you'd do something about that, eh?" – "Yeah, what if they steal everything from *your* sheds?"

"Well, as far as I know, they haven't taken anything yet and have camped on a pretty useless piece of land," I stated loudly to them all, "the kids don't play down there anymore - they are all up at the Bury. So we have no reason to be aggressive towards them."

I took another look across the field; I could see two young lads had seen us. One was peering at us through binoculars, and the other appeared to be calling towards the caravans. I could feel my heart rate increase once again as more figures started to appear in the doorways of the caravans and those working on their van also turned their heads towards us.

I took a deep breath, "Time to go. Please keep that gun and those garden tools well out of sight!"

"How many?" said, Nigel, as I sat down beside him in the car, and he drove away slowly.

"I don't know? Twenty teenagers and adults, maybe more."

We rounded the corner of the clubhouse, and Nigel aimed the

van towards the right side of the camp. As we slowly headed across the damp mud, a group started to form between us and their caravans. Scruffy-looking teenagers fetched equally scruffy and aggressive looking dogs that snarled, barked, tugging against their leads.

Nigel continued in a straight line until we were about thirty metres away, where he turned quite sharply to the left, across the path of the waiting group. Then he stopped some twenty metres away. I guessed this was so he could both make a quick exit and that the side of our refrigerated trailer, with 'Big Fridge.' printed on it, was facing them.

Maria's cautionary words suddenly entered my head; 'Think carefully before you act' and 'learn to recognise who your friends are'. I sat there for a few moments considering the risks. "Here goes!" I said. I reached back and hauled the heavy sack of corn onto my lap before climbing out, "Wish me luck!"

Nigel looked at me seriously, "Scratch the back of your neck if you need to make a run for it."

As I rounded the front of the van and hauled the sack over my shoulder, I realised I'd never heard so many words from Nigel in one sentence before, and I found myself grinning as I approached this ugly group, whose numbers now exceeded thirty.

"Hello!" I said boldly, as I tried desperately to maintain my smile.

"Wus in the sack?" A young guy struggling to hold a lead with a Pitbull-like dog attached demanded. I had expected an Irish accent but instead thought the young man sounded Eastern European.

"Is that a working refrigerated box you got there?" Asked a

middle-aged bald man, who with a group of three others walked, past me, and directly towards the Nissan and its trailer. One deliberately shoulder-barged me as he passed.

"I have got corn for your chickens," I said, my voice quivering slightly, "I was hoping you'd give me some eggs, preferably *not* thrown at me! And, yes, that is a working refrigerated trailer. Yours is broken, and you guys maybe need to trade?"

The men approaching the trailer retreated a few paces, as Nigel stepped out of the Nissan and stood with his arms folded facing them.

"Woah! He's big fella; he's not a local boy, is he?" The bald man asked, his face right in mine, "Is he why you're so bold?"

"You're from London?" I asked, trying not to appear phased by his aggressive invasion of my personal space.

"And, you aren't from these parts neither," he stated, "away lads!" he yelled suddenly, causing me to jump and him to smile, "what's your name, jumpy?"

"I'm George," I put my hand out, nervously.

"Del," he said ignoring my offer of a handshake, instead putting his hand around my shoulder and pulling me towards the caravans as the mob and their dogs reluctantly dispersed, "we are traders, and we do 'ave a problem keeping our stock frozen. Is it you who has all the village lights burning, and maintains that trading Manor?" He pointed in the rough direction of the Manor.

"Er, yes. I'm George Craven; the centre *was* my idea I suppose," I was hoping he might recognise my name and it would somehow give me added kudos, but it didn't seem to mean anything to him.

"Can I relieve you of that?" He prodded the heavy sack I still had over my shoulder.

To be honest, I'd have been relieved just to have got rid of its weight and bulk even if I got nothing in return for the seed, but I did say, as I put it down, "Got to be worth a good few eggs that?"

Del didn't answer my question he just said "Thank you." but something had changed; something subtle, he was no longer menacing, and although many pairs of eyes were still watching me from doorways and misted windows, I no longer felt in imminent danger. I looked ahead and could see that Del was leading me towards a caravan where a plump woman - who reminded me a little of Doris Day; but with grey hair. She had enormous earrings; was wearing what looked rather like a pantomime white witch's costume. She was leaning casually in the doorway with a curious expression. As we got closer, she waved Del away.

Del stood his ground, "This is George Craven, you're right, he *is* from the Manor. He's come with a fridge trailer some three meters long, and some corn for our chickens." Del obviously wanted to stay and continue to be involved, but she waved him away again, this time, more forcibly, and with a hard stare.

I stood looking up at her while trying not to look at her enormous cleavage, as she continued to block the doorway above me. She tilted her head to one side questioningly and eyed me up and down, but she said nothing nor beckoned me in. I felt I was somehow being tested or analysed. She took a deep breath and looked skywards.

My eyes flicked down to her bosom for the briefest of seconds, and straight back to her face, which had instantly lit up into a big smile, "And, there it is!" she proclaimed in a Welsh accent "Nice aren't they, now? Even gay men can't resist havin' a sneaky glance! You held out for quite a while! Now you can squeeze your tiny frame past these lovelies as you come in!" She stood to one side, leaving me plenty of room to get passed, but she narrowed the gap as I got to the top of the three little wooden steps, ensuring I rubbed past her heaving breasts with my chest as she turned and pushed me into the caravan with them. She laughed as I uttered an embarrassed, and almost inaudible, apology.

"Aw... Sorry, George, I was only toying with you, and that was a little unfair of me, wasn't it now?" She grinned as she waved an open hand towards one of the two long bench seats, made of studded blue leather.

I ignored her question, and instead asked one of my own: "I was expecting Irish accents, but I've heard Eastern European, London - and you're from Wales!"

"We are a mixed group, mostly Latvian." She opened a cabinet above the opposite seat exposing a row of unusual-shaped bottles of brightly coloured drinks with foreign labels, "Would you like a drink to toast our new partnership?"

"Um, no." then I quickly correctly myself - thinking I been rude: "Sorry... No, *thank you*, it's just a little early for me."

"Oh, it's not all as bad as it looks!" she said, closing the door, "Now you won't say no to a proper Romany tea, now will you?" She headed for the kitchen area at the front of the caravan and lit a gas ring for the kettle. I took the opportunity, while her back was turned, to look down to the other end of the caravan; It was curtained off with a pair of yellow curtains with gold trim. Through a small gap between them, I could see the light of some flickering candles, and a bed with shiny, bright purple linen. All around the caravan, on every spare inch of wall, was a photograph or memento, each carefully positioned so that they were equally spaced. There were lots pictures of groups around fires, others showing proud people posed with dogs or horses - many with rosettes.

"We have picked up a few Irish over the years, but it seems to be their nature to bring trouble back to the camp and so they had to take to their own path. Then Del and I hooked up, and we became fish traders," She said as she readied the pot. "Oh, I'm Fenella - or Nella to my friends - and, you... You are George?"

"Um, yes. So, you and Del are..."

She turned abruptly, her sudden change of expression to dismay stopping me.

"No," she said as she pulled cups from a cupboard, "Del and I are respected elders, but I don't share this caravan if that's what you were asking? Del picked me up from a group of Travellers in France. He'd taken a Latvian bride, many years before that. My husband, Tom, he died suddenly, see? I needed a complete change of lifestyle and had been bouncing from one group of Travellers to another since I left Wales. I never really settled in until I found this group." She came and stood in front of me, making me feel small again. Then with two fingers under my chin, she gently lifted my head and studied me closely, "Aw, you don't look like a 'George', now, is that really your birth name?" She stroked the back of her hand down my cheek," I've told you my story, I think you've one of your own?"

"I was christened Simon," I admitted, wondering how on earth she could tell? "but I left that name behind in another life," I shifted back in the seat as far as I could - her closeness was making me very uncomfortable, "I've been known as George for over five years now. Oh, and I didn't mean to pry about your relationship, it's just I thought ..."

"You thought I might drag you off to my bed?" she laughed, Oh, George, you've not the stamina to last an hour in my company!" She stood back grinning, "Aw! I'm just playing with you see? Hmm… 'Simon' … Yes, I can see why you ditched that name, but why George? Hmm, now 'Craven' that's a good strong name that is, but is that yours either? By birth I mean?" She asked as she headed back to check on the tea.

"Not really, I was adopted. My step-parents said I could keep their name, but that it was OK to change it when I was sixteen," I explained, wondering why we were talking about names and not trading.

"Well, I think they'd have had a job stopping you changing it at sixteen, but did you change it?" She asked, as she returned to the kitchen area and poured tea into two bright white cups with delicate gold gilding.

"No, Craven was *their* name, I did briefly toy with changing it to 'Raven' after some old kid's program starring Phil Daniels that my step-dad showed me once, but I'm glad I didn't now.

"Aw no! You can't be a 'Raven' without jet black hair! Milk but no sugar I'm guessing?"

"You have milk!" I asked, having not been offered a drop for many weeks.

Fenella smiled, "It's from frozen, but all our milk and fish are defrosting rapidly now that our van's broken, but you knew that, didn't you? We were trading the fish as we went around, mainly for diesel for the boats and vegetables for us and the fishermen themselves." She handed me the tea in the pretty little cup, "Was all so much simpler when we just bought the fish with cash and just sold it for a profit!"

"Thanks," I said as she put the tea down, "How much fish do you need to get rid of?" I asked.

Fenella smiled, "I knew as soon as I saw you dragging that thing onto the field that you'd be asking that! Saw us in a pickle and thought you'd take us for a ride, did you? Well, I guess you want, more or less, all we have? That'll be about 600Kg of gutted fish. But, you see, that leaves us with nothing and no way to continue trading. I hope you weren't planning on loading up your trailer with all we got and thought we are so desperate as to accept a sack of corn in exchange?!" She peered at me suspiciously.

"No, absolutely not!" I replied quickly and earnestly, "we want you to continue to go and get fish and for that, you'll be wanting *our* refrigerated trailer. Now that's got to be worth your fish! – All I ask is that you deliver what you've got now, less any you'll need for yourselves, to the Manor and, next time you're in the area, park up, and we'll trade our vegetables for your fish. Make this an on-going arrangement. I've got two hundred-plus mouths to feed, so we could probably take all you can carry once a month. We have a cold room, under the house, as well as enough power to keep fridges and freezers running. Our problem is that we have no spare vegetables to trade now; we need just a few more weeks for them to grow."

Fenella's expression changed, she appeared to be hiding near excitement, "George, I'm impressed! I must admit to having misjudged your motives somewhat." Then she looked doubtful, "We still have a problem; you see, we had to provide 100 litres of diesel for the boats for them to load our van with the fish, and we need some ourselves. Now, our van is quite a bit bigger than your trailer, but we're still going to need some diesel. We have to travel further and further to find any. It's becoming scarce, you see? Can your much larger population still scavenge enough for our needs?"

I wasn't going to mention the fact that we'd got two fuel tankers hidden away, "I think we have about 80 litres you can have, provided you give us empty containers, so our guys can continue to scavenge. We know places where we can keep getting diesel for quite a while."

"Oh, is that locally?" Fenella asked.

"No. There's very little locally - you're right there." I responded, hoping this woman couldn't read my thoughts!

"I see," she winked, "I'll have to discuss this with Del and the others. You'll be coming back at noon."

"Oh, em, yes. You can't make the decision yourself?" I asked hoping to save time and wrap up the deal then and there.

Fenella laughed as she stood up, "I'm not the Gypsy Queen, you know! I've become more their spokeswoman; I used to deal with the local radio when they came knocking, try to dispel a few myths and correct the gossip. Try to undo the damage some of our kind persistently tar our brush with. Anyhow, now, I've found out what you have and what you want, Del and the boys will discuss your offer, decline or tailor it more to our liking, see? Then three of us will negotiate directly with you," she pointed to my forehead, "Aw, you never finished your tea, there'll be more drink at noon, oh, and bring your haggling hat!"

As I stepped down from the caravan, I could smell fish being cooked on the steamy fire. Nigel was standing next to Del and a very petite young woman, who appeared to be talking excitedly to Nigel. All three were eating baked fish from blackened wraps of silver foil. As I approached, Nigel grinned. "Nice!" he said, as he held out the fish for me to try.

I took a pinch of the hot, steaming white flesh. It came away easily and tasted rich, not just of fish - I could taste and smell more subtle flavours; lemon, rosemary as well as pepper. I had not eaten anything better than canned fish for many weeks, and my mouth almost sang with pleasure on receiving this simple delicacy.

Del, patted me on the back as I greedily reached for more, and Nigel quickly withdrew his fish, "Steal fish from the jaws of a shark would ya?!" he joked, as Nigel took a step back to defend his meal further.

"Here, take these. The deal is done for the corn." Del handed me two boxes, a dozen eggs in each.

The thin young woman said something in Latvian like, "Varak Zivis?" and offered me her fish. I smiled and nodded and took a piece. I quickly realised that this was a different kind of fish, thinner, and with a more delicate flavour, there seemed to be an unusual yet very pleasant undertone of vanilla, "Vanilla?" I asked.

The woman nodded and said two long sentences, all unintelligible to me.

Del nodded to her when she said a few further words to him, "She's shy of talking to strangers herself. She can speak English, but she's saying that she cooks the fish; that one," he nodded to Nigel, "is mackerel, and hers is sole. She cooked them both, and she says 'yes', there's vanilla and lime with the sole."

I smiled at this tiny woman "They are both very nice, and I'd very much like the recipes!"

Del, looked at me seriously, "You can add them to the list of things you want us to trade. When ya comin' back?"

"Twelve, noon," I said slightly taken back by his abrupt answer.

"Then you'd best be gone. Is that trailer cooling?" He pointed to our car and trailer.

"Er, no it's not plugged in," I replied.

"Well don't you think you should be readying it? Assuming you want to be taking our 'very nice' fish away in it?" He gave me a hard shove in the back, towards it.

I thought I'd leave it to Fenella to explain that's was not what I planned, and hoped his mood would be kinder when we returned, and that he appreciated the trailer was actually for *them*.

As I climbed back into the car with Nigel and carefully placed the eggs in the foot well, I felt a gentle tug on my arm. I looked back to see the thin Latvian woman, smiling and offering another, even bigger, foil-wrapped piece of fish as she nodded into the car. I took it gratefully, smiled, and said, "Thank you," very clearly, "I wish I knew the Latvian for *thank you*," I said to Nigel.

"Paldies." replied Nigel quietly, as he did up his seat belt.

Before I could react to Nigel's apparent and unexpected language skill, or test this word on our new Latvian friend, Del shouted angrily, "Monta!"

The little woman jumped and looked scared. Then gave us a little wave, and a wonderfully cheeky smile, before running obediently back to the camp.

"She's nice." stated Nigel.

As we rounded the clubhouse, we encountered a smaller

group of villagers; James Granger was still there, and Simon Duguid had made his way back but was no longer in uniform.

I wound the window down, "I see you've changed, Simon!"

"Those type of people had no respect for a uniform, even when I could have called for backup," he stated, "probably just antagonises them now," he shrugged as if resigned, "you've still got the trailer... Are they not going to leave?"

I smiled, "Not just yet," I handed the hot fish out to him, "share that around. I'm coming back here at noon to discuss getting a lot more of the same, and to invite then back on a regular basis!"

James Granger was grinning from ear-to-ear, he clearly understood, and took the fish from Simon, who seemed far from happy and was trying to give it back. But before he could protest further, I added, "Now, please don't do anything that might upset these people, they are already frustrated at being at a disadvantage, and I don't want them wound-up before I come back."

James and the others were behaving like hungry birds, all pecking away at the hot fish with their fingers, James offered the fish to Simon again, but he rejected the offer with a scowl and walked off angrily.

"Ah, don't you go worryin' about him, he's just bitter because he's losing his authority, he'll come round as likely has it," James said, with his mouth full.

As we left, James threw the empty ball of silver paper through my open window, and he laughed as it hit my ear, "You might want to see how much silver foil you've got in stock, George?" he called out.

"That's a good idea!" I said, remembering that Molly had managed to get Paul to trade ten, 200-meter, rolls of foil that she'd nicked from the Blackhorse kitchen. She'd convinced Paul it was exceptionally useful and had effectively swindled him out of 10 food tokens for it. Maybe now, that deal wasn't so bad?

We'd need it and maybe the Travellers would too? "Remind me to bring a couple of rolls when we come back," I said to Nigel, who appeared to be sitting with his arms crossed angrily.

"That fish was for me," said Nigel, unhappy that I'd given it away. I told him I doubted it was meant for him, and that by sharing it as we did, we had helped them to appreciate why we didn't want to be fighting with the Travellers.

Nigel dropped me off at the gatehouse, and I walked up the drive with the eggs. Outside the portacabin, there was the usual queue of people with bags, wheelbarrows and shopping trollies bringing goods and garden produce in, while others were collecting items from the sheds. Today, as with most days, Andrea, Phillip, Jason, and two of the young 'stable girls' as I called them, were helping to value and sort produce, and exchange tokens as they were presented. I stopped on the drive by the garages where I could see that Arthur and Melissa were loading batteries onto the cart. Stuart had arrived with a group of children he'd taken out blackberrying. Excitedly, they were each trying to show Arthur how many they'd collected. Some were also proudly showing off their scratches, with mouths and chins purple with fruit that somehow hadn't made it into their baskets.

I stood listening to the happy voices and watched this little scene for quite a while. Suddenly the importance of a successful trade with the Travellers dawned on me: We desperately needed that fish, and I had to be prepared to offer maybe more than it was worth to ensure that I secure it, but not so generous that we'd be unable to afford subsequent trades.

"George! Are you OK?!" Karen was running down the steps from the house towards me, causing Melissa and Arthur to turn and also notice I'd returned. Karen ran all the way up to me and gave me a surprisingly tight hug.

"Mind the eggs!" I said holding them aloft, "and I'm alright, just suddenly a bit squashed that's all!"

"I saw you just standing there, without Nigel, and I thought that you'd been hurt!" Karen blurted out.

"No one's been hurt, and I've got good news." I waited for Arthur and Melissa to join me before I started to explain what had happened. My explanation interrupted by the children, now eager to show me their baskets of blackberries. Eventually, Stuart sent them back towards the portacabin, so Paul could display their finds on the fresh food stall that had had little other than limp rhubarb on it for many days.

As I expected, Melissa, Stuart, and Karen were happy with my proposed trade. They accepted my explanation as to why we'd need to give them diesel, and maybe some silver foil too, as a sweetener. Arthur, though happy that they had fish, thought that the 'Damn Pikeys' were 'robbing us blind' stating that the refrigerated trailer alone was worth much more than the fish. He suggested that we could take the trailer and some diesel directly to the fishermen ourselves. But Stuart was quick to point out that we'd probably become victims of road pirates and possibly the Travellers too if we attempted that. Arthur back-tracked- just warning me not to be more generous than necessary and to make sure they kept to their side of the deal, by not giving them the trailer until the fish was at the Manor. To keep Arthur happy, I said I agreed, though I thought I'd not insist upon that because our new trading partners would know we didn't trust them, and it would likely harm the chances of future trading. I just hoped that Arthur was wrong.

Noon seemed to come so quickly; in the back of the trailer, I had packed ten ten-litre tanks of diesel and one of petrol. In the back of the car, hidden under a blanket, I'd stashed two more cans of diesel and two of the large rolls of silver foil. I had found myself hunting through the hardware shed for additional items. There was a professional set of ceramic kitchen knives; I hid those in the glove box, too.

Word had got about that we were heading out to the Travellers' site again, and that I could be returning with fish. There was quite a crowd down by the gatehouse as we left, wanting to wish us luck, and some telling us to be careful.

Among them was the elderly woman; she appeared by my window and insisted I took her wooden cross, "Take this and God will protect you from evil." she said, as her hands shook, and her eyes burning with absolute belief.

"Thank you." I said, putting the cross in my breast pocket, "I'll be sure to bring it back safely."

Nigel shot me a disbelieving look, and I just shrugged at him and said, "Well, it can't do any harm, can it?"

The wind had picked up when we got back to the cricket club, the smoke was worse and blowing straight at us from the far corner. It was travelling low across the ground preventing us from seeing the camp at all, and meaning we would have to travel blind through the thick smoke to get there.

"I think they're burning wet leaves," I peered into the smoke, unable to make out anything.

Without saying a word, Nigel turned the van around and back out onto the road. Briefly, I thought he had abandoned the trade, and I could well understand why. But he turned left onto Gainford Road and through Ingleton, turning left just before the church. Here the road narrowed to a rough track. We were coming out into the same field but much closer to the camp and we were no longer blinded by the smoke, and could see the camp and the new fire on the field some 20 meters to the left. Two teenagers were emptying large buckets of leaves onto it, causing the fire to choke and create billowing clouds of white smoke.

"That's deliberate." I stated as we sat there, watching.

"It's almost twelve." Said Nigel pointing at the dashboard clock.

"OK, drive up quickly, park between the fire and the camp, and sound the horn just before we stop. Same as before; I'll scratch the back of my neck if I'm going to need to make a run for it and I'll try not to be lured into a caravan this time."

The two boys were so engaged in feeding the fire and laughing to themselves, that our car horn made them both jump. They turned, and looked frightened on discovering we were now between them and their caravans. They first started to run around the front of our car, then, deciding it would be safer running around the back, changed direction and ran around us in a big circle.

As I disembarked, I could see Del, sitting on a chair facing the field, laughing. He continued to grin as I approached and the two boys disappeared amongst the caravans, way off to my right, "Ha, ha!" He said, "You sure gave them a fright," then his face changed to a false seriousness, but you're late, and that's gonna cost ya!"

"Despite your smoke, we're not late," I stated, "and from the smoke can I assume you no longer want to trade?" I said, pretending to be disinterested.

"What?" Del stood up as another man, and Fenella approached, "Oh, you know boys will be boys, that fire wasn't nuffin' to do with us." He turned his chair around, and I saw three more, now all facing each other, around an upturned crate with a bottle and four shot glasses. Del beckoned me towards them as the others sat down. "Sit, we'll knock out a trade."

A tall and gaunt man with jet black hair, a sharp nose, and eyes that were so dark brown they almost appeared black, sat opposite me. He eyed me up and down before nodding to Del and saying something in Latvian.

"George, this is Uldis - he is Monta's father," Del nodded towards the man with the dark eyes, "sorry, he does not speak much English. And Nella, you have already met." He nodded towards Fenella, who had changed into a dark grey dress and completely dropped the flirty act.

"Now we should drink!" Del announced. Fenella poured what I think was a spiced vodka and, though I thought it was not a great idea, I joined them in tipping the liquid down my throat in one go. Fenella immediately refilled the glasses, with my attempt to put my hand over my glass being defeated by her swift actions, as the liquid burned my throat and I struggled not to choke.

"George is offering a refrigerated trailer and eighty litres of diesel for 500 kilogrammes of fresh fish," Fenella announced.

Before I could contest the amount of fish now offered, Del spoke; "The trailer offered isn't new, and its capacity is only half that of our current van. The amount of diesel offered is less than we usually give the fishermen, and George is not offering any vegetables. Therefore, I suggest he must increase his offer significantly - who is in agreement?"

Not surprisingly, Fenella, Del, and Uldis all raised their hands.

I sat back and shook my head before speaking out. Clearly this group was playing games and would always be able to out-vote me, even though I doubted Uldis was fully understanding the details. "Well, the trailer we are offering is *working* and is, therefore, better than any bigger one that doesn't. My offer was for the 600 Kg of fish you have. The fishermen, as I understand it, were asking 100 litres of diesel to fill your bigger van. What was it you said, Del? 'Your van was twice as big?' So, I should be offering 50 litres of diesel for them to fill the trailer. I accept that we don't have any vegetables to offer right now, but the extra 30 litres of diesel should cover that. Therefore, I state that our offer is fair and that the 240 people I represent all agree with me." I crossed my arms, hoping this action would somehow show determination.

"Drink!" Said Fenella, as she pushed the glass into my hand and the others all threw back their vodka. Reluctantly, I drank down the strange liquid and again grimaced as Fenella quickly refilled the glasses.

Del spoke urgently and forcefully, in Latvian, to Uldis, who eventually nodded before Del turned back to me, "George, you must improve your offer if you wish to trade. We will increase our offer to include Monta and 550Kg of fish; for that we expect 200 Litres of diesel, 100 litres of petrol and 100 of your meal tokens."

I was confused about the inclusion of Monta and assumed they meant her recipes. I also didn't realise they knew of our meal tokens, but if given these, it would ensure they would come back for future trades. My problem was I didn't have any with me, and the amount of petrol and diesel they were asking for was suddenly excessive. As I considered how to reject this request, Uldis called out "Monta!"

From somewhere behind me Monta appeared, came around slowly and stood behind her father, smiling but looking a little nervous. She had also changed her clothes and was wearing a thin, pale blue dress, that exaggerated her tiny frame and clearly outlined her pert little breasts. Uldis spoke again and pointed at me. To my complete surprise, she came over and just sat on my lap, putting her arm around my neck.

"Woah!" I exclaimed as I gently slid her off by slowly standing up, "I really only wanted her recipes!" Then addressing her father directly, I said slowly and clearly, "She is beautiful, but I'm sorry, I have someone." I looked into her dark, sad-looking, eyes as she turned away from me to face her father once more.

Uldis didn't look at all happy, but Monta did seem to be a little relieved as her father angrily sent her away. I felt sorry for her as she left, she obviously didn't have the freedoms other girls of her age took for granted; I wondered if she wanted to leave before her father traded her to someone equally badly matched, and I was left feeling guilty that I'd rejected her. Maybe I should have accepted her; then told her she was free to leave and find a man for herself?

Del, Uldis, and Fenella spoke in Latvian for a few minutes. Del seemed angry with Uldis, and Fenella was trying to calm him down.

Feeling isolated, I thought I'd better speak up again to try to smooth things over; "I will increase our offer." I said loudly, interrupting their argument, "I'll give you the trailer, 100 litres of diesel, 20 litres of petrol, and a 200-metre roll of aluminium foil for cooking fish. For that, all we want is 600 Kg of fish delivered to the Manor and your word you will return to trade fish for diesel and vegetables at your *usual* rates. This is a one-off special offer to allow you to continue to trade with the fishermen. It's very generous and one I can't repeat. If you reject it, we will use the trailer to trade with the fishermen directly. Now I believe this is a very fair offer and is the maximum I'm authorised to make. So… take it or leave it!" I am still not sure how much the alcohol influenced my decision to announce this 'take-it-or-leave-it' offer, but I do remember instantly doubting my decision, thinking it was rash.

Del shook his head firmly, but Fenella smiled and translated my offer for Uldis, who then slowly nodded. Fenella then said, "I'm sorry, we really only have 550Kg of fish remaining. Who here agrees to George's offer?" Fenella asked. She and Uldis quickly put their hands up. Del looked at me with an expectant twinkle in his eye. Suddenly I understood, and I raised mine too. Del winked and with false reluctance, he then raised his also and then roared, "Drink!"

This time, we clinked our glasses together before drinking down the liquid that had strangely become more palatable.

Del poured us each another, and the bottle was drained, "To the future!"

I repeated, "To the future!"

"Priekā! said Uldis and Fenella together.

So it was agreed; we should take the fish back in the trailer, and we would then return it once we'd unloaded it. Del was surprised to find the diesel was already waiting in the trailer, "You were mighty sure you'd do this deal, weren't you?" he asked, as we hauled the heavy cans out, "You negotiate well!"

I just grinned, knowing I'd still got more stashed in the car. I called for Nigel to bring a roll of foil and the set of ceramic knives from the car. Maybe the alcohol had softened me; I felt happy with the trade, and once the fish was loaded up, I presented the knives to Del as an extra gift, that he accepted gratefully and with some surprise.

I felt euphoric as I got back into the Nissan, we'd got a good deal and made some new friends who'd regularly bring us fish. The Ingleton Manor trading centre was back on its feet. I felt that nothing now could stop us.

"We got all the fish! A sweet, sweet deal!" I said to Nigel as I buckled-up. I was very pleased with myself as we pulled away, "We just need to bring this trailer back once we've unloaded it."

"Palikt zems!" Nigel said.

"Ha, ha! – What's that? Latvian for 'cracking a good deal, George - You are a superstar'?!" I laughed, on a high from the good result and, probably the alcohol too, "How come you know some Latvian, Nigel?"

"It means 'stay down', I learn languages from tapes," Nigel glanced over to me, his face stony and severe, as the car left the rough track and joined the smooth tarmac road that led past the graveyard and picturesque church.

"What's up with you? – we got the fish!" I gave Nigel a questioning look. Nigel's serious expression was soon explained:

"Hello!"

Startled, I turned to the back of the car to see Monta rising from behind our seats. Her face lit up with a child-like, cheeky smile. "I come too," she giggled, putting her finger up against her pouting lips and making an exaggerated shushing sound, "to be for Nigel." her smile widening further as she looked at him adoringly.

"Oh, Shit! – Stop the car!" I yelled.

Nigel hit the brakes hard, and poor Monta screamed as, unrestrained, she was thrown forward between our seats, her thin dress ripping apart at the front as she became wedged tightly between our seats with her arms pinned behind her. She urgently struggled to both free herself and cover herself up.

I quickly averted my eyes and pulled my seat forward to release her.

Nigel gave me an angry stare, "Why did you yell stop? Look what you did!"

I turned to the back where Monta was holding her dress together with one hand, and shaking, was examining her shoulder, that already looked sore. "I am sorry, Monta, we *can't* take you." I said forcefully, intentionally not leaving either her, nor Nigel, in any doubt.

She looked so petite and helpless as a single tear rolled down her face. She looked questioning at Nigel. Her pitiful expression contorted into one of fear and intense disappointment mixed with puzzlement. She turned to me, and letting go of her dress, sank to her knees, with her hands together as if in prayer, "Please!" She begged, but not wide-eyed and flirty as I'd come to expect from Melissa. This wasn't a rehearsed expression; her face was screwed up in genuine anguish as if her whole life depended on upon my answer.

I had to turn away from her, "We've got to take her back. Right now, Nigel" I stated. Then I realised we couldn't possibly just return her, not with a gaping dress and bruised shoulder, "Oh shit, shit, shit! Well, Melissa will have to find a new dress for her, she's about her size, *then* we bring her straight back with the trailer."

Nigel and Monta began an urgent and desperate conversation in Latvian, at one point, early on, she looked at me and just exclaimed 'No!' as she shook her head frantically.

I got out of the car and looked back towards the field to check no one from the camp was pursuing us, I was hoping that they hadn't realised she had gone. "Don't go anywhere!" I insisted, "I'm going to walk a bit, clear my head, and decide what to do." I looked at Nigel, "Nigel, do even you know how old she is?"

Nigel translated my question, and a long answer came back from Monta, who rattled away in a quite forceful tone. "She's twenty-two and says she has the right to go where she wants," Nigel said.

"Twenty-two! Really? So, she said goodbye to her family, and waved to them as she left, did she?" I asked while shaking my head with frustration.

"She wasn't able to, they won't approve." Nigel answered.

"You realise we've got to bring this trailer back for them, don't you Nigel?"

"Do we?" Nigel asked flatly.

I just shook my head and climbed through a gap in the hedge, into the churchyard. Looking at the church, I remembered the old lady's cross and pulled it out of my pocket; "Come on then... give me a sign!" I spoke out loud to the cross, "What should I do, feed the 200 or save the girl and *really* piss off the Travellers?" I had to dismiss Nigel's idea that we simply just didn't go back; keeping the fish, trailer, and the girl. That would, almost certainly, lead to violent retribution against the people of Ingleton, and probably the Manor too. That left three other options as I saw it: We could return with the trailer and deny knowing where Monta was, or when we deliver the trailer, we admit to having her and try to pay for her, or… we just say 'sorry, we found her in the back of our car' and return her.

I hated the idea of effectively buying her – that just wasn't right, but then neither was returning her, knowing that she didn't want to be with them and that they'd probably only trade her to someone else another day.

That ment denying we'd got her – lying to them, and lying to her father who might be distraught? But what if they'd not noticed her gone when we delivered the trailer? What would they assume or do when they later discovered her missing? These thoughts and options circled in my head as I dismissed each of them in turn before, desperately reassessing each of them again.

"Bloody Hell!" I shouted out loud, "And you're no help!" I threw the cross towards the Church. The good feeling, I had entered the Nissan with had completely evaporated. And yet, I instantly felt bad about throwing the cross and went to retrieve it, hoping it wasn't damaged.

"Has your God deserted you?"

I jumped and spun around to see Fenella had crept up behind me.

"I wondered how far you'd get? I saw Monta sneaking into your car and the big man hiding her in the back," she said.

"What? But, why didn't you say something to Del or her father?" I asked, "You let her go, and now I'm right in the shit!"

Then I heard the car door close, and saw Nigel looking over the hedge, "Nigel, you stay right there!" I called out, still angry with him for causing this dilemma.

"Well, I didn't stop her because she went of her own free will," Fenella explained calmly, "you didn't take her - she left. I have just told Uldis that she hid in your car and that you weren't aware of it. He and Del are worried that, once you discovered her, you'd not return to complete the trade. So, I said I'd follow you and explain that you must still complete the transaction. Also, that Nigel has to come back and ask Uldis for his blessing to marry her."

I laughed, "What, he has to marry her? – They only just met this morning!" I exclaimed, realising that Nigel had ignored my instructions and was scrambling through the hedge.

"I'll do it!" he said urgently as he got to us, "I'll tell him now."

"Wait-up Nigel! You only just met her, you can't possibly want to marry her!" I protested as I struggled with this new but utterly bizarre solution.

"I will *not* send her back!" Nigel stated, quite aggressively.

"George, listen to me," Fenella took me by the shoulders and turned me to face her, "you don't understand their culture, Uldis is *not* a bad man, but he *will* severely punish Monta if she returns, or has to be taken back by force. However, if she is to marry, and Uldis has been trying to marry her off since she was fourteen, then he will be happy for her. It was Del's idea to try to trade her away, Uldis never really approved. She was so late maturing; you see? Our girls are usually paired up long before they are sixteen, but Monta - she didn't develop into a woman until she was twenty, even then she was so tiny and shy, no one wanted her. She's twenty-two now, and that's unacceptably late to marry for those in our community. If Nigel asks for her hand, Uldis will be delighted! He will shower him with gifts and, most importantly, Monta and Uldis can remain friends. Her mother died in childbirth, you see. Nigel understands all this - can't you?" She gave me a very questioning stare as Monta appeared through the hedge and, looking scared, ran to Nigel's side.

As Nigel put his arm around her, I looked at this odd couple; A large black man in his late thirties, and this tiny waif of a girl who looked a lot younger than she actually was. Yet I could see that somehow they were matched, and despite having met only that morning, there was already a deep, unspoken, bond between them.

I sighed loudly, and shook my head in false disapproval, "Oh, what-the-heck... Congratulations Nigel!" and, smiling, I put my hand out.

Monta's little face lit up again, Nigel's broad smile appeared, and he shook my hand firmly, "Thank you, George!"

Fenella, with tears running down her face, added, "I'm so happy for you Monta my dear, but I am going to miss you so, so much." Monta hugged Fenella tightly, "Oh dear, whatever happened to your dress?"

"My fault; I yelled 'stop the car' when she popped up, and she got stuck between the front seats. We were going to replace it at the Manor. Would you like to come back with us and see our operation there?"

Fenella declined the invitation, instead explained that she'd better go back to the camp and prevent them from forming a raiding posse. She also advised that Nigel should take Monta with him when he talked with Uldis.

Monta was both in awe, and looked a little frightened, as we drove past the no longer working fountain, the many sheds and people, towards the Manor. As her eyes widened, she also sank further into her seat, "We are to live here?" she asked quietly, and with obvious trepidation.

I laughed, "No!" You and Nigel will live in that little cottage we passed on the way in – the gatehouse. I used to live there; it's very nice!"

Monta appeared slightly less worried but was reluctant to leave the car once we stopped. Nigel coaxed her out, offering a helping hand and whispering some calming words in Latvian.

Arthur, Melissa, and Karen had all come out as we arrived - eager to discover how, or if, the deal had gone through. The appearance of Monta, shyly holding her skimpy dress together, certainly raised some eyebrows! But Melissa soon took her under her wing, and they went off together to find a replacement dress.

Arthur was happy with the trade, but thought Nigel's imminent marriage to a 'Pikey reject' was 'madness!' Fortunately, he was wise enough not to express his opinions in Nigel's company. After storing all the fish in the freezers and cool room, Nigel and Monta returned to the traveller's camp with the trailer. I did offer to go with them, but Nigel said that he should be the one to talk with Uldis and that he'd prefer to do it without any help.

"Ah, George," Arthur caught me as I was heading towards the library where the CB was set up, "Paul was finding it difficult valuing the fish. Karen suggested that he just quote the same, one token value for each 250-gram portion," He looked at me over his glasses, "if you don't agree, you'd better head straight to the portacabin."

"Er, no that sounds fine." I answered, "we maybe need some scales and some way to divide the fish and pack it in the cellar? We can't be having everyone traipsing down there; the fish won't stay cool with the door constantly opening and closing. Maybe we should prepare portions and transfer them to the freezer in the portacabin?"

"Right you are," replied Arthur, with a nod and a wink, "I'll ask Jason and Phillip to organise that. I can see you look a bit tired, George, where were you heading? To check-in on Richard at Lincoln?"

"Yes, I missed our usual noon contact, and I am a bit worse for wear - the Travellers' method of negotiation involves much alcohol!" I admitted.

Arthur grinned, "Well, my boy, you got a bloody good deal and surprised a good many of us sceptics, myself included. I remain a bit worried about that Monta girl being here, and her motives, but I'm sure Nigel can sort her out if she turns rogue. I will leave you to it," Arthur pointed at the CB radio with his stick and turned to go. "Oh, by the way," Arthur stopped in the doorway, "Phillip reported that the cameras caught someone scaling the gate last night, may have been one of our new 'friends' on a reconnoitre, the guy can be seen climbing back, apparently without carrying anything. Stuart said that someone broke into the Bury last night too, but he didn't think anything was missing from there either."

"Oh, right." I hoped it wasn't the Travellers; I wanted to feel we could completely trust them, "It probably wasn't the Travellers, but maybe tonight we should stay up and monitor the cameras live?"

"Well, I'd perfectly understand if you take a nap before then, George, your eyes paint a weary picture!" He winked again and left.

"Ingleton to Lincoln, anyone receiving?" I yawned and stretched, expecting to have to wait a while for a reply. Arthur was right; it had been a mentally challenging day and that strange foreign vodka at midday didn't agree with my wish to stay awake. I leant forward and pressed the button on the microphone again, "Hello Lincoln; this is Ingleton with some news! Come back?"

I closed my eyes and put my head on my crossed arms on the desk. Just as sleep began to fade my senses and my eyes started to close, I was startled by the sudden reply from the CB, "Hello, is that George?" A woman's voice came over the radio.

"Oh, yes, it is. Hello, who's that?" I asked.

"Hi, this is Linda; Richard's sister. We've had an incident here. A bad one. I'll see if I can find Richard, he should explain what's happened."

"Oh, is everything OK?" I asked, noting that Linda sounded upset.

"No, no it really isn't. We've been done over. I'll get Richard." The click as the radio went silent seemed so much more final than usual, and I was suddenly fully awake, with concern about this little, offspring community so far away.

A few minutes passed before the radio clicked again and I heard Richard's familiar voice. However, his usual upbeat and jokey tone had been replaced by one of complete disillusionment, "Hello, George, Lincoln is over and out I'm afraid."

"What's happened? I thought you'd got everything working so well? Is everyone OK? Over," I asked, desperately wanting more

411

information.

"Marauders came; Two flatbed trucks, two guys riding in the back of each with shotguns followed by a couple of motorbikes. They just crashed through the gates, yelling, 'The Marauders are here!' They threatened to kill anyone who wouldn't help them load up all our food onto their damn trucks. They shot one of the students when he tried to be a hero, he's badly hurt, and we're trying to get him to Norwich hospital now, we've heard it's still operating. Over."

"Oh shit, Richard, they got everything? What did the student do? ... Over."

"Benny was up by the hives and must have seen what was going on. He took a frame heavy with bees from a hive and threw it through the open window of one of the trucks. They did abandon that truck pretty quick, but the guys on the back both shot him as he ran away. Those who'd gone in to ransack the house, ran out and started shooting randomly as we all just ran for it in all directions. Luckily no one else took more than a few bits of shot. We then watched helplessly from the surrounding fields as they loaded what they could onto the one truck. Then, before they left, one of the bastards took a dump into our well. So we have no clean water unless we climb to a spring almost a mile away. I think we're done for, mate, and I'm afraid they'll be back for their truck. Although, we have just used it to block the entrance and let the tyres down. Over."

"Oh, Richard! I don't know what to say. Can you somehow put spike strips or something on the road to stop them coming back?
... Over."

"We were talking with the farmer about digging a trench that their farm vehicles could get across but not the marauder's trucks. They want us to try to continue and have given us a shotgun. But I'm for quitting, as are about half those here. I've also got some bad news for you; I'm really so sorry... I had taken one of your Ingleton Manor Trading Centre posters, just for ideas and to show Linda what we'd set up there. Well, it *was* on my desk, and it's gone. I think the Marauders must have taken it. So I'm sorry; they might be heading up to you next. Over."

I knew we could not defend the Manor against an attack by armed and organised groups. I had simply hoped our isolated location would protect us from such gangs. We had heard some radio news reports, and much gossip, about gangs who had started out raiding homes and small shops, but who were becoming more organised, and were taking on whole communities and farms. The government had introduced rushed legislation allowing the police and army to stop these gangs by deadly force, but they were already stretched trying to protect food warehouses, supermarkets, and the road network from pirate gangs.

"Look, Richard, it's not your fault. You couldn't possibly have known this group of shitheads would raid you. And, you have given us some warning. There is also a chance they won't know which Ingleton to go to; they might end up on the other side of Yorkshire! There's never been anything on our posters saying, 'County Durham'. And, we could hire James Granger, he has some shotguns. Maybe we could let it be known, on our next posters, that we are an armed and defended community?" I didn't want Richard to feel responsible, he obviously had enough problems of his own. "Do you think they will bother or risk coming back to the same community, especially if, excuse the pun, they've been stung there once already? Over."

"Oh, I just don't know? These bastards might only attack those who are unprepared, but if they do come back, they will be firing first, and that's for sure. We certainly don't have excess food to trade with you now, though there was quite a lot left on that

413

second truck, enough to get by. Right now I'm for quitting and maybe coming back to join you but, I don't know… maybe we are all still in shock?"

I could hear Linda insistently saying something to Richard in the background.

"Linda said we should check with you first: That it's OK just to roll up with another forty people and that we shouldn't be making any decisions today. Maybe tomorrow we'll put it to the vote? I've heard more self-sufficient communities have formed around fishing villages near The Wash, we could maybe up-sticks and head there? Over."

Richard and I spoke for another hour: I told him that he'd be most welcome to come to Ingleton where there were plenty of abandoned houses in the area. I also told him about our new friends and suggested that they could also supply his community with fish. As the conversation continued, I could tell that Richard wasn't as defeated as he first sounded. It was evident he was terribly upset by the attack, but that he wanted to repair the damage and continue. I found myself relating his feelings to those of my own mood change that same day.

By 'over and out', we were both in better spirits. Richard was still very concerned about security, his injured friend Benny, and the two who had set off with him to seek treatment in Norfolk. I was also worried that these marauders had a copy of our poster, and we could be getting a similar visit from them ourselves.

There was quite a commotion coming from the hallway when I finally stood up and stretched. The noise had slowly been building over that last hour. My first thought, when I saw people passing out boxes of fish, up from the cellar to the front door, was that the marauders had arrived already! I briefly panicked and felt guilty that I'd just chatted on the radio rather than issuing urgent warnings.

However, it quickly became clear that all the chatter was happy, and I could also hear music coming from outside.

Nigel and Monta had returned, and the whole community seemed to have returned with them. Several fires were burning on either side of the drive; I'd never seen so many people gathered together at the Manor. Stuart was playing the guitar along with a couple of the Travellers. Melissa and the three stable girls were singing and shaking tambourines. I saw some children, Fenella, and Del dancing with Arthur and Nigel! People were rushing about with wood for the fires, others were wrapping fish in foil, yet more were tending to pieces already being cooked.

Karen, Molly, and Monta were all seasoning fish on a long pasting table and then passing them to others who were queuing expectantly. Through all this, children ran and chased each other, screaming excitedly as they dodged and occasionally collided with themselves or into the legs of others. Further down the drive, I could see that Phillip, Jason, and Andrea were doing a robot dance around the raised edge of the fountain and a small group of children and teenagers had gathered around them and were clapping. Beyond them, yet more people were arriving to join this spontaneous party; some were carrying fold-up chairs - others had picnic blankets - yet more were carrying guitars. All here to sample our new supply of fish, and jumping at such a rare chance to celebrate anything. The sun had even managed to appear from behind the clouds, and the scene in front of me resembled a village summer fête, something I thought I might never see again.

I still blame the alcohol I'd had earlier, and my lack of sleep for what happened next: As I stood on the top of those nine stone steps, looking down at so many happy people, my legs suddenly gave way, I sank to sit down on those cold steps and I wept uncontrollably.

After a short while, Melissa must have seen me; through blurry eyes I could she was running up the steps towards me. I hurriedly wiped my eyes on my sleeve and attempted a smile.

"George, what's up? She asked as she sat down next to me.

"Oh, nothing really, Mel," I sniffed and waved an open hand across all the joyous activity in the garden below, "it's just all this… This spontaneous joyfulness, after the day I've had, I felt emotionally overwhelmed - just for a minute there. I'm OK really."

"You have been looking stressed lately, George. I wanted to ask you what was bothering you, but Karen was always nearby, and she'd probably not appreciate me showing you any concern. But, I do understand the relief you must have felt when you came out and saw all this. Oh, talk of the devil, here she comes!"

I followed Melissa's now hardened stare to where Karen was excusing herself from fish preparation duties and stern-faced, was picking her way through the crowd towards the steps, "Yes, you'd better go, but thanks for understanding."

As Melissa left, she said, "I'll say I came to ask if you wanted a drink, the Travellers have brought some beer, did you know?"

"No, I didn't. I really could do with a glass, though!"

"OK," she said as she skipped back down the steps only to be intercepted by Karen, who caught her arm and pulled her to a stop. A few words were exchanged before Melissa walked off into the crowd, without the spring in her step she'd had only moments before.

"So, what did *she* want?" Karen asked coldly as she stood

over me.

"She came to ask if I'd like a beer." I replied as I stood up, "She said the Travellers had brought some."

Karen peered into my face, "I think the beer has all gone, and you look like you've been crying. What did she say?"

I shook my head, "It's got nothing to do with Mel." I thought the honest explanation I'd given Melissa wouldn't be appreciated by Karen, so I switched stories; "It's Richard's community in Lincoln; it was attacked today by armed marauders. They smashed through their gate with trucks, took a load of their food, and shot Benny twice. He's badly hurt, and they are trying to get him to a hospital that's hopefully still operating in Norwich. I was upset for them."

"Oh, my God!" Karen's face softened, "and here we are having a party! Come on, "she put her hand out," you do deserve a beer, I'll see if Del has any left," Then she looked at me questioningly, "you knew this 'Benny'?"

Del saw me coming, and ran to shake my hand firmly, before I needed to admit that I'd not heard of 'Benny' before that day, "I've reserved a beer for you, my friend." Del said, grinning broadly, "that refrigerated trailer will make a big difference to us
- and is much appreciated - and now, we come here to eat all the fish we gave you for it, to celebrate!"

"Tell him about the marauders." Karen prompted.

"Oh, I thought we were celebrating Monta and Nigel?" I winked at him, "and, we're only serving you lot the fish that smells a bit bad!"

417

Del laughed, but his expression soon changed to one of concern, "What's this about marauders?" he asked.

We all stood together while I explained to Del what Richard had said. I also suggested that if Richard's community did continue, they could become another customer for his fish. Del then walked with us to a cooler box Uldis was sitting on. I saw Melissa was dancing and flirting with a group of young lads from the Traveller's camp, and Nigel, in another group of men, was holding a glass of beer in each hand and was being goaded to drink them both down.

Uldis stood and gave me a warm hug, while Del pulled a four pack of beer out of the box he'd been sitting on. He offered one to Karen and Uldis, then said firmly to Karen, "Man talk. Goodbye."

I thought she would be sure to protest, but she simply snatched the beer and cast me a brief disapproving look, before winking and walking off.

Del and I walked around the perimeter of the rear garden, as we discussed the attack on Richard's community, and the security at the Manor. He said that there had been many stories of a group that originally had four flatbed trucks and several cars as well as motorbikes. They had been attacking small towns, villages, and trading communities as they headed northeast from Wolverhampton. They had apparently taken heavy casualties and lost some vehicles when they clashed with a large group of road pirates on the A1 near Carlton-on-Trent. Del suggested, that if they were now down to just one truck and a couple of bikes, that they no longer posed much of a threat unless they recruited more people. He asked if I had encountered a group that had taken over the Appleby Manor Hotel, their leader was apparently a guy named Mick who was driving around in a bright yellow Hummer and who's game was trying to ambush people on the A66. "They quickly buggered off when they saw us lot coming!"

Del said proudly.

"So that's where Mad Mick ended up! I wondered what had happened to him? Apparently, he had threatened to attack and take over the Manor, but I guess our numbers were too great for him to tackle?" As I said this, I noticed that Melissa and Monta were also now walking together in the garden. Some 20-meters behind them, like a stalking pack of animals, a group of three teenage boys from the Travellers camp were following them.

"Probably. He looked like a waste of space - and his gang all seemed quite a bit younger than him," Del said, "I've met his kind before."

"Oh, that's definitely Mad Mick!" I replied, "a big guy when his little mates are by his side, but a complete coward on his own. I owe him a punch in the face; he broke Richard's nose and attacked Melissa," I pointed out Melissa, who was now walking with Monta down the side of the east avenue.

"Oh now, she's a real beauty she is! More than a few of the young men in our troop have spotted her, including those three," he nodded to the girls' stalkers, "and any would be happy to take her off your hands! Surprised you've not taken her for yourself, although that Karen is a bonnie lass too. You still not married yet?"

I sighed "Oh… been there – done that!" I stopped to look as the girls walked the boundary along the far side of the   garden, "She *is* lovely, though she's only just sixteen, so too young for me."

Del gave me a very odd look, "I'll never understand you Gaugo folk, you makes up so many rules, just to keep you from being happy!"

"Different cultures, I guess." I stated, not wishing to have this argument all over again.

"Ey-up! Those girls is all excited about summink, over there." Del pointed across what had been the lawn, to where the end of the East Avenue meets the boundary at the fence.

In the fading light - and I couldn't make out what they were pointing at from such a distance - Melissa was waving at me, unusually frantically, almost begging me to come over, "I guess we are going over there!" I said, as we changed direction and quickened our pace.

As we go closer, I noticed that the boys had stopped walking, and had gathered together at the entrance to the avenue. Melissa was pointing directly to the green, plastic coated, chain-link fence. I still couldn't see anything wrong with it, until she tugged it, to reveal that it had been cut vertically down from near the top, right down through the rabbit fencing that was tacked to it at the bottom.

"Oh, someone's been in," I stated, looking at the damage, "that's been cut recently."

Mel looked straight at Del, "Is this down to any of your lot?" She asked.

"Mel!" I said, caught out by her very direct accusation.

"No, it's alright," Del responded, "she speaks her mind rather than muttering sarcastic hints - I always prefer that. But, my dear, this is too neat for us, and too far from your sheds. We'd have come over the gate, or cut through the fence in the front. I can guarantee this is not one of us. This is someone who wants to come and go regular, or maybe has staked out the gaff and who plans to return another day. You losing inventory?" Del

420

turned to me for an answer.

"Well, no, not really," I answered, "some people do take a little more than they are entitled to, but our inventory isn't far adrift. We did catch someone scaling the gate on camera, but they went back over without a bag or anything we could see."

"Maybe they knew you had cameras, collected what they wanted, and left it here by the hole in the fence to collect later?" Del suggested, "though I still don't get why this hole is so far from the road. Is there another road over that way?" Del pointed past the fence.

I shook my head.

Melissa answered, "No, nothing but a couple of fields before you get to the edge of Ingleton, you know, where the cricket ground is. Funny we haven't had a break in until your lot turned up?"

This time, Del did turn on Mel, "That's the kind of underhand accusation that will earn you a punch in the face, my girl! Now, I've given you my word we had nothing to do with this," He took her by the shoulders, "and I don't expect this type of prejudice from one as young as you!"

Monta then spoke softly, "Melissa, you make me sad, thinking that of us."

Mel just stood there, looking confused.

I was equally surprised by her repeated accusations, "Mel, only this morning you were speaking out against those who jumped to conclusions about Travellers. Why now we are friends and trading partners, have you switched sides?"

Mel didn't say anything for a few seconds; she just looked vague and distant. "Sorry," she said, finally, before suddenly sitting heavily on the ground, "that's not really what I believe, it's just that suddenly finding this hole in the fence, and I think that Black Balsam that Davis gave me… I'm sorry! It's made me feel all weird!"

Del's face suddenly turned to anger, and he swung round to the group of boys behind us, who were already retreating, "Davis!" yelled Del, startling Melissa and making me jump.

The boys all ran, but one stopped and, head down, slowly turned around, "What's up Del?" He called back, nonchalantly.

"Get here, now!" Del roared, and he pointed to the ground in front of him. The boy slowly began to walk towards us.

"What's Black Balsam?" I asked quietly.

"Riga!" Del replied, "Bloody strong, foul, near toxic, Latvian Vodka - 70% proof, and I bet you that lad's carrying a bottle of water!"

Del grabbed the boy's arm and pulled him in close and, sure enough, behind his back, Davis had been holding a bottle of water that fell to the mud with a dull thud.

"70%?" Mel asked, looking up vaguely, "I had a big cup full, he said it was just punch!" Then she reached for the water.

"No!" Said Monta and Del in unison.

"That's the thing about that stuff - it's so strong it doesn't really get straight into your system, just wears you down, confuses you and makes you damned thirsty. Davis here arrives with a nice bottle of water, a few gulps later and a young girl is nearly unconscious."

"Oh, I didn't know that!" Davis pleaded, "Really, I didn't know it was that ..."

Del, without warning, shut Davis up with a mighty blow to his stomach, as the boy folded, his arms tightly across his middle. Del kicked him, hard, right between his legs, causing him to topple over in agony as he desperately tried to gasp for breath.

"You're out!" Del yelled, "By mornin' light, and don't let me ever see you again!"

Davis nodded, as he lay in the damp mud, tears streaming down his face.

Melissa had turned away and started crying, Monta knelt down to put her arm around her, whispered some comforting words, and pulled her up before, leading her back towards the Manor.

"Make sure someone stays with her, and that she's laying down when she does take water." Del called after them, "and make her drink lots of water!" Del then turned to me, "Now, George, if she had been married or chosen to marry at fourteen, then this wouldn't have happened - your culture and its rules cause more problems than it solves!"

"I don't agree. And, that was rough justice in my book, Del - but your community has its own rules, I guess?" I said, still in shock over his swift and harsh punishment of Davis, who was still squirming on the ground as we left.

"You think we should do it your way; call the police, gather statements, hire solicitors, get social services to do a report, go to Court, have the decision appealed, repeat at enormous cost till the cows come home? No, the punishment should be dealt out as soon after the crime as possible – that's our way. You wouldn't beat your dog a week after it stole your food, would you? – it's the same with people, they respond better to instant justice without calling on a bunch of 'do-gooders' who will make pitiful excuses for them, make them out to be some kind of a victim while trying to make the actual victim look like they were somehow asking for it!"

"Del, I have to admit, you make a good argument, but I didn't need to see what you just did - and poor Melissa certainly didn't!" I said.

"Yeah," Del nodded thoughtfully, "I accept that maybe you're right there, but at least this way she knows it been dealt with - properly – our way." Del glanced over to me as we walked back, "We are very different people, George, and we'll never agree on everything. But you don't have the police force, nor courts, to rely on now, so you need to consider what justice *you* dish out when you catch whoever cut your fence or steals from you. What are you gonna do if you capture the marauder who shot that geezer at Lincoln?" Del shook his head and grinned, "George, I do like you. I like you a lot, but God alone knows how you've survived this long – you are as soft as shit and, believe me, you're going to have to toughen your attitude if you don't want to get over-run."

"Well, maybe I *have* got some thinking to do?" I said, "I'll have a chat with Arthur and Karen, but we'll probably just agree to resolve situations as, and if, they occur. Now, as the light's going, how about you help me to wire up that fence?"

"Sure, just answer one question first," Del stopped me by grabbing my shoulder quite firmly. "remembering we're working together now, so I'd appreciate a straight answer?"

I nodded, almost in resignation, wondering what new conundrum Del was going to set before me.

"As Travellers we get to pick up news and gossip as we go, one story in particular is of interest, and I wondered if you knew anything about it?"

"Go on…" I said.

"Rumour 'as it that farms, mostly those in the south, have been sent fully loaded fuel tankers, to ensure they keep producing food. Do you know anything about this?" Del's eyes probed mine for a hidden reaction.

I gave him a reaction; I grinned broadly before laughing and shaking my head. Then I asked simply, "Do you often ask questions you already know the answer to?"

Del laughed too, "OK so do you know of any farms nearby that have got any?"

"I'll tell you how it is, Del: You're asking if we work with a farm who has a little more fuel than they need?" I shrugged, "Well, yes. We take any excess and trade this with you, for your fish, some of which goes to back to the farmers. However, neither the farmers, nor we, will appreciate anyone else knowing this, nor anyone trying to take more than they can spare. You understand?"

"Perfectly," Del patted my shoulder, "I was just trying to make sure that, when we come back to trade, you'd definitely have enough to pay us. I promise that we'll not disclose this to anyone else or try to take it ourselves. That's not how we operate. But, Nella, she sensed you had access to more than you were letting on."

"Yes, she's exceptionally intuitive that one!" I stated, "Now, let's get that wire!"

It was very dark when we finished repairing the fence by torchlight, and there was a chill in the air. The smoke from the dying fires was drifting slowly towards Ingleton. Here and there lay discarded balls of silver foil that Andrea was gathering up into a bin liner. Everyone else seemed to have gone; the party was over, and the garden was almost silent again. I took a deep breath and filled my lungs with the cool, damp air. Then I noticed the outlines of Nigel and Monta, arms wrapped around each other, silhouetted against the security lights by the gate as they disappeared into the gatehouse together.

"Young love..." said Del quietly, "Look, I'd best be going. We'll try to get one of those CB's and let you know, in advance, when we're coming back next, but it'll probably be early in the new year." Del turned to look at me, "You look exhausted, George - long day?"

"Yeah," I yawned, "and tonight I've agreed to stay up and watch the cameras live. See if we can catch whoever it was who climbed the fence last night."

"Phew! – rather you than me. Goodnight, George! And good luck!"

I don't think it took more than about 40 minutes of staring at blank screens to put me to sleep. However, Phillip had set up an alarm that mimicked the call of a cuckoo if the movement detectors on any of the cameras detected activity. At just after 1am, I woke with a start at the urgent sound of a cuckoo. I rubbed my eyes and stared at the dark screens; only the gate camera had been activated, and the image was black and grainy. I reached for my walkie-talkie and waited for the security lights to be triggered. Sure enough, the lights came on, and a slender, hooded figure could be clearly seen dropping down to the ground on the inside of the gate.

"Anyone still awake? Urgent! We have an unwelcomed guest at the gate. Repeat, we have an uninvited guest at the gate. Over."

The figure ran forward, disappearing from the field of view of the first camera. I waited both for a reply to my message and for the second camera mounted on the wall of the gatehouse to trigger. But nothing happened.

"Oi! Wake up sleepy heads – we have a trespasser! – Over."

The security lights timed-out and my only active screen went dark again.

"Come on, you bastard, trigger another camera!" I said out loud.

"Anyone awake if not – WAKE UP!!" I shouted into the walkie- talkie.

My eyes flicked from one blank screen to the next, urgently willing the intruder to trigger another camera.

"Hello?" a timid voice came back over the walkie-

talkie. "Who's that?!" I asked, not recognising the

voice.

"Oh, I'm Claire, the owner of Casanova," came the reply.

"What?" As far as I knew; Arthur, Phillip, Melissa, Nigel and Karen were the only people who had been issued walkie-talkies, "Who on Earth is Casanova?"

"Sorry, I'm looking after Melissa, she's not very well. Casanova is my stallion, the Cleveland Bay… Oh, is that George? … I mean the brown horse that pulls the battery and water cart."

"Right. OK, so are you in Melissa's room?" I asked my patience wearing thin.

"Er, yes. But, well, she's a bit drunk, sorry!" came the reply.

I sighed, the screens were now all blank and my only contact, and an unlikely source of help, was one of the stable girls, "Yes, I know, I need you to turn left out of her bedroom door and knock on the second door on you left, got it? Over."

"Sure, that Mel's Dads' room. What should I say?" Claire asked, sounding a little more confident but forgetting to let go of the talk button this time.

The cuckoo alarm sounded again, and the camera hidden in the base of the fountain flicked on. The figure was now heading cautiously up the drive, paying particular attention to the sheds to his right. In his hands, he held what appeared to be bolt cutters and this time there *was* a bag on his back.

"Oh, shit! Sorry!" Claire said as she let go of the talk button.

"Don't worry, just tell Arthur that we have an intruder and that I need him with his walkie-talkie down here to monitor the cameras, then wake Karen, she's in the room directly below yours - Mel's - you know what I mean!"

"OK, I'm on it." Came the chirpy reply, then the radio clicked again, "Oh... Over." she added.

The figure turned off the path and headed towards the shed nearest the house and out of view again. "So much for thieves choosing to rob from spud and carrot," I said out loud, he's going for the canned produce or the petrol!"

"Oh, come on people!" I called into my walkie-talkie desperately, before realising that I could hear my own voice from the doorway. I turned to see Claire standing there, fully dressed with her boots ready in her hand. I recognised her as the very pretty brunette, stable girl, that Karen had jabbed me in the ribs about; after she'd caught me following her with my eyes as she rode up to the Manor one morning. "Morning Claire, er, there was no need for you to get dressed and come down."

She smiled, "Well you're a man down and I can run pretty fast, you might need me!" She said as she bent down to put her boots on.

Arthur was down next, in his dressing gown and carrying his walkie-talkie, "Gathering the troops to repel borders are we, eh, George?" Then he looked at Claire and back at me, "Er, most of the troops are AWOL, are they?"

"Seems so. Karen should be coming down soon, but I can't raise Nigel, and Phillip is at Langdon, and he's not always able to pick these up," I waved my walkie-talkie.

Karen then appeared in the doorway, yawning and not looking at all impressed.

She was in her nightwear but was wearing shoes and carrying a coat, "How many?" She asked, looking unimpressed at Claire.

"Just one, a skinny guy in a hoodie, er, this is Claire and apparently, she can run fast, so let's go! Arthur is going to tell us whenever he pops up on a camera, but for now, I think he's going for one of the sheds at this end."

"Ah, lights have just gone on in the gatehouse, "Arthur said as he sat down, "Nigel should be joining the party."

"Better late than never," I said, "now everyone, except Arthur, turn down your walkie-talkies, so our coms don't alert this guy, and no unnecessary talking, just report when you see him, OK? Arthur, can you just tell Nigel, when he untangles himself from Monta, to just to walk slowly up the drive? He'll trigger the gate lights and let this guy know the exit is blocked."

Arthur nodded, "What are you going to do if you catch him, George?"

"I don't know, bring him here I guess? It's your house after all!" Del's warnings of the previous evening suddenly had greater meaning.

The three of us filed out into the cold night air, as Arthur issued his instructions to Nigel. Then the radios fell silent as, with much anticipation, we headed down towards the fountain, our eyes all scanning the sheds to our left. We all froze when the gate lights came on, and we could see the outline of Nigel with his heavy Maglite torch walking towards us. Suddenly there was movement from the sheds; A figure darted to our side of the closest shed and peered around the corner of it towards the gate.

"He's there!" called out Karen, as she pointed urgently.

The intruder heard her and turned to see us. Running behind the shed, he quickly disappeared between the others. Without saying anything, we all ran towards the sheds. Claire was indeed fast, and reached them well before Karen and I could, "You go right," I said to Karen, "I'll go left." Unquestioningly Karen obeyed.

"He is on the far left heading towards the gate," Arthur stated over the radio, "Nigel, come in from the drive and cut him off."

There was a brief shriek from Claire, "He's just ran back past me!" she shouted out, forgetting her radio, "Back down

430

the middle."

Both Karen and I made the same decision to move in towards
the middle path. As we met, we saw the man running towards
us, with Claire close behind him. On seeing us, he slid to a halt
and turned sharply towards the drive. He grunted as he cracked
his shoulder on one of the water butts as he stumbled out of
sight. Karen and I both turned right to try to cut him off. Claire
shot out of the gap just in front of us, and we nearly collided,
"Where did he go?!" Panted Claire, "he must have run out from
here."

Karen and I both shrugged, "No?" I said, "Arthur, can you see
anything? Over."

"He ran towards the drive between canned and dried foods with
Claire on his tail; he must be hiding very close to where you all
are now. Over."

Nigel appeared from between the next two sheds, "I found
these." he held up a pair of bolt cutters and an empty rucksack,"
Then he pointed the cutters towards the door of the shed
opposite us.

I tried the door; the large padlock was intact and holding firm. I
looked back at Nigel questioningly.

"No, there!" said Nigel as he advanced, holding the cutters out,
more clearly indicating the water butt we were right next to. It
was glistening with water and the ground around it had splashes
and small puddles. The lid wasn't quite on properly, and we all
realised we might have captured a very desperate intruder. We
stood back as Nigel flipped the heavy round black plastic lid off.
Then I felt nervous disappointment; we'd just uncovered an
over-flowing water butt. The water was almost still and lapped
the brim gently. We all came forward and peered into the dark
water. Nigel switched his torch on, and we all jumped at this

sudden new light, then laughed at our foolishness as he directed the beam into the water. The surface reflected most of the light onto the shed wall and revealed little below a couple of inches of the green, ribbed sides of the container. A few hoverfly and mosquito larvae could be seen darting and dancing around near the surface, attracted to the new light.

I let out a deep breath, "So where the heck *did* he go?" Nigel withdrew the torch and shrugged.

"We could split up again, and keep looking?" Claire suggested.

I picked up the water butt lid and started to replace it when, without any warning at all, the surface of the water suddenly erupted into a huge column of white water that showered all of us. Claire and Karen both screamed and ran, I fell backwards, narrowly avoided hitting myself in the face with the heavy lid. Nigel, however, stood his ground and pointed his torch at our unwanted visitor as he choked and gasped for breath while looking around at us in absolute terror.

It took a full minute for this bedraggled and shivering black man to stop panting, and to gain enough strength to haul himself out of the cold water. Then he just sank to the base of the water butt, cowering, his hands over his head as if expecting a beating. Karen and Claire both returned, their eyes filling with pity and concern realising that this young man was no real threat at all.

Surprisingly, while I stood wondering what to do or say next, Claire knelt down by the man, offered him her hand and said, "Can we get you inside into the warm? My name's Claire."

Karen jabbed me in the ribs again and nodded urgently towards the man, "Come on, George, you're in charge!"

"Yes," I agreed, "sorry. Hello, I'm George," I too knelt down as this man peered at us and slowly dropped his arms, "we aren't going to hurt you. Come on let's get you up and into some dry clothes. Karen, there's one of my gardening jumpsuits hanging in the garage, can you get it for me?"

Nigel escorted our non-speaking guest to the spare room for a shower, and Karen duly supplied him with my spare set of gardening greens. I waited with Arthur and Claire in the library for him to be brought back down, and for Karen to prepare a big jug of steaming cocoa to warm us all up.

At 2.30am, a reluctant figure appeared in the doorway of the library wearing a set of gardening greens that were too short for him.

With his head bowed, he went straight up to Arthur, knelt before him and offered his hand, "I'm sorry Sir," he whispered, "I don't deserve your kindness."

Arthur took his hand, "Please stand up. My name is Arthur Quail, what would yours be, young man?"

"Dale," replied the man as he stood up, his head still bowed, "I'm Dale, Dale Bello, and I'm sorry, Sir, for trying to steal from you."

"Dale, why did you cut the fence behind the house?" I asked.

Dale turned to me, "I'm sorry, but I didn't cut any fences. I climbed over your gate," his eyes were probing and darting around nervously.

"We are not trying to interrogate you, Dale, please do take a seat. Have some of Karen's delicious cocoa, it is made with powdered milk, I'm afraid." Arthur said.

Karen poured him a mug and handed it to him, as he nervously sat down.

"Thank you." Dale said quietly, "You are not at all as I expected. Do you have much powdered milk?"

Karen sat next to him, and asked, "Powdered milk? – Oh! … Were you looking for baby formula?"

Dale nodded, "My wife gave birth to our first baby a week ago, but she's got too thin to make milk, so I was looking for any juice or powdered milk, or soup - anything really."

Karen put her hand over her mouth in shocked surprise, "Oh my God, where did she have the baby? Is it a boy or a girl?" Then more urgently, "Where are they now?"

"Why did you not, simply come in during the day and ask?" Arthur enquired, before Dale could answer Karen's question, "Why did you creep in a night and try to steal it?"

"I'm sorry, Sir," Dale replied, "I was told you were, well, that your group here, isn't 'friendly' towards foreigners - I didn't see any coming in or out."

Nigel coughed loudly.

"Well, except him!" He nodded to Nigel, "and I thought he was just security."

"Just security..." Nigel repeated under his breath.

"Dale, my dear boy, you are not completely wrong;" replied Arthur, sincerely, "I have harboured a large number of prejudices, mostly passed down from my father, and from his before that. I have fought with my daughter and my trusted advisor here, about gays but recently, I have had my eyes prised open by recent events and encounters. This PCP thing has caused me have a complete rethink. You might think this strange, but maybe this crisis is what Great Britain needed; a sharp kick up the behind. Push old farts like me into the 21st century, and get us all to re-evaluate what the crucial things are; like food, lighting, community. What I am trying to say is; what you heard was probably entirely correct, but just a little out of date. – I have had to adapt, and change with the times. You are as welcome here as anyone else, so is your wife and new-born. Now tell me about the birth and where we can find them now? Your wife must be very anxious."

I remember thinking, as Arthur made his little speech, that it was such a shame Melissa wasn't there to have heard it. She'd have been so proud of him.

Dale slowly and calmly explained how they had left Newcastle when the maternity unit was abandoned, and the smell of the unburied dead and the smoke from burning buildings became too much to bear They had walked almost as far as Durham when another family, in a minibus, saw them and kindly picked them up. This family intended to go to York because their daughter had become very unwell after falling and hitting her head while playing. They had heard that the hospital in York was still open, and was being protected by the police and civilian forces. They didn't get that far though; road pirates forced them off the road just north of Darlington.

Dale explained, as if exhausted of all emotion, how the pirates took what little food they had, and then drained the minibus of all its fuel. So, on foot again, they crossed the A1 hoping to get to Barnard Castle and any kind of medical help. Without looking up from the floor, Dale told how their little girl had died the following morning, and that her parents stayed behind to look for a spade, so they could bury her by the side of the road.

At this point in his story, Dale looked up at Arthur and said solemnly, "You might think this PCP thing is good for Great

Britain? I can tell you, Sir, that for most people, it is not. You might have it really good here; I saw you having a party today while others are dying from drinking contaminated water, or starving to death."

"Dale," I interrupted, noting his comments had clearly hurt Arthur, "we do what we can to support about 240 people, we have struggled too and came very close to failing. We can't help everyone, but our doors are open to all willing to either help us, or learn to help themselves. Arthur didn't mean PCP has been good for everyone; he knows it's turned some people into complete monsters, and caused many to suffer great hardship."

"Yes, OK," Dale replied thoughtfully, "I understand. Those last remarks were tainted with some jealousy, and also some frustration with myself for breaking in before daring to ask you for help. Please forgive me, Arthur?"

"Ah, no harm was done, my dear boy, Arthur replied, "now, where can we find your wife and baby?" Arthur asked, "Karen can go and fetch them. You can stay here tonight, and we'll find you an empty house nearby tomorrow. We have not got a baby in our community; I am sure you'll be inundated with offers to babysit!"

"They are at the end of a footpath just opposite your gate. Go carefully; they are lying down wrapped in a blanket." Dale cautioned.

"Oh, my God! Poor darlings," Karen said, as she put her coat back on, "I'll go and get them now. Oh, what's her name?"

"Precious," replied Dale proudly, "it's Precious."

"That's a lovely name. And your baby?" Karen asked.

Dale didn't answer for a few seconds; a single tear ran down his face, "We haven't named her yet, we were so unsure that she could survive that we didn't want to give her a name."

Karen, squeezed his shoulder affectionately, "I understand, but we will do whatever we can to keep you all healthy - we have a pharmacist among our number, and she has brought with her quite a few drugs and treatments - I don't know if she has any vaccines, though? I'll go and get her tomorrow, to check your wife and baby over. She's the closest thing we have to a doctor."

"Thank you, thank you so very much, you've given me hope, and I'm so very sorry I tried to steal from you." Dale replied earnestly.

"I'm not needed here now?" Nigel asked.

"You can go, Nigel," Arthur answered, "and Dale, I don't want to hear any more apologies, but if you need help choosing a name for your baby? How about 'Hope'?

"Hope Bello?" Dale said as he considered the name, "New-Hope Bello! ... I like that!" Then, for the first time, we saw Dale smile.

Nigel was grinning too, "New-Hope – Lovely!" and he turned to leave, "I'll walk with you to the footpath, Karen." Nigel waved his torch.

"Thanks, Nigel." Karen said, looking a little relieved.

Arthur then asked Dale what he did before the grass

died.

"I am - well I was - an electrical engineer, and had been installing solar panels and their switch gear."

Arthur and I looked at each other and grinned.

"Can you convert a grid-tied system to allow the panels to supply a house?" I asked, "At the moment we are reliant on an old diesel generator that charges batteries all over the place, and does the house lighting and keeps the fridges and freezers running. But, we'd really like to be able to use our solar panels to take some of the load."

Dale smiled again. "I am sure I can. I will need some equipment, but I know where it's stored; there's a warehouse this side of Newcastle. There is everything there except panels. We ran out of those soon after this crisis started. I will need to look at your system first, though, just to make sure I can adapt it."

"You're hired!" Arthur announced, "your wages are to be food, and scavenger parties out looking for baby milk; I do not believe we have any? Now, I am missing my pillows! Goodnight, Dale - and you two." Arthur pointed to Claire who had, long since, fallen asleep with her cocoa still in her hand, "What was she doing here anyway? – Oh, never mind! Goodnight!"

I gently took the cup of cold cocoa from Claire's hand and, borrowing Arthur's blanket from the conservatory, covered her up. I did not have the energy to carry her up to the top floor, and also, I didn't want to risk her waking up half-way up and screaming!

I warmed a can of tomato soup up for Dale, who was very grateful, and we waited for Karen to return with Precious and the baby. I couldn't find anything more suitable for the baby, and hoped that would be alright.

Precious was indeed very undernourished; she came in looking exhausted and bedraggled, but she still clung firmly to the bundle of clothes that wrapped her baby. She ran to Dale, and they hugged.

"These are good people, they will feed us and will try to find milk for the baby," Dale said in a calming voice.

Precious just nodded in acknowledgement, then to Dale she said: "I was so worried when you didn't come back. I saw people running, lights going on and the big man with a torch, I didn't know what to do!"

"It's OK, my love, they caught me but they are nice people, they will look after us, and I have a job!"

Running her hand over his green overalls, she whispered: "What happened to your clothes?"

"I'm going to show them straight up to their room, and bring them some food and drink," Karen said to me, "you go off and get some sleep too, George - you've had a long day."

Chapter 14 – Parallel Worlds

"It 'd be nice if the sun came out right now," Dale explained. He was shouting over the noise of the generator. At Dale's request; Philip, Jason, Arthur and myself had all gathered in the cellar. We were looking at a new and complex maze of wiring. Not only that; Dale had also installed bright LED lighting panels in the tunnel and corridor. The chain of bulbs hanging from the ceiling had long gone. New switch boxes and control panels dominated the wall before us. "When the sun shines," Dale continued, "the generator will automatically shut off, and the solar panels will take over. Even in today's poor light, those panels are still charging all your batteries."

Dale grinned, clearly proud of his achievements. "It's all fused, just as it was before. If the mains did come back on, then only this single lamp," Dale pointed to a bare bulb on the wall, "and the fountain on the front drive will come on. If that should ever happen, then you'll have to switch these two manually, to off and *then* - that one - on. It's vital that both those two are off before that is turned back on." Dale insisted. "In fact, I'm going to ask Mel to print a big label for those switches."

"So what's powering the house lights now?" James asked as he tried to follow the multitude of cables that were spread across the wall like a disorganised London Underground map.

"The solar panels are topping up those twenty-four fixed batteries," Dale answered, pointing to the original bank of batteries, "those are now completely isolated from the generator. So all the house lights, the gate, and cameras are now solar powered. You've just got to remember that you can no longer charge the villager's batteries during the night, even when the generator is running."

"I don't get it," Phillip stated, "what's that new set of batteries doing?"

"That's the clever bit," Dale said, "because you are running all those fridges and freezers, the generator had to run all the time. Now, the generator charges that second set, and automatically switches off when they are charged. Those batteries, via that invertor," he pointed at another box, "power the fridges and freezers. When they drop down to 20%, it will switch back on to recharge them… unless the solar panels are working, then *they* will charge them! That's why I needed so many automatic switches. I've never wired up such a complex system anywhere!"

Arthur had been leaning on his stick all this time, listening intently, and nodding occasionally. "Well, my good man," he said finally, "I have little idea what half of this does, and I am not sure I actually need to know *how* it all works, but I can tell you that my father would have been so excited by all this. You see solar power was a dream of his, but he died long before it became a practical reality. Dale, you have worked exceptionally hard down here in all this heat and noise. Now I understand why it took so many months to complete. I am sure we are all going to benefit from your efforts. I only wish you'd chosen to break in earlier… you could have saved us a lot more diesel!"

As we all filed back out through the long passageway to the stairs, Arthur held me back. "Ah, George, may I have a minute?"

"Sure, what's up?" I asked.

"Two things; as you know, the Travellers are delivering again tomorrow. Can I ask you to oversee the negotiations personally this time? I think the deal we got in April was nowhere near as good as the deal you agreed to in January. They almost cleared us out of root crops, *and* what was left of our nuts. The vegetarians, those who still won't eat fish!" Arthur shook his head in bewilderment, "Well, they have complained that there were no eggs in that trade and that their only source of protein is beans and broccoli. The latter which has suffered rather, with all the rain we had around Christmas."

"Yes, I'm sorry. I choose the wrong day to drive Dale around looking for parts. I thought they weren't arriving until the following week. They did take advantage of Paul and Monta, and I do intend to have a strong word with Del about it! What's the other thing?"

"Good man! Now, yes… The 'other thing'; well, I don't wish to pry into your personal lives, but with everyone under one roof, one does tend to notice things," Arthur looked slightly embarrassed, "and, well, I've noticed that Karen seems a little unhappy - well distant lately. Is there anything I can do?"

I'd also noticed that Karen, while she continued to work hard, and said all the usual pleasantries, wasn't herself; we were not so close, and she seemed permanently frustrated and short tempered. I found myself avoiding her by helping out on the allotments or going out on water and battery deliveries.

"I'm not sure you *can* help?" I said solemnly. "It started on Christmas day: When we got up, we found Paul had sneaked out, abandoning his stocking. She saw Nigel and Monta with Paul when she opened the curtains. They were all up on the hill flying a kite they'd acquired for him. Paul was laughing and running about, as happy as could be. This seemed to trigger something in her. Later when she gave him that laptop that she'd got Phillip to build, he rushed straight off to show it to Nigel. I think she feels that somehow Paul has replaced her - that she's been undermined by two, slightly odd people who don't speak to *her* much at all. I must admit that even I feel slightly jealous of their relationship; they do behave just like a little family. I barely get to say two words to Paul now, and those

442

are usually just 'good night,' often after he's gone to sleep."

"Parallel worlds," Arthur stated, "those three rarely share a word in our dimension, but together they chatter away, laughing and joking with one another. You and Karen both need to realise that you remain very important to Paul, to all of them. Yet although you are not quite 'tuned-in' to their world, you *are* the bridge that links them to it."

"Jesus, Arthur, that's a bit deep!" I sighed, "but you're right. It's as if they speak a different language, or are on a slightly different frequency. Should I talk to them, or discourage Paul from spending so much time with them?"

"Oh, my dear boy, you don't think Karen's not already considered that? She knows Paul is now happier than he's ever been. A good mother won't want to interfere, or break that up. She just wants to be included, to be part of it. She… well, you both, feel isolated and need to find a way share Paul's new happiness. Have you talked with Karen about this?"

"No." I slowly shook my head trying to find words to explain why: "I guess I didn't want to upset her further. I've been treading on eggshells for months now."

"May I be so bold as to tell you what I think, even though you are probably not going to like it?" Arthur asked before he started chewing on his top lip again.

I didn't want to hear what I think I already knew; I'd rather just have plodded along with my head in the sand, but I found myself nodding. Arthur had become a friend, and he was older, and certainly wiser than I thought I could ever be.

"Just a little brandy survived Christmas; I think we should finish it off in the drawing room. Too much air in the bottle isn't good for it, you know?" Arthur winked.

The brandy tasted warm and rich, and it left a pleasant burning sensation on my tongue. "That's so much better than that Latvian crap we traded so much good kale for," I stated.

"Maybe," replied Arthur, "but even that's all gone. How's Richard doing? I hear he's better now the army have secured the A1 as far as York, I hear they are even clearing drains and that 'your' marigolds, clover and mint are growing on some of the embankments!"

"He's OK - they have dug a new well! They still haven't heard anything from the two who tried to get Benny to Norwich Hospital. But at least those marauders met their match when they ran into Warcorp Tanks on the A66. I still think they were heading here you know! But that's not why you wanted to talk to me is it?"

"Ah, no my dear boy, I was just trying to bide time and let the brandy do its good work. Here, let's empty the bottle, I can't abide capping such a small drop.

Arthur drained the bottle into our glasses, and I noticed he was sucking on his lip again.

"Come on Arthur, out with it!" I said goading him on. "That Dale, he's a real asset, isn't he? Did you know that Precious has finally agreed to name that darling baby 'Hope' after all? She was never going to accept 'New Hope', and I can't really blame her." Arthur sat back and made himself comfortable in the big leather chair.

I just gave Arthur a blank stare. He had something to say, but was stalling.

"OK, I will just come out with it; You and Karen, well since Christmas you have been, well you don't even seem so comfortable in each other's company. You have said that she has a problem with Paul spending so much time with Monta and Nigel, and I can understand that, but why are you two also in trouble? To be honest, you never seemed a very romantic couple, but now... well, now there is a void between you. You appeared closer when you *weren't* a couple. I am concerned because, I, no... *we*, all need you both. You are the backbone of this community. I hope you don't mind me asking? But is there anything I can do to get you back on the right track? Even if that does mean you going back to just being friends?"

Arthur was saying exactly what I thought he would; he could see what I'd been feeling, and thinking, for some time. I didn't want to have to deal with our issues, and had been avoiding both them and Karen. I had reached the conclusion that Karen had wanted me only as a father figure for Paul. I did love her, but maybe I loved her more as a friend? Now she was losing Paul to Nigel and Monta, did she need me at all? Or was this all just my imagination and unjust anxiety? Arthur was sitting opposite me, and was patiently waiting for my reply.

"I'm sorry Arthur, thanks for the brandy, but can you finish mine?" I pushed the glass towards him, "I need to resolve this myself. I can't keep dodging the issue, nor expect you solve it for me. I must sort this out with a clear head. Karen and I used to talk so much more before we shared a bed. I miss my gatehouse; I miss my bar, my stupid old Pacman machine and..."

"I know..." interrupted Arthur, "There's a point where helping a good friend becomes self-sacrificial, and too much self-sacrifice can lead to self-destruction. Find her now and talk. See if you are able to resolve things, or agree to change things. I believe I have said all I needed to."

"Thanks, Arthur. You've given me the shove I needed. Do you know where she is?"

"She was heading for the kitchen earlier. Paul was in there with Monta. Phillip said she was teaching him to cook, and that they were preparing a special, grand late-evening meal for us all. Molly will help, but has gone to Gainford to take some food to her parents. They are *still* refusing to move to Ingleton!"

"OK, thanks again, Arthur."

I peered around the kitchen door. Monta, was there and so was Paul with a big paper chef's hat on, but Karen was nowhere to be seen. I headed up to our room where she'd often retreat to when she was unhappy.

"What's the matter?" I asked on seeing that Karen was lying face down on the bed, her face deep in the pillow.

She spun around and stood up aggressively to face me, "Who me? Oh, nothing. Nothing at all! Paul, who I thought was *my* son? Well, he chose to spend the whole morning with Nigel, delivering water. Then, he went to the portacabin with Monta. He's showing her how to run his spreadsheet, did you know? It's the same one he thought *I* couldn't understand. You remember how I was made to feel this big," She held up her thumb and forefinger close together, "when Melissa understood Paul better than me? Well, guess what? Now even those dumb bastards Nigel and Monta seem to as well!" Karen sat back down on the bed heavily. "I don't know what to do; I just don't feel included anymore - and where have you been all this week?"

I sat down next to her. "I kind of know how you feel," then I justified my remark before she could react, "I thought I'd made a connection with Paul, and was only too pleased to play at being 'the father figure', but I hardly see him to talk to, either."

"Yeah, but you can just walk away anytime you want," Karen said dismissively, "if you've not already done that? I'm not 'playing' at being his Mother, I *am* his Mother! It seems that just because I'm not some dumbfuck like Nigel, or that outcast Monta, that I'm excluded from his life. What can he hope to learn from *them*?"

"Wait up Karen!" I couldn't let her rant go completely unchallenged, "Firstly; I hope *you* need *me* too, and that I can't just 'walk away' anytime, as if I was some spare part? Secondly; there is no one better to provide security than Nigel, and even Molly agrees that Monta is the better cook. They are certainly not 'dumbfucks' and Paul is happier than I've ever seen him."

"Oh, it's always about *you*, isn't it?" Karen retorted, "well, why don't you just walk before you get pushed? I told you I don't *do* love, and while you might, it's not reserved for me, is it?"

We sat next to each other in silence, both staring at the floor. I was waiting for some kind of a retraction or an apology, but nothing more was said. Ten minutes passed, where she waited for me to respond and I hopefully, waited for anything - a simple hug would have been enough.

Eventually, I stood up. Turning to her I said, with as little emotion as I was able; "I'll ask Arthur if I can move into the spare room upstairs. But know this, I came up here to offer you support. You clearly don't want either my help, nor company. I think you know that, other than Arthur, you're my only consistent friend here. So I hope we can still be friends, and maybe just go back to the way things were?"

Karen continued to stare at the floor, and I headed towards the door. Just as I turned to close it, she looked up. I stopped. She produced a drained smile and with glistening eyes, she murmured, "Yes, please, I'd really like that."

I remember standing at the top of the stairs, wondering where I could go? I so wanted to run down to the solitude of the gatehouse, or anywhere I could shut myself in and be alone with my thoughts. I needed to work out how I actually felt. I wasn't heartbroken, it was more ashamed, disappointed in myself and alone once more. I decided to explore the loft space above the garage again. I'd maybe read one of those books that Peter had left up there. I didn't get that far, though; Andrea excitedly called up to me, "There are rabbits in the back garden, George! At least two of them. That James bloke, the one who brings the pheasants; he's here with his shotgun and Melissa is going crazy because Arthur has asked him to shoot them!"

A worthy distraction, I thought, "I'm on my way!" I called down.

"Alright, alright! So how do you usually get rid of them?" James Granger was replying to Melissa as I got to the hall.

"George!" Melissa said turning to me, "Tell them how you trap them, or how we run them out of the gate!"

"Hi, James, Arthur. Er, yes; I do try catching them, but I don't catch many," I admitted, "we do have better luck just walking in a line towards the open gate. Run them out, then try to find out where they got in, and seal it back up."

"I'd prefer to shoot them; then they rarely come back! But I'd be as happy to help?" James offered, "Will five of us be enough?"

"Oh, am I helping?" Andrea asked.

"Yes, to both questions." I answered, "We'll walk along the edges in two groups, meet down at the lake then walk in a line towards the front. Just do not to chase them down into the meadow, else we'll never find them!"

"They might try to double back through the croquet lawn, or run

448

around the shed or garages." Melissa offered excitedly, "George and I chased one out on our own, a couple of years ago!"

"We will have to go now; it's nearly nine and the light's fading fast, and they are so difficult to see in the gloom." I said as I marshalled everyone out. "Mel, you've done this before, can you take Andrea and James down the left side. Arthur, you and I down the right?"

"Right you are, young fella!" replied Arthur as he picked up his stick.

As we were passing the West Avenue, Arthur asked, "Did you get to have a chat with Karen?"

"Yes, but I was no help. Would you mind if I move into the spare room on the top floor?"

Arthur patted my back, "Oh, my dear boy, things didn't go at all well then? But, of course, you can have the room."

"Thanks, Arthur." I replied, then, to try to change the subject; "Look at all the clover and dandelions that have come up! We might need to mow the lawn after all!"

Arthur was wise to my tactic, "So you do not want to talk about it? That's OK. Just remember that I am always here if you do. As for the 'lawn', don't you dare mow it! We have had eight months of brown mudflat, this patchy green with flowers is a vast improvement. If you could pull up the nettles spreading up from the meadow, though, and the topiaries at the front desperately need a trim. I'm sure there's plenty of chaps from the village who'd be happy to help for a few meal tokens."

"Yes," I replied. Then I caught sight of two rabbits, "Look!" I pointed to the middle of the lawn just above where it drops into the meadow. Melissa's group had already seen them, and were

449

moving in trying to prevent them running down towards the meadow. Arthur and I did the same. The rabbits, now aware of us, hunkered down, almost vanishing.

"You do appreciate that my running days are over, George? I'll wave my stick and shout, but fast walking is my limit!"

"Yes, Arthur, I know. You can track back up the middle though, and turn any that double-back."

"They're off!" replied Arthur, as he started to nod.

The two rabbits sprang off together, first directly towards the meadow, but Melissa sprinted to cut them off, forcing them to turn sharply and run directly towards the house. "Keep them running!" she yelled.

Melissa joined me, jogging up the right, while Andrea and James raced each other up the other side. The rabbits hesitated in front of the house and briefly tried to run back, but we closed the gap and continued advancing on them. Before long, they ran through the croquet lawn and kitchen garden, before bounding straight down the drive. Nigel joined the chase and shut the gate as the rabbits ran out, only to have to open them again as Molly returned.

Arthur and James had only got as far as the front steps. It was there we all gathered to report our success, and excitedly chatted about the chase as we regained our breath. James gratefully accepted Arthur's invitation to join us for the evening meal - although he still insisted that it would have been better to have shot the rabbits and eaten them. Nigel nodded gravely in agreement. However, Melissa was very restrained and didn't rise to their provocation. She did suggest it was too dark to look for holes in the fence, and offered to help me early the next morning.

I was relieved to find that Karen was in the bathroom when I returned to 'our' room to change. I quickly and quietly gathered my only suit, together with as many of my clothes as I could manage. I took these up to my new room at the far end of the top floor. As I went past Melissa's room, she came out wearing a sweeping, long, blue gown.

"Oh, hello! - I thought you were Molly or Monta." she said, "I told them that they could use the spare room to get changed in. I guess they are still preparing the meal?" Then she looked at my bundle of clothes, "Oh, *you* were going to change in there? … Why not use my room? I'm done, really."

I was glad she chose not to question what had happened, though she seemed to understand, "Thanks, Mel. Your dress... well, you do look very lovely."

With a sympathetic expression and wide eyes, she stopped me as I passed. Without saying anything, she just squeezed my arm gently and offered a weak, knowing smile and a nod before she left. I felt that in those fleeting few seconds, Melissa had silently shared with me a deeper compassion and understanding than I had ever known before.

Arthur greeted me as I entered the rarely used dining room, where the table was laid with white cloth napkins, and silverware all set out perfectly. It reminded me of Arthur's 60th birthday.

"Ah, there you are, George, I think that Monta, Molly and Paul have done wonders, don't you?" Arthur stated proudly. Then he whispered, "It may raise a few questions, my dear boy, if you don't take your place beside Karen. So, I thought that if I set you one apart, at this end, then young Paul can sit between you and so kill two birds with one stone?"

"Yes, good idea, though Paul will want to sit by Nigel and Monta no doubt!"

"Well, I did have a little word with Nigel." Arthur said, as James entered with Andrea, "Ah, nice to see you both - please would you take the two seats there." he indicated the seats towards in the middle. Then returning to a whisper, he continued, "I just said that Karen was feeling a little down, and that she'd really appreciate Paul's company this evening."

"Oh, thanks, Arthur. You are most incredibly understanding, and a good diplomat to boot!"

I took my place as the others filed in. Karen was the last to arrive and sat, as directed, one place away from me. She didn't catch my eye, and just nodded when I complimented her on her dress. I counted four empty place settings but thought that was a mistake as only the three preparing the food were absent.

Paul, Monta, and Molly then proudly brought in the food, presented in decorative tureens and matching casserole dishes. They'd managed to acquire potatoes, peas, green beans and cauliflower to accompany the many fish dishes.

Arthur, who was sitting between Melissa and James Granger at the other end of the table, stood up as they took their places, leaving the chair to my right vacant. "Without a doubt, you three have done splendidly," he said, "let's raise a glass of this lovely Ingleton apple juice, to our two cooks and their guest Apprentice: To, Molly, Monta and Paul!"

We all stood, raised our glasses, and I led a round of applause.

Arthur continued as we sat back down, "Before you tuck into this quite remarkable fayre, I would like to remind you all that we are very fortunate indeed; other people are still without food today, and many others have perished since this crisis began. I would very much like to take this opportunity to thank those who, from the very beginning, planned, contributed, and organised this. I think we should give special thanks and raise a glass to Jason, Phillip and Dale for their technical support and sheer hard work. Unfortunately, Dale is unable to attend this evening because Precious is unwell." We raised our glasses again, and I looked at the vacant seat. "Also, credit should be given to Andrea, Karen, Melissa and young Paul, who tirelessly keep everything running smoothly, without complaint or question." We raised our glasses and chanted their names as I began to think I'd got away without similar embarrassment. "Last and not least, the two people who did so much of the original work, and who conceived the Ingleton Manor Trading Centre: "Please stand, and raise your glasses to George, and our special guest this evening – Richard from Lincoln!"

As everyone stood up, I turned to see Richard, nonchalantly leaning in the doorway behind me, grinning from ear-to-ear.

"Richard!" I exclaimed in complete surprise as I stood up and hugged him as the others laughed and clapped, "I had no idea! Arthur, you dark horse! How did you get here, Richard?"

I let Richard go, so he could take his place as everyone sat back down.

"I came up with the Travellers and am going back with them on Tuesday. I've been hiding in the portacabin all day. Boy, this place is so busy! How many are you serving now?"

Arthur coughed loudly, "Excuse me; I think we'd better tuck-in before the food gets cold. Everyone, please help yourselves!"

"Hang on, just one more moment," I announced as I stood up. "We've forgotten to mention one person; someone who facilitated everything. A special person - a friend to us all - who financed this venture. A proud man who has shared his house, and his garden, with so many… To Arthur – Lord of Ingleton Manor Trading Centre!"

"To Arthur!" Everyone echoed loudly.

As we chomped on the wonderful food, I caught up with Richard. I told him how we now fed almost three hundred people including a few who had fled the Boxing Day flooding at Appleby and Penrith. Richard told how he was trading with three other self-sufficient communities since the main roads were secured. His community hadn't grown very much because there were no empty properties nearby. However, despite the setbacks caused by the marauders, Richard also considered his community a success.

"I wonder how many communities have survived this, and how many people the government are managing to keep alive in the cities?" Richard asked, "I keep hearing on the radio, how they promise to provide food to both power and water workers, but I have not heard of anywhere that has power or running water."

"I've heard that parts of Edinburgh have got both power and water, and Bristol too, but rumours aren't facts." I replied. Then I heard a defeated sigh from my left. I turned to see Karen watching Paul head off with Monta. "I think he's just gone to help bring in the desserts." I called across to assure her.

"Oh, I hope so." she replied, "All he's talked about is his cooking. I'm so proud of him; he's remembered all the ingredients; I just wish I'd been the one to teach him."

"I know, but he is including you by telling you all about it." I stated, though I was sure she knew that already.

Karen just smiled slightly, "I'll help gather the plates." she said, and got up to help clear the table.

"Hey, Nigel," Richard called across to Nigel, who along with Molly was tucking into a second portion of fish, "Your new young lady, Monika, she's a real little cutie! You struck gold there, my friend!"

Nigel looked up, nodded with a grin, "Monta, her name is Monta."

At the other end of the table, Arthur suddenly stood up, "Those damn magpies keep tap-tapping away at that window." He headed for the glass door that was behind heavy cream curtains, and flung one open to scare the birds away.

Melissa laughed, "Oh Daddy, you can hardly hear them, let them be!"

What happened next is not etched into my memory, it's more permanently burnt in like a brand. Nothing can stop me recalling every little detail over and over again.

Richard tapped me on the arm and whispered, "I see Arthur is still a loveable old eccentric!" But I ignored him, because I'd noticed that Arthur was standing as if frozen. He was just staring, blankly, straight out into the darkness. Then the flash, the explosion: Both curtains billowed right up almost to the ceiling and were splashed with red. As Arthur started to fall backwards, I became aware of the expanding cloud of white smoke and the thousands of fragments of glass that were flying through the air, bouncing off the walls, and raining on the far end of the table. I don't actually remember hearing the sound; I felt it like a shock wave and my ears hurt. Arthur hit the floor heavily; he didn't raise his arms and made no attempt to break his fall. James, who was nearest to Arthur, put his hands over his head and flattened himself onto the table, while Melissa and her chair fell over towards Karen, who had just entered carrying a huge, red, yellow and orange jelly. She fell backwards too, as the flying glass tore into the jelly she held in front of her.

I still wonder if time had somehow slowed down? I vividly remember having the strangest of thoughts, as the chaos unfolded before me. I clearly remember being thankful: Thankful that Arthur hadn't put his hands up to where his face had been. He never got to feel what I had seen; that his chin, cheeks, nose and eyes had all been blasted away. Also, that he hadn't tried to break his fall, so he was either already dead, or was unconscious and so felt no pain.

As the smell of the gunpowder reached my nostrils, I tried to assess who else was injured. James was slowly raising his head off the table; he had cuts to his left hand and cheek. I couldn't see Karen but hoped the jelly had protected her face and eyes from the flying glass. Then, unbelievably, I was thinking about getting a dustpan and brush to clear up all the broken glass!

Nigel was the first to react sensibly - he ran straight to the door leading towards the kitchen closing it, just as Monta and Paul appeared. He shouted something through the door to them.
Molly was still sitting but was choking on her food and looked terrified. Andrea ran out of the door behind me. I think she was screaming – her mouth was wide open. James stood up, took a brief look at Arthur, and grimaced. He shouted something to me then went to help Melissa up. Melissa was so pale and looked dazed and confused as she was led towards me. Nigel was pulling Karen up with help from James. Jason ran past James, who put an arm out to try to stop him. Jason stood looking down at Arthur and was promptly sick. James was shouting at me again, and I realised that I was just standing motionless, being absolutely no help to anyone. Richard spun me around by my shoulders to face him, and he shouted, "Gun? – Where is Arthur's gun?"

I shook my head; I knew that, as well as being in Arthur's room on the second floor, I had no idea where he kept the key to the gun safe. I became aware of more noises, mostly muffled by the ringing in my ears that was slowly clearing. Karen looked badly injured, but as she wiped the jelly off, it became clear she was shocked but unhurt. James then ran past me into the conservatory. I realised where he was heading, and ran after him. He had the hidden cupboard open by the time I got there, Bloody croquet! Where are the guns?" he shouted as he turned to me angrily.

"We don't have any. Arthur has one, but it's locked away upstairs, and I don't know where he keeps the key."

"Ah, Lord, that leaves just me with a single barrel 28 bore - I'll get it from my car. George, you must pull yourself together and stop Melissa seeing Arthur's face. Get her a brandy or something."

I wondered if Arthur had finished the brandy he had poured in the drawing room earlier. Sure enough, both glasses remained. I poured them together and resisted the temptation to gulp it down myself, as the commotion continued in the dining room.

Andrea had returned, she was standing just outside the door and visibly shaking. Not wishing to enter, she was holding a duvet cover. "George," She handed me the cover as I went in, "please put this over Arthur - he *is* dead, isn't he?"

"Yes. I'm afraid he is..." I replied, taking the cover, "Oh, Andrea, I think Nigel sent Monta and Paul down to the portacabin. I don't know what they know? Please would you go down there and check they're alright, stay with them, and make sure they don't come back here?"

Andrea nodded and headed for the front door. Karen was trying to comfort Melissa while dabbing her forehead and ear with a napkin where she had cuts, "You *really don't* want to see him," Karen insisted, "remember him as he was, not how he is now."

I handed the brandy over and whispered to Karen, "Try to get her to drink some of this."

Richard was pouring water for Molly and Jason, who both looked like they would be sick.

Phillip came back in through the broken door. "It was Mick!" he announced, "Look!" He held up a post-it note, "This was stuck on the outside door handle. It says 'For Sandy a eye for a eye!' That's got to be Mick - he's an illiterate bastard!"

"You can't know it was him!" Karen said sharply.

"Surely it must be?" said Richard, "You never got Peter's note to Sandy, George?" he asked.

"No, I've not seen her since last year, Mick took her off to the Appleby Manor Hotel, and that town became a no-go area after he teamed up with a load of delinquents from that detention centre."

James came back with his shotgun as Nigel climbed in through the window with his torch in hand.

Nigel came over to us, "It's that guy with the yellow Humvee, and he won't be going anywhere fast," He held up a bright yellow Humvee key fob. "He's cut a hole in the fence by the West Avenue, looks like it's been repaired there before? He dropped these climbing back through."

"Right, let's get him!" Said Richard, "he may not even realise he's dropped his keys yet. Let's find that car and wait for him."

"You got a problem shooting him, James?" I

asked. "Be my pleasure." James answered coldly.

"No! You can't. Just let him go. He won't come back."
Karen pleaded.

"What? Are you mad?" screamed Melissa, "Mad Mick just
killed Daddy! Kill him - do it now! And Sandy too, if she's with
him!"

"We'll use my car," said James, "who's coming with me?"

I stepped forward, as did Phillip and Richard, but Nigel
shook his head, "I'll stay here in case he comes back, looking
for his keys."

"No!" yelled Karen, as we started to leave.

"Karen, why the heck not?" I asked, getting impatient to get
after Mick.

"You just can't. Don't kill him, please!" Karen begged.

"He killed my Daddy!" Melissa hissed, "What the fuck is
your problem?"

"Come on," said James, "he might get away if we stall
any longer."

As one, we marched out, but just as we got to the front door
Karen fell to her knees and yelled after us, "He's Paul's
father!" then more quietly, "Mick is Paul's dad… you can't."

I couldn't believe what I was hearing, nor understand why she would make up such a story. "You and Mick?" I asked, as I went back to her, tears now streaming down her face.

Melissa had followed her out. "Are you fucking mad? You went out with Mick?"

"No!" sobbed Karen, "No…" She looked me in the eyes, then looked back down to the floor. Almost in a whisper she wept, "He raped me. Mick raped me on my 18th birthday."

There was a moment of silence before Melissa hissed, "So, that's another reason to kill the bastard!" she pointed at the door, "Go and get him now!"

"You didn't report it?" I asked, torn between the anguish and distress of the two women. Helping Karen up, I guided her into the library for a seat while beckoning Melissa to be patient.

Karen took a napkin offered by Jason and wiped her eyes, "I told Simon Duguid about a week later, but he said I had no evidence. I didn't know he was Mick's dad then. Later, when I realised I was pregnant, I knew I had proof and by then I also knew Simon was Mick's dad. Simon begged me not to either terminate the pregnancy, nor turn Mick in. He said Mick had learning difficulties - that he wasn't really to blame - and that he'd help me look after the baby. He said this was the only chance he had to be a grandfather. He found, and started to pay half the rent for that bungalow."

"So, it was Simon you were talking to on the phone that morning?" I asked, suddenly understanding Karen and her moods better than I ever had before.

Karen nodded and put her head in her hands.

"Karen," Richard spoke softly, "Paul doesn't know, does he?"

460

She shook her head. "No."

"Mick is never going to be a father figure for Paul, is he? He's a thief, a rapist and now a murderer. Why would you ever want to share that with Paul?" Richard asked.

As Karen struggled with the question, I looked up at Melissa. Her eyes had glazed over, she was very pale, and was slowly toppling forwards. I just managed to catch her as she fell, head-first, towards the back of Karen's chair.

"She's in shock," stated Richard, "someone should get her to bed, and stay with her."

"I'll go," offered Molly, "if someone can carry her up?"

As she was already in my arms, I cradled her limp body and carried her up. Molly pulled back the covers, and I gently laid her down. I recall hoping that she'd never wake, saving her from reliving the dreadful memories of that evening.

"Yours?" Molly interrupted my thoughts as she handed me my work clothes that were still on her bed.

I offered no explanation, and Molly didn't press me for one. Very little seemed to matter other than my desire to both get Mick, and try to understand Karen's reasoning.

"So you thought that at some point he'd grow up, change, and you could then introduce him to Paul?" Richard was asking Karen as I came back down.

Karen sighed, "That's never going to happen, is it?"

"You know we can't just let him go," I said as calmly as I could, "not now. Think of Melissa. And Arthur was a good friend to all of us here. Surely, Paul would be better off just never knowing who his father is… or was? He certainly doesn't need to know what he did to you or Arthur. Having learning difficulties just doesn't excuse his actions."

Karen gave the tiniest of nods. "Go, but not Sandy, leave her."

"Of course. I'll bring Peter's note; in case she *is* there."

"Come on!" said James, ever more impatiently.

"Here." Nigel handed me the key fob.

"Thanks. Oh, Nigel, did you send Monta and Paul down to the portacabin?"

Nigel shook his head, "No. Gatehouse - they play Pacman."

We all bundled into James's Land Rover and we sped down the drive. The lights were on in the gatehouse, giving me some comfort that Monta, Paul, and Andrea were all safe.

The silence was abruptly broken, "Stop, please!" Phillip said urgently as we slowed for the gate to open, "Sorry, I can't do this; I've just realised that we are about to kill someone! Please just let me out? I can't do this." Phillip had already opened the door before anyone answered. Richard looked like he was questioning his decision too, and it was only then that I fully realised and questioned what we were actually planning to do, myself. Was this yet another of my rash and stupid decisions?

Richard pulled the door shut again and turned to me as the car started to move again. "We do *have* to do this, don't we?" he asked, with a worried look.

"Bloody Hell!" called back James, "You not pussyin' out too, is yer?!"

"No." I said quietly, "You don't have to do this Richard, but I do. I must. For Arthur and Mel, I have to..."

Richard solemnly nodded. "Yes... For Arthur."

James slowed the Land Rover and switched the headlights off, "Keep your eyes peeled for anyone on foot, or that yellow Humvee."

"He doesn't usually do anything alone," Richard warned, "there might even be other vehicles?"

We had reached the end of the lane and turned left onto Ford Dyke Lane. The road ahead climbed gently towards Ingleton. We stopped by the turning for Langdon but saw nothing and continued on for another couple of minutes in silence. Then, just as the 30 speed restriction signs for Ingleton came into view, silhouetted against the summer's night sky, we saw the outline of a large vehicle parked on the left of the road. James cut the engine, rolled to a halt and gently applied the handbrake. There was some movement; it appeared that one, possibly two people, were just beyond the vehicle where the stone sign marks the boundary of Ingleton.

"Don't slam the doors!" James instructed, "You two walk along the right side of the road, arm-in-arm like. Make out you're a couple, he won't be seeing you clearly till you gets close. I'll go up on the left, but I'll be the other side of that hedge, in the field. I knows it well."

Richard and I crept out of the car, and looked at each other with slight apprehension.

"Come on darling," whispered Richard, "you can be my bitch!"

At any other time, I'd have found his glib remark funny, but as we walked up the hill in that humid night air, I wasn't amused. I was terrified, and I could tell that Richard was too; more so when James silently disappeared through the hedge, and Richard tightened his grip on my arm. Slowly, we walked up the hill towards the back of the stationary car. With our heads down, our eyes scanned the hedges and verges for any shadow or shape that could be a hidden killer. We walked over yellow strips in the road that warned cars to slow. Neither of the figures in front of the car matched Mick, so he was either still on his way back from the Manor or was hiding, waiting to ambush us.

"We are creeping up on Mad Mick's car, we know he has a gun, and we're armed with nothing," Richard said in a serious and hushed voice.

"Shush, look! There are *two* people in front of that car; A tall woman in a dress! And look, the shorter one, that could be Sandy?"

"They're both looking towards Ingle; I don't think they've seen us," Richard whispered, "that short one is a boy I think? Is he holding the taller one and pushing her down onto that sign?"

"Oh shit, I wish they'd see us before we get too close," I replied. Then I thought I heard a sound like someone treading on gravel behind us, I glanced around hoping to see James, but no one was revealed in the darkness. We kept going in silence. The Humvee got bigger as we got closer, and it appeared grey in the poor light. We were now so close there was no point remaining arm-in-arm. As I gave Richard a little nudge and started to pull my arm away. I was relieved to see that was no one else in the Humvee then shocked when I realised that tall woman, sitting on the Ingleton sign, was Andrea!

464

"That's far enough girls! Put your hands up." With my heart in my mouth, we slowly turned. Mick was on the verge behind us to our left. He was pointing a double-barrelled, sawn-off shotgun straight at us. He walked around us confidently, towards the Humvee, keeping the weapon trained on us.

"So which one of you two gay arseholes, has my keys?" he asked.

Richard pulled away from me and took a step forward. Instantly Mick raised the gun and pointed it directly at his face. Richard raised his hands above his head and retreated a step.

Andrea struggled, her hands tied behind her back. Despite attempts by the considerably shorter lad to hold her, she got up, dragging him round to face us too. Her mouth crammed with some lacy material, she was unable to speak, yet her eyes spoke clearly of the horror she was experiencing. I recognised her captor too; it was the Latvian boy, Davis.

Mick stood in front of the others by the side of the car. "I'll shoot her first if you don't answer. Now, toss the keys over here, or I'll blow her legs off and bring her down to his height." He aimed the gun at Andrea's feet. She closed her eyes and turned away while Davis, scared he'd also be hit, let her go and stood away.

"I have your keys, Mick," I stated urgently. I felt sure he was about to shoot. I had already realised that, unfortunately, the large Humvee was between the hedge James was behind, and Mick.

"Toss them here now or she gets it." Mick indicated the floor by his feet.

"You let us all go, and we have a deal." I called back loudly, "I'll throw the keys down just in front of your car, and we'll all just run away when you go to get them."

"I give the orders!" shouted Mick, "You really 'ave 'em?"

I held up the keys.

"Wait," said Richard, "Andrea's not wearing any shoes."

"What happened to her shoes, Davis?" barked Mick.

"I took them off and threw them under there." He pointed under the Humvee.

"The shoes don't matter!" I whispered urgently to Richard.

Then Richard understood, "Just throw them now," he called out loudly, "Andrea can run in bare feet."

Without waiting for agreement from Mick, and ignoring Andrea's fierce head shaking, I threw the keys as far as I could in front of the car. They flew over Andrea landed with a slight chink, just beyond the Ingleton sign.

As soon as Mick started to walk briskly towards them, I yelled, "run!" and ran to Andrea to help her run with her hands still tied behind her. I expected to hear a gunshot, but all I heard was Mick laughing.

Then he started to chant, "Run rabbits, run rabbits, run, run, run..."

I turned back to see Mick had raised his gun again and was aiming at us as we ran.

"Mick's gonna kill yah, with his gun, gun..."

This time, I did hear the bang and saw the intense flash of light.

Andrea and I fell forward together, both landing heavily on the hard tarmac. Ahead of us, Richard dived, head-first into the hedge on the right.

I heard a cartridge land on the floor as the shotgun was broken, and then a solid click as the breech snapped closed again.

Then I heard Mick screaming in agony, and I couldn't wait for the second shot. I looked back to see James advancing on Mick's fallen and writhing body.

"Finish it!" I yelled.

James didn't look up. He calmly placed the barrel of the gun to the back of Mick's neck. "Arthur was a friend. You are a cowardly, worthless piece of shit, that nobody is going to miss." he said coldly.

I turned away as James fired, but was relieved that the screaming instantly stopped and that Mick was dead. I don't think I could have grieved for Arthur while he was still alive.

Richard scrambled out of the hedge and he helped Andrea up and cut the cable tie that bound her wrists with his pocket knife. She pulled the ball of wet fabric out of her mouth and threw it behind her. She was shaking and breathless, so much that I sat her back down on the verge behind the car, "I'll find your shoes." I said, "You're safe now."

"What about the lad?" Richard asked, pointing at Davis, his hands held above his head as he cowered on his knees by the car door.

James took the keys from Mick's bloodied hand and the sawn-off shotgun that was by his side. He walked up to Davis and

467

yelled "Boo!" right in his ear.

Davis recoiled and started to beg for his life. James ignored him. "You hurt?" he asked Andrea, as, still shaking, she replaced her shoes.

"No, I've not been hurt, just bloody terrified," Andrea put her hand up, and James pulled her up, "Monta and Paul weren't in the portacabin," she continued, looking at me accusingly, "*he* was!" she pointed to Davis, as she stood up and marched over to him.

"I'm sorry, Miss," Davis pleaded, still on his knees, "it was Mick's idea to gag you..."

Andrea drew her hand right back and swung it hard and fast, straight into Davis' face. "Pervert!" she yelled, as her weighty slap bowled him over.

I went over to him, and he curled up on the floor with his hands over his head. "Davis?" I tried to pull him up, but he was convinced he was about to get a kicking and tried crawling under the Humvee. "Davis, get up!" I yelled. "I need you to do something for us."

Unconvinced, Davis slowly stood up trembling with fear.

"I'll get my car." offered James, "don't go soft on him."

I shot him a quick nod and turned back to Davis as Richard joined me. "Peter's note?" he asked.

"Davis, do you know Sandy? Sandy Rutherford - she's

about twenty-one, your height, with jet black hair like yours?"

"Yes, Sandy was Mick's girl," Davis said questioningly, "she left him for another, last week. Mick came here to avenge her Grandfather. It was Mick's desperate attempt to try to get her back. She continuously called Mick 'useless' for not doing anything." Davis, along with Richard and myself all turned to look at Mick's lifeless body. "She controlled him completely," Davis said quietly, "he was never in charge, he was like her puppy."

"Loyal, but not very bright." Richard stated.

Suddenly I felt overwhelming compassion and regret. Just a few moments earlier I'd felt satisfaction that Arthur's killer had been executed and that justice had been served. I had even been considering leaving his body in the ditch for the animals to devour. "We've just killed a man with learning difficulties." I stated.

Richard put his arm around my shoulders. "George, don't beat yourself up. Mick was also a rapist, and he chose to try to impress Sandy by killing a lovely, unarmed man in his late sixties. He knew right from wrong, learning difficulties or not."

I took in a deep breath. "Yes... but we will cover his body, and I'll go and tell Simon where he can find his son." I turned to Davis, "You can have that Humvee and go back to your mates at Appleby if you promise to do the following; firstly, you drive me to Simon's house, it's just the other side of Ingleton by the school. Then you help him bury or burn the body if that's what he wants. Agreed?"

"I'll do anything. I promise." Davis said earnestly. "What else?"

I took Peter's note out of my pocket and handed it to him,

469

"That note is from Sandy's grandfather. Two lives could have been saved if she'd read it earlier. It is imperative that you give her this note when she's on her own. I need to trust you to do this. Only once she's read it, tell her that Mick lost his life for killing Arthur."

Davis sincerely promised he would do as instructed. As James drove Richard and Andrea back to the Manor, I climbed up into the Humvee and prepared to make the most difficult of house calls. I had little time rehearse what to say; we were turning into Manor Close just five minutes later.

Simon opened the door in his dressing gown. He read my expression immediately. He just stood there, looking utterly depressed and beaten, even before I started talking. He said nothing when I told him that Mick was dead. He only shook his head sadly and bowed it further when I told him that Mick had killed Arthur at the Manor. He nodded in agreement when I offered Davis's services to recover the body. Without a word, he went in to put his clothes and boots on. He returned carrying two spades.

No one spoke as we drove back, but Simon took a sudden intake of breath, and put his hand over his mouth when the headlights exposed Mick's body by the Ingleton sign.

"I'm going to leave you to it," I said flatly, "we have a body to attend to as well. Davis, *please* do not forget that note."

As I started to walk towards the Land Rover, Simon spoke for the first time; "This… this is all my fault." he said in a broken voice, clearly on the edge of tears, as he looked down at his son's body.

I turned back to Simon and stated clearly and with much bitterness: "Yes, it *is*."

Chapter 15 — Life Goes On

Saturday, at 12 noon, Melissa and her friend Claire gently tugged the harnesses of the two horses. The cart, carrying Arthur's coffin, juddered and started moving slowly. The quiet chatter of the crowd became hushed as the procession began to move.

Richard and I walked on the right side, while Karen and Paul, were on the left. I had been staggered when greeted by a crowd of over three hundred, who had gathered in the carpark and road by the Black Horse.

The whole community had been shocked by the news of Arthur's death. But they had also worked, as one, to help organise an almost royal send-off. In just three days, a coffin had been beautifully crafted from oak panelling found at the Bury.
The two horses had been groomed to perfection - even their hooves had been varnished.

The late July sun reflected and glinted on the many brass bridle clips and tack. The rhythmic clip-clop of the hooves on the road was the only sound I could hear.

Melissa was walking directly ahead of me in a bright yellow summer dress. She had issued instructions that we should not wear black or dull colours; instead, she insisted that the parade should be a colourful tribute. I contrasted this with Arthur's tweed jacket and cap that laid across his coffin, held in place with his favourite, silver-topped stick.

I was so glad I couldn't see Melissa's face. She was so very brave; leading the procession with her head held high. But I knew that she was likely on the verge of tears - as was I.

Glancing back, I could see the crowd forming into an orderly procession behind. The roadside and houses had all been decorated with flowers or bunting. More people stood either side of the road, and some tossed flowers or tributes onto the cart as we passed.

Ingleton's colourful houses reminded me of a picture postcard, especially with so many brightly-dressed people standing in front of them. But two figures wearing black hoodies caught my eye; Standing a little apart and further back than everyone else, they looked out of place. I turned and nodded to them, hoping they'd nod back and identify themselves. One meekly nodded back, giving nothing away. The other, who I think was a young woman, slowly mimed blowing a kiss. I initially assumed towards Arthur's coffin. Then I wondered, indeed I hoped, that this hooded pair were Davis and Sandy and that the kiss was a 'thank you' for her grandfather's note.

Simon Duguid stood alone at the end of Manor close, his head bowed. Melissa noticed but did not turn to acknowledge him, as she had done to others she recognised.

As we turned right into Gainford Road and proceeded up the gentle slope, I was surprised to see James Granger ahead. He was waiting by the side of the road, holding a single red rose. To my complete amazement, Melissa stopped the cart just before the Ingleton sign. While Claire held the horses, she walked alone, up to James, as the procession stopped.

Melissa took the single rose and knelt to place it on the stone, close to where Mick had died. While she remained kneeling, I struggled to believe that she possessed such forgiveness. I was reminded that I had chosen to bring the wooden cross with me. I felt for it in my pocket. I had hoped to see and return it to the old lady who had lent it to me. I'd not seen her since December, and I felt guilty that I still had it.

As Melissa slowly walked back, she caught my eye. She managed a weak little smile and walked right up to me, "George, would you please walk with me, I'm feeling a little wobbly."

"I would be honoured," I replied, "you are doing really well, and that last gesture... well, Arthur would have been so proud of you."

"I do hope so?" She seemed unsure, "But I know exactly where I am going to break down;" she whispered, "it's when I see all those flowers and messages."

I nodded, "Yes, that's an incredible display, considering there are no flower shops." I knew exactly where she meant: The fountain in the middle of the drive had become an impromptu memorial. Villagers, the Travellers, farmers, and traders had left flowers, tokens, poems and messages. That morning, there were so many that Stuart and I had to move some of them to allow the cart to pass. The job had brought us both to tears, because we felt compelled to read out the touching messages on all those we moved.

Nigel and Monta stood either side of the open gates as we entered the garden. Melissa had asked that only a small number of people to attend the burial, and it was their duty to guide the others around the fountain memorial, and back out. The travellers had organised a public wake on the cricket ground, where we would join them again later.

Ahead of us lay the impressive display of flowers and messages, all around and over the fountain. I felt a sudden lump in my throat, and Melissa's grip on my arm tightened.

"They are so beautiful," she said, tears streaming down her face. I was ready with a clean hanky and offered it to her. She dried her eyes, as a single tear rolled slowly over my own cheek.

On seeing this, she quickly and gently just dabbed it away for me. By then the flowers and tributes were all behind us.

Melissa had agreed to Richard's suggestion that the vacant space at the end of either the East or West Avenues, would make a good final resting place for Arthur. She suggested that a memorial or statue could be erected at a later date and that the end of the other avenue could be dedicated to her mother.

It seemed apt that Melissa's fountain was in the middle, and tributes to Arthur and Jayne would be so far apart. I'm sure that neither Melissa nor Richard missed that interpretation.

Gathered at the end of the East Avenue, as well as those who had attended Arthur's last meal, were; Stuart, Claire, Del, Fenella, Dale with Precious, and Hope. Reverend Kenneth said some rather dull, but nice, things about Arthur. Melissa stepped forward but was unable to speak. Richard took over, taking her notes, putting his arm around her as he read the few words that Melissa had written. She'd written how she had, only quite recently, really got to know and love her father and how he was key to saving the new community at Ingleton.

As Arthur's coffin was lowered into the dark hole, Melissa was led away by her friend, Claire. She had been brave for long enough.

Richard had volunteered to help me fill the hole once everyone else had left. As we shovelled in the soil, he told me that his sister had agreed that he could remain at Ingleton for as long as was required. For this, I was very grateful. I had often described Arthur as the 'oil in our machine'; he sorted out disputes and was the man everyone had gone to if they had either a complaint or suggestion. I knew that Richard was equally capable of fulfilling this role and that I should learn how to do the same.

Richard was keen to join the Travellers at the cricket ground, where they had offered to cook anything anyone brought along and had acquired barrels of beer. I felt drained, and although I didn't want to miss Arthur's wake, I didn't have much energy; I hadn't had more than a couple of hours' sleep since Arthur had been killed, and I wasn't in the mood for the Travellers' loud hospitality. I told Richard that I might join him later. I felt like going down to the lake and just sitting on my rock, with my thoughts and guilt, so I headed back to my room to change.

Claire was about to leave as I got in, "She's in her room, and wants to be left alone," Claire warned, "she won't be going to the wake."

I thanked her for all her help, both for preparing the horses and for being such a comfort to Melissa. She gave me brief, sincere smile and said while looking straight into my eyes said, "She needs you too, try to keep her from withdrawing into herself."

As I changed into jeans and a t-shirt, I could hear intermittent sobs from Melissa's room. I took heed of Claire's warning and left her alone to grieve. From my window, I could see smoke rising from the fires on the cricket ground, and watched Claire as she slowly led the horses towards the gatehouse. I found myself torn between going to the wake and staying behind. It was then I noticed a solitary figure crouching by the flower-covered fountain. I squinted to try to recognise who it was. I then quickly recovered the wooden cross from a pocket in my discarded clothes - it was the old lady again.

"Good afternoon, George," she said as she slowly stood up, "so many lovely messages here, your gardeners are clearly not only growing food!"

"Hello, sorry... I don't know your name?" I waited for her reply, but she just smiled warmly, "I have brought you your cross back - thanks for lending it to me."

"Did it help you?" She asked.

I was going to say, 'no,' but I didn't want to upset her, and Fenella *had* shown up to resolve my dilemma, just after I threw it at the church. "It gave me some comfort." I decided to reply as I offered it back.

She grinned, "Oh, well, in that case, my dear, you surely should keep it?"

"Er, no. I certainly shouldn't; just three days ago, I was involved in the execution, without trial, of Arthur's killer. So, I must insist you take it back," again, I offered the cross.

"Oh, I see," she sadly took the cross back, and clutched it tightly in her frail hands, "I would question who could have tried him? But was this 'execution' an act of hatred or revenge?"

"Not hatred, but revenge? Yes," I sighed, "when this crisis is over, I will turn myself in to the police and accept my punishment."

"Have you read *this* message?" The old lady picked up a small posy of dark red hesperantha.

I recognised the flowers as both those growing in the borders around the conservatory, and as Arthur's favourite flower, "No, but I know it will be from - Arthur's daughter, Melissa."

"Let me read it to you," she whispered, "It simply reads; 'Daddy, I love you.' That's fewer words than all of these other messages, but don't you think it means so much more?"

Suddenly too emotional to speak; I knew my voice would crack, as the lump in my throat swelled. I had made a very conscious decision not to read Melissa's last message to her father, so I just nodded.

"Love is *always* a good thing," the old lady took my hand and squeezed it between hers, "it is more powerful than both hate or revenge. Only forgiveness can ever compete with love. I believe that you helped to end Michael Duguid's life out of love. I also think that you may have already turned yourself in? Did you not report it to Simon Duguid, who was his father *and* is a police officer? Why not wait and see if Simon can forgive you, or will turn you in? Surely, there can be no better person to judge your actions?" As she let go of my hand, I realised that she'd surreptitiously passed the wooden cross back to me.

As I looked down at the cross in my hand, the old lady started to walk, very slowly towards the gate, "Goodbye, George. Should you find yourself at a junction and your future looks uncertain; do consider the signs, but always let your heart be your guide."

"Right? ... Look, I'm going to the cricket ground..." I called after her, "I can give you a lift somewhere?"

She turned back laughing, "Oh, I'm not going your way, George! But you are a considerate man for offering."

I hurried back to the garage to borrow the RAV-4. I couldn't just leave the old lady to limp along so slowly, wherever she was going. I'd soon catch her up and then insist on giving her a lift.

She'd already made it out of the gate by the time I'd got there, "She can walk faster than I thought" I said to myself. However, when I got to the end of the lane, I'd still not seen her, and could now see half a mile in each direction on the Ingleton Road. I sat in the car and started to question my sanity. I concluded that either this frail and weak old lady was fighting her way through the now very overgrown, and steep, footpath, or she didn't exist and was merely a figment of my troubled imagination.

I turned around and drove slowly back up the lane, checking the daisy covered verges carefully in case she had fallen. I got out by the gate. Dense undergrowth obstructed the footpath and its sign. Clearly nobody had travelled that way for many months.

24th September: 'Drone lands.'

We had only just finished reshaping the last topiary, and Richard was still high on a ladder when he called down, "Look, there's a drone, and this one is circling the garden." He pointed his shears to the west.

The little shape turned sharply and disappeared behind the house. I ran around to the croquet lawn just as it landed in the middle. It was a massive drone - over a meter square - and I was wary of it. A small lens on its underside swung up to face me. Then as Richard joined me, a plastic box on its back popped open.

We'd heard many people tell of seeing drones flying to and from Edinburgh, speculating that they emanated from London. But this was the first to stray this far from the path of the A1.

Richard took a closer look, "Property of the British Government. Recharge if red light flashes. Instructions in the wallet below," he read out loud. "I can't see a red light," he added, "But there's a CD in the box labelled 'For the personal attention of Arthur Quail."

"Can you hear me?" I called out.

Richard turned and looked at me. "What do you mean? Of course, I can!"

I nodded back towards the drone, where the camera now moved up and down three times.

"Oh!" Said Richard as he stood back.

I took the CD out of the box, and the camera tracked my movements. "Arthur Quail died eight weeks ago." The camera slowly lowered and pointed towards the soil. "Do you know who I am?"

"Wicked!" Paul had seen the drone landing, and had joined us, "Make it fly!"

The camera 'nodded' again.

"Should Melissa and I look at the CD?"

Again, the drone acknowledged.

Realising that he wasn't required, Richard said, "I'll go with Paul, to the portacabin - we'll be there if you need us."

I found Melissa sitting on 'my' rock by the lake. She'd spent many hours there since Arthur had died. Sometimes we'd sit there together recalling 'the good old days' and even had the odd laugh about the fish she'd put in my boot, or the time she sewed up the bottom of my gardening trousers. Other times, like on that day, she just wanted to sit alone with a book.

"Hello, come for a chat?" she asked.

"No, not today; a drone has landed with a message on a CD," then I said more quietly, "it was addressed to Arthur, but those controlling it say we should look at it." Sounding disinterested she replied, "I saw the drone flying around, but didn't realise it had landed. OK, let's see what Maria wanted Daddy to do? I bet you any amount of food tokens that it's from her!"

Then, as we walked back through the, now golden-brown, meadow, she asked, "What do you miss the most about life before PCP? Not people, just things we can't get or see anymore?"

"Oh, I don't know? Maybe cheese, or just the smell of cut grass? – I bet for you, it's social media?"

"No! If *that* ever comes back, I might use it to find out who's still alive, but I'll never waste so much time on that again!" She paused, "I miss the sheep, and lambing on the hill, and vapour trails in the sky."

"Wow! – Vapour trails? I'd have never thought of that. I do hope someone has managed to keep sheep alive somewhere, and they can repopulate."

I realised that Melissa was walking much more slowly. "You've slowed down Mel, are you not keen on playing that message?"

She stopped walking, "Oh, I'm just not sure I want to hear 'Hello Arthur! – That's all. I'm being stupid, aren't I?"

"No," I put my arm around her and guided her back towards the house, "not at all. I'll be with you, and ready with a tissue. I perfectly understand."

The CD launched a program that offered three options: Arthur Quail, Andrea Parker or Nigel Haywood. Melissa clicked on 'Arthur's button, and password box appeared.

"Oh," I said, "I wonder if the drone can indicate what his password is?"

Melissa just started to type, "It's bound to be 1874 dash 1965," she said as she hit the return button confidently, Churchill's birth and death years." She explained, "he used the same password for everything!"

A video started to play.

"What did I tell you? – Maria Trellis!"

The picture showed Maria sitting very upright, behind a grand desk, "Hello Arthur, I trust you are well? I've heard that you have built a thriving trading centre at Ingleton, and I apologise that my duties here do not presently allow me to visit." Maria paused to read from a script, "I don't know if the news has reached you yet, but I am now your Prime Minister. My work continues to stabilise food production and supply. In April, we secured communications with China and Indonesia, and imports of rice, beans, and nuts are now arriving. These are being distributed from Hull, Ipswich, Southampton, Plymouth, Newport, and Toon. This, together with our homeland production, and our newly secured transport network, means we should able to support our remaining population, estimated to be just over 35 Million. Please deliver any surplus food you produce to your nearest distribution centre at the Port of South Shields.

I also require the services of both Andrea Parker and Nigel Haywood.

Instructions for them are included on your disc. I would like to thank you for your support, Arthur. I look forward to seeing you again when everything settles down." The screen returned to the original menu.

Melissa's and my reactions to Maria's brief message were very different;

"I hope Nigel can bring Monta with him?" Melissa asked, "Poor Paul, he is *so* going to miss those two, and Karen will miss Andrea - they share all the cleaning, cooking and trading-counter duties."

"Yes..." I said, "But, she said, '35 million', I thought our population was about 64 million?" I shook my head sadly. "Have we really lost close to 30 million people to a grass virus? We've been so lucky here."

I became aware that Melissa wasn't replying, she clearly didn't feel we'd been so 'lucky', so I put an arm around her. "Not completely lucky, I know... I'm sorry!"

She rested her head on the top of my arm, "It's OK," she whispered, "please don't feel you have to walk on eggshells when you talk to me. I know you miss him almost as much as I do. And, we *have* been lucky. It's just that I'm afraid that this is all slowly coming to an end, not just the crisis, but what we have here. It was so special. We've already lost Daddy, and now Nigel, Monta and Andrea are going. Richard is going back to Lincoln next month too - The house is emptying again."

"Yes, I know what you mean." Then I laughed, "But, I can't wait to tell Karen that her 'claim-to-fame' is that she once threw plates at the Prime Minister! Do you know what you are going to do when, or if, things get back to normal?" I probed, wondering about my own prospects, "Will you sell Ingleton Manor and up sticks to London or Edinburgh?"

"No," Melissa replied firmly. "Daddy wouldn't have wanted that. I thought that I could rent parts of the house out as self-catering holiday accommodation. Maybe sell the farm houses to the farmers, quite cheaply because their families helped in this crisis and for generations before. Use that money to modify the house for guests. And, don't worry, I want you to stay on as my

Head Gardener, and Richard, he could re-join us too, anytime he wants. Claire could help manage and promote the Manor as holiday accommodation"

"Wow, you actually have been thinking a lot about the future, haven't you?" I gave her a little squeeze before letting her go, "I'd love to stay, that's for sure!"

"I haven't just been sitting on my rock and crying you know," Melissa smiled, "though I have done quite a lot of that too. Daddy was only 30 when his father died, and he had to take over the Manor. I will just have to do the same at 17."

"Oh God, I'm so sorry; We completely forgot your birthday!" I exclaimed, "The 10th of September. I should have remembered!"

Melissa laughed, "Well I'm sure we forgot yours too, and I wasn't in the mood to celebrate. So, I'm glad you forgot. Just don't you ever do it again!" she punched my arm. Something she hadn't done for simply ages. That simple, light-hearted action told me that Melissa was recovering.

"OK I promise not to forget again!" I laughed, rubbing my arm as if it hurt, "What about Karen and Paul, though, can they stay on at the house?"

"Yes, if she's happy to stay on as the cleaner, I do worry that Paul will need special schooling and that they'll have to move away too, though. Only time will tell, I guess? Now George, time to get Nigel and Andrea in here to get their packing instructions!"

Late July - 3 years later:

The low morning sun was reflecting in the formal pond's
fountain, scattering the light into miniature rainbows that
danced across the walls of the little gatehouse like demented
butterflies. Arthur smiled. He was sitting at the end of the bed,
laughing and pointing at them.

"Morning my darling," yawned Melissa, as she turned over and
planted a long kiss in the middle of my chest, "has our little
monster been awake long? Oh, do look at Arthur! – he's
pointing at all those little prisms. He's very alert this morning.
Ew, but someone's nappy needs changing, doesn't it? – And,
Mummy thinks it's Daddy's turn! – And, Little Arthur knows
that Mummy's always right, doesn't he? – Yes-he-does!"

Arthur beamed, bounced excitedly, and pointed at her.

"Oh, but look… Daddy thinks that Little Arthur wants
Mummy to do it!" I joked.

"Well, if Daddy does it, and then puts him back in his cot,
then Mummy might say to Daddy, *I think I'm ready to let Daddy
try to make another Little Monster!*"

"I'm on it!" I said, springing out of bed, much to Arthur's
amusement. "She's kept me waiting a very long time you
know, Arthur!"

"Oh really?! So, you've never kept me waiting then!" She grinned
cheekily, "Anyway, Mrs Trellis does want all young couples to try
to produce two or more children – and she who must be obeyed
…" laughed Melissa.

"Yes! – Maybe later, we could take Arthur over to Keswick, to see Andrea's new grass and the sheep there? I know he's way too young to remember it, but I'd really like to see them too!"

Melissa sighed, "Hmm, OK, but don't laugh if seeing it makes me cry – it's been over five years since I've seen any grass and it's going to bring back a lot of memories!"

"Yes, me too…" I sighed deeply, "but I need to see it for myself and it has become a major tourist attraction – who would have ever predicted that five years ago? – Come to Keswick and see some grass!"

I'd finished changing the nappy, and lowered Arthur into his cot, when I jumped at the urgent buzzing of the doorbell. "Oh God, don't tell me… another guest has forgotten the internet password, or has tripped a fuse!" I unhooked my dressing gown from the door, "Don't you dare move!" I said, pointing to Melissa, who looked equally frustrated by this interruption.

I hurriedly put on my dressing gown as the doorbell sounded again. The buzzing was immediately followed by repeated rapping on the glass.

"Sounds urgent!" Melissa said, "Maybe they can't work the remote control?" Melissa called after me, "or have lost their key?"

I hesitated by the bedroom door, I looked back at Melissa looking so seductive and happy in our bed. It suddenly occurred to me that Simon Duguid may have called the Police; naming me as one of those responsible for his son's death. Was this to be the last time I see my new family looking so young and happy?

I blew both Melissa and Arthur a kiss before I closed the bedroom door behind me, took a deep breath and prepared to face my fate.

Bang, bang, bang! My early morning visitor was now banging the door with their fist. This was clearly *not* one of our guests from the Manor. Shaking with fear, I took a deep breath and slowly opened the door…

As the door swung open, I was greeted by a smartly dressed woman bearing an impatient and very confused expression. Though she did look vaguely familiar, I didn't immediately recognise her.

"Oh, good morning, George? I am more than a little confused," she glanced down at my dressing gown and shook her head in disapproval and frustration. "I've just come from the Manor, and a man there - I have absolutely no idea who he was? Well, he suggested that Melissa was to be found *here* in the gate house!"

"Lady Jayne!" I exclaimed, wide-eyed, my mouth agape.

"It's Jayne *Cavendish*," she said firmly, "Now, George, I've had an exceedingly long and difficult journey. Please tell me *now* - where I may find my daughter?"

The End

About your Author: Richard T Weston

Richard is dyslexic but does not complain about this condition. Not diagnosed until his 20's he has learnt to live with it and, for most of his life, hide it.

"Dyslexia has held me back, but it won't hold me down."

His mother, May 'Murray' Weston was herself a creative writer, gaining a BA Hons in her mid-seventies. She refused to write Richard's story for him, saying to Richard: "Dyslexia is a good excuse not to write, but it is not a good reason."

Richard's principal occupation has revolved around photography: Starting as a colour printer in Stevenage, then portrait photographer, he moved to photographic retail, managing a shop in Hitchin for several years. He acquired his own camera shop with processing lab in Letchworth in 1992 and expanded into mail order in 1995 becoming the UK's first eBay PowerSeller with his username 'a.bargain'.

In 2010, disillusioned with the declining direction of the photographic trade and online marketing costs, he decided to leave the 'rat-race' to become a gardener. Gardening not only freed him from the stresses of a complex business; it allowed him to enjoy the natural environment, spend more time with his family and also research this book. His narrating character morphing from a civilian grounds man on an RAF base to a Lord's gardener.

Turf Wars was originally inspired by his Environmental Science teacher; Mrs Nicola Edwards, at Nobel School, Stevenage in 1977. After she eloquently described the fragility of a food-chain, Richard made his first scribblings.

Four times he returned to this evolving story but, each time he was unhappy with the end result and consigned it to the trash bin. But the story just wouldn't go away. It continued to evolve as Richard found himself researching the many possible consequences of the loss of all grasses and what could take their place.

In August 2015, while gardening with his Son, Richard suffered a TIA (a mini-stroke), for several minutes he was unable to recall the names of even his closest family. While he has fully recovered, a fear that he might suddenly lose all memory of his story pressured him to try once more. This time he did more research and created a full time-line and detailed character descriptions before he started to write.

In October 2015 Richard drafted Turf Wars and discovered that his writing flowed onto the pages with greater ease. Ten months later he was finally happy with his work, and published it as an eBook for Kindle on Amazon. He awaits his first reviews with some trepidation and hopes to attract the attentions of a professional publisher and distributor.

In October 2016, Richard also wrote an eBook describing writing with dyslexia. Written in a casual, humorous and autobiographical style; he offers tips and advice for dyslexics who may wish to write and also for educators to maybe better understand this unusual condition.

WHEN LIFE DEALS YOU MELONS – Writing with Dyslexia is available in eBook format only from Amazon now.

There is also a spoof Facebook page like that Melissa set up. Available only while we still have power and access to the internet!

Ingleton Manor Trading Centre – Facebook Page
www.facebook.com/IngletonManor

Feel free to post comments and have some fun with the characters!

For publishing enquiries, foreign language rights and permission requests contact the author at richardweston247@gmail.com

RT Print Publishing is owned and operated by the Richard T Weston

THANK YOU!

I sincerely hope that you enjoyed reading my first novel as much as I did writing it.

If you have, then please, tell your friends and family about it.

I'd also appreciate an honest Amazon review – Thank you!

Richard T Weston

I need to give my cover designer a special mention:

Nick Hare of Nick Hare Design, first read this book before drafting several unique designs. He communicated very well throughout the entire process accepting that I kept adding or removing elements and suggesting minor tweaks.

I highly recommend his affordable services.

nickharedesign.com

Printed in the UK by Biddles – www.biddles.co.uk